THE OLD GRAY
WOLF

ALSO BY JAMES D. DOSS

Coffin Man

A Dead Man's Tale

The Widow's Revenge

Snake Dreams

Three Sisters

Stone Butterfly

Shadow Man

The Witch's Tongue

Dead Soul

White Shell Woman

Grandmother Spider

The Night Visitor

The Shaman's Game

The Shaman's Bones

The Shaman Laughs

The Shaman Sings

JAMES D. DOSS

THE OLD GRAY WOLF

MINOTAUR BOOKS ✖ NEW YORK

THE OLD GRAY WOLF. Copyright © 2012 by James D. Doss. All rights reserved. Printed in the United States of America. For information, address St. Martin's Press, 175 Fifth Avenue, New York, N.Y. 10010.

www.minotaurbooks.com

ISBN 978-0-312-61371-6 (hardcover)
ISBN 978-1-250-01809-0 (e-book)

First Edition: November 2012

10 9 8 7 6 5 4 3 2 1

When they are ready, this is for
Summer
Bry
Moriah
Walker
Savannah Rose
and
Nathan

THE OLD GRAY
WOLF

PROLOGUE
HESTER "TOADIE" TILLMAN

No; please do not ask. It would be less than charitable to explain how the unfortunate old soul got tagged with a nickname which suggests froggish features. Ninety-year-old ladies are not without vanity, and are entitled to their privacy.

But that polite designation might be misleading. In the interest of trustworthy reporting, it shall be noted that not everyone in La Plata County who has encountered Mrs. Tillman would characterize her a bona fide *lady*. Probably not one in ten of them. Perhaps not one. Truth be told, the mean-spirited old crone is believed by more than a working quorum of duly registered voters to be a black-hearted, spell-casting witch—for which dubious craft there is no overwhelming market in South Central Colorado. Yes, this does sound like deliberately titillating gossip, and so it may be—but maliciously disseminated rumors, barefaced hearsay, and silly tittle-tattle are occasionally relevant to a significant current event, as is the case at this very instant, about a mile and a minute north of the Ignacio city limits on Route 172. Which is not a nice place to be if one is either trapped inside a severely damaged automobile or attempting to console the mortally injured citizen within it. Which unhappy duty has fallen upon one . . .

OFFICER DANNY BIGNIGHT

The aforementioned constable is a respected employee of the Southern Ute Police Department and a reputable (if displaced) member of the Taos Pueblo, which venerable New Mexico community boasts the largest continually occupied apartment building in the United States of America and (as far as we know) the vast entirety of the Western Hemisphere. But that advertisement is an aside for which remuneration is unlikely, so let us get right to the grisly business at hand—which is an unforeseen and jarring encounter between Hester "Toadie" Tillman and Danny Bignight, which follows a far more jarring encounter between the sturdy motor vehicle Ms. Tillman was a passenger in and a medium-size ponderosa pine. No contest.

Even as we speak, the elderly reputed witch is about to be pried from the wrecked Dodge pickup—the very same conveyance that her granddaughter was driving when a bald front tire (the one on the passenger side) meandered onto the shoulder to roll over a pointy chunk of gravel and pop (ka-boom!) like a pricked balloon. For the record, the driver will depart in the first of two waiting ambulances, which will (sirens screaming, emergency lights flashing) roar away speedily to Durango's Mercy Regional Medical Center. Therein, she will be expertly treated in the ER and survive with a one-inch scar to cleft her chin. This mark will serve as a lifelong memento of the accident and a reminder not to use the rearview mirror for applying shocking pink lip gloss whilst exceeding the posted speed limit.

But enough about the granddaughter; back to Hester "T" Tillman.

As a brawny state trooper applies the hydraulic Jaws of Life spreader-cutters to the crushed vehicle's roof, Officer Danny Bignight is doing his level best to comfort the old woman *whom he is deathly afraid of.* Mrs. Tillman has a few words to say to this latter-day Good Samaritan who would just as well have passed her by if underpaid SUPD cops had the same options as Bible-time priests and scribes. Happily, the attending police officer is not the immediate object of her dreadful declaration; Bignight is merely Toadie's intended messenger. The alleged brewer of sinister potions and caster of evil spells has a menacing communication for one Daisy Perika, who shall be introduced in due time. But let it be said right up front that compared to Miss Daisy P., Hester T. is a sweet, purring, furry little pussycat.

This so-called pussycat, still trapped in the crunched-up Dodge pickup, hissed at the public servant, "Now listen to me, Danny Bignight—you pass what I've got to say on to Daisy *word for word*, or my curse'll fall on you and all of your family down at Taos Pueblo."

"Yes, ma'am." As the cop listened to the message for Daisy Perika, he broke into a cold sweat, his soulful eyes bulged like big brown bubbles in the white of an overfried egg, and his stomach churned sourly. As one might expect, Danny Bignight also swallowed hard.

Following her final declaration, Toadie cackled a crackly laugh, hiccupped—and drew her last breath. Or—as old folks long ago used to say on dark nights in the flickering yellow light cast by kerosene lamps—she *gave up the ghost.* Where a particular given-up ghost goes and what it does when it gets there remains an open question— and one that is relevant to a forthcoming unnerving event which will create no small disturbance.

By the time the state trooper and an EMT had pulled the aged woman's warm corpse from the totaled pickup and loaded it into the second ambulance, which was perhaps six minutes after Toadie's final hiccup, Danny Bignight had retreated into the sanctuary of his SUPD unit and locked the door. As he wiped perspiration from his forehead, the Southern Ute police officer knew what Job One was: *I'll go see Aunt Daisy right away!*

No, Daisy Perika is not Danny Bignight's aunt. As it happens, every Southern Ute on the res and most of the Hispanics and Anglos who reside in and around Ignacio apply the title Aunt to the crotchety tribal elder, who is more or less infamous in her little corner of the world, and mighty proud of it. If you were to ask Daisy, she'd tell you that if those do-nothing bureaucrats in Washington, D.C., were really on the ball, that honorary first name (Aunt) would be printed in U.S. government ink onto her ragged old Social Security card, but they are not (on the ball) and it is not (printed there).

Please—don't get Aunt Daisy started on the subject of government. Wild-eyed anarchists everywhere tremble at her heartfelt threats against all shapes and forms of authority—and her stated intent to

". . . push on the pillars till I bring the temple down on all those #%$*! parasites." (Including those wild-eyed anarchists, who—seen through Daisy's gimlet eyes—are merely hopeful bureaucrats in disguise.)

CHAPTER ONE

THE UTE ELDER'S WILDERNESS HIDEAWAY

Imagine yourself miles from the nearest human settlement, hiking along a dusty trail. All cares forgotten, you are whiling away a balmy autumn day in a wilderness which is both picturesque and forbidding. To the north, a slight blue haze shimmers over round-shouldered mountains. From those ancient peaks, miles-long brown mesas stretch out like a fallen giant's fingers, clutching at crumbling earth. Between the steep sandstone cliffs of those flattened heights, the patient forces of nature have worked for hundreds of millennia to shape the landscape that you see today. Gurgling little springtime streams, gray winter rains freezing in sandstone cracks, and howling grit-laden winds—all those relentless forces have combined to carve out deep canyons, wherein are multitudes of secluded, shady glades where direct sunlight has never beamed an incandescent ray on lichen, moss, or fern, nor shall it ever. Away to the south, beyond the mesa's grasping fingertips, the sun-drenched topography is gradually transformed into a jumble of rugged hills, isolated buttes, rolling arid prairie, and huge patches of nasty badlands that provide suitable habitat for those scaly, slithering serpents who will (when they are of a mind to) hiss, rattle—and then fang you.

But let us not be overly concerned about where we are stepping. (That coiled object half concealed in the dead grass is probably a discarded hank of manila rope. Or so we hope.)

This image is etched indelibly on your consciousness? Good.

While distracted by the panoramic Big Picture, you have passed right by the most important feature of this remote landscape. We refer to the well-known residence of that notable citizen who—excepting a few fleshless exceptions to be described in a moment—is the only human soul who has a settled homestead within the vast neighborhood already described, which comprises approximately forty-four square miles of the Southern Ute reservation.

But do not fault yourself for this understandable oversight. But just so you'll know where to look should you ever pass this way again, Aunt Daisy's home is situated *right over there.* Yes, on the sunny side of that low ridge and near (very nearly *in*) the yawning mouth of *Cañón del Espíritu,* wherein (so the tribal elder assures us) dozens of ghostly presences lurk. (We refer to the aforementioned "few fleshless exceptions.") Not only do these spirits *lurk,* they also (so Daisy claims) often appear to her in a more or less bodily form. Why are they drawn to the cantankerous old woman? There is no one-size-fits-all answer. As each year of our lives is recalled by unique events and distinguishable seasons, so the spirits have their various and sundry reasons for rubbing elbows with Daisy. But, that said, the lonely souls of the long dead reveal themselves to the Ute shaman primarily for the purpose of conversing with a warm-blooded human being. And the oftentimes cold-blooded Daisy Perika is, in a somewhat twisted sense, what a roving poker player might call "the only game in town." Way out here at the mouth of Spirit Canyon, the Southern Ute tribal elder is simply the only person around.

Except when she has company.

Which Daisy does at the moment. Which fortuitous circumstance enables us to focus our attention on three more of the four primary participants in the forthcoming adventure—which has already begun (only they don't know it). Namely . . .

CHARLIE MOON, SCOTT PARRIS, AND SARAH FRANK

By way of introduction to those who have not yet been formally introduced to the citizens listed above, they are, respectively:

The amiable nephew of the notoriously cranky Southern Ute tribal elder. Charlie is that long, lean, lanky fellow who is toting Daisy's circa-1935 leather suitcase from her front door to his Ford Expedition. Mr. Moon is a former SUPD officer, a part-time tribal investigator, current owner of the Columbine Ranch in Granite Creek County—and sometimes deputy to Scott Parris, a tough ex-Chicago cop who is chief of the Granite Creek Police.

The aforesaid tough cop has opened the rear hatch of the SUV and is pushing a cardboard box in between a heavy toolbox and a gallon jug of well water. What's in the cardboard box? Four quarts of Daisy's homemade peach preserves, two loaves of m'lady's baked-in-her-oven rye bread, three pints of green-tomato relish, some leftover walnut fudge, and miscellaneous other delectables to spice up the meals at Charlie's ranch. Parris has the enviable distinction of being one of the few Caucasians (*matukach*) whom Daisy Perika is fond of, which means that she does not spit in his eye just for the fun of it. Speaking of eyes and distinctions, the blue-eyed lawman is also the only paleface who has seen physical evidence of that legendary dwarf who presumably resides in the shadowy inner sanctum of Spirit Canyon. (Several years ago, the white man spied some tiny footprints in the snow.) Gently suggest to Daisy that these might have been the paw prints of an adult raccoon and she will very likely knock your block off and then kick it down the road a furlong or two.

Sarah Frank is that lissome youth who has just locked the front door of Daisy's house and is now approaching the automobile to help the tribal elder into her customary seat behind the driver, i.e. Charlie Moon. Speaking of whom, the twenty-one-year-old Ute-Papago orphan (Sarah) lives in the continual distress of being deeply and passionately in love with Mr. Moon, who—when he bothers to reflect on the pretty, willowy young lady at all—thinks of Miss Frank as his semiadopted daughter.

These cursory introductions complete, we return to the action already under way—which has to do with Hester "Toadie" Tillman's designated messenger, who is on his way to deliver the alleged witch's threat to Aunt Daisy. Will Officer Bignight arrive after they are long gone? Hard to say. We hope not. If Danny doesn't take care of business today, there's no telling what the consequences might be. (The tension is almost palpable.)

But wait a minute . . . About a quarter mile away to the east-northeast, isn't that a puff of dust on the lane? Yes, it is.

CHAPTER TWO

SUPD OFFICER DANNY BIGNIGHT ARRIVES AT DAISY PERIKA'S DOMICILE

Which visit was, in itself, sufficient to annoy the edgy old woman—who was eager to depart with Charlie Moon, Scott Parris, and Sarah Frank for a month-long stay at the Columbine Ranch. Daisy was, in fact, already settled into the backseat of Charlie's Expedition beside the Ute-Papago girl and waiting impatiently for the men to get in, close the front doors, and "Get this big bucket of bolts rolling north!" when Bignight's SUPD unit pulled up and lurched to a neck-jerking stop.

Daisy scowled with understandable suspicion. *This'll be about some kind of trouble.* In her long experience, sworn officers of the law rarely came calling to bring the glad tidings that a penny-pinching old woman who'd bought a one-dollar ticket in Someone or Other's Annual Fund-Raiser Raffle had won First Prize (a brand-new, dark blue F150 pickup). Or even Twentieth Prize (a two-pound box of old-fashioned cherry chocolates, which you hardly ever saw in the store anymore and which sugary treats Daisy's mouth fairly watered for).

Officer Bignight emerged from the official tribal vehicle, hitched up his heavy black leather gun belt under his slightly bulging belly, and waved a fond salute at his former Southern Ute Police Department comrade.

Well aware that his aunt was eager to get on the road, Charlie Moon ambled over to meet and greet his old friend. "Hello, Danny."

"Hey, Charlie." Having noticed the old woman hunched in the backseat of Moon's big SUV, Bignight recognized a welcome opportunity for passing the well-known buck. "Uh, I can see you folks are about to leave, so I'll just let you deliver a message from Hester Till-man to Aunt Daisy." He cleared his throat. "It was Hester's last words before she . . . passed on."

"I'm sorry to hear that, Danny." The devout Catholic Christian closed his eyes, crossed himself, and murmured a prayer for the sad old woman's soul. This done, Moon made the standard inquiry: "How'd she die?"

The SUPD cop described the pickup accident.

The world-class poker player had no difficulty reading the fear in Bignight's eyes. "What was Mrs. Tillman's message to Aunt Daisy?" Some kind last words to terminate their lifelong feud, Charlie hoped.

Bignight provided Moon with a brief summary.

Having no intention of passing on such a silly threat to his elderly relative, a disappointed Charlie Moon passed the buck right back to its rightful owner. "I think you'd better tell Daisy yourself." One of the few Southern Utes who didn't believe in witchcraft explained without even the hint of a smile, "Hester might not like it if you used me as an intermediary."

This reminder had the hoped-for effect. *Charlie's right—that old witch told me to tell Daisy myself.* Danny Bignight inhaled a deep breath that swelled his barrel chest. *I might as well get this over with.* Hitching up his sagging gun belt again, he approached the Colum-bine SUV with a tip of his hat at the open window where Daisy sat, and mumbled the perfunctory greeting: "How are you?"

"I'm fine as frog's hair," Daisy snapped back. "Now tell me what's on your so-called mind so I can get away from here."

This coincidental amphibian reference served only to elevate Big-night's anxiety. *I'd better get this right—ol' Toadie is probably floating around somewhere close-by, listening to every word I say.* Leaning close to the open car window, the reluctant messenger enlarged on what he'd told Charlie Moon about Hester Tillman's untimely death. "Then, she said, 'Now listen to me, Danny—you pass what I've got to say on to Daisy Perika *word for word,* or my curse'll fall on you and all of your family down at Taos Pueblo. You tell that mean old Indian woman that if she don't show up at my funeral and shed some salty tears on my account—I'll come back and haunt her to death!'"

Expecting a vile expletive or at least a throaty oath, the bearer of bad news backed away from the Expedition. "I'm sorry, Daisy—you know I don't think you're mean, but I felt like it was my bounden duty to come out here and tell you exactly what Toad—what Hester had to say."

The old woman waved off this apology as if it were a black housefly buzzing about her wrinkled ear. "Don't worry about it, Danny— Toadie always was a big windbag, and one who had to get the last word in."

Oh, I hope she didn't hear that! After glancing right and left, Bignight shifted nervously from one booted foot to the other. "So . . . are you gonna go to Mrs. Tillman's funeral?"

"Maybe. If I have the time." Charlie Moon's aunt shrugged. "I might go to her burial too, and hang around till after both of the hired mourners are gone and the workmen have shoved dirt over the six-foot-deep hole in the ground and made a nice, smooth mound."

The worried cop sighed with relief. "That'd be awfully nice of you."

"Yes it would." Daisy grinned wickedly. "And it'd be *fun.*"

Officer Bignight knew that he shouldn't ask. *She'll say something awful.* Without a doubt. But, like a hungry trout presented with a plump cricket, Danny Bignight could not resist the clever old angler's bait. "Fun?"

"Sure." Daisy Perika's black eyes sparkled wickedly at the cop. "It'd be great fun to *spit on Toadie's grave.*"

An optimistic citizen might assume that the irascible old soul was merely making a tasteless jest. (The same optimist might also draw an inside straight.) But whether Daisy's vulgar threat is to be taken literally—or is merely an attempt to tweak an already nervous Officer Bignight—only time and opportunity will tell.

In the meantime, more-urgent matters demand our attention. Indeed, the malignant seed of the oncoming calamity is about to be planted in one of those salt-of-the-earth Rocky Mountain munici-palities where the thin air is so wonderfully exhilarating and down-right *nutritious* that a hardworking man who breathes it can live on nine hundred calories of beef and beans per day, and a lean long-horn can get along on about two dozen mouthfuls of alfalfa hay. (Or so they say.) Yes, we'd all like to go there and stay. Directions? Well, this particular all-American high-altitude community is positioned along the final fifty-mile lap of the drive from Aunt Daisy's wilder-ness home on the Southern Ute reservation to Charlie Moon's vast cattle ranch.

If you're not sure that you can navigate your way there, do not fret—we'll take you to this fine example of a wholesome western cow town, and show up just as the unseemly hostilities are about to com-mence.

CHAPTER THREE

1322 COPPER STREET
GRANITE CREEK, COLORADO

Which is where personal correspondence to Bertha's Saloon & Pool Room should be addressed. But no junk mail, please; be advised that this is a strictly first-class joint.

First of all, there is the matter of firearms restrictions—pistols with sissy mother-of-pearl handles may not be brought onto the premises, and permissible (manufactured in the USA) sidearms must be holstered and in plain view. Carbines and shotguns are to be checked at the door.

Violence which might lead to destruction of Bertha's property is looked upon with disfavor. The use of pool cues, billiard balls, or heavy beer mugs as weapons is forbidden and a large sign suspended over the bar advises customers that FISTFIGHTS MUST TAKE PLACE IN THE ALLEY. Even outside, there are unwritten rules of decorum: eye-gouging and groin-kneeing are discouraged unless a combatant is severely provoked.

Moreover, Bertha's Saloon & Pool Room enforces strict rules to ensure proper hygiene. Customers are not permitted to spit on the barroom floor, and the brass spittoons are emptied once every month or more frequently if they're full.

Impressed? Of course you are.

And you will be pleased to know that the establishment caters to uppity professors from Rocky Mountain Polytechnic University, armed-and-ready GCPD police officers, cheerful county-government officials, clear-eyed cowboys, honest truck drivers, and local entrepreneurs of all stripes. The proprietor does not welcome shifty-eyed grifters, high-plains drifters, whining panhandlers, slithery pick-pockets, loudmouthed louts, or any other sort of disreputable riffraff you can think of. (Take careful note of this management bias, which is relevant to what is about to transpire.)

The owner, general manager, and chief bartender is (as you would expect) Bertha herself—and this teetotaler runs her profitable establishment with all the keen attention to detail of a certified public accountant. To flesh out this 240-pound character (who lifts weights on her coffee breaks), we shall specify that she is known as Big Bad Bertha Bronkowski, or "B-to-the-Fourth-Power" to her mathematically inclined customers from the university, who generally abbreviate that imposing appellation as B^4 or simply The Power. You begin to get the picture.

One final brushstroke: the lady is not entirely dedicated to making a buck—all work and no play tends to make Bertha lethargic and moody. For the benefit of occasional amusement, B^4 pinch-hits as bouncer. Sadly, her rep being widely known hereabouts, the lady has few opportunities to demonstrate her efficient technique. Which is why the artiste secretly pines for the appearance of an offensive out-of-towner.

As it happens, the pined-for subject is about to appear—the fun about to begin.

Enter one LeRoy Hooten.

Literally. He has just passed through the same sort of swinging doors that adorned Miss Kitty's world-famous Dodge City saloon. (Recollect Matt Dillon, who shot the same gunslinger dead at the beginning of every episode. Also recall his limping deputy, Chester, and ol' Doc what's-his-name.) But we must return our attention to Mr. Hooten, who is about to initiate a small disturbance. B^4 has spotted the fellow right away and decided that the scruffy-looking citizen is definitely a member of that class of seedy entrepreneurs who are not welcome in her place of business. She has a remedy in mind, but such enjoyments are to be savored. The proprietor bides her time.

· · ·

LeRoy Hooten ambled along the bar, eyeing Bertha's worthy customers as a weasel appraises plump chickens who look ready for plucking. Almost immediately, he spied a likely specimen who was sipping
mincingly at a Coors Lite as if he hoped to make it last all night—or
at least until closing time. Hooten, whose presence exuded a noxious
blend of odors, eased himself onto the stool beside an amiable gent
and (conveniently shedding the weasel metaphor for another) presented a possum's toothy grin and a friendly greeting. Hooten's "Hiya,
buddy" and burp were delivered with a rancid breath that might have
staggered (if not felled) a privileged-class ox who was accustomed to
grazing in vast meadows of fragrant wildflowers.

Grimacing, the gassed victim tottered on the stool as if he might
topple off and fall dead to the floor. (This reaction was somewhat
overdone. To date, no one in Bertha's respectable establishment has
ever expired from sudden exposure to a combination of exuded gas-
tric odors and extreme halitosis.)

Unfazed by this less-than-gracious reception, Mr. Hooten observed that his throat was "dry as Mojave sand" and observed that a
beer would do him no end of good. Sadly, he did not have "two dimes
to jingle in my pockets."

The honest citizen was trying to decide whether to (1) buy the
odorous, odious fellow a brew and make the best of the situation or
(2) to advise the smelly bum to take a hike to the Salvation Army HQ
and get a shower, when the aforementioned Bertha—who had been
wiping a table with a wet dishrag—materialized behind LeRoy Hooten and inquired what the matter was.

What Hooten did next exhibited poor judgment, but in his defense
it shall be stipulated that he had just arrived in town on the back of a
flatbed truck that was used to haul cattle to market. That convenient
conveyance smelled of livestock dung, urine, and other unidentifiable
secretions. The effects of this means of transport had not served to
enhance his admittedly meager intellectual powers.

Turning, the vagrant glanced at the large woman, and said with a
supercilious sneer, "Get lost, fatso—me'n the gentleman are talking
about beer."

Bertha was almost overcome with gratitude. Her bouncer's skills had not been exercised much of late, and now Fate had provided fresh material of the choicest kind. In the interest of not pandering to the unsavory cravings of those who enjoy gratuitous violence, the gory details shall not be dwelt upon. Suffice it to say that B^4 grabbed Hooten by his grimy shirt collar with her left hand, the equally grimy seat of his trousers with her right paw, and before you could say "Look at 'er go!" had given the malodorous pestilence the old heave-ho through the swinging doors, which continued to swing for some seconds after LeRoy Hooten's startled expression had encountered the cement sidewalk and (following a yard-long skid on hard-frozen snow) his thick skull had impacted with a red fire hydrant that did not budge.

This summary ejection from the premises (though merely an average performance for Miss Bertha) was welcomed with enthusiastic approval from her audience, including a heartfelt "Bravo!" Also a "Way to go!" and a "Bertha's number one!" to which high praise the performer responded with a grateful, girlishly shy smile. She felt immensely blessed to have an upper-class clientele that was capable of appreciating the finer nuances of her art. The lady's charming modesty served only to encourage her admirers, who began stomping their cowboy boots and hooting earthy salutes to their heroine. There were also shrill whistles, boisterous howls, and raucous laughter that could be heard half a block away.

But not by Mr. Hooten, who was unconscious on account of a concussion, which is no laughing matter. Despite the blood leaking slowly from a tiny artery in his brain, the injured man returned to his so-called senses within about a minute. No one noticed when, with the support of the helpful fireplug—beside which vagrants and loiterers were not allowed to park—the dazed man managed to push himself to his feet and stumble away in a state of confusion, which he summed up succinctly: *Where am I and what's going on?* His first guess was, *I musta fell out of an airplane and landed in this little burg.* Being an analytic sort, Hooten took into account the fact that he was chilly. *I bet I'm in Maine—or maybe Minnesota.* He was not so disoriented as to totally misunderstand his predicament: *I'll freeze to death if I don't get something to eat and find me a warm place to sleep.* This was a reasonably accurate estimate of his predicament, and one that is bound to arouse at least a tad of sympathy. But not to worry; the plucky ne'er-do-well knew just the remedy: *I need some hard cash.* As he staggered past a greasy-spoon diner and glanced at a DISHWASHER WANTED sign in the window, his course of action was a no-brainer: *I'll bump into some rich sucker and pick his pocket.*

The unfortunate malefactor did not know where he had landed. Though there were perhaps a dozen citizens in Granite Creek, Colorado, who could be categorized as rich, not one of them was a sucker, and poking your fingers into any of these bad hombres' pockets was a good way to lose them. But, as it happened, not one of Mr. Hooten's dexterous digits was in the least danger of being lopped off by a bone-handled Bowie knife. Within minutes, he would select a victim from that supposedly less-dangerous gender and commit a felony that was related (first cousin) to that venerable craft of picking prosperous gentlemen's pockets.

CHAPTER FOUR

A SUITABLE SENTIMENT FOR AN EPITAPH

As they motored down Copper Street in Moon's Expedition, neither the lean, keen-eyed Indian behind the steering wheel nor Scott Parris (in the passenger seat), nor sweet little Sarah Frank (in the backseat), nor Charlie's aunt Daisy Perika (seated beside Sarah) took any notice of Mr. LeRoy Hooten, who—in search of a promising pocket to pick—was headed in the same direction as they were, though not at the posted speed limit of twenty-five miles per.

Accustomed to his role as chief of police, Parris barked an instruction to his part-time deputy and pointed. "Pull in at the Smith's parking lot." Suddenly remembering that he was a guest in Moon's car, he added quickly, "If it's no trouble."

"Not a bit." Wanting some elbow room, the amiable rancher selected a space about fifty yards from the few dozen vehicles that were clustered near the supermarket's entrance.

As if she had intended to pick up a few things herself, Daisy snorted. "Why didn't you park in the next county?"

Ignoring his relative's caustic remark, Moon addressed his buddy: "You intend to do some last-minute shopping?"

"Yes I do." Parris was unbuckling his seat belt. "I was just adding up all the times you've fed me at the Columbine, and all I've ever brought with me was a big appetite." Free of physical restraint, he opened the car door. "Tonight, I'm providing the dessert."

"That's very thoughtful," Moon said.

"And it's about time," Daisy snapped. "I've baked you enough pies to keep a big family of hogs fed and fat for a year."

Parris leaned to gaze at the feisty old woman. "I was thinking about some ice cream."

"In this weather?" She feigned a shiver. "Just *thinking* about ice cream is enough to freeze my gizzard."

"Then I'll get a couple of pies that we can warm up in the oven—"

"Store-bought pies taste like warmed-over cardboard," she muttered. "I wouldn't feed one to a starving coyote that came scratching at my door."

Parris was determined to please. "So what would you like?"

"I'd like for you to close that door before I get a bad case of frostbite!"

Scott Parris had known the tribal elder for too many years to take offense. Tipping his felt hat with a boyish smile, the beefy cop shut the car door and began his downhill stroll to the supermarket.

Realizing that there was nothing to be gained by upbraiding his irascible auntie, Charlie Moon held his tongue. *I'll get some ice cream and pie, too.*

Twenty-year-old Sarah Frank could not resist lodging an oblique protest. "I think Mr. Parris is very nice to buy ice cream for—"

"Hah!" Daisy shot back. "You'd think rabid foxes was nice until one of 'em put the bite on you." This off-the-wall assertion was an effective conversation stopper.

Pleased with her witty self, the aged combatant settled back into the cushioned seat and sighed with unconcealed satisfaction. She was promptly rewarded with a slight twitch in her lower back, which part of Daisy's anatomy was wont to gave birth to excruciating muscle spasms. Sure enough, the twitch sharpened to an agonizing pain. Was this the just reward for her misbehavior? Perhaps. Daisy Perika grimaced. *Before this happened, I was having a good time.*

That was it (a Suitable Sentiment for an Epitaph):

BEFORE THIS HAPPENED
I WAS HAVING A GOOD TIME

But these words were not suitable for Daisy's gravestone.

Then for whose polished granite slab?

A pertinent question, and one whose answer eludes us. But only for the moment.

Of this much we may be assured: before the first gray glow of dawn, one pretty tough customer will be in the market for an inscription on her (or his) tombstone.

CHAPTER FIVE

A CAUTIONARY TALE

The caution referred to is directed particularly to those young folk who aspire to a satisfying career in law enforcement. (Bless their innocent hearts.) But who among us has not occasionally daydreamed about wearing the spiffy uniform, toting a deadly weapon, and tearing around town on a government-provided motorcycle? Not to mention the intellectual stimulation of detecting a sly crime-in-progress, the visceral thrill of the subsequent chase, and the soul-filling gratification of arresting a dastardly criminal—thus saving some upstanding citizen from suffering an act of mindless violence and/or the loss of valuable personal property. And add to those rewards the heartfelt appreciation of said upstanding citizen who has been served and protected by the courageous, clear-eyed constable on patrol.

Ninety-nine percent of the aforementioned youths will, of course, yawn at the forthcoming lesson (provided free of charge) and return their slack-jawed attention to the latest computerized diversion wherein the cherished goal is to maim or kill the maximum number of digitally simulated fellow creatures. But for that one-in-a-hundred young whippersnapper who will pay close attention—the Granite Creek chief of police is about to demonstrate the folly of youth's vain ambitions.

HIS UNEXPECTED ENCOUNTER
WITH THE CRIMINAL ELEMENT

As Scott Parris slogged his way slowly across the snowy supermarket parking lot, the off-duty policeman's mind was occupied with thoughts about this evening's dessert. Mrs. Parris's little boy had never met a pie he didn't like, and he could not make up his mind about what kind. *I'll just close my eyes and grab a couple off the shelf.* Which left the matter of ice cream. *Two half gallons will be more than enough for the four of us.* The uncomplicated fellow would have been happy to settle for chocolate and vanilla, but there were about two dozen flavors to chose from, and that plentitude obliged him to make a carefully considered decision. Nearing the Smith's entrance, he was mulling over the relative merits of strawberry, butter pecan, and peach. Not an easy choice: each of these flavors was a taste-bud-titillating treat. Parris's pleasant mullings were interrupted by the muffled patter of hurried footsteps somewhere behind him. Instinctively, the cop glanced over his shoulder—to spot a slender figure dressed in black who was high-stepping it along the slippery parking lot. *Where's that Gomer goin' in such a hurry?* He turned to get a better look, just in time to see the sprinter snatch something from a grocery cart parked by the left rear fender of a sleek Cadillac. Something white. *It's a purse!* The woman whose handbag had been pinched was occupied with a fidgety little girl and several bulging plastic bags that she was stuffing into the Caddy's trunk—which was why she had not noticed the brazen theft.

Write this maxim down in blood and commit it to memory:

On or Off Duty, a Gritty Ex-Chicago Cop
Does Not Hesitate to do His Bounden Duty.

In less time than it takes to tell about it, Scott Parris was on a dead run after the purse thief. Sad to say, Charlie Moon's best friend was well past the flower of his youth, and carrying about sixty pounds more than the young man he was chasing. Add to that the fact that the grade was slightly uphill and what it summed up to was No Contest—the skinny criminal was putting an increasing distance between them. By the time Parris was within a stride or two of the Cadillac, he was puffing like an overloaded pack mule ascending La Veta Pass. Too winded to think and relying entirely on instinct, he wished that he . . . *had a rock to throw at that thieving bastard*. But he did not, and popping a shot at a petty perpetrator's back was not strictly kosher, so the cop improvised right on the spot by grabbing the nearest object at hand, which was a can of black-eyed peas from a lady's shopping cart. (That's right—the very same lady whose purse had been snatched.)

On this occasion, unlike the last, both the mother and the daughter were aware of the blatant thievery.

Blissfully unaware of their wide eyes and gaped mouths, and recalling his days on an Indiana high school football team, Parris got a firm grip on the can with his trusty right hand, slowed to a light trot, and prepared to assume the classic stance and make that once-in-a-lifetime pass.

Outraged, one of the victimized citizens (Momma) yelled, "You bring that back, you big fat thief!" The other (sweet little Betsy Lou) commenced to jump up and down and scream shrilly, "Call the po-leece, Momma—call the po-leece!"

Was Scott Parris jarred by this verbal abuse? Not a bit. Your sure-enough, steely-eyed quarterback does not allow himself to be distracted by murderous threats from the hulking defense, much less flustered by rude yells from the bench, away-team fans with blood-lust in their hearts—or the opposition's wild-eyed cheerleaders who would dearly love to beat him to death with pink pom-poms.

The GCPD chief of police stopped dead still, raised the hefty (sixteen-ounce) can of black-eyed peas over his beefy shoulder, made a hasty estimate of where his uncooperative receiver would be when the missile arrived—and *let 'er fly*. Being a realist about his athletic prowess, Parris figured his chances of hitting the target were about one in twenty. Which, given the dismal twilight visibility and the decades that had passed since he'd last launched the ol' pigskin, was somewhere on the yonder side of optimistic.

But the over-the-hill athlete had given it all he had—*look at it go*!

Up into the glare of a parking-lot light, to an apogee where it paused for an infinitesimal instant, then down . . . down . . . down.

Clunk!

Thud—thud!

Why both a "clunk!" and a "thud-thud!"?

An understandable query from those with Inquiring Minds. A detailed explanation is hereby provided:

The "clunk!" was the satisfying (to Parris) sound of the can smacking the fleeing miscreant squarely on the back of his lice-infested skull.

The initial "thud!" was made by the fleeing thief's body as he slammed face-first onto the parking-lot pavement.

Which raises the delicate issue of the secondary "thud!"

It happened like this. The spot that Scott Parris had selected for his game-winning pass was on a patch of what is popularly known as black ice, which is not a nice place to get set up for a long toss—especially when your footwear is a brand-new pair of Roper boots with slick-as-snail-spit leather soles. This unfortunate combination was the root cause of Parris's hard fall—flat on his back.

What little wind he had left after the sprint was completely expelled from his lungs and the sudden experience of asphalt slamming him in the spine like John Henry's nine-pound hammer driving a railroad spike into a crosstie was sufficient to daze our hero for a fleeting moment. Call it six seconds. Which was enough time for sweet little Betsy Lou—ignoring her mother's yelled warnings to "stay away from that thieving white trash, honey—he's probably all doped up and packing a knife!"—to arrive at the scene of the police chief's mortifying accident and begin whacking enthusiastically at the prone man with her little white purse, which was an adorably cute girl-size version of her mother's expensive leather fashion accessory. All the while, the mother was yelling, "Police—somebody call the police!"

When Betsy ran out of steam and could no longer manage a healthy swing with her purse, she glared down at Parris and said, "You give my momma her black-eyed peas back *right now* or I'll kick you a good one!"

He couldn't and didn't and she would and did.

Wincing at the sharp pains in his ribs, Parris gazed up at the darkened heavens and offered a heartfelt prayer. *Please—somebody just shoot me.*

We may be thankful that Betsy Lou was not packing a classic .44 caliber Remington derringer in her purse. But being bereft of a deadly weapon did not discourage her—spunky as they get, she kept right on kicking his rib cage.

The farce continued for quite some time, but there is no need to document the chief of police's humiliation in excruciating detail. Enough has been reported to provide the cautionary element of this small episode, which was . . . We have forgotten. But it had something or other to do with the importance of a young person's career choices, and the unparalleled satisfaction of public service—what with mediocre wages, doubtful health and retirement benefits, a generally ungrateful citizenry, and . . .

Never mind.

Accounting, computer science, and animal husbandry are worth considering.

CHAPTER SIX

WHERE WAS CHARLIE MOON DURING ALL THE EXCITEMENT?

Another pertinent question, and one that shall be dealt with forthwith. Up until the instant when the thief snatched the purse from the lady's shopping cart, Mr. Moon was seated behind the wheel of his parked Expedition, chatting with Sarah and Daisy about what flavors of ice cream Scott Parris would select. (The rancher leaned toward strawberry or butter pecan, Sarah hoped for pistachio, and Daisy opted for chocolate or vanilla because "that *matukach* cop has got about as much imagination as a cue ball.")

As soon as the purse was purloined and Parris took off after the purloiner, Moon eased himself gracefully out of the SUV. As the chief of police was about to make the soon-to-be-legendary pea-can pass, his teammate was positioning himself for the interception. No, not to receive the can of black-eyed peas. The hopeful interceptor had placed himself directly in the purse thief's path. Like the instant quarterback, Parris's sidekick harbored no hope that the missile would come anywhere near its intended target, much less actually connect and clunk! for a head-shot that would knock the felon flat onto his face.

Which wildly unlikely event was, as we know, precisely what Moon witnessed. Along with Parris's almost simultaneous flop onto the parking lot.

Within a few easy strides, the long-legged Ute was standing over the fallen felon.

When the dazed miscreant turned onto his side and muttered a curse, the deputy got a good look at the profile of the designated "suspect"—and caught a whiff of his distinctive aroma.

The disoriented man, white purse still firmly in hand, rolled onto his back and gazed at the tall Indian with frank curiosity. In a tone that hinted of righteous animosity, he inquired, "Did you knock me down?"

"No I did not," Moon said softly. "But if you get up before I tell you to, I'll be glad to oblige." He aimed a forefinger at the stolen property. "Let go of that purse."

"No." Sitting up, the perpetrator shook his shaggy head. "I won't."

Bemused, Moon asked, "Why not?"

Shaggy-head clutched the booty to his thin chest. "Because it's mine and you can't have it."

"Well, I suppose a grown man's got a right to do as he pleases—but won't you feel kinda silly struttin' around town with a lady's purse hangin' over your shoulder?"

The felon scowled. "Are you insinuatin' that I'm some kinda sissy?"

"The thought never occurred to me, mister. But not everyone in Granite Creek is as broad-minded as I am. So, to avoid any unnecessary embarrassment, why don't you set the purse aside—and then get up real slow-and-easy-like."

The feisty fellow did get up, but he would not give up the white purse, perhaps because it was genuine Moroccan tooled leather—and might have been a sure-enough Gucci worth a wad of hundred-dollar bills. But that amounts to unwarranted speculation about undisclosed motives. What can be asserted with complete assurance is that as soon as Shaggy-Head was on his feet, he tossed the heavy purse at Moon's face, and a knife flashed in his hand—with which cutlery he made a savage slash at the deputy, slicing a genuine buffalo-horn button from Moon's new shirt. For this little piece of work, his wages were a hard uppercut that put his lights out right on the well-known spot; and for the second time in five minutes and the third time in twenty (remember Bertha's toss through the saloon doors?), LeRoy Hooten took a sprawling fall. As his already-cracked skull hit a Please Leave Your Shopping Carts Here steel signpost, the unfortunate purse thief was down for the count and then some.

At about the time Hooten hit the deck, Sarah Frank showed up at

Moon's elbow—ready to throw a punch of her own should the knife wielder pose any further threat to *her man*. Moon's aunt arrived a moment later to mutter a Ute curse at the malefactor, the gist of which was that he was inferior to certain slithering vipers and loathsome amphibians. Leaving the unconscious fellow to his dreamless sleep, the trio strode to the spot where Scott Parris remained lying on his back. Charlie Moon's best friend was enormously relieved that his pint-size, hard-kicking persecutor had been forcibly removed by her distraught mother. As the Ute and two of the three important women in his life approached, the white Cadillac was pulling away—the excited child shouting shrill imprecations behind a closed window.

Charlie Moon squatted beside his fallen friend. "You okay, pard?"

"Sure. Fine as frog hair. I just laid down here to take a short siesta." A parking-lot light in his eyes, Parris was unaware of the ladies' presence.

"You sure picked a hard, cold bed to lay down on."

"It's all a matter of perspective." The cop grimaced. "To me, it feels soft as a mattress stuffed with baby-duck feathers." Parris managed a painful grin. "Did you see that long throw I made?"

"Sure did. That was some dandy pitch."

"Did I kill the purse-snatching son of a bitch?"

"Seems unlikely." Moon glanced back at the purse snatcher's prone form. "He got up and gave me some trouble."

Scott Parris had no doubt of the outcome. "So you decked him."

"Mmm-hmm. Now what can I do for you, pard—d'you want a hand up?

"Huh-uh. What I want is some chocolate and vanilla ice cream."

Daisy Perika snickered. "I told you so."

Parris blinked at the Ute elder's shadowy figure. "And apple and peach pie."

Moon: "You still got ice cream and store-bought pies on your mind?"

"You bet." Parris's mouth watered; his stomach growled approvingly.

"I'll take care of the purchase soon as you're back in the car where you can warm up some. But in the meantime—" Moon helped his friend to a sitting position, "let's get you forked-end down."

As the dizzy man got onto a pair of unsteady legs, a GCPD black-and-white with blue-and-red emergency lights flashing pulled into the supermarket parking lot. "Looky," Parris said, mimicking the little girl's shrill voice. "The po-leece has done showed up to arrest me for stealing food from that poor lady in the white Caddy. I grabbed a can of . . . of something or other." *What was it that little girl said—black beans?*

Right on cue, the dented steel cylinder came rolling down the slight incline. The container stopped conveniently at the toe of Charlie Moon's left boot. "Black-eyed peas," the deputy said.

CHAPTER SEVEN

A PREMATURE CELEBRATION

Despite the hard fall the chief of police had taken while making that long toss across the supermarket parking lot and—against enormous odds—connecting with the purse snatcher's skull, Scott Parris hardly noticed the ache in his ribs. Matter of fact, GCPD's top cop was in an upbeat mood. During the evening meal at the Columbine, he regaled his small suppertime audience with how "mighty fine it felt to throw the game-winning pass."

Daisy Perika smirked at her favorite *matukach.* "See if you can pass me the biscuits without dropping the platter."

Parris's right arm did not fail him: he performed his mission with masterly precision and a touch of athletic elegance. "You want me to pitch you the butter dish?"

"No thank you." Charlie Moon's aunt selected the choicest of the golden-brown biscuits. "You'd better slack off before you hurt your elbow."

Chuckling, the white cop turned to his Indian friend, who had also counted coup. "You ain't said a word about decking that scum-bum."

Moon shrugged "There's nothing to tell." The hungry man sliced a meaty right triangle off his T-bone. "That petty thief was dazed from being conked with the can—and he was about half my size."

The exuberant chief of police did not appreciate this display of modesty in his deputy. "But the lowlife pulled a knife on you and practically sliced your—" Parris paused when he noticed Sarah cringe.

Moon had also noticed. "The guy was so spaced out, he couldn't have peeled a potato without cutting his fingers off." The reluctant warrior winked at Sarah, then grinned at his best friend. "That thirty-pound little girl who beat you up with her purse could've handled him with one hand tied behind her back."

"I don't know about *that*." Parris frowned as he buttered his third biscuit. "But she sure was a feisty little brat—kicked at my ribs like an Arkansas mule. If you hadn't come to help, she'd probably have done me in."

Daisy smiled at the memory of the spunky girl-child. "When her momma came to the police station to get her purse, did she take the can of pinto beans?"

"Black-eyed peas," Parris corrected. "No, she did not—that can is tagged and locked up in the GCPD evidence room."

"I bet it won't be there next week." Moon stirred a second spoon of Tule Creek Honey into his coal-black coffee. "Those black-eyed peas will end up on your mantelpiece—along with other memorabilia of your many exploits as a fearless lawman who always hits what he aims at."

You're right about that. "There's nothing wrong with a man taking a souvenir now and again." Maybe there wasn't, but Parris's sunburned face blushed to a deeper shade of red. "I'll buy the woman another can of peas."

And so it went, with Sarah Frank uttering not a word and Daisy edging in a barbed remark whenever the opportunity presented itself. With the possible exception of Miss Frank, a good time was enjoyed by all. When it was time for dessert, the young woman removed a pair of warmed-up pies from the oven, then opened the freezer to get the two half-gallon containers of ice cream.

While the menfolk were leaning toward apple pie and vanilla ice cream, Sarah thought she would treat her sweet tooth to a thinnish segment of peach pie.

Daisy Perika stoutly refused dessert. "No store-bought pie for *me*. And I don't know how anybody but an Eskimo could eat ice cream in cold weather like this."

Sarah was about to slice the pie when—and such interruptions seem almost inevitable—the mobile phone holstered on Parris's belt warbled a familiar tune. Not a surprise—he had expected a call from the GCPD dispatcher. He pressed the instrument to his ear. "H'lo, Clara—have we ID'd that purse snatcher?"

"Yes sir. One LeRoy Hooten. Born in Oak Park, Illinois, in 1992. Young as he is, Mr. Hooten has a record a yard long."

"A real bad boy, eh?"

"A born loser. Car theft. Assault and battery. Drug dealing. Been in and out of jail since he was sixteen."

"He'll find out that the revolving door stops in Granite Creek." Parris grinned across the dining table at Charlie Moon. "Purse snatching. Evading a lawful arrest. Assaulting my deputy with a deadly weapon. Mr. Hooten will do some serious time in the Colorado clink."

"Well—I don't think so . . ." Her voice trailed off.

Parris steeled himself. "So what're you trying to tell me, Clara?"

"I'm sorry, sir." The dispatcher took a deep breath. "Approximately ten minutes ago, Mr. LeRoy Hooten was pronounced dead in the Snyder Memorial ER."

The cop's ruddy face blanched. "Did you say . . . *dead*?"

"Yes sir. Cause of death is uncertain, but the ER doc says it was probably due to a concussion that caused internal bleeding in the brain. Death sometimes occurs immediately after the injury, but depending on how fast the blood is leaking, it can take hours." A heartbeat. "The neurologist who usually checks the cranial CAT scans is at home with the flu, but the digital files have been uploaded to the Internet for a radiologist in Australia. We should know something more definite in a few minutes."

The deflated lawman closed his eyes. "Do we have a next of kin to notify?"

"Not yet, but a couple of officers are working on it." Clara Tavishuts added, "With a transient like Mr. Hooten, it might take few days to locate a parent or sibling."

"Thanks, Clara." Disconnecting, Parris gave his host a barely discernible nod.

The lawmen got up from the table and drifted listlessly down the hallway to the parlor, where Scott Parris filled Charlie Moon in on what the deputy hadn't already guessed. "I suppose getting slammed on the noggin with a can of black-eyed peas ain't nothing to laugh about."

"That can you tossed probably wasn't what killed him." Moon stared at a heap of dying embers in the fireplace. "When he pulled that blade on me, I guess I hit him harder than I needed to—and when the fella went down, he banged his head against a signpost."

Miles away, and at the very moment when the remorseful lawmen were speculating about which of them had dealt the death blow to the late LeRoy Hooten, the person actually responsible for the unintentional homicide was serving a Budweiser beer and a light California white wine to a Rocky Mountain Polytechnic English-literature professor and a long-haul trucker from Butte, Montana. (Yes, respectively.) The 240-pound bouncer had dismissed LeRoy Hooten from her mind as soon as his odorous presence was outside her high-class saloon. B^4 was laughing loudly at a coarse joke the university professor had shared with the trucker.

But do not leap to the conclusion that Big Bad Bertha Bronkowski was a woman without tender feelings toward her victims. If she had known that the barfly bum had died from being flung through her swinging doors and headfirst into a sturdy fire plug, she would have definitely lost some sleep about it. Maybe forty-four winks. Maybe four.

DESSERT?

The two half-gallons of ice cream and the store-bought pies were untouched after the supper that had ended so abruptly for Charlie, Scott, Sarah, and Daisy. And would remain so until . . .

12:10 A.M.

Which was when a sleepless Daisy Perika rolled out of bed, pulled on her faded red bathrobe, and toddled down the hallway to the headquarters kitchen for a stealthy postmidnight snack. The ravenous old lady finished off a sizable chunk of lightly microwaved peach pie—à la mode, of course. (No, *chocolate* ice cream.) After swallowing the last morsel, she licked her lips. *That sure hit the spot.* To underscore this earnest compliment, the aged gourmand added a healthy burp.

BAD NEWS TRAVELS FAST

And like a ravenous vampire bat lusting for blood, even in the middle of the night.

It had begun like this: about six minutes after LeRoy Hooten's black heart had ceased to beat, an enterprising ER X-ray technician at Snyder Memorial Hospital (Myra) learned from a chatty ambulance driver (Pete) that the purse snatcher's demise had resulted from an unfortunate encounter with the county's best-known lawmen. The young lady, who had been ticketed by a lesser-known GCPD cop for running a Stop sign and issued a second citation for employing a string of colorful obscenities to characterize the officer's parentage, saw an opportunity to get in a good lick at the local gestapo.

During the wee hours, the vengeful insomniac (who had dropped out of journalism school at a fine Ivy League university) settled down in her tiny studio apartment on Knapp Street and tap-tapped out a sparsely parsed three-hundred-word summary of LeRoy Hooten's wrongful death at the hands of a couple of cops who (so she said) had a history of brutalizing less-fortunate citizens. To this lurid piece of fiction, the wide-eyed lass added the most suitable image of Scott Parris and Charlie Moon (together) that she could find online and posted her article on two of the major social-networking sites. In the grainy, five-year-old, black-and-white newspaper photograph, the lawmen friends were posed with drawn six-shooters—laughing about a shooting-gallery contest they had won at the county fair. (First prize, for which they were much obliged, had been a meal for four at the best barbecue restaurant in Granite Creek County.)

The spread of the X-ray tech's posting was what the virtual community calls "viral." By morning, the story was picked up by one of the cable networks. Neither Moon nor Parris got a gander at the eleven-second report, which—with the photo—portrayed them as a couple of chuckleheaded cop-clowns who enjoyed beating up on any down-on-his-luck bum who hit town.

It was an unfortunate development, which would produce grim consequences.

LET US SLIP AWAY FOR A REFRESHING CHANGE OF SCENERY

Why would we do that when the panorama on Charlie Moon's spread is picture-postcard perfect?

Because aside from an unwary cowboy getting gored in the groin by a playful three-year-old Hereford bull, a boisterous brawl in the Columbine bunkhouse where an ornery, big galoot known as Six-Toes will be decked by "Little Butch" Cassidy, and a rusty old windmill that gets wrecked by a passing whirlwind that presumably had nothing better to do than twist useful machinery into a pile of metallic junk—not a lot will happen around Charlie Moon's ranch for the next few days, which quiet interlude will provide a fine opportunity to drift away toward the sunrise and find out what some interesting and enterprising folks are up to on the yonder side of the muddy ol' Mississippi. That does not narrow down the locality sufficiently? Then let us say north of the wide Ohio and eliminate all of Dixie (which is regrettable). Even more geographical specificity is called for? Very well; we shall further limit the neighborhood to a location well south of Chicago and a tad west of Indiana.

What could happen in the Land of Lincoln? Just about anything.

Ask any steely-eyed hombre you happen to bump into in Bozeman, Cheyenne, Leadville, Socorro, or El Paso and he'll tell you that those quiet, polite midwesterners create a whole lot more trouble per capita than ten thousand hornets in a nest that some reckless passerby wearing a White Sox cap casually whacks at with a baseball bat.

But we all know that was an unwarranted exaggeration that borders on being regionally prejudicial. After all, how many folks do you know who would deliberately disturb a colony of edgy insects who are armed with seriously barbed stingers and know how to use them?

Really—*that* many? Well. Perhaps you ought to consider emigrating to Tombstone, Dodge City, or Islamabad.

But back to the urgent question, which (in case it has slipped your mind) is: who is this imprudent passerby who is about to take a swing at the aforesaid metaphorical nest? You may, if you are so inclined, spend precious hours in vain speculations, or—turn the page and find out.

CHAPTER EIGHT

MISS LOUELLA SMITHSON, PRIVATE EYE

As to what name she goes by, let us qualify: this particular Miss Smithson is Louella on her driver's license, Ella to her few friends, and Ellie when Granddaddy Ray Smithson calls her to supper. (When on a hot case, the lady often assumes a convenient alias—a moniker with just a dash of pizzazz.)

Now to the issue of vocation. Is Louella-Ella-Ellie a bona fide, fully qualified, licensed private eye? Not really; the lady is more or less playing the part. Pretending, if you like. Admittedly, she does make a few dollars running down the occasional missing person (an out-of-work ex-husband who is behind in alimony payments, or a wife who has run away with her high-school sweetheart). Small potatoes some will say, but a novice cannot launch her career by pursuing those high-profile offenders on the FBI's Ten Most Wanted list. Even so, Miss Smithson has high hopes of becoming a big-time bounty hunter—and then penning a bloodcurdling account of her encounters with real-life criminals that will make Mr. Capote's *In Cold Blood* seem anemically pale in comparison.

A somewhat lofty ambition for someone of ordinary talents—perhaps even unseemly? Maybe so—but who are we to arch a critical brow, or for that matter to pose so many vexing hypothetical questions?

A PI is what Louella Smithson imagines herself to be, and here in the good old U.S. of A. a lady may practice whatever self-deception happens to strike her fancy. This born-in-the-heartland citizen is endowed with an inalienable right to envision herself as a hard-boiled detective, a gimlet-eyed gumshoe, or even a pistol-packing-momma bounty hunter who always gets her bad man *and* collects a humongous reward. And whenever she's of a mind to, Miss Smithson can drift along in daydreams about her primary ambition—which is to become a bestselling author of hair-raising accounts in that ever-popular genre known as True Crime.

But do not assume that the lady is detached from reality. Her stern paternal grandfather has taught Ellie that no worthwhile goal is ever achieved unless one ruthlessly disciplines both mind and body, concentrates on a specific long-term goal, puts in many long, hard hours—and never, *ever* gives up. These are words that she lives by, and why—at this very moment—our plucky entrepreneur has parked her old blue-and-white Ford Bronco about six miles north of Millport, Illinois, on the crest of an eighty-foot promontory known by locals as Noffsinger Ridge. Which elevated vantage point is directly across the paved highway from the Logan County Picnic Grounds. (Which is where the happy congregation of Mount Pleasant Methodist Church is congregated to enjoy their annual outing.) Which inevitably raises the nonhypothetical question: is Miss Smithson fascinated by highly competitive games of foot racing, the poetry of slow-pitch softball, and the haphazard tossing of yellow plastic horseshoes? Does her mouth water at the very thought of tables spread with barbecued pork, fried chicken, honey-baked beans, and a half-dozen varieties of potato salad? Check the little box by *No-sireebob.*

The young woman would have preferred to park her rusty SUV directly across the highway from Mrs. Francine Hooten's oversize dwelling—where, with the aid of her trusty binoculars, Louella could have peered through the front windows of that residence. In highly contrived fiction, such a convenient spot would have been thoughtfully provided for the private eye, but in real life that choice real estate was a wide-open pasture with no place for a PI to hide. To make matters worse, it was presently occupied by about two dozen head of cud-chewing Holstein milk cows. This harem was chaperoned by a dangerous-looking bull who would have gladly charged a Sherman tank had the tracked vehicle invaded his territory.

Accepting the deuces she had been dealt, Miss Louella Smithson did not whine about her less-than-optimal observation point. She patiently surveilled the Hooten driveway—in anticipation of witnessing the arrival of a legendary assassin. No, not just any legendary assassin who might happen by. Our hopeful bounty hunter has a yen to spot the very same killer whom the aforesaid Mrs. Hooten was rumored to have hired some years ago to rid Chicago of a plainclothes copper who'd gunned down her brutal, drug-pushing, mobster husband, who had lead poisoning coming, and make that a serious overdose. What brings the pseudo–private eye to the neighborhood at this particular time? Like so many of modern life's misadventures, you may blame it on the Internet. Miss Smithson routinely googles to find any morsel of knowledge that might enrich her bulging file on the Hooten clan. (This process is more difficult than you might imagine; the USA and Canada boast hundreds of salt-of-the-earth Hootens who are credits to their communities—and no kin whatever to Francine.)

For months, there have been nothing but dead ends, but quite recently Miss Smithson's number came up and she yelled "Bingo!" The cause of her excitement was that blog heaping abuse on "that brutal pair of Colorado lawmen" who had killed Francine Hooten's only son with a can of black-eyed peas and/or a sharp left hook. As a result of this report, the hopeful young woman had driven almost four hundred miles overnight to stake out the Hooten estate on the hunch that history might be about to repeat itself. If it does, the young entrepreneur plans to follow the suspect known to the FBI only as "Cowboy" and make a positive ID on the shadowy character. That in itself would be a fantastic accomplishment, but would she be satisfied? You know she wouldn't. Sooner or later, if all goes well, our ambitious private eye plans to effect a "citizen's arrest." If all goes well.

In the meantime, all she can do is wait atop Noffsinger Ridge and hope. Hope that Francine has already employed the same assassin. Hope that Cowboy will actually make a showing. Hope that she will be able to tail and ID said Cowboy. Forget about arresting an armed and extremely dangerous felon; the odds of all these hoped-for preliminary events converging in Miss Smithson's favor were somewhere in the neighborhood between astronomically low and dead zero. That being so, she dismissed all negative thoughts of improbability from her mind.

So was Louella Smithson having a good time? Ask any private eye you know about stakeouts, and she'll tell you they're about as much fun as watching ragweed grow in malodorous back-alley trash heaps.

Nothing of interest had occurred until some twenty or so minutes ago, when a motor vehicle showed down on the country road. The shiny automobile (so she thought) looked a little bit *out of place*. Don't ask her why; even amateur PIs just *know* these things. Wishfully, Miss Louella Smithson had watched the sleek gray Ford sedan slow . . . hesitate as the driver presumably took a look at the happy gathering of Methodist Christians . . . and pass by.

Not much, but it was enough to catch Louella's eye and cause her hopes to soar. *That'll be him!*

Perhaps. She would have to wait and see.

It is gratifying to report that minutes later, the same vehicle had returned and turned into the picnic grounds to park among the dozens of sedans, SUVs, and pickups already clustered there. Miss Smithson had gotten the merest glimpse of the driver exiting the automobile, and seen only an indistinct figure though her binoculars as the *person of interest* strode away from the boisterous picnic and through a thickly wooded area. *He's keeping out of sight!* And here was the clincher: the suspect was proceeding in a *southerly* direction. Yes, toward the boundary of Mrs. Francine Hooten's thirty-four-acre property, which abutted the Logan Country Picnic Grounds.

Despite this promising development, Louella was frustrated—and not without cause. First of all . . . *I didn't even see enough of the driver to know whether he's fat or thin or short or tall—much less get a look at his face.* On the plus side, she had gotten a glimpse at the Ford sedan's license plate, which was definitely from out of state. This would have canceled out her failure to get a good gander at the suspect *if* she had been able to read the plate—which was smudged with mud—which was suspicious because the rest of the automobile glistened like it'd just been run through a twelve-dollar automatic car wash. *He rubbed mud on the plate so somebody like me couldn't read it.* Having nothing nutritious to chew on, the lady settled for sour grapes: *It's probably only a rental car, so even if I had the plate number all I could do was trace it to Avis or Hertz or whatever.* Which probably wouldn't be of much help, because . . . *If the driver is a seriously professional criminal, he wouldn't have used his right name when he rented the car.* And Miss Louella Smithson had several other aggravations to contend with. The worst of these was her worry that . . . *The driver might not be who I hope he is.* Sigh. *He might even be another private eye, come to spy on Francine Hooten.* But that possibility was a real downer, and Louella-Ella-Ellie was determined to believe that the newcomer *was* the legendary Cowboy Assassin. And not without good reason: *Things just feel right about this.* Never underestimate the efficacy of that mysterious talent commonly referred to as "a woman's intuition."

Among her secondary aggravations was:

There's no telling when he'll drive out onto the highway again—I could be waiting here for hours and hours. Which annoying possibility was complicated by the grim fact that . . . *I drank almost a whole quart thermos of coffee and now I've got to pee but there's no place to go and if he don't show up soon I'm liable to— Oh, no!*

(Oh, yes.)

There were additional aggravations that might have been worthy of mention, but under the embarrassing circumstances, our highly distressed snoop has forgotten all of them.

CHAPTER NINE

HER ESTATE ON THE BANKS OF THE WABASH

Francine Hooten's property might aptly be named The Hornet's Nest, but no such luck.

It is nothing fancy: a mere thirty-four acres comprised of briar-choked forest and weedy pasture without any fat livestock to crop it down. The dwelling is a 130-year-old Victorian mansion that is sorely in need of new shutters, a replacement shingle here and there, and a few dozen gallons of white paint. But, humble though it may be, the stately old manor is hearth and home for the recently deceased purse snatcher's widowed mother. Speaking of whom, the semiparaplegic Francine Hooten is a shameless Anglophile who enjoys tea and crumpets in the afternoon, rereads Jane Austen most evenings, knows all the latest gossip about the royal family, and would have a moat (complete with drawbridge and crocodiles) encircling her castle if the persnickety county building code did not prohibit it. Such an extravagance is well within her means.

It is worth mentioning that Mrs. H. has two employees. These are Miss Marcella Clay (Mrs. Hooten's maid, cook, and opinionated companion) and pale, beady-eyed, ever-suspicious Cushing—m'lady's English butler. Truly—we do not jest. Cushing is the real McCoy, and straight from Merry Olde England—whence he emigrated to the USA following a brush with the legally constituted authority. That sordid incident involved suspected illegal possession and use of a firearm on behalf of Lord So-and-So, who had encouraged the hired help to discourage a cheeky commoner who was poaching salmon from m'lord's private lake. Nothing could be proved against

Cushing, on account of the fact that the alleged pistol was ditched in the River Tyne by the alleged shooter. Nevertheless, Mr. C. is unlikely to qualify for a cherished Green Card, seeing as how Scotland Yard has provided a thickish file of uniformly uncomplimentary information regarding said Brit to the U.S. Department of State, Federal Bureau of Investigation, and Bureau of Immigration and Naturalization—copies of which have found their way into the files of the Illinois State Police and the Logan County Sheriff's Office.

Though dimly aware of the fact that he is not overwhelmingly welcome in King George's former colony, Cushing is determined to make a go of it in the fabled Land of Opportunity. To that end, he has been displaying that sterling all-American quality that is so valued on the west side of the pond. We refer to the attribute popularly known as Get Up and Go, which in this instance involves doing more than a butler is paid to. Here is an illustrative example: despite the fact that the task is not listed as one of his official duties, the surly anachronism serves as his employer's armed-and-dangerous bodyguard. Old habits die hard.

A PREARRANGED RENDEZVOUS

Accompanied and aided by her live-in maid and companion, wheelchair-bound Mrs. Hooten exited a rear servant's entrance where the century-old cedar door stoop had been replaced with a gently sloping concrete ramp.

As was his habit, Roman-nosed, hawk-eyed Cushing watched from the kitchen window.

With her ever-present and seldom-used telescoping walking stick gripped tightly in her lap like a club, the testy woman pulled the brown blanket she was wrapped in tighter around her thin shoulders. Feeling more comfortable in the chill, humid air, Francine barked an order: "Take me to the rose garden, Marcella."

"Yes, ma'am."

"I intend to spend some time there." She added acidly, "Alone."

The long-suffering employee smiled. "Whatever you say." Marcella enjoyed these brief trips out of doors. The tall, big-boned woman pushed the oak-wheeled chair as easily as if the conveyance were empty and the grade on the flagstone pathway dead level. The incline was, in fact, noticeably uphill and the live cargo tipped the scales at 156 pounds. "If I've said it once, Miz Hooten, I've said it a hunnerd times—you oughten to be so stingy. I swear—you could be Jack Benny's penny-pinchin' granmammy."

The invalid responded tartly, "I believe you have complained about my frugality more than fivescore times, Marcella." The voice from under the gray headscarf was gratingly raspy, like the harsh shriek of a file being drawn across the dull teeth of a rusty cross-cut saw. "But if you don't mind getting to the point, what is the focus of your concern upon this particular occasion?"

"Well, I'll tell you—a rich lady like yourself ought to buy herself one a them *motorized* chairs to wheel around in."

"I could purchase a dozen battery-operated carts, Marcella, but what can I say?" Mrs. Hooten said it: "I am incurably old-fashioned, and frugal to a fault."

"You're *that*, all right." Her paid companion snorted. "But I still say—"

"Besides, if I indulged in such conveniences as motorized wheelchairs, electric dishwashers and such, what would I need to keep you around for?"

"Hah! Who'd cook your meals and pick up after your messy self—*and* stack your dirty dishes in that fancy 'lectric dishwasher." Marcella's broad face flashed a dazzling smile. "And don't go tellin' me that you could hire somebody else to take care of you—you know well as I do that nobody around these parts'll work for you 'cause you're such a bad-mouthed ol' grouch and you don't pay enough wages to keep a mouse in cheese and crackers."

The maid's employer smirked. "You certainly don't show any visible signs of starvation."

"That's because I help myself to all those goodies in your pantry. This mornin' at about two o'clock, I got up and toasted about half a loaf of white bread—and I spread fancy apple butter over ever' slice and I et it all before I went back to bed!"

"I have always suspected you of committing petty larcenies at my expense, but I do wish you had not confessed. Now I shall feel compelled to count the silverware daily."

"You go ahead and do that—all I steal is food."

Mrs. Hooten smiled. *Dear Marcella is so entertaining.*

The maid pushed the invalid toward a picket-fence gateway that opened into a circular garden which pressed halfway into a forest of oak and maple. Their daily little game and the pathway had about played out. "It's cold enough out here to freeze my shadder to the ground; I don't know why you won't stay inside by the fireplace like a normal old crank."

"I am not an old crank. I am an aged recluse." Francine surveyed her tiny hideaway, which was surrounded by a thick hedge. "Call me eccentric."

"I'd call you silly, 'cept you'd cut my pay to maybe one greenback dollar an hour."

"An option that I shall consider if you do not mend your meddling ways. But enough of this silly banter; I require a few minutes' respite from your company." Remembering her expected guest's instructions, Francine added, "Wheel me around to the opposite side of the fountain, Marcella, and turn the chair so that I am facing the house."

This order was carried out without comment.

"Thank you kindly. Now, you may leave me."

Marcella gave the disabled woman a worried look. "D'you have that little gadget with the red button?"

"I do." Mrs. Hooten pulled back her scarf to reveal the plastic pendant hanging from her neck. "When I have soaked up enough solitude to satisfy me, I shall buzz for you. Now depart this instant." After glancing at her wristwatch, she added by way of inducement, "That inane television show that you adore came on two minutes ago."

"Okay, I'm gone." The sturdy woman from the Missouri Ozarks patted her employer on the shoulder. "But if I don' hear that buzzer buzz in a hour, I'll come out here and wheel you back inside whether you want to go or *not*!" Having had the last word, Marcella stomped away on the flagstone pathway.

A damp, fetid breeze played with dead leaves.

Empty minutes ticked away toward yesterday.

The pale woman was as immobile as the lichen-encrusted iron porpoise that had long ago ceased to spew water into the fountain, which bone-dry ornament was the dreary centerpiece of a garden where a dozen untrimmed rosebushes that bloomed in June were now but a withered memory of warmer, happier days. The dismal effect had not gone unnoticed by the widow who had recently been deprived of her only descendant; the wheelchair's occupant evaluated her surroundings thusly: *This place looks like a scene from an old black-and-white horror movie.* Some eighty yards away, at her shambling, nine-gable Victorian home, the rear screened door slammed shut behind the maid with a bang. *Actually, this little garden spot would make a nice cemetery.* Francine's twisted smile was bittersweet. *Perhaps I shall have LeRoy buried here.* A long, weary sigh. *Before too long, I will lay myself down beside my only son . . . who has been such a disappointment.*

As she mused about converting her shabby rose garden into a family graveyard, Francine Hooten's imagination might well have conjured up the spirits of other members of her close-knit circle who had passed on. Such as the husband who had been shot dead by the Chicago plainclothes cop. Also Francine's brother, who'd run afoul of a rival South Side gang—and whose body had never been found. *Those Oak Park thugs probably set poor Buford into a fifty-five-gallon drum of cement and dumped him into Lake Michigan.* The sudden impression of a *presence* jolted Francine from her reverie. She had sensed neither sight nor sound, merely the slight stirring of another living creature. Her raspy voice rattled a hoarse whisper: *"Are you there?"*

The reply, from somewhere behind her, was immediate: "I am."

"You're on the far side the hedge—completely out of sight?"

Her visitor took no offense at this pointless query. "Certainly."

"Did our intermediary explain why I require your professional help?"

"There was no need to." There was a hint of a smile in the reply. "I manage to keep up with current events."

"Well, just to be sure we're on the same page, it's about—"

"Your son LeRoy, who died after being injured by those two small-town policemen in Colorado."

"Yes. Officers Parris and Moon." She ground her teeth at the memory of the cops' grinning faces on the television screen. "You are well informed." Francine inhaled a deep breath of the chill, dank air and expelled the frosty mist with a compliment: "I appreciate that job of work you did for me a few years ago."

"Thank you. It is my specialty." The gun for hire added, "You should also appreciate the fact that my rates are high—'exorbitant' would not be an overstatement."

The invalid assumed a haughty expression. "Despite my reputation for being miserly—when it comes to important matters, I always go first-class."

"I am pleased to hear it—a vulnerability to flattery is one of my few weaknesses."

After the partners in crime enjoyed lighthearted laughs, the assassin said soberly, "Assuming that you agree to my standard fee—I can give you my personal guarantee that both of these men will be dead within ten days."

"That would be gratifying—if their immediate demise was what I had in mind."

Judging by the brief silence, the person concealed on the forested side of the hedge might have been slightly taken aback. "What *do* you have in mind?"

After explaining her intent in some detail, Francine added, "I want those two grinning cops to suffer—like I am suffering. But I don't want either of them killed—not until I am in my grave. Then, you may feel free to deal with them in any manner that suits you—at my expense, of course. I will arrange payment through our trustworthy intermediary."

"Very well. Unless one or both of them gets in my way, I won't harm a hair on their heads while carrying out the immediate assignment. And after your death, I will dispose of them promptly." Two heartbeats. "But I suggest that you consider the cost—this will be a complex, dangerous task—and even more expensive than my usual work."

"Name your price."

The assassin did. Including a substantial advance for "miscellaneous expenses."

The old woman caught her breath. Held it. Then: "Agreed."

"Then consider it done." A pause. "There is," the concealed visitor said, "one last thing."

"What might that be?"

"In the pawpaw tree, there is a bird feeder hanging from a branch—within easy reach."

"I am well aware of that fact. I am the benefactor who provides expensive seed for my famished little feathered friends." Francine's mouth puckered into an expression that suggested a porcine smile. "May I assume that you have placed something there for me?"

"You may. And it is to be used only in the case of an emergency."

"Oh, my—a cyanide capsule?"

"Nothing quite so dramatic. Just yesterday, I purchased a matched pair of inexpensive mobile telephones. One for myself, the other for you. I will keep my instrument for . . . let us say . . . two weeks." Two heartbeats. "If something should come up that I absolutely *must* know about, you may call the only number listed in your telephone's directory."

"I understand." Francine Hooten's eyes were focused intently on the feeder. "But such an eventuality seems unlikely."

"Let us hope so."

CHAPTER TEN

HOW MARCELLA (NOT THE NAME ON HER BIRTH CERTIFICATE) IS USING HER TV BREAK

Is Mrs. Hooten's maid enjoying her afternoon television show? In a word—no. In seven more: she cannot stomach *I Love Lucy* reruns.

The Sony portable television in her second-floor bedroom is turned on, the volume set loud enough to be heard downstairs by the nosy butler—and by Mrs. Hooten, should the lady of the house return unexpectedly. Marcella has withdrawn to a third-floor storage room where cherished family heirlooms (along with miscellaneous other junk) have been deposited for a hoped-for posterity that—with Le-Roy Hooten having met his untimely end in Colorado—will never be born to inherit. Yes, even mean-down-to-the-marrow mobster moms look forward to darling grandchildren on whom they can dote.

From where the maid was seated in a dusty, purple velvet armchair, she could peer from one of the mansion's rear, east-facing gables. Her sober gaze was presented with a vast, misty vista of forest where the winding ribbon of the Wabash River was shrouded under a vaporous layer of gray, undulating mist. This domestic worker, who earned some eight hundred dollars per month plus room and essential victuals, had little interest in hardwood forests or silty midwestern watercourses, but even if she had, Marcella could see neither the foggy Wabash nor the trees—excepting a few dozen oaks and maples behind the rose garden's bushy hedge. Her tunnel-vision glare was limited to a patch of earth some ten yards in diameter, her alert mind occupied with delectable suspicions. *Unless I'm badly mis-taken, the old girl didn't go out there to enjoy some quiet time.*

The maid removed a miniature radio receiver/audio recorder from her apron pocket, unwound a twisted cord that was plugged into the instrument, and pressed the tiny microphone on the other end into her right ear to listen intently to—nothing. What she heard was not dead silence . . . merely a slight whisper of static. Marcella checked the receiver. *I know the thing is turned on.* So what was wrong? *Either this piece of junk has crapped out on me—or the bug I planted in the old woman's walking stick has gone on the fritz.* There was another possibility, which did not bear thinking about. But she did. *Or the rubber plug at the tip of her cane has fallen off and the bug's lying in the pathway—right in plain sight.* She leaned closer to the window, squinting in a futile attempt to see the thing. No matter. Brash as a pit bull on an overdose of steroids, spunky Marcella always dealt with dangerous issues straight-ahead and up front. *When I go out to wheel the old reprobate back in, I'll spot the rubber gimmick, pick it up, and push it back onto Mrs. Hooten's walking stick right under her nose—and get a well-deserved compliment for having eyes like an old-time Indian scout.*

All well and good, but before that award-winning performance could be pulled off, there was a more immediate problem to be solved: *One way or another, I've got to make a recording of whatever she says to whoever shows up.* And she knew just how to do it.

Before the invalid in the wheelchair had opened her mouth to say a word, Marcella removed another instrument from her purse. She focused the miniaturized, gyroscope-stabilized digital video cam-era's zoom lens on Francine Hooten's wrinkled face, centered the frame on the old woman's mouth, and pressed the Record button. The maid was delighted when the woman began to speak. Marcella shifted her gaze from the camera's LCD screen to peer out the win-dow. *I don't see anyone, so whoever she's talking to is keeping well out of sight.* Which was good news. Honest visitors do not sneak around like thieves—concealing themselves behind bushes. But just in case the lowlife did show his face, she set the camera to record a somewhat that might be. *The frumpy woman has probably lost a two-dollar plastic earring.*

A small drama, unworthy of his interest. But, having nothing of importance to occupy his idle time and in need of some mild cerebral exercise to stimulate his underemployed intellect, the butler (who carried a 9-mm Beretta semiautomatic in his inner jacket pocket) made up his mind to find out what Marcella was looking for along the pathway.

FOLLOWING THE COWBOY ASSASSIN

As we now know, Mrs. Hooten's caller was the very same infamous hired gun whom Miss Louella Smithson had hoped would show up. But the "Cowboy" designation calls for a comment. Here it is: despite the fact that the Federal Bureau of Investigation has a fat file on the suspect, the criminal's identity has not been ascertained by the nation's premier law-enforcement agency. This being the case, the title of the Bureau file is "Cowboy Assassin." (No, the shooter does not specialize in popping lead at western horsemen who wear broad-brimmed hats and high-heeled boots with jingly steel spurs mounted thereon.) "Cowboy" refers to the assassin's *reported* choice of apparel. But be forewarned: the evidence along this line is thin and might prove misleading. We trust that more shall be revealed as events unfold.

Despite the humiliating failure of her bladder's sphincter muscle, Louella Smithson had neither left her post nor given up hope of identifying the sinister person who'd parked among the Methodist vehicles and then slipped away on foot in the direction of Francine Hooten's sprawling house. *He's got to come back to his car sometime, and when he does I'll be right here.*

You may embroider this motto onto your linen napkin:

Patience and Persistence Pay

And indeed, things were beginning to look brighter. About five minutes after Francine Hooten had completed her conversation with the hired killer, Miss Smithson spotted the shadowy figure again—this time advancing on a northerly course to the Logan County Picnic Grounds, where everyone was chowing down on succulent, slow-roasted pig flesh, delicious, deep-fried barnyard fowl, and a variety of tasty and indigestible side dishes that are far too numerous to enumerate. Was the amateur sleuth ecstatic? Yes indeed. *This time I'll get a good look at the rascal!*

Parked in the slowly graying shade atop Noffsinger Ridge, Louella Smithson had her binoculars carefully focused and, to minimize the inevitable jittering, her elbows resting steadily on the steering wheel. When the vehicle exited the picnic grounds and turned in the northerly direction whence it had originally come, she was treated to a glimpse of the profile of the person of interest. The most impressive feature was the driver's cowboy hat—which attire was not all that unusual in southern Illinois. Unfortunately, the wide hat brim had—from Louella's elevated vantage point—concealed the upper portion of the face from her view. The features she did get a glimpse of—a moderately strong chin, a determined mouth, and the tip of a pointy nose—had struck her as rather ordinary. Not exactly what you'd expect for a cold-blooded killer. But, having read about Baby Face Nelson and any number of other homicidal brutes who did not fit Hollywood's notion of seriously bad guys, she was neither greatly surprised nor the least disappointed. As far as our make-believe detective was concerned . . . *I just know it's him!* And, more hopeful still—*I'll know that nose and chin when I see him again.* Stowing the binoculars in her pink purse, Miss Smithson started the V-8 engine and eased her blue-and-white 1989 Bronco slowly down the ridge in low gear before easing the old bucket of bolts onto the blacktop. *All I've got to do now is stay way back so he won't know that anyone's tailing him.*

Though the Bronco was almost a quarter mile behind the departing vehicle, the driver under the six-hundred-dollar, made-to-order cowboy hat spotted the big SUV right away. Its presence in the rearview mirror raised no immediate concern, but professional assassins who she mumbled, "I'll fuss at that silly ol' lady for stayin' out in the cold so long."

It would never do the trick in Atlanta, Vicksburg, or Little Rock, but it was sufficient to deceive her singular audience. On her way to retrieve Mrs. Hooten, Marcella kept an eye peeled for the bug, but didn't get the least glimmer of anything resembling a rubber plug. She prayed . . . *Oh, please please please let it be on the tip of her walking stick.* As all those who petition the Almighty know, sometimes the answer is no. Which observation gives the game away. Yes, sad to say, when the maid approached her employer, the bug's rubber enclosure was *not* on the tip of Mrs. Hooten's titanium walking stick.

All the way back to the rear door of the Hooten mansion, as Marcella's mouth kept up a running commentary on the folly of "an ol' lady like you exposin' her feeble self to cold, damp weather," the special agent's sharp eyes flicked left and right, examining every inch of the dead grass beside the path. What did she see?

Nada. Zilch. Naught.

Which is to say—not what she was looking for. Which was vexing. Sufficiently so to cause the maid's speech to drift out of character— but only in her thoughts. *Damn. That thing must've grown wings and flown away!*

As wistful characters in novels said in bygone days, "Oh, would that it had."

THE BODYGUARD

Yes. The butler who is endowed with good old Yankee get-up-and-go is on the job.

As the maid looked right and left and speculated about walking sticks' airborne rubber tips, she was observed by the ever-alert Cushing, whose primary mission was to protect the missus of the house from bodily harm, problems with John Law—and deceitful employees. At his lookout post by the kitchen window, the Brit expatriate took note of the American maid's nervous examination of the ground. *It looks like Marcella is searching for something.* He wondered idly what broader view. Marcella was understandably pleased with her ability to improvise right on the spot, and things went fairly well, except that from time to time an elm branch clustered with dead leaves was wafted by a pesky breeze to temporarily block the video camera's view. Despite this aggravation, the resourceful operative was able to document the movement of Francine Hooten's lips for more than half the words her employer uttered. Right up to . . . "But such an eventuality seems unlikely."

When Francine's mouth finally clenched in its usual scowl and stayed that way for quite a while, the maid realized that the conversation was over and her summons imminent. Marcella pulled a mobile telephone from her pocket. Like the cheap telephone the assassin had left for Francine Hooten, this top-of-the-line communications device was reserved for serious business. After using a delicate cable to link her miniature Japanese video recorder to the telephone, she punched in a memorized ten-digit number and placed the call.

Almost immediately, a computer-generated monotone on the other end said, "Connection made. Please provide ID and password."

Marcella recited her six-character alphanumeric identity code and confirmed it with this week's password (*thunderstorm*).

"You may proceed," the robo voice said.

After making a terse, factual report, she downloaded the video camera's digital memory—all of which was duly recorded on the other end. When she had completed the task, the maid said, "Goodbye," which would automatically break the connection. She slipped the mobile telephone back into her ample apron pocket and put the video camera into her purse.

This communication had required precisely seventy-two seconds.

When the buzzer in the kitchen sounded a minute later, Marcella Clay (aka FBI Special Agent Mary Anne Clayton) was downstairs at the back door. The Emory University graduate put on her dull, slack-jawed smile, exited the house, and sallied forth to wheel Mrs. Francine Hooten back into the warm comfort of her home. Falling into character, the counterfeit maid assumed her southern accent as what that might be. *The frumpy woman has probably lost a two-dollar plastic earring.*

A small drama, unworthy of his interest. But, having nothing of importance to occupy his idle time and in need of some mild cerebral exercise to stimulate his underemployed intellect, the butler (who carried a 9-mm Beretta semiautomatic in his inner jacket pocket) made up his mind to find out what Marcella was looking for along the pathway.

CHAPTER ELEVEN

FOLLOWING THE COWBOY ASSASSIN

As we now know, Mrs. Hooten's caller was the very same infamous hired gun whom Miss Louella Smithson had hoped would show up. But the "Cowboy" designation calls for a comment. Here it is: despite the fact that the Federal Bureau of Investigation has a fat file on the suspect, the criminal's identity has not been ascertained by the nation's premier law-enforcement agency. This being the case, the title of the Bureau file is "Cowboy Assassin." (No, the shooter does not specialize in popping lead at western horsemen who wear broad-brimmed hats and high-heeled boots with jingly steel spurs mounted thereon.) "Cowboy" refers to the assassin's *reported* choice of apparel. But be forewarned: the evidence along this line is thin and might prove misleading. We trust that more shall be revealed as events unfold.

Despite the humiliating failure of her bladder's sphincter muscle, Louella Smithson had neither left her post nor given up hope of identifying the sinister person who'd parked among the Methodist vehicles and then slipped away on foot in the direction of Francine Hooten's sprawling house. *He's got to come back to his car sometime, and when he does I'll be right here.*

You may embroider this motto onto your linen napkin:

Patience and Persistence Pay

And indeed, things were beginning to look brighter. About five minutes after Francine Hooten had completed her conversation with the hired killer, Miss Smithson spotted the shadowy figure again—this time advancing on a northerly course to the Logan County Picnic Grounds, where everyone was chowing down on succulent, slow-roasted pig flesh, delicious, deep-fried barnyard fowl, and a variety of tasty and indigestible side dishes that are far too numerous to enumerate. Was the amateur sleuth ecstatic? Yes indeed. *This time I'll get a good look at the rascal!*

Parked in the slowly graying shade atop Noffsinger Ridge, Louella Smithson had her binoculars carefully focused and, to minimize the inevitable jittering, her elbows resting steadily on the steering wheel. When the vehicle exited the picnic grounds and turned in the northerly direction whence it had originally come, she was treated to a glimpse of the profile of the person of interest. The most impressive feature was the driver's cowboy hat—which attire was not all that unusual in southern Illinois. Unfortunately, the wide hat brim had—from Louella's elevated vantage point—concealed the upper portion of the face from her view. The features she did get a glimpse of—a moderately strong chin, a determined mouth, and the tip of a pointy nose—had struck her as rather ordinary. Not exactly what you'd expect for a cold-blooded killer. But, having read about Baby Face Nelson and any number of other homicidal brutes who did not fit Hollywood's notion of seriously bad guys, she was neither greatly surprised nor the least disappointed. As far as our make-believe detective was concerned . . . *I just know it's him!* And, more hopeful still—*I'll know that nose and chin when I see him again.* Stowing the binoculars in her pink purse, Miss Smithson started the V-8 engine and eased her blue-and-white 1989 Bronco slowly down the ridge in low gear before easing the old bucket of bolts onto the blacktop. *All I've got to do now is stay way back so he won't know that anyone's tailing him.*

Though the Bronco was almost a quarter mile behind the departing vehicle, the driver under the six-hundred-dollar, made-to-order cowboy hat spotted the big SUV right away. Its presence in the rearview mirror raised no immediate concern, but professional assassins who do not pay close attention to what is occurring in their immediate vicinity are not likely to survive long enough to see their first gray hairs sprouting—much less to retire to an idyllic beachside residence in Maui, Bali, or Key West.

Puttering along at a mere forty-five miles per hour, Louella Smithson realized that she was gradually closing on her suspect. *He must've slowed down.* The edgy PI eased off on the accelerator pedal until the Bronco's speedometer needle jittered around the 40 mark. *I hope he's not onto me.* Playing it safe, she pulled into a small service station—one of those nostalgia-provoking ma-and-pa operations with a seventy-year-old Coke sign rusting away in the window and a sturdy cane-back rocking chair on the front porch. *There. I'll give him time get out of sight, then get back on the road again.* And she would.

While Louella waits for a few heartbeats, there is breaking news to report at Francine Hooten's domicile. Indeed, the troubles there began some six minutes ago, which requires us to rewind the clock by that amount—and begin at the beginning.

CHAPTER TWELVE

AN UNFORESEEN AND ALARMING DEVELOPMENT

After Marcella deposited a chilled Mrs. Hooten in the parlor by the blazing fire in the sandstone hearth, the meticulously vigilant maid returned to the third-floor storeroom to make sure that she had not left the slightest telltale evidence of her recent clandestine presence in that rarely visited space. After the FBI undercover agent had moved the purple velvet armchair so that its maple legs were positioned precisely over their former dustless prints and picked up a long-dead moth that she had stepped on and smashed flat, she reached over to straighten the grubby lace curtains at the window—and glanced through the dingy glass to see Cushing strolling along the pathway toward the rose garden. In an instant, the roles of suspicious butler and spied-on maid were reversed. *What's that sneaky little twerp up to?* She thought she knew, and Marcella's heart literally *stopped*—skipping a beat as the beak-nosed Englishman stooped to pluck something off the ragged edge of an unclipped hedge. A dark something, about the size of a rubber plug that belonged on the tip of Mrs. Hooten's titanium walking stick. There could be no doubt about it: *He's found it.*

She might have hoped that the butler would not realize the significance of what he had discovered and decided that she would stick around and see it out to a final showdown—come what may.

Such follies are for amateurs and absurd characters in lurid novels—not for professionals who want to blow out the candles on their next birthday cake. Her training kicking in, Special Agent Mary Anne Clayton turned to descend the stairway two steps at a time. Before she had reached the landing on the second floor, the lady had removed the mobile phone from her apron pocket and connected to a memorized emergency number where a human being would pick up the phone. She held her breath for three rings, then breathed again when the anonymous voice said, "ID, please." She responded in a *Right Stuff* monotone that did not betray the slightest hint of her apprehension, "S. A. Clayton."

"Please state your request."

"Evacuation."

"Say again?"

"S. A. Clayton—Evacuation. Plan One."

"Roger, Clayton. We're on top of it."

And that was that.

A BEARER OF BAD NEWS

Pleased with the important business she had conducted in the rose garden, Mrs. Francine Hooten was comfortable by the fireplace— and relaxed. Very much so. Indeed, her head was drooped, and she was almost dozing when her rest was interrupted by a polite, "Excuse me, madam."

Raising her chin and opening her eyes, the lady of the house murmured irritably, "What is it, Cushing?"

"This." He presented an open palm. "I found it lodged in the hedge, at the edge of your rose garden."

She leaned forward for a closer look. "Is that a pint Mason jar?"

"Yes, madam." The butler cleared his throat. "But the jar is not what I discovered in the hedge. I thought it prudent to seal the found object inside this handy glass container."

He can be so damn irritating. "Are you going to tell me *why*?"

"Ah—but that is the very point."

"Cushing—you are beginning to get on my nerves." She blinked at the black object in the pint jar. "What on earth is *that*?"

"A small, black rubber cap." Her bodyguard pointed his finger at the tip of her walking stick, which lay across her lap. "I believe it belongs on the end of your cane—it must have fallen off during your recent visit to the flower garden."

Francine took a look at the naked tip of her telescoping support. "No doubt." She got a good grip on the titanium cylinder. "If you do not tell me *why* you have put the rubber thingamabob in the Mason jar, I shall feel compelled to whack you with my stick."

"Whack if you wish, madam." A smirking pause. "But before you resort to unseemly violence, I suggest that you take a closer look at the rubber cap." He offered her the jar.

As she squinted through the thick, curved glass, the woman's lips closed tightly, then pursed to say, "Oh my."

Cushing nodded. "You have no doubt noticed that a coin-shaped metallic device has been pressed inside the rubber cap."

"I have noticed." She looked up at her employee. "Is that what I think it is?"

Cushing nodded. "Without the least shadow of an inkling of a doubt."

"But . . . who could have put it into my cane?"

"I can think of only three possibilities." The butler, who was somewhat of a literalist, cleared his throat. "Firstly, yourself." Without smiling, he added, "Which conjecture seems sufficiently unlikely as to demand immediate dismissal."

"Thank you, Cushing." Her lips curled in a wry smile. "Please proceed."

"Secondly, myself."

"I will keep that prospect in mind. Then am I to conclude that Marcella—"

"It does seem quite likely, madam—especially in light of certain ancillary evidence which supports such a hypothesis."

"Please explain."

The butler tilted his bald head to indicate the south side of the towering house. "A moment before I entered the premises, I observed your maid entering the detached garage. A moment later, Marcella departed in her hideous little German motor vehicle. She turned north on the paved road, and seemed to be in rather a hurry. Unless you have just dispatched the woman on some urgent errand. . . ." He let the accusation hang in the air.

"I see." The purse snatcher's momma sighed. "Too bad. I was rather fond of her."

"If you like, madam—I will be pleased to take the Rolls and deal with this distressing matter—*personally*." He patted his concealed jacket pocket.

The dead-mobster's wife shook her head and replied firmly, "Thank you, Cushing, but no." Francine Hooten knew just what to do.

Her butler did, too. "Yes, madam." After making a slight bow, her discreet employee withdrew to prepare a steaming pot of extrastrong English breakfast tea and a silver tray of dainty biscuits.

CHAPTER THIRTEEN

THE DISCONNECT

Miss Louella Smithson, who pulled into the ma-and-pa filling station to avoid being spotted by the assassin about a quarter mile up the two-lane highway from the picnic grounds, is precisely where we left her. But not for long.

Having counted to ten, Miss Smithson pulled onto the road again—and stared in stunned disbelief at the ramrod-straight section of blacktop stretching for miles ahead of her. The two-lane was as empty as a grinning politician's election-day promise. She gave the thirsty Bronco a tasty gulp of gasoline, then slowed to cast a hopeful glance at a deserted farmhouse. Except for an antique tractor rusting away in the front yard, there was no sign of a vehicle. "Damn—I've lost him!" Major bummer. *I should've counted to five.*

The dejected gumshoe had two options. *I can give up the chase and slink home to Kansas City like a wimp-sissy amateur who doesn't have an ounce of confidence in herself. Or . . . I can go with my hunch and drive all the way to Granite Creek, Colorado. If I spot Cowboy's car there, I'll ID the bastard before he murders the cops and then spit in his face when they put the cuffs on him.* Or (and this scenario was preferable), *Maybe they'll just shoot him down like the mangy, egg-sucking dog he is!*

You know what she did. But before we have time to applaud the spunky lady's fortitude and pluck, another serious player is about to take center stage—one who has gotten a good look at the woman behind the wheel of the aged Bronco.

A CRITICAL REVERSAL OF ROLES

As the sleek, silver-gray Ford sedan with Oklahoma plates emerged from behind the deserted farmhouse and pulled onto the paved highway, the driver stared at the slowly receding Bronco and considered the possible downside: *She has certainly gotten a look at my rental car and might have read a portion of the plate number despite the mud.* Which was no big deal. Tracing the car back to Avis would produce a Visa number on a stolen card, which would lead the snoop nowhere fast. *So I'll ditch the rental at the St. Louis airport, use another bogus credit card to buy an airline ticket to Denver or Colorado Springs, where I'll rent myself another set of wheels. After a good night's sleep, I'll motor over to Granite Creek, do the job, and be out of town before those hick cops know what's happened.*

All well and good.

But the seasoned pro could not dismiss that proverbial worst-case scenario. *The nosy bitch might have gotten a good enough look at me to recognize my face next time she sees me.* And (though this seemed like an awfully long shot) . . . *She might be waiting for me in Granite Creek, ready to ID me for the police.*

A vexing situation, but challenges do serve to keep one's edge razor-sharp. It also helps to have a sense of humor. "What *is* the world coming to—me being tailed by a *woman!*" Finding some comedic relief in the tense situation, the so-called Cowboy Assassin laughed out loud.

A typically sexist attitude? In more commonplace circumstances one might reasonably conclude so, but in a dicey situation where the presumed chauvinist lout pays the rent by offhandedly murdering fellow citizens—does it not seem somewhat nitpicking to dwell upon such relatively minor issues as political correctness? And who among us, whether deliberately or without intent to offend, has not committed a similar or equivalent transgression—including Miss Louella Smithson?

But enough of these pesky semirhetorical questions. The urgent issue at hand is (in a manner of speaking not intended to cast canine aspersions on either party) that *the fox is now following the hound.*

Or would have been—except for the interruption.

A MINOR COMPLICATION

The person referred to as "Cowboy" did not flinch when the cheap cellular telephone warbled like a robin choking on a knotty earthworm. *I really must reprogram that piece of junk for something less grating on the nerves.* With a wan smile, the assassin answered the presumably urgent summons: "So soon?"

Francine Hooten's unmistakable raspy voice responded, "My apologies. I have grave concerns about one of my employees, who has apparently been taking an unseemly interest in my personal business—and possibly, in *yours*. Even as we speak, she is headed north in a pale green Volkswagen Bug." A pause. *Or do they call them Beetles?* "Will you be able to resolve this troublesome issue—per our agreed financial arrangement?"

Cowboy smiled as the described automobile passed. "Consider it done." *I do lead a charmed life.* "Goodbye."

CHAPTER FOURTEEN

IN THE MEANTIME, WHAT'S HAPPENING
AT THE COLUMBINE?

Probably not a whole lot, but a Rocky Mountain westerner who stays away from his natural habitat for too long—even in the pleasant environs of rural southern Illinois—tends to get homesick for alpine peaks that keep their winter frosting on all summer long, lonesome cowboys who sing sad songs about love gone wrong—and stream water so crystal clear that Mr. Rainbow Trout stands out like a multicolored mitten dropped on a snowbank. Not to mention that thin, chilly high-country air, which is a surefire elixir for just about every ailment known to those altitude-deprived folk who spend their lives no more than a few hundred feet above sea level.

PREVIOUS REFERENCES—A THUMBNAIL
SUMMARY UPDATE

The unwary Columbine cowboy who got gored by the bull is recovering at Snyder Memorial Hospital in Granite Creek, and assuring every pretty nurse who'll listen that upon his return to Charlie Moon's ranch, he is going to de-horn that danged Hereford with a butcher knife. And if a ten-inch blade don't get the job done, he'll have a go at it with an ax.

Six-Toes (that big, stupid galoot who got decked by "Little Butch" Cassidy during the knock-down-drag-out bunkhouse brawl) is suffering from a dislocated jawbone and missing a pair of molars and a front tooth, which makes it hard to chew a wad of tobacco and hit the red coffee can when he spits. Mr. Cassidy is suffering from a sore right hand, and the bitter regret that he didn't hit Six-Toes hard enough to break the halfwit's neck.

The whirlwind-wrecked windmill? That had looked like a total loss, but the Columbine blacksmith—a brawny man with hands big as catcher's mitts and hairy forearms like cedar posts—has been known to work wonders with mangled machinery. The smithy is convinced that he can repair the damage, and despite Charlie Moon's doubts about the outcome—is about halfway there.

Which gets us around to those three souls who reside under the roof of the two-story log headquarters building. It's a long way past sundown, but let's look in upon them.

SARAH FRANK

Shhh. (The young lady, who went to bed worried about the man in her life, seems to be deep in the sweet, dreamless sleep of the innocent.) *Seems* to be. But in Sarah's melancholy night-vision, she is driving her red Ford pickup away from the Columbine and Charlie Moon—forever. And compared to a week or maybe two, that's a long time to be gone.

Never mind. Now and again, anxious young folk tend to suffer from excessive angst. But they get over it. Usually.

DAISY PERIKA

Charlie Moon's irascible auntie is not numbered among the innocent, and the troublesome tribal elder finds herself dead center in a straight-out nightmare.

There is no point in going into the nitty-gritty details, but it may be of interest to know that Daisy is dreaming that she is present at Hester "Toadie" Tillman's funeral. This aged woman has attended more wakes, funerals, and burials than an acre of gnarly old piñon trees has knots, and there's nothing about such gatherings that is even slightly nightmarish for one with so much experience in saying her goodbyes to the dearly departed, or for that matter, shouting a hearty *hasta la vista* to those señors and señoritas whom she is glad to have seen the last of.

But even for Daisy P.—who is accustomed to seeing dead people in broad daylight and talking to them about this and that and whatnot—it is somewhat jarring when the person you are viewing in the luxuriously quilted casket is also standing beside that costly coffin, and making complaints. In the case of Daisy and the elderly lady who had been trapped in the wrecked pickup, their conversation went something like this:

Daisy (politely): "Pardon me for asking, Toadie—but how d'you manage to be two places at one time?"

Hester: "This ain't my actual funeral, Daisy—it's a silly dream you're having." A miffed expression. "I bet you won't even bother to show up at the real send-off."

Daisy: "Oh, I might—if I'm not too busy doing something important."

Hester: "Like what—trimming your toenails?"

D.: "That's not a bad idea." A smirk. "When other folks show up to celebrate your going away, I might be at home clipping an ingrown nail on my big toe."

H. (shaking a finger at the smart aleck): "I sent Danny Bignight to warn you, Daisy—you'll be sorry if you don't show up to mourn at my funeral!"

D. (regretfully): "I'm already sorry, Toadie."

H. (doubtful): "Are you—really?"

D. (nodding): "You bet! I'm sorry your momma and daddy didn't get run over by a Greyhound bus when they was five years old."

H. (transformed into a hideous toadstool with a thousand bloodshot eyeballs, every one of them glaring at her hateful enemy): "I'll *get* you for that!"

D. (rolling her two eyes): "Being dead hasn't made you any more likable."

Not much of a comeback for acid-tongued Daisy Perika, but she may be excused for being somewhat off her usual form. Even those who have dreamed of being trapped in the center of a railroad trestle bridge (over a deep arroyo filled with snarling grizzly bears, six-foot rattlesnakes, and millions of purple scorpions) with two humongous steam-engine locomotives approaching from opposite directions at ninety-nine miles per hour to smash the dreamer flat as a fritter will be compelled to admit that Daisy's confrontation with a thousand-eyeball toadstool was, at the least, unnerving. Charlie Moon's aunt opened her eyes and groaned. *Well, I'm glad that aggravation is over.*

But it wasn't. Not quite. Hester "Toadie" Tillman's impudent threat to return from the grave and haunt her rankled the tribal elder. *If she so much as shows her homely face, I'll make that silly old woman wish she'd never died in the first place.* The tribal elder's mouth gaped in a soul-satisfying yawn. She snuggled her head into the feather pillow. *Now I'll get me a healthy dose of shut-eye and forget all about ol' Toadie.*

And so she would.

Until the next haunt came along.

CHARLIE MOON

Daisy Perika is a tough act to follow, but for the sake of triangular symmetry, the third member of the small family shall be visited.

As it happens, the tribal elder's nephew has not yet fallen asleep. The hardworking stockman has a lot on his mind. Some pleasant things to think about, some otherwise. Here is the list:

His pretty sweetheart, Patsy Poynter.
The gored cowboy at the hospital.
The trouble Six-Toes is always creating.
The sinking price of beef on the hoof.
The rising costs of operating the Columbine, and . . .
The sudden realization that his quarterly tax report is overdue.

Those folks who always see the bright side might say one out of six ain't so bad, but they have probably never tried to make a decent profit raising cattle.

Number seven was a more or less neutral issue. We refer to a recent offer Mr. Moon had gotten a from a consortium of Las Vegas investors to buy the Columbine Ranch—which formal proposal expired in six days. The stockman began to mull it over. *If I sold this big ranch for the price those high-rollers quoted, I could buy that dandy little three-section spread on the Gunnison.* It was well-watered, and not only that . . . *I'd have enough cash left over to last me for the rest of my life and then some.* He hung a Cheshire cat smile in the darkness. *I might raise a few quarter horses just for fun, but*—and this was a solemn promise—*I'd never work hard another day in my life.* He nodded as well as a man can whose head is reclining on a firm pillow. *I'd turn in my deputy badge to Scott and my tribal-investigator badge to Oscar Sweetwater. Why not? Scott don't really need a deputy and the tribal chairman hasn't given me a job to do for almost a year.* Then, there was Moon's immediate family to consider. *Daisy and Sarah would enjoy a little horse ranch on the Gunnison just as much as being here on the Columbine.* Which raised another issue: *I wonder what Patsy would think about raising horses.* Which, quite naturally, got him to thinking about the prettiest lady in Granite Creek County.

This general line of middle-of-the-night mulling continued for quite a while, until—as a man does from time to time—the Ute sat up in bed and flat out made up his mind. *I'm going to do it.*

Which raises the burning question:

IS HE *REALLY* GOING TO DO IT?

It would appear so. But don't go betting your best boots and Mexican saddle on it.

The issue seemingly settled, Charlie Moon has stretched out on his bed again and is about to drift off to sleep, but by the time the sun comes up and he wakes up, the rancher mostly likely won't remember very much about these wee-hour musings. And even if he does, he'll probably shake his head and wonder, *What got into me—to even* consider *such a thing?*

Of course, there's always the onion-skin-thin chance that he really will. (Do it.)

CHAPTER FIFTEEN

THE WELL-OILED MACHINERY OF GOVERNMENT HAS BEGUN TO HUM

Comforted by this assurance, we shall not fret about the potential troubles brewing for Charlie Moon and Scott Parris. Somehow, the lawmen will muddle through; they always do. In the end, things will turn out all right. Unless they don't.

Which government?

Uncle Sam's, of course—the one in Washington, District of Columbia, on the Potomac. Comprised primarily of the Executive Branch (headed by a POTUS who knows precisely what to do and always acts decisively), a bicameral Congress whose sole intent is to look after the public interest, and a Supreme Court whose members are dedicated to preserving the original intent of the U.S. Constitution. Not to mention more bureaus, departments, administrations, and offices than a centipede could count if she had twenty toes on every foot.

Oh, very well—fret if you must. But the widely held view that the feds cannot get *anything* done right or on time borders on the very edge of cynicism—and strictly speaking is not true. Not one hundred percent of the time. Despite the best obstructive efforts of those hundreds of thousands of dedicated bureaucrats who had jobs for life and elected officials who had benefits beyond the fondest dreams of the average working citizen—every once in a while, things do fall into place, and promptly so. And all because of a modest proportion of highly dedicated public servants among both feds and government contractors who put in long, hard days—and without a penny of overtime pay—all with minimal appreciation from the aforemen-tioned average working citizen.

Recall, by way of sterling example, FBI Special Agent Mary Anne Clayton, aka Marcella Clay, who—at considerable risk to life and limb—made the clandestine video recording of Mrs. Francine Hoo-ten's mouth whilst the bereaved purse snatcher's momma was utter-ing felonious instructions to a hired assassin. And recall how the undercover agent had (via mobile telephone) transmitted the video data stream of the old woman's moving lips to her Bureau contact. A creditable day's work for a government employee, but her labors were not complete. When the butler discovered the misplaced "bug" on the garden pathway, the so-called Marcella Clay had alerted a Bu-reau handler of her intention to withdraw immediately from the Hooten residence. A pretty good performance for an underpaid fed, and though the daring FBI operative was definitely the star of act one of that melodrama, there were other players (yet to step onstage) who deserve our appreciation.

Only hours after the data was received, it was processed (so that only Mrs. Hooten's mouth was digitized for analysis) and then trans-mitted to four internationally recognized experts—three of the hu-man species, the fourth belonging to no known biological category. A trio of deaf-from-birth lip-reading experts (located in Greenville, South Carolina, Medford, Oregon, and Medicine Hat, Alberta) eye-balled the processed version of Francine Hooten's mouth forming words unheard except by the speaker and the unseen (alleged) assas-sin. All three of these contract lip-readers recognized the words *Paris* and *moon,* and naturally assumed some sort of French Connection with lunar overtones that suggested an astrological element.

While the humans were watching Mrs. H.'s thin lips form sylla-bles, a skilled MIT-educated computer scientist in the Hoover Build-ing in D.C. was uploading the digitized video frames into a souped-up HP parallel-processor desktop wherein the latest version of a custom-developed Bureau software (LIPanalyze IV) would compete with the three human professionals. It was not so much a matter of who would win the game—a distinguished linguist at the University of

Texas in Austin (who reads lips while conducting her all-deaf Sunday-school class at a congregation of happy Presbyterians) would review the four independent reports and produce a written summary of Mrs. Hooten's "most probable" remarks.

But before you begin bemoaning the slowly turning wheels of the federal bureaucracy—be advised that the entire process was completed in twenty-two hours flat. How's that? Go ahead, admit it—doesn't knowing how the government's toothed gears twirl and mesh make you feel measurably better?

You want to know what happened to the Sunday-school-teacher's report? (Bringing up such issues is in poor taste, and suggests a distinct lack of patriotic fervor.) The report was *distributed,* of course.

Who (if anyone) on the distribution list would actually take time to read the document, what action (if any) would be initiated—and who (if anyone) would carry out the prescribed action?

Very well, if you insist on exhibiting nitpicking negativity.

The answer to all three questions is: FBI Special Agent Lila Mae McTeague.

Those who know the formidable lady will be visibly impressed, but if you've never heard of this remarkable public servant—that just goes to show how little recognition a really top-notch fed gets for working six days per week for an average of about twelve hours a day. More to the point, Scott Parris is acquainted with McTeague, and so is Charlie Moon—the slender Ute rancher's acquaintance with the lady being of a much more personal nature than that of the brawny *matukach* chief of police—whose relationship is strictly professional and not always friendly.

For those who desire clarification about Mr. Moon's connection with the drop-dead gorgeous fed, here is a tidbit of nonmalicious gossip to chew on and digest: once upon a time, Charlie and Lila Mae came *this close* to a merger of the martial kind. No, reverse the order of *i* and *t* to make that *marital.* (Sorry—one of those embarrassing Freudian slips of the typographical category.) Where were we? Oh, yes—recalling the potential Moon–McTeague amalgamation of some years past. Alas, as is so often the case—the deal fell through at that proverbial last minute. And all on account of a smart-aleck, quarter-wit Columbine employee (one Six-Toes) who didn't know the difference between wholesome cowboy humor and stupidity. And still don't. Doesn't. Whatever.

But we digress.

The point is this: the FBI is deadly serious about nailing Francine Hooten's tough old hide to the late Mr. J. Edgar's barn door. With so many critical irons in the fire, why is the Bureau heating up still another one—and just to put a pathetic invalid mobster's wife into the well-known clink? Thank you for asking. One cannot be absolutely certain, but the federal cops might be especially hot under the collar because one of their own has, as the odd saying goes, "gone missing." Not a solitary word has been heard from Special Agent Mary Anne Clayton, aka Marcella Clay, since Mrs. Hooten's employee called in the evac code and presumably hit the road to Terre Haute to meet a Bureau team dispatched from Indianapolis. The lady has, in a word—vanished. Dropped off a cliff.

No doubt with an enabling push from that miscreant known to the FBI as the "Cowboy Assassin."

But this is not exactly a morale booster. What we need is a few minutes of R & R from the dark, seamy side of life—a pleasant diversion in the bright sunshine. Which suggests some lovely spot where yellow butterflies flutter by, happy little bluebirds sing their tiny hearts out, and good, honest, salt-of-the-earth folks are occupied with having themselves an innocent good time. The Methodist picnic in Logan County would do the trick, but that congregation of upstanding citizens has long since packed up their high-calorie leftovers, softballs and bats, and plastic horseshoes—and gone home.

Never mind.

There are bound to be some other solid citizens hereabouts who will fill the bill.

Aha! There are—word has just come in about a fine old gentleman and his wholesome grandson. They are enjoying one of those memorable days that inspired Mr. Norman Rockwell to illustrate covers on the old *Saturday Evening Post* with nostalgic and heartwarming scenes that remind aging romantics of what Small Town USA life was once like in the Lower Forty-eight. For those who slept through four years of high school except for lunch breaks and Pep Club, this was before the toasty-warm Sandwich Islands and the Seward's Folly deep-freeze were admitted to the federal union. Which celebrated historical events occurred in nineteen hundred and fifty-nine A.D. (On January 3 and August 21, respectively.)

CHAPTER SIXTEEN

A BIG CATCH

Eighty-year-old Grover T. Washington was seated in the narrow end of an aluminum bass boat, happily running his trotline, which was submerged across a narrow section of the Wabash. What made the old man so doggone happy was not only a fine catch of channel catfish (not one of those slippery rascals was under three pounds) and a respectable assortment of drum and carp, but the fact that his twelve-year-old grandson was along for the fun. "Uh-oh," he muttered through his gray, tobacco-stained beard as he tugged at the taut line. "Feels like we got us a shore-enough big 'un!"

The blue eyes in the boy's charmingly freckled face bulged, and his changing voice croaked as he said, "What is it, Granddad—one a them hunnerd-pound jug-head catfish that lays on the bottom, just waitin' for somethin' tasty to drift by that he can swaller?"

"Could be, sonny—them lazy old buggers don't put up much of a fight." *But this feels like dead weight.* He shrugged and sighed. "More likely, it's just a waterlogged poplar stump, or a rusty old 'frigerator that some jackass dumped into the river, or—" He got his first look at a portion of the catch, and dropped the line before the boy could see the monstrous thing he'd hooked. With admirable presence of mind, Grover muttered, "Damned old log." He motioned to the boy in blue overalls. "Row us back to the bank. Before I get this line untangled, I'll need to get some special tools from the green tackle box."

"Okay, Gramps." As the man-child leaned into the oars, he licked his chapped lips. "Can we have us a riverside fish fry afore we go home?"

The elderly man did not respond.

"Granddad?"

"Oh—I don't think so." The dispirited angler glanced at his wrist-watch. "We'll have our fish fry at home. While I'm tending to business here, you hoist this string of fish over your shoulder and take the shortcut across the cornfield."

The boy's face fell. "Why can't I ride home in the pickup with you?"

"Because you need to go tell Grandma that I'll be running late. I need to get my line untangled from that danged old log."

A suspicious expression shadowed the lad's honest face. "Why don't you call her on your cell phone?"

Danged smart-aleck kid. "Because if I do, she'll start pestering me with silly questions—just like somebody else I won't mention!"

"Okay, then." The youngster grinned as he tied the bass boat to a sycamore limb. "But I'll tell Gran'ma what you just said." And lickety-split, off he went with the catfish, drum, and carp.

Even before his grandson was out of sight, Grover Washington put in a 911 call. When the dispatcher asked what the emergency was, the grim fisherman described the horrific thing that was entangled on his line.

The sheriff and his deputy showed up in fifteen minutes flat, and an Indiana state trooper was not far behind. What did the lawmen find?

A cinder-block-weighted corpse that might never have been discovered had a strong undercurrent not taken it a few miles downstream to a fateful encounter with an aged fisherman's trotline.

The preliminary finding was that the body was that of a forty-five-to-fifty-five-year-old Caucasian female, who'd had her throat cut. Even in rural southern Indiana, a few such unfortunates are never identified, and those that are rarely attract overmuch attention by those in the upper echelons of law enforcement.

This instance would prove an exception.

A subsequent examination by the McLean County Medical Examiner's office would lead to a positive identification: FBI Special

Agent Mary Anne Clayton, aka Marcella Clay—until quite recently, maid and live-in companion to Mrs. Francine Hooten.

Despite the Bureau's best efforts to connect the homicide to the purse snatcher's momma, and the telephone record of the undercover agent's hurried departure from the Hooten residence, there would not be a shred of solid evidence to support an indictment—much less a conviction.

Very depressing. Let us leave Indiana and the tree-lined Wabash banks behind.

And go where?

How about—a far piece west of here, in sunny Colorado, where most rivers are too shallow and transparent to conceal the corpse of an adult Caucasian female. But for the moment, we shall not visit Granite Creek. (We have friends in Pueblo.)

CHAPTER SEVENTEEN

THE TOWN LAWMAN'S DAY OFF

Scott Parris is the lawman in question, and he had taken a day of precious vacation to spend with his best friend in the whole world. Why? Because Charlie Moon had asked him to, that's why. Which, as answers are wont to do, raises still another question. Which is: why did Parris's deputy make such a presumptuous request of the busy chief of police, who saves up his vacation days like wild-eyed old misers hoard gold coins? Because the owner of the Columbine had made up his mind to *do it,* and was determined to reveal his life-changing decision to Scott Parris so that they could celebrate with a big day on the town down in Pueblo. The Ute could not wait until tomorrow, which—as we all know—never comes for some of us. Anyway, when Moon proposed the impromptu holiday, Scott said, "Let's go," and they took off on a joyride. Had a danged good time, too.

Which wasn't very hard to do, because these were uncomplicated men who enjoyed ordinary pleasures, like paying a call on Fat Jack's Tack and Leather, where one of the westerners (the paleface) bought himself a fancy pair of Moroccan ostrich-hide boots and the other one treated himself to a Made in America leather gun belt. About the time stomachs had begun to growl, the hungry men drove over to that dandy Cracker Barrel on the north end of town to enjoy fried chicken (Parris) and a double order of fried catfish (Señor Luna). For the benefit of those on strict diets, we will not describe either the side dishes or their outrageously scrumptious desserts, which Parris and Moon walked off on Twelfth, Seventeenth, and Elizabeth Streets before dropping in at dusty old Polecat Joe's 1950s Pawnshop, an establishment that specialized in previously owned bone-handled pocket knives, sooty old Mexican silver, miscellaneous and sundry hand tools, vintage musical instruments, and, for those who don't want to buy somebody else's old junk—a selection of brand-new items. Scott Parris bought himself a pocket-worn Case stockman's folding knife just like one he'd lost on Pigeon Creek some fifty-odd years ago. The Columbine Grass's dexterous banjo player purchased a set of Nashville Special finger-picks for his nimble fingers.

After the most fun they'd had in quite some time, the lawmen said a heartfelt adios to Pueblo and—

But wait a minute. An honorable mention must be made of an incident (the most fun they'd had in quite some time) that, though of no great importance, did serve to add some spice and vinegar to their already dandy day.

HELL-CAT HARLEY, SNAKE-EYE, AND SWEET MAURICE

Right up front, it should be noted that the three scruffy thugs thudding along on matching black Harley-Davidson motorcycles were what you'd call *new boys in town*, and like so many of their ilk—they figured they were about to have their way in Pueblo. (Not all insane folk are in lunatic asylums.)

These entrepreneurs had parked their pulsating bikes outside Polecat Joe's profitable establishment with the intent of conducting some customary business—i.e., beating Joe's head to a bloody pulp, emptying the semifamous pawnshop's cash register, and roaring away with raucous wa-hoos! and shouts of "the Bad Black Wolf Pack has struck again!"

With this stimulating adventure in mind, the uncouth youth were pleased to find only one vehicle parked out front. Charlie Moon's wheels. (Polecat Joe, a U.S. marine Iraqi war vet who topped out at about five-seven in his GI boots, kept his black Hummer parked out back and a matched pair of loaded-for-bad-asses .44 Colt six-shooters holstered on his hips.)

H-C Harley, self-appointed leader of the pack, eyed the Expedition's Columbine Ranch logo and spat. "Anybody who'd paint a purple flower on his SUV is a damn sissy who drinks his beer through a straw!"

Snake-Eye signified his agreement with a demented snicker.

A slope-browed ape-man of few words, Sweet Maurice replied with 10 percent of his vocabulary: a heartfelt grunt.

Cutting his Harley-Davidson's ignition, Harley said, "Let's go in and get it, brother Wolves."

As they entered the dimly lighted pawnshop, the pupils in the doped-up bikers' eyes did not dilate appreciably behind their dark sunglasses, which may be one reason why the thugs made the potentially fatal error of picking a fight with an overweight, late-middle-aged white man, his skinny Indian friend—and the extremely dangerous proprietor behind the counter, whose round, little-boy face barely showed over the top of a glass case that was filled with antique carpenter's tools.

As it happened, Scott Parris, Charlie Moon, and Polecat Joe had noticed the sinister-looking trio the instant they pulled up in front of the pawnshop, where robberies were attempted by ignorant out-of-towners two or three times every year—most of whose carcasses were removed by unsympathetic emergency medical technicians, pronounced seriously deceased at the ER, then transferred to the morgue.

The boss biker swaggered up to the counter to sneer at the proprietor. "I'm Hell-Cat Harley." He jerked a thumb to draw attention to his sidekicks. "This here is Snake-Eye and that's Sweet Maurice. We're here to kick ass and take what we want." He punctuated this announcement by spitting. *On the counter.*

Parris rolled his eyes and whispered, "Here we go again."

The Ute neither moved nor said a word.

His concealed hands itching on the ivory-handled butts of his silver-plated six-shooters, Polecat Joe smiled. "Don't stand there all day—make your play."

Not before Charlie Moon had his say. "Hold on just a minute, Joe—me and Scott can handle this."

Before the eager-for-action proprietor could voice a righteous protest, Parris chimed in. "Which of these scum-bums do you want, Charlie?"

Moon took an appraising look at the momentarily speechless opposition. "I'm still a little full from lunch, pardner. You feel up to taking the two big ones?"

"Piece of cake." Eyeing the available weapons, Parris selected a old ash ax handle. "I'll have a go at Hell-Cat and Snake."

"Good choice," Moon said. "While you knock their ears off, I'll grab a hold of Sweet and stuff his pointy little head into that twenty-gallon brass spittoon which ain't been emptied in thirty-nine years." Which he commenced to do straightaway.

As they used to say about Major League home-run hitters, Scott Parris "laid the wood" into the other two before the startled side-kicks quite realized what was happening.

It would be gratifying to report that the fight was over in six seconds flat and that was that, but in real life things don't generally work out so nice and clean. While Hell-Cat was felled by Parris's first blow and would not regain the least glimmer of consciousness until three days of dreamless sleep had passed, Parris's attempt to poleax Thug Number Two was a glancing blow that served merely to arouse Snake-Eye's understandable ire. The big bruiser threw a roundhouse punch that caught the Granite Creek chief of police square in the jaw. This made the cop wielding the ax handle plenty angry.

Mr. Moon also had his hands full. Sweet Maurice (already a slippery character) objected to being drowned in several gallons of aged-in-brass spittle. The miscreant managed to wriggle his way out of the gigantic spittoon and bite Charlie Moon on his leftmost cowboy boot, which (thankfully) Sweet's yellowish canines did not penetrate—elsewise the Indian might have expired from the infectious effect.

The rest of the brawl wasn't quite so pretty as the outset, and neither the delightfully gratuitous violence nor its official aftermath need be amplified upon herein. It is sufficient to stipulate that four worthy representatives of the Pueblo PD arrived to cuff and haul away the injured, and that Polecat Joe would complain about being unduly deprived (by Moon and Parris) of his inalienable constitutional right to shoot the three lowlifes stone-cold dead and then jump up and down on their corpses with his combat boots whilst bellowing that soul-stirring U.S. Marine anthem about the Gates of Tripoli, etc. One can sympathize with the feisty fellow's point of view, but do not feel overly sorry for the pawnshop proprietor. Before the year is over, P-Joe will be all alone when several other thuggish tourists drop by to commit a misdeed, and he will release all his pent-up fury upon those unwary felons. Feel sorry for them who won't live to tell the tale, and (if you like) for Hell-Cat Harley, Snake-Eye, and Sweet Maurice—it'll be a long time and then some before the Big Bad Black Wolf Pack is back on the road again.

What about the two off-duty cops who took care of business with considerable enthusiasm? Despite some bruised knuckles (Moon) and a loosened molar (you know who), the one-minute scrap really capped off a fine day in a fun town for Charlie and Scott.

But where were we when the pawnshop fight broke out?

Oh, right. The Colorado cops credited with brutally killing a purse snatcher were leaving town.

After the most enjoyment they'd had in quite some time, the lawmen said a heartfelt adios to Pueblo and headed back to Granite Creek in Charlie Moon's Expedition. Mr. Banjo-Plucker was (despite his sore knuckles) in the mood to pick two or three upbeat breakdowns ("Foggy Mountain," "Hamilton County," and "Fifty-seven Chevy Pickup"—the latter selection a fast-moving piece composed by Mr. Moon himself). Its being against local ordinances to operate a motor vehicle whilst picking a banjo, Parris agreed to serve as designated driver.

It was to be a fine, scenic drive and worthy of description, but we shall skip the breathtaking travelogue and skip ahead and over to the so-called Show Me State (MO), where something even more interesting than skull bashing with ax handles, head stuffing into disgustingly filthy spittoons, and knuckle-bruising fisticuffs is about to occur.

CHAPTER EIGHTEEN

THE CONVERSATION

While rolling westward on I-70 in Missouri, and only a few dozen miles short of Kansas City, Miss Louella Smithson pulled off the congested thoroughfare and into a busy truck stop. After filling the thirsty Bronco's big tank, she parked by one of those huge, noisy dispensers of tasty-as-cardboard burgers, greasy red chili, gristly chicken-fried steaks, and mighty fine apple, cherry, and meringue pies "Like Your Mom Used to Bake"—and coffee strong enough to make your bloodshot eyes pop. It was the sort of eatery that hungry, sleepy, long-haul truckers fondly refer to as "a first-class choke-and-puke." Reason enough for a chronically dyspeptic diner not to enter therein, but the hopeful bounty hunter/author had additional reasons for remaining in her aged SUV. Desperately needing someone to discuss her plans and problems with, Miss Smithson initiated a conversation with her clever twin sister, Stella—who was Ella's *very image.* (The one that looked back from the Bronco's cracked rearview mirror.)

Miss Smithson did not kick the chat off right off the bat with an ice-breaker greeting like, "Hi, Stella—how've you been?" She got right to the point with: "I'm going to Granite Creek to talk to Chief of Police Parris."

Sis-in-the-Looking Glass: *Okay, so you go chew the fat with the Colorado cop that dropped LeRoy Hooten with a can of peas—what, exactly, are you going to tell him?*

"Well, I intend to—"

A customer exiting the restaurant with a red toothpick dangling from his lips and a blue Ford cap on his head grinned and winked at the young woman who was talking to herself.

Mildly embarrassed at conversing with her reflection, Miss Smithson glanced left and right before whispering a response from the corner of her mouth: "After I've told him who I am and why I'm in town—which is to do some background research for my true-crime book with Chief Parris and Deputy Moon as the heroes and—"

Hah! That's a flat-out lie.

"No it's not!" *It's a teensy-weensy little lily-white fib.* "I have *dozens* of pages of confidential notes on the Hooten family's criminal activities that the FBI would just *die* for, and soon as this job's done, I plan to get started on a manuscript that I've been outlining for months—"

You're also planning on losing six pounds of ugly belly and butt fat, and have been since year before last.

"Okay, Skinny Saint Stella Smithson—I'll tell Chief Parris the whole, unvarnished truth."

Her mirror image had assumed a luminous halo. *And what's that, pray tell?*

"Well . . . that I'm tailing a notorious, anonymous assassin who's probably on his way to Granite Creek and—"

You aren't tailing anybody, kid—you lost Cowboy back in Illinois and you couldn't find him again with both hands if he were sitting in your lap. The image looked past Louella at the Bronco's dirty rear window. *For all you know,* he *could be following* you.

"No, he's not, and *please* don't interrupt! I'll be completely up front with Chief Parris and suggest how we can pool our resources to identify and arrest the assassin and—"

What a crock of you know what! Sis rolled her eyes. *What resources? You wouldn't recognize Cowboy if you tripped over his boot toe at high noon in front of the Dead Dog Saloon. And on the off chance you did happen to figure out who he is—it'll be the cops who'd do any arresting.*

"Those are minor details." The flesh-and-blood sister sniffed. "Chief Parris is bound to be interested in a criminal who's been sent by Francine Hooten to murder him and his Indian friend."

This is really feeble, Sis. D'you actually think a hard-nosed small-town cop who kills a thief with whatever canned goods are handy would buy a dopey story like that?

"I guess not." *Stella is always right.* Long, melancholy sigh. "He'll figure me for a weirdo who oughta be strapped into a straitjacket."

At the very least. But I'm here to help, not criticize—so read my lips: what you need is a plausible story and impressive credentials.

"Which I don't have. I'm a run-of-the-mill missing-person tracker who's trying to work my way up to first-class bounty hunter and then write a book about it . . . someday."

We both know that, and it's truly pathetic. Now use your so-called brain—how does Little Miss Nobody impress a cop who's met up with more nuts than Mr. Planter ever put into cans?

Her uppity twin was beginning to wear a bit thin. "I don't have a clue—please give me a big, fat hint."

I'll give you two. First—go for the teensy-weensy little lily-white fib about doing research for your bestseller book. It's lame as a three-legged llama, but a hick cop might just fall for it. Now listen close—here's number two: wrangle an introduction to Chief Parris from an upstanding citizen who commands respect in the law-enforcement community.

"Okay. Like who—the U.S. attorney general?"

The annoying reflection rolled her eyes again. *If you don't know, I'm not about to tell you.*

Louella glared at her insolent sibling. "One more hint wouldn't *kill* you."

All right, here goes: it's been a long time since you telephoned our favorite granddaddy.

The hopeful bounty hunter clapped her hands. "Of course—ex-Texas Ranger Ray Smithson!"

CHAPTER NINETEEN

TWENTY-NINE MILES WEST OF PLAINVIEW, TEXAS, MORE OR LESS

Which is about halfway from Plainview to Muleshoe and a good seventeen miles on the yonder side of Halfway. If you make it to Earth you've gone a tad too far, pardner—which is not the thing to do in the Lone Star State. If these directions are confusing, maybe you were headed to Floydada, which is in the other direction entirely.

But never mind. Ray Smithson is a crusty old retired Texas Ranger who'd rather be left alone with his two fat beagles, four gaunt longhorns, and one worn-out old saddle horse who answers to the name of Colt .45—which is why Ray does not encourage visitors except for his granddaughter Ellie, who drops by when she's so lonely she *could just die*—or doesn't have enough hard cash to pay the rent, which happens more often with every year that goes by. Times are hard for quite a few young folk and for some old ones, too—but ol' Ray's tough as seventy-nine-year-old buffalo jerky and his granddaughter is also pretty gristly.

THE CALL FOR HELP

Ray Smithson was in his living room when the old-fashioned wall-mounted telephone rang. Having just mended a saddle that was twice as old as his horse, the silver-haired senior citizen was going through his fishing-tackle box—checking the inventory of barbed hooks, lead sinkers, cork bobbers, nine-pound test line, and the like. He greeted the jangling intrusion with a salty curse, grunted himself up from a painful squat on the hardwood floor, and strode sorely to the telephone. *It'll be some fast-talking clown trying to sell me a maga-zine subscription.* "Hello!"

"Hi, Granddaddy—it's me."

"Well . . ." He arched a bristly eyebrow. "It's been a long while since I've heard your voice."

"Uh . . . I've been kinda busy." His mild rebuke had stung. "So what're you up to?"

"I'm fixing to go fishing," he said through a smile. "What's keep-ing you so danged busy?"

"Oh, you know the drill—same old same old."

"No, I don't know." The old straight shooter detested meaningless double-talk. *I wonder what Ellie wants this time.* "Where're you call-ing from?"

"Western Missouri. I'm pulled over at a truck stop on I-70."

Mr. Smithson smiled; it helped some to have a fix on his unpredict-able granddaughter. "That's not far from Kansas City—you home-ward bound, or headed east?"

"Coming home. I'll stop tonight for a few hours' sleep." Her voice took on a proud, professional tone. "I'm on a job."

Ray Smithson posed the expected query: "Doing *what?*"

"Gathering material for my book."

"Which book is that?" *Last time, it was a damn silly romance about vampires and whatnot.*

She read the old man's mind. "This one's nonfiction. It's about a hired killer and a rich old woman with Chicago mob connections. And . . . I need a little favor."

"Sure you do." The over-the-hill lawman paused for a dry chuckle. "You never call me up to say, 'How're you, Granddaddy Smithson—I miss you so much that I just had to find out if you're still alive or bur-ied out behind the horse barn after you got stomped to death by a snorty longhorn who did you in just for the fun of it.'"

"I'm sorry." She was. "I'll stop by after my work is finished." She wouldn't.

"So what's the flavor of the favor?"

"I'm on my way to Colorado—a small town called Granite Creek—and I need an introduction to the local chief of police." She paused for a breath. "I was hoping you could put in a good word for me. You know, about how I'm doing research on a really *great* book that'll put his little Rocky Mountain cow town on the map, and how I'm your favorite granddaughter and—"

"You're my *only* granddaughter. Why're you *actually* going to Colorado?"

"Does that matter?"

"Damn right it does. You want me to do you a favor, you tell me straight out what you're up to. And don't think you can fool me, Ellie—I'll *know* if you try to hold something back."

He would, and she knew it. *Granddaddy Smithson could always see right through me.* "Okay. Here's the lowdown. A few days ago, Chief Parris and his deputy killed a purse snatcher and—"

"Good for them. But why do you want to write a book about a common purse snatcher who got his clock stopped by a couple of Colorado cops?"

"Because the purse snatcher was one LeRoy *Hooten*."

"Never heard of the thief."

"If you'd ever lived in Chicago, you'd have heard about the Hootens."

"I wouldn't hang my John B. Stetson lid in the Windy City for all the twenty-dollar bills it'd take to fill a Rock Island Line boxcar."

"Okay," she snapped. "If you don't want to know about LeRoy Hooten, that's fine with me."

"Sorry, Ellie." *She's sure got her hot-blooded-momma's temper.* "It won't be easy, but I'll try to keep my trap shut."

"Thank you." Having already let the well-known cat out of the bag, Louella Smithson did not hesitate to make her brag. "When I saw the story about the purse snatcher on the Internet and found out *who'd* been killed—and there was this picture of these two cops *laughing* like they were happy about having done the deed—I knew that Leroy's mother would be *furious*. Which is no small thing, because Francine Hooten has serious mob connections—including contacts with knuckle draggers who'd kill their own grandmother for a hundred bucks." She paused to let that sink in.

It did, and hit bottom. His brow furrowing into a worry frown, Ray Smithson seated his lanky frame on an uncomfortable straight-backed oak kitchen chair that he kept by the telephone for long conversations. "I'm listening."

"Here's the thing—Francine has a history of getting even with cops who kill her kinfolk—and LeRoy was her only son. So I had a hunch that she'd call in some heavy heat. The *heaviest*. And somebody that she's contracted before." Dramatic pause. "I'm talking about the same executioner who's rumored to have killed a Chicago police detective for Francine—the one the FBI calls 'the Cowboy Assassin.'"

"The *what?*"

"Oh, Granddaddy—you are so *out* of it!"

"That's what I've been trying to tell you." The retired lawman grinned at his image of an exasperated granddaughter. "I've never heard of no cowboy—"

"He's not necessarily an *actual* cowboy—the FBI hung that tag on the assassin after a witness saw someone wearing a cowboy hat leaving the scene of a gangland execution in Newark."

"All hat, no cattle." The old Texan chuckled.

Pointedly ignoring the gibe, Louella continued, "And the feds found what looked like cowboy-boot impressions at the scene of two other mob-related killings—one in Gary, Indiana, the other near Detroit. This Have Gun—Will Travel is a deadly Mr. Get-Even who's paid big bucks to rub out mob enemies."

"You seem to know a lot about this particular outlaw."

"Sure I do—and that's what'll help me track him down and collect over *two hundred thousand* bucks in reward money when he's arrested, charged, indicted, and found guilty by a jury of his peers." Louella smiled at the thought of a panel of twelve citizen-assassins hearing the case against Cowboy. "Not to mention finding a major publisher for my red-hot book about how I tracked down and identified a legendary killer for hire that the FBI couldn't lay a finger on."

Despite an understandable pride in his gutsy granddaughter's ambitions, Ray Smithson felt obliged to offer a snort of the derisive sort. "You've been watching too many back-East cops-and-robber shows on the TV."

"You think so?" Louella's voice was slightly shrill. "Well, think about this: while I'm wasting time begging you for a teensy-weensy little favor, Cowboy is probably already on his way to Granite Creek to pull off a couple of cop killings. And I not only know that he's driving a Ford sedan with Oklahoma plates—*I got a look at the assassin's face.*" She blushed at the exaggeration. *Well, sort of.*

This reference to some thug in a western hat murdering brother lawmen made Ray Smithson's stomach churn. "Did you get a good enough look to pick the suspect out of a police lineup?"

"Well . . . maybe." *And maybe pigs can fly.*

Ray Smithson closed his gray eyes. *With a little bit of luck, Mr. Cowboy is headed back to Oklahoma to work on his memoirs.* "I hope you're wrong, Ellie—because if you're right, you're likely to get yourself into some seriously bad trouble."

"You worry too much."

"You don't worry enough. I've got a bad feeling about this, Little Miss Smart-Britches—now you be extra careful."

This sage warning was met with the expected girlish laugh and the assurance that she knew how to take care of herself. To this confident assertion, Louella Smithson appended a ten-year-old girl's "please please *please*" request: would her favorite granddaddy in the whole wide world place a call to the chief of police in Granite Creek and portray his favorite granddaughter as an up-and-coming true-crime author? "But don't mention anything about Cowboy—I'll take care of that part myself."

"Okay." As he sometimes did when flustered, Ray Smithson reverted to his West Texas lingo: "But if this Okie cowpuncher is comin' a-gunnin' for those two Colorado cops, they oughta be told right away—"

"No! Don't you dare say a word. I need your help, not your inter-ference." A pause. "I'm sorry, Granddaddy. I didn't mean to yell at you—but this is really, really important to me."

"I know."

"Besides, Cowboy'll need a few days to set up the hits and I'll show up about the same time he does. And I promise you—if for any reason I'm running late, I'll call the chief of police and tell him all about the killer who's coming to town. But if you spill the beans before I show up, there's always the chance they might arrest Cow-boy without any help from me—and take all the credit."

"Well . . . I suppose they might." *And I sure hope they do.*

She read the old lawman's mind. "Promise me."

"I promise I'll call the Granite Creek PD—and not tell them any more than is absolutely necessary."

"Thank you, Granddaddy." This was not quite the ironclad prom-ise she wanted, but Louella realized that she had pushed her formi-dable grandfather about as far as he would go. "Now will you please please *please* make the telephone call *right this minute*—before you wander off to your favorite fishing hole and forget all about it?"

"I'm not quite as senile as you think I am." The world-weary old man shook his head at the image of his impudent, imprudent, ador-ably lovable granddaughter. *One way or another, I know I'm going to regret getting mixed up in this nonsense.* "I'll make the call to Granite Creek PD right after I dial up Information and get a number for the police station."

Another laugh. She informed him that there was no need for that.

After the old man had found the stub of a yellow number-2 lead pencil and the back of an AARP Insurance envelope to scribble on, Miss Louella Smithson recited the GCPD telephone number for her favorite granddaddy—and the names of the lawmen ("Parris with two *rs*") who were responsible for the death of the purse snatcher.

"I've never heard of this Parris cop." A hint of his former smile returned. "But I've sure heard tell of Mr. Charlie Moon."

"Wonderful. Now please call Chief Parris right away."

"Consider it done."

"Love you, Granddaddy." Kiss-kiss sounds. "Talk to you later."

The sudden silence aching in his ear, the old man blinked twice at the plastered wall before he rehung the telephone. *She's the last family I've got in the world—I'd sure hate to wake up some morning to hear the phone ringing—and some stranger's voice telling me my little Ellie has been shot dead by some Okie outlaw.*

Ex-Ranger Ray Smithson pulled a sealed pack of unfiltered cigarettes from his shirt pocket and stared at it. *I've been carrying this around for almost a month.* Defeated, he opened the pack, removed a white cylinder, put it between his lips, and touched a butane lighter to the tip. Inhaling deeply of his drug of choice, he immediately coughed up a lungful of carcinogenic smoke. *If something else don't put me six feet under first, these damn cancer sticks are going to be the death of me.* The nicotine addict tossed the offending cigarette into the fireplace, and then the pack from his pocket. The smoker's melancholy sigh might have been a dry, West Texas breeze drifting over the parched prairie. *This ain't no way for a man to live. Aside from a cigarette now and again, about the only enjoyment I get out of life is from going fishing.* The retiree took a long, hopeful look at his open tackle box. *And from talking with Ellie every few months.* But there had been little pleasure in today's conversation. *Now my granddaughter has asked me to withhold important information from a brother lawman.*

Every once in a while a man has a critical choice to make, but Smithson had spent a lifetime *doing the right thing* and he was not about to change. The old-timer made up his mind to just do what came naturally. Like telling that Colorado chief of police what he needed to know about a cop killer who might already be on his way to Granite Creek. Which would be a pleasure unadulterated by the least regret. Smithson grinned. *Any hombre behind a tin star who kills a purse snatcher and then laughs about it is my kind of lawman.*

After he made the phone call to Scott Parris, the ardent angler would have another easy decision to make. *I can either go fishing, or . . . go fishing.*

And so he would, bless his honest soul.

CHAPTER TWENTY

PARRIS AND MOON GO ROLLING HOME

Their fun in Pueblo concluded but still relished like the sweet after-taste of a favorite dessert, the off-duty lawmen were a mere six miles shy of the Granite Creek city-limits sign and motoring along about as happily as a pair of best friends can. How happily is that?

Chief Parris (the beefy fellow behind the Columbine Expedition's steering wheel) was bellowing at the top of his lung power, and Deputy Moon (the skinny Indian in the passenger seat) was booming out about as loud in a range somewhere between bass and baritone, all the while plucking like a pro (which he is) at his Stelling Golden Cross twanging five-string banjo. ("The Yellow Rose of Texas.")

This unadulterated cheerfulness continued for about three miles more and about as many minutes, before the boisterous singing and red-hot banjo plucking ceased.

WILL HE REALLY DO IT?

Homeward bound and close to town, the celebration of Charlie Moon's big decision was about to wind down. It is worth mentioning that while the rancher's joy was unconditional, for Scott Parris the festivities were more than a little bittersweet

The man who was driving Moon's SUV sighed. "Charlie, can I ask you a really personal question that'll probably annoy you no end?"

"Nope. Don't even think about it."

"Okay, here it is: are you *really* gonna go through with it?"

"Sure I am." *I should've done it years ago.* The musician rested the stringed musical instrument on his knee. "It's high time I made a big change in my life, and this is the right decision."

"Well . . . maybe so." To emphasize his doubts, Scott Parris shook his head. "You know that old saying: 'If it ain't broke, don't fix it.' And the way I see it, you've already got yourself a mighty good setup. You own maybe the finest ranch in the state, and—"

"There's no *maybe* about it, pardner. No other cattle operation in Colorado can hold a candle to the Columbine."

"Which just goes to prove my point." Parris crossed over the center line to pass an old, rusty pickup loaded with split piñon firewood. "The main point I was going to make is that you're a free man—you're your own boss."

"And I still will be when I settle down on that nice little horse ranch on the Gunnison. And since I don't intend to make any serious money by raising a little string of rodeo stock, that outfit will be even better than the Columbine. I won't have any hardheaded employees to give me the miseries." The Indian grinned at his best friend. "No man who has a cranky foreman, an unpredictable blacksmith, and about four dozen wild-eyed cowboys on the payroll is his own boss—he only *thinks* he is."

Parris snorted. "You know what I mean."

"Sure I do," Moon said with a boyish grin. "But I'm going to be a happier man than I've ever been."

"For a few weeks, maybe." The chief of police looked in the rearview mirror at the firewood truck. *I don't think that old Chevy pickup had a license plate.* But it didn't matter. *I'm off duty and aim to stay that way until tomorrow morning.* He gave Moon a sly sideways glance. "I'm afraid you'll wake up some fine morning and say, 'I should have listened to ol' Scott when he tried to talk some sense into my head— what was I *thinking*? I had a life of perfect freedom—not to mention considerable stature as owner of the finest ranch in Colorado. But what did I do when things was just peachy? Why, I sold my ranch to a bunch of Reno hotshots and got myself all wrapped up in this dinky little horse ranch that don't make a thin dime, not to mention that I went and got me a—'"

"Don't mention it."

"Whatever you say." Parris suppressed a mischievous grin that was trying hard to twist his lips. "But I bet you'll be having second thoughts." He counted off three heartbeats. "Within three months of closing the deal."

Though his buddy's strategy was entirely transparent, the least hint of a wager was irresistible to the compulsive gambler. "Don't keep me in suspense, Mr. High-Roller—how much do you want to lose?"

"Two bucks?"

"Hah! Is that the best you can do?"

"Okay." Parris jutted his chin. "Twenty."

"Now that's more like it." The Ute twanged a banjo string. "You're on."

As the instigator of the wager eased the Expedition into light Granite Creek traffic, a comfortable silence settled between the good friends.

This peaceful interlude would not persist, and all because (wouldn't you just know it) someone's mobile telephone had been signaled to warble a familiar tone and alert the chief of police that his dispatcher had something of importance to tell him. Did Scott Parris respond? Not a chance. When the boss was on vacation, so was his mobile telephone, which was turned off. This sensible precaution was to prove futile. No matter how hard he tries to hide on his day off, an experienced dispatcher knows where to find the chief, and how to get his ear.

Deputy Moon's phone buzzed in his pocket. It was Charlie's day off, too, so Scott Parris's trusty sidekick checked the caller ID before taking the call. "It's Clara."

"Don't answer it!" the chief of police snapped.

Deputy Moon assumed a virtuous expression. "I feel obliged to."

Parris shot a hateful glare at his fun-loving buddy. "Why?"

"Well, for one thing—me'n Clara Tavishuts are members of the same tribe. And for another—"

"Oh, go ahead then. But tell your fellow spear chucker that I'm not here. If she don't believe that, tell her that I'm stone-cold dead."

"Whatever you say, boss." The deputy pressed the button. "Hello, Clara."

Miss Tavishuts helloed Charlie Moon back, and asked to speak to the chief of police if he was close at hand.

"Sorry I can't help you, ma'am—Scott said to tell you he's not here and if you don't believe that fabrication—that he's 'stone-cold dead.'"

Granite Creek's top cop groaned.

The dispatcher laughed, and proceeded to give Charlie Moon the general lowdown.

"Sure, I know who he is." *That tough old lawman's famous in Texas and has a big rep all over the Rocky Mountain west.*

"He's holding on long distance, Charlie—would you mind giving your phone to Chief Parris?"

"I'll be more than happy to." Moon passed the instrument to his companion. "It's for you, pardner."

Heaving a heavy sigh, the driver pressed the infernal machine against his ear. "I'm driving Charlie Moon's big gas hog, so it ain't legal for me to be talking on a mobile telephone— Goodbye!"

"I promise not to tell a cop," Clara Tavishuts said. She added in a no-nonsense tone, "But just to set a good example, you ought to pull over and come to a complete stop."

Muttering a curse, Parris pulled over to the curb. (A yellow-painted curb, beside a shiny red fireplug and a prominent No Parking sign.) "What's up, Clara?"

Miss Tavishuts responded in her professional monotone, "You've got a phone call from a Mr. Ray Smithson in Texas."

"Ray Smithson, huh?" Parris's brow wrinkled into a frown. *I'm sure I've heard that name before; maybe he's somebody I know.*

"Mr. Smithson says it's urgent that he speak to you, and he sounds like a solid citizen— Uh-oh, I've got a 911 call flashing on line three. May I patch him through to Charlie's cell phone?"

"Sure—put 'im on."

CHAPTER TWENTY-ONE

THE EX-TEXAS RANGER'S REQUEST

The old man's voice that crackled in Scott Parris's ear was not familiar. "Chief Parris—this is Ray Smithson. I'm calling from my place out west of Plainview, Texas. . . . I'm a retired lawman."

Parris was stunned. *Of course—the legendary Texas Ranger!*

Louella Smithson's granddaddy waited for a response. "Say—can you hear me okay?"

"Yes *sir*—copy you loud and clear." *Wow—this is like getting a call from Wyatt Earp!* Not quite, but Parris's hyperbole was understandable.

"I expect you're a busy man, so I'll try to keep this short."

"Take as long as you like, sir."

"Thank you kindly, but I don't have a lot of wind left these days. I guess I still smoke too many cigarettes"—the caller paused for a raspy cough—"so I'll just tell you that my granddaughter Ellie—her given name is *Louella* Smithson, and years ago when she left Plainview for Kansas City, she started calling herself 'Ella.' Sorry, I guess I've already gotten off the track. Point is, even as we speak, Ellie's on her way to Granite Creek. She should show up in a day or two."

I wonder what this is all about. "I hope she enjoys her visit."

"I hope so too, but Ellie has some business to tend to."

Parris didn't like the sound of that. "What kind of business?"

"A law-enforcement issue that she's interested in. Since I used to wear a badge, my granddaughter figured it might help some if I called and introduced her to you." Smithson's croaky chuckle betrayed a mild embarrassment. "She figures that an intro from a brother lawman might help her get started off on the right foot—if you know what I mean."

"Uh, yes sir." Parris thought he knew exactly what his "brother lawman" meant. *He wants me to entertain his granddaughter while she's in town. Show her around. Take her out to dinner. The whole ball of beeswax.* A mild frown found its way to his brow. *What a bummer.* But he couldn't say no. "Can you tell me where Miss Smithson will be staying?"

"No. But I expect she'll be calling you soon as she gets there—to set up a meeting."

"Not a problem, sir." Parris blushed at this half-truth.

"I sure appreciate it. Ellie is awfully anxious to talk to you."

Parris's frown furrowed deeper. "About what in particular?"

After an embarrassed pause, Smithson said, "My granddaughter's writing a true-crime book and she figures you might be able to help her."

I might've known: folks who don't have anything better to do write dopey books or call radio talk shows ten times a day—or find some other way to make a general nuisance of themselves. "Uh—help her how?"

"Oh, I expect she'll want a few pointers about modern police procedure—that kind of thing. But Ellie doesn't want me to discuss her *personal* business."

"She prefers to tell me about it herself?"

"Well . . . let's say *up to a point.*" Ray Smithson's wry smile could be heard in his voice. "But that gal knows how to keep her secrets. And me, I've promised to keep mum . . . more or less . . . if you understand what I'm gettin' at."

Parris did. "Would it help if I pressed you a little?"

"Nope—my lips are stapled shut." The old man's grin was as loud as a jumbo firecracker at 2:00 A.M. "But if it'll make you feel any better, go ahead and give it your best shot."

"All right." Parris cleared his throat and repeated Smithson's earlier question to his granddaughter. "What's she really up to?"

"Oh, I couldn't tell you *that*—but I will go so far as to say that I'm a little bit worried." There was a brief silence while he tried to think of the best way to put it. "Ellie's smart as a whip, but she tends to be headstrong and overconfident—a combination that's likely to get her into some trouble. I'd sure appreciate it if you'd kinda keep an eye on her."

"I'll do my best." Parris glanced sideways at Moon's dark profile. "Without any direct reference to her personal business in Granite Creek, might I ask what line of work your granddaughter's involved in—besides writing books?"

"You might at that, and I'm glad you did." The sly old Texan's voice took on a conspiratorial tone. "Ellie pays the rent by tracing missing persons. But what she really wants to do is become a big-time bounty hunter."

"You telling me she's tracking some seriously bad actor?"

"No, I'm not tellin' you anything of the sort—and I'm also not telling you that Ellie figures this bad actor is headed directly for your fair city—and that he'll probably show up in a couple of days."

Uh-oh. "I hope she's wrong about that."

"You and me both. And I'd never think of telling you that tracking the rascal down and writing about her experience in a book ain't enough for Ellie, or that she's hoping to help you arrest this criminal and then collect a big reward when he's put in the lockup for good."

Big uh-oh. "Bounty hunting is a dangerous profession."

"Yes it is." A discreet pause. "I sure hope you won't ask me *who* Ellie thinks she's following to Granite Creek and *why* she figures he's gonna show up in your jurisdiction."

"I wouldn't even think of inquiring, sir. But if you happen to drop a small hint, I'd be a danged fool to ignore it."

"Oh, I'm not likely to do a thing like that. My high-strung grand-daughter would throw a hissy fit if I happened to mention that this fella she's hoping to make a big rep on is a sure-enough bad outlaw who's already murdered a Chicago police officer in cold blood."

The ex-Chicago cop grimaced. "I can see why you wouldn't want to bring up a thing like that."

"Then you'll appreciate why I can't say a word about how Ellie thinks that he's comin' a-gunnin' for you and your buddy."

More than a little taken aback, Parris blinked at the Expedition windshield where plump, plopping snowflakes were beginning to make wet spots. "Uh . . . which buddy is that?"

"Why, Mr. Moon, your deputy—who else? And I'd appreciate you not asking me any more questions, Chief Parris. I've already said too much."

"Yes sir."

"And there's no need to 'sir' me every time you open your mouth, young feller—I'm just a wobbly old cowboy with one boot at the edge of an open grave and the other on a nanner peel. Call me Ray."

"Understood." *Sir.* "And you can call me Scott."

"Agreed."

"Just one last thing, sir—uh, Ray—could you describe the vehicle Miss Smithson is driving?"

"I can, unless she's traded that gas hog in. The last time she stopped by my place, Ellie was in her rusty old Bronco. And I'm not talking about one of those lightweights that Ford rolled off the assembly line; Ellie rolls around in one of them big brutes, an '88 or '89. Blue and white. Spare tire mounted on the tailgate. Oh, and Missouri plates."

"Thanks." Parris had committed the information to memory. "And don't you worry about a thing. I'll call you when your granddaughter shows up, so you'll know she got here okay."

"I owe you one, Scott." A wheezing cough. "But don't bother to telephone me—I won't be at home. I'm about to set off on my last fishing trip before serious winter sets in down here. I'll ring you up in a few days to find out how Ellie's getting along." A pause. "Well, it's almost suppertime—I got to go burn me some beans and bacon. G'bye for now."

"Goodbye, Ranger Smithson." *Sir.*

CHAPTER TWENTY-TWO

THE DEPUTY HAS OTHER PLANS

After Scott Parris had returned the telephone to Moon, he pulled out of the illegal parking spot. Motoring along toward the center of town, the chief of police recited the essentials of Ray Smithson's end of the conversation to Charlie Moon, including the description of Miss Louella Smithson's SUV.

As was his practice when listening to bad news, the taciturn Ute held his silence until his friend was done. And then some.

Which silence irked Parris. "Well, what do you think of them apples?"

Moon took some additional time to roll the thing over in his mind. Finally: "I think I'm only a part-time deputy. I'll do whatever comes up if it's reasonable. When push comes to shove, I'll shoot bank robbers dead, pull drunk drivers over and throw their ignition keys into the ditch—I'll even put a ticket on a nun who spits on the sidewalk if she gives me any nasty backtalk. But looking after visiting authors who play at bounty hunting is way beyond my pay grade."

"What about this bad outlaw who might be comin' to town to rub us out?"

"If and when this Mr. Eraser shows up, pard—you let me know so's I can keep out of sight."

The thought of Charlie Moon hiding from a bad guy made Parris's big face split into a toothy grin. As a young lady jaywalked across Copper Street while chatting into her cell phone, he stomped on the brake and scowled under his bushy brows. *What do these kids use for brains—steamed cauliflower?* "You figure this Miss Smithson is some kind of airhead who sees a crazed killer behind every boulder and bush?"

"No I don't." Moon smiled at the oblivious youth who was snarling both lanes of traffic. "But it's possible that this so-called true-crime author specializes in romantic fiction."

When the citizen with the cell phone was on the sidewalk, Parris pulled away. "Is this your way of hinting that you don't intend to help me escort our guest around town?"

"That's about the size of it, pard."

The chief of police assumed a sad expression. "That cuts deep—my straight-arrow deputy copping out on me."

"I need to get used to not being a cop anymore." Mr. Moon beamed like the brightest moonbeam you ever saw. "With all the spare time I'll have on my hands, I intend to concentrate on activities I really enjoy—like raising fine quarter horses, winning twenty-dollar bets, and making lively music." Parris's longtime sidekick hit another lick on his stringed instrument. But the whole truth be told, the man who was looking forward to the biggest and best-ever change in his life had something far more important to do than raise horses, win wagers, and pluck banjo strings.

Scott Parris did not disapprove of Moon's intent, but he had not expected his friend to make the big plunge right away. In his experience, the Indian tended to mull over major decisions for a long while. A month at least. Sometimes a whole year.

What had inspired Charlie Moon to make his move so suddenly? Only a confirmed cynic would suggest that it was the twenty-dollar wager with Parris. Possibly because he was stimulated by the present conversation, the Ute was suddenly accosted by one of those pesky "inner voices" that gets us into so much trouble:

Do it now, *before you chicken out!*

Mr. Moon nodded. *Right. I'll do it tonight.* On the other hand, it was getting late in the day. *Tomorrow will be okay.* He mouthed his next thought in a whisper: "That'll give me some time to think just how to go about it."

Which calls for a parenthetical comment: ("Time to think" is a powerful antidote to decisive action; Moon's life-altering plan was beginning to look a bit iffy.)

His buddy's enigmatic whisper had not gone unnoticed by Scott Parris's keen right ear. The driver shot his characteristic sideways glance at the suspect deputy. "What'd you say about thinking?"

"I'm thinking I feel a song coming on." But not with bare fingers. After affixing the newly purchased finger-picks to his limber digits, the poker player who was betting his entire stake on the turn of a facedown card commenced to pluck strings and sing. Sing what?

What else? "Jack of Diamonds."

CHAPTER TWENTY-THREE

THE FOLLOWING MORNING
(HE FINALLY DOES IT)

The inevitable climax to this emergent crisis had been brewing for quite some time, and one way or another—the thing had to be settled today.

After a mostly sleepless night that was punctuated with vexing dreams about a rabid fox nipping at his bare feet, Charlie Moon rolled out of bed at the first cold gray glow of dawn to pull his britches, socks, and boots on. Half dressed, he exited his upstairs bedroom into the hallway and climbed the pine ladder into the headquarters loft. Fighting the shivers in that chilly, dusty space, he dialed the combination on the Columbine's old Mosler safe, opened the eighty-pound door—and removed a small box that contained the symbolic hope of his future.

Before Daisy Perika and Sarah Frank were up and about, the hopeful man had perked a pot of black-as-tar coffee, fixed himself a stick-to-his-ribs breakfast of three fried eggs, a thick slice of ham, and some warmed-over biscuits from yesterday. Though he had no appetite, he wolfed it all down like a soldier who was going to need all the strength he could muster for a desperate take-no-prisoners mission.

Whatever else may have occurred between Moon's early rising and his eventual arrival at the Granite Creek Public Library at 9:00 A.M. on-the-dot (which was when the front doors were unlocked) is not of any consequence and shall be omitted.

Except to note that from their bedrooms on the first floor, both Daisy Perika and Sarah Frank had heard Moon tromp along the upstairs hallway and climb the ladder into the attic.

Daisy rolled over on her other side and sighed. "The big gourd-head is gonna do it." Which raises two questions: *Do what?* and *How did she know?* The answers are (respectively): *We'll soon find out,* and *Daisy knew what her nephew kept in the attic safe.*

Sarah Frank knew, too. Like Daisy, she remained snuggled in under the quilted covers while Moon had his breakfast, but the moment he closed the front door behind him, the young woman sprang out of bed. Clad in her blue-and-white-striped pajamas, Sarah sprinted down the hallway and across the parlor to a west-porch window. She arrived just in time to see the Expedition make a tight U-turn in the Columbine headquarters yard. *I bet I know what he's going to do.* She did. But, short of snatching a Winchester carbine from the gun rack and shooting Moon dead before he was out of range, there was not a thing Sarah could do to prevent him from *doing it.*

She watched the automobile roll down the ranch lane and rumble across the timbers of the Too Late Creek bridge. As Moon passed the foreman's residence, a small cloud of frosty dust billowed behind the SUV to produce a foggy yellow barrier between the despairing youth and the man in her life. *Oh, I just* hate *him!* Sarah's hands knotted into brittle little fists that could've knocked the knotty head clean off a wooden Indian.

9:01 A.M.

The prettiest reference librarian Moon had ever laid eyes on was warming up her computer terminal when she became aware of a silent someone who was casting a long shadow over her shoulder. Ever ready to assist a reticent member of the reading public, the sweet lady turned to present a reassuring smile to whoever might need her help. The lady's smile upped from "professional glow" to hundred-kilowatt knock-your-socks-off intensity. "Oh, Charlie," she said. "It's you."

He managed a weak grin. "I know."

How to describe her laugh at this minuscule witticism? Imagine six dozen little silver bells tinkling on Ye Fairie Queen's ankle bracelet as she dances among acres of iridescent wildflowers. Moreover, Patsy's blue eyes sparkled merrily. "What brings you to the library so early?"

A pertinent question, and one that the overly tall Indian cowboy did not want to answer right on the spur of the moment. "Uh . . ."

Poor Charlie . . . he looks like he's going to be sick. Losing the smile, she inquired with all the tenderness of a mother addressing her three-year-old son, "Do you feel all right, sweetie?"

Being an accomplished multitasker, Moon swallowed hard—nodded—and responded thus: "Let's get out of here."

"What?"

He enlarged on his notion: "I need a breath of air."

Patsy detected the hint of a greenish tint on his dark face. *Oh my God—he's going to throw up!* Ejecting herself from the cushioned armchair, the panicked librarian took the gangly man by the arm and ushered him to the rear door (the nearest of the exits), which (thankfully) was equipped with a photo-detector mechanism that opened the portal when they were within three paces. This emergency egress was also (unfortunately) equipped with a loud buzzer, which was intended to attract attention to those slippery citizens who (rather than check items out in the designated manner) opted to sneak library property out the back door. Both the photo-detector door opener and buzzer worked flawlessly. As soon as they were on the redwood deck that overlooked the creek that had given its rock-hard name to both the county and the town, Moon leaned on the painted pipe railing and inhaled a refreshing gulp of air.

Patsy squeezed his sinewy arm. "Do you feel better now?"

He responded with another nod.

Head librarian Miss Parsons (who rarely missed a trick) had noticed the unseemly commotion even before the 140-decibel buzzer sounded, and had concluded immediately that Granite Creek County's most prominent rancher, best friend and deputy to the chief of police, enthusiastic banjo player, manager of the Columbine Grass bluegrass band, and longtime boyfriend of Miss Patsy Poynter—was looking more than a little queasy. Stepping smartly over to a spotless window that was situated between a matched pair of microfilm readers, she gazed upon the couple and shook her head. *I know what this is all about.* And, like Daisy and Sarah, Miss Parsons did know. Which knowledge was helpful to the curious lady, because Mr. Moon and his sweetheart were addressing each other in adoring looks and whispers.

(Sorry. Even if a head librarian or a fly-on-the-outer-wall could have picked up an endearing phrase here and there, it would be indiscreet to repeat a single word.)

As she watched their lips move, Miss Parsons nodded knowingly. When Mr. Moon removed a small, velvet-covered box from his jacket pocket, she sighed and rephrased her earlier conviction in a whisper: "I *knew* that's what he was going to do." Watching the tall, dark man open the box and remove the diamond ring and slip it onto the woman's finger, the elderly spinster felt a wetness gathering in her eyes. When Patsy began to cry and the couple embraced like the rapturous lovers they were, Miss Parsons's vision blurred with tears.

Brief though it may be, this account shall be deemed sufficient.

CHAPTER TWENTY-FOUR

MR. MOON BREAKS THE BIG NEWS

Like any important announcement at the Columbine, this earth-shaking revelation (think 9.3 on the Richter scale) was bound to be divulged in the dining room—at suppertime.

Sarah Frank had little doubt that her more or less secure life was about to absorb an unprecedented jolt; what she did *not* know was . . . *How will I react?* Little Miss Stiff-Upper-Lip promised herself that there would be no tears. *I'm twenty years old now—not some silly teenager who runs away to her bedroom to bury her face in a pillow and bawl like a calf who can't find its mother!* This was simply how the cookie had crumbled; there would be no hysterics. *I'll say: "I'm very happy for both of you, Charlie—I know you'll have a wonderful life together."* And to top that off in first-class fashion . . . *I'll smile at the big bonehead like I really mean it.* (She was only about two notches away from applying Daisy Perika's heartfelt "big gourd-head" epithet to the object of her vexation.) Speaking of whom (Mrs. P.):

Daisy also knew what her nephew was working his way up to, and knew just what she'd do. *I'll laugh in his face and tell him, "Of all the dumb things—"*

And she probably will, but anticipating Daisy's insults is a risky business, and even if she imagines it word-for-word, repetitions tend to be tedious. So we shall wait for the actual event.

Of the trio, the normally steady-as-he-goes Charlie Moon was the least sure of himself. Whether or not breaking the young woman's heart would have done less damage at a more propitious time and in a more private venue—those present for the impending earthquake shall never know. Not that Charlie Moon had given the matter of Sarah Frank's feelings a great deal of thought—but, like his proposal to Patsy, the thing simply had to be done. The long, tall Ute refused to admit to the reality of the Ute-Papago orphan's affection for him. This was a futile exercise in self-deception; deep down where he had tried to strangle and drown the truth, the essence of it kept bubbling up to disturb his peace. But worrying about what *might go wrong* was not the Cowboy Way, and, like pulling an aching tooth or branding a bawling year-old heifer, the stockman figured the best thing was to yank the danged molar or press the sizzling iron into the tender flesh *right now* and be done with the hurtful business. Nevertheless, the clueless tribal investigator (who honestly believed that . . . *This'll hurt me a lot more than Sarah*) hesitated. To put it more bluntly, he dithered. Also dawdled. And hemmed and hawed. Even *vacillated,* which is virtually unheard of in Granite Creek County.

But eventually, and without the slightest get-ready-for-this preamble, Moon mumbled the dreadful words: "Uh . . . me and Patsy have decided to tie the knot." Which reminded the prospective groom of a promise he had made to his betrothed. Meeting Sarah Frank's blank stare with a sickly smile, he said, "And Patsy asked me to pass on her request for a special favor."

The young woman's dry lips hissed a death-rasp whisper. "Favor?"

The hopeful groom nodded. "She'd be real pleased if you'd agree to be one of her . . . uh . . ." *What do they call them?* "Bride-somethings."

"Brides*maids,*" Daisy snapped.

"Oh, right." Charlie Moon told them something he *did* know, which was the date and time of day for the big event. And the fact that the wedding would take place at the Columbine, in the headquarters parlor.

A conversation stopper?

For Sarah, yes. A half-swallowed piece of prime Columbine beef stuck in her throat.

For Daisy, Moon's announcement was her cue. She laughed with all the scorn she could muster, then said, "Of all the dumb things you've ever done—this one sure takes the layer cake!"

Prepared for some such observation from his no-punches-pulled auntie, Moon smiled at the irascible old relative.

Aggravated by this good-natured response, Daisy shook a fork at her annoying nephew. "Mark my words—that white, blue-eyed *ma-tukach* hussy will make your life so miserable you'll wish you'd never been born."

"Well, if she does, I ought to be able to manage." He winked at the wrinkled tribal elder. "I've had some training."

"Hah—you just *think* you have." Daisy paused for a derisive snort. "You can get away from *me* for days at a time, but when it comes to a wife—not that I'd expect you to know because you've never had one—being married is a full-time job." The old crone grinned to display her few remaining peg-shaped teeth. "First thing you know, that yellow-haired gal will have a rope around your neck and you'll be followin' her around like a whipped dog."

What was Sarah Frank doing during what passed for witty repartee in the Columbine headquarters dining room? Choking. Literally.

Being directly across the table from the chokee, Daisy was the first to notice Sarah's distress. "Slap her on the back!"

Immediately grasping the situation, Moon applied a sound thwack between Sarah's shoulder blades. The result of which shall not be described in nauseating detail. Who wants to hear about a sweet young lady's inevitable response to this well-intended assault? None of us, that's who. Descriptions of projectile vomiting are off-putting—even when the projectile is merely a smallish piece of partially chewed beef, which—having been expelled from her throat—sailed directly across the dining table to land in Daisy's coffee cup. *Ker-plop!*

What one may say without offending delicate sensibilities is that the experience was extremely mortifying for Sarah, that Charlie Moon was embarrassed for the young lady, and that Daisy Perika cackled like an old red-combed hen who's just been told an off-color joke by the lusty barnyard rooster.

It was do-or-die time for Sarah, who was obliged to offer a lady-like apology for spitting her beef into Aunt Daisy's highly caffeinated beverage—and make her noble speech to Charlie Moon about how happy she was for him and Patsy, the wonderful life they were bound to share, et cetera. So did she "do"—i.e., come through with flying colors? No. She died.

Miss Frank got up from her chair, walked calmly out of the dining room and down the hallway, entered her darkened bedroom, closed the door softly, fell onto the bed—face in the pillow—and bawled. But, to her eternal credit—not like a calf who cannot find its mother. More like a twenty-year-old china doll whose delicate heart has been fractured into a zillion smithereens. *Oh! I'll never be able to look Charlie Moon in the eye again.*

An exaggeration. But not by much.

And I hate him and Patsy Poynter and I hope they choke to death on their wedding cake and I'll be there to laugh and clap my hands and yell, "Have another slice!"

Not very nice, but she meant it. Every malevolent word. But, as we all know, the white-hot heat of such youthful passions passes once angry lassies have had time to think things through.

On occasion, though, what *we all know* proves to be . . . not entirely true.

CHAPTER TWENTY-FIVE

CHARLIE MOON TAKES A NIGHTTIME WALK

Where to? Let's watch and find out.

There he goes, across the parlor, through the front door, across the redwood porch, and down the creaking steps. He strides purposefully across the dusty headquarters yard, down the dirt lane, and across the Too Late Creek bridge—to the foreman's residence.

What for?

Most likely, to conduct some ranch-related business with his second-in-command. It might be interesting to listen in, but eavesdropping will have to wait. Sarah Frank is also about to take an after-sundown stroll and the young lady's urgent business trumps Mr. Moon's.

THERE IS A TIME FOR LEAVING

Resembling a numb sleepwalker—or an insubstantial, imagined phantasm in someone's dream—Sarah Frank seemed to almost *float* out of the Columbine headquarters. Only barely conscious of her surroundings, the terribly unhappy young woman was moved by some deep, instinctive impulse toward the river—where perhaps peace was to be found in its cold, rolling waters. For how many faltering heartbeats did she stand alone on the pebbled bank, staring unseeingly at midnight-black waves and snowy froth where the stream broke over mossy boulders and heaps of smooth rocks? Sarah had not the slightest notion, and the issue of bits of time measured by man-made chronometers never entered her stunned young mind.

Even so, her precious moments—like lustrous pearls slipping along an invisible string—were not wasted.

ON THE BENEFITS OF PEACEFUL SOLITUDE

Sarah Frank loved the vast, open spaces of Charlie Moon's Columbine Ranch—from the spruce-studded Buckhorn Mountains on the east to the rugged Misery Range, whose jagged peaks pierced and bled the setting sun. At the first dusky hint of evening, she would often slip away to conceal her willowy form among a cluster of chattering aspens that had congregated near the riverbank. Marvelously uplifted by the joyous, uproariously glorious stream that laughed its way to the western sea, the girl would close her eyes and pretend that she had slipped back a thousand thousand years to an era when there was not another human soul between the oceans. The Ute-Papago orphan would be—for an eternal moment—entirely, blissfully secluded. But young ladies who are alone for more than a few heartbeats tend to get lonely, and wherever Sarah's imagination might transport her to, the essence of Mr. Moon's soul was obliged to follow.

Tragically, almost unutterably romantic? Perhaps.

But on this evening, her isolation was complete because . . . *It's all over now.*

A TIME

The gentlest of breezes touched the aspen branches and murmured to her, *For everything, there is a season.*

Sarah's head nodded; her lips whispered back, "A time for every purpose under heaven."

The slight movement of night air caressed her black hair. *A time to be born . . .*

"And a time to die."

The breeze was stilled; a sly serpent's voice spoke to her: *A time to kill!*

"No." She closed her eyes. "A time to heal."

Thus rebuffed, the demon departed . . . until a more opportune time.

The breath of night returned. *A time to weep.*

"And a time to laugh." Unable even to smile, the young woman sighed. "And a time for leaving." So said Sarah. *But not before I serve as Patsy's bridesmaid—and wish Charlie and his sweet wife all the happiness in the whole world.* And after that? *Then I'll leave.* A salty tear appeared in her eye. *But where will I go?* The lost soul considered her options. *For a month or so, I could stay in a dorm room at the university.* And after that? *I'll go back where I came from.*

Which was where?

Sarah could not return to the Papago reservation in Arizona. *Both of my grandparents are dead, and my other relatives there treat me like I'm . . . a stranger.*

Which suggested spending a few months with Marilee Attatochee in Utah. *Aunt Marilee is nice, and was always kind to me, but . . .* But Sarah had never been content in Tonopah; the very thought of returning to that windswept desert community almost made her shudder.

Before coming to the Columbine and being close to Charlie Moon almost every day, where had she ever been truly happy? *Nowhere.*

Except for one place . . .

I could go down to the res and take care of Aunt Daisy. The old woman certainly needed looking after, and Daisy Perika's remote home in the arid badlands of the Southern Ute reservation was a perfect retreat for a young woman who'd lost the only man she'd ever loved or ever would. Every meter and mile of the tribal elder's wilderness retreat held a special enchantment for Sarah, from the yawning mouth of *Cañón del Espíritu* at first light until the evening shadow of Three Sisters Mesa had spread a fuzzy blanket of gray twilight over the sleeping landscape.

Yes, spending a few months with Charlie Moon's aunt might be just the Rx for what ailed Sarah Frank.

But it's not like I have to make up my mind right this minute. The dreaded marriage was almost a month away. *Three weeks and six days.* She glanced at her wristwatch. *Minus about nine and a half hours.*

It would appear that the therapeutic river had done a first-rate job.

Not that Sarah was entirely (or even 95 percent) cured, as when an infected wisdom tooth is dexterously plucked out by a plucky dentist wielding chrome-plated pliers, or a troublesome gallbladder is deftly severed by the skilled surgeon's stainless-steel scalpel.

Nevertheless, the love-struck girl was definitely on the mend.

Which is not necessarily to say, as if abruptly consigning this deathless romance to oblivion, "The End." After several decades spent hanging on to to this spinning globe by one's fingernails, one learns to be cautious about making confident prognostications.

It is not only that our lives tend toward complexity; as you may know from playing bingo, purchasing lottery tickets, or trusting your favorite TV weather forecaster—the outcome of any process you might want to mention is aggravatingly unpredictable. Which willy-nilly property sometimes pencils big surprises into what we thought was a well-scripted play.

More jarring still, these bolts from the blue sometimes appear to be highly contrived, which—to some of us—suggests that someone concealed behind the scenery is pulling strings now and then. Managing the performance. Even picking winners and losers . . . Dare one say *stacking the deck*?

What was that from fifth row, center—did someone mutter, "God forbid!"

CHAPTER TWENTY-SIX

CHARLIE MOON'S DIFFICULT MISSION
AT THE FOREMAN'S RESIDENCE

It was one of those decisions that he'd been putting off for a couple of years or more, but the thing had to be done tonight—right on the spot, and without any rambling preamble.

So the rancher sat in his foreman's parlor for about an hour, sipping strong coffee, nibbling at Dolly Bushman's delicious warm-from-the-oven chocolate-chip cookies—all the time chatting aimlessly with Pete about the dry weather, the price of beef, and those two new Mormon cowboys from Utah who didn't drink a drop of whiskey, utter the least swearword, or get into fistfights if they could avoid it, but when push came to shove, those clean-cut fellas could stand their ground with the biggest, toughest, meanest cowpunchers the Columbine had to offer and give as good as they got. Whenever the boss ran out of other things to talk about, he'd drift back to the weather. Charlie Moon covered just about every subject a man could think of except the one that was on his mind and *had* to be broached before he could leave.

Not that Pete or Dolly Bushman was the least bit fooled.

Pete (suspiciously): *Charlie's working his way up to somethin'.* (With a nervous twitch in his left cheek): *Somethin' that I won't like to hear.*

Dolly (with motherly empathy): *Poor Charlie wants to tell us some bad news but he just can't make himself do it.*

But by and by, Moon could and did.

Not the upcoming wedding. *I'll tell them about my engagement to Patsy later on.* What he was obliged to say would be sufficient for the evening. After clearing his throat twice, he lowered his grim gaze to the cold coffee cup. "I've had a pretty good offer from some investors that want to buy the Columbine."

The foreman and his wife froze like marble statues.

Pete: *Ohmigod—I'm out of a job!*

Dolly: *Dear God . . . what will we do?*

Swirling the tepid black liquid in the bottom of Dolly's fine china cup, Moon felt like a drowning man who wasn't going to come up. Not for the proverbial three times—not even once. "If the deal goes through, they'll want to keep you on as foreman."

Pete Bushman let out the breath he'd been holding till his lips were turning blue.

The buyers *wanted to* because that was how Deputy Moon had laid down the law. The consortium had protested that it didn't make good business sense to take on an old, over-the-hill straw boss and his ailing wife, but Charlie Moon had stood firm on the point. "Pete Bushman gets an ironclad contract for twenty years or there's no deal. Period."

Not sure that the Bushmans would want to work for a bunch of city folks that hardly knew the difference between a heifer and a steer, Moon offered his foreman an option: "Or, if you and Dolly want to, you could move over to the Big Hat for the same wages." He raised his gaze to their faces. "There wouldn't be much stock to look after unless you wanted to keep some for yourselves—the main job would be to look after my smaller ranch. Protect my investment."

Pete had known the good-hearted Ute too long to be fooled. *Charlie's offering to put us out to pasture.*

Dolly found her voice. "If we was to go over to the Big Hat, would we be working directly for you?"

"Sure." Moon nodded. "For as long as it suits you." He added, "The Big Hat's not for sale."

She looked at her stricken husband. "Let's go over there, Pete."

The tired old man shrugged. "Whatever you say, Dolly."

"I say we move the minute Charlie says it's okay."

"Go as soon as you like." The Indian looked from one pale face to the other. "Try the place out before you make up your minds. Make sure you'll be happy there."

Pete Bushman let out a long sigh and turned to gaze at his help-mate. "Let's you and me take a run over there tomorrow and look things over."

As the old woman smiled, a teenage girl looked out from her tear-filled eyes. "It'll be fun, Pete—moving to a new place and setting up housekeeping again."

Grateful for this happy outcome, Moon put the delicate cup onto Polly's battered coffee table. "Let me know how the Big Hat works out for you." The tall man eased his lanky frame up from a lumpy but comfortable armchair. "If you're of a mind to, you can always stay right here and run the Columbine for the new owners."

CHAPTER TWENTY-SEVEN

ON THE DETRIMENTS OF PRIDEFUL BEHAVIOR

Which deficiency, though always simmering just beneath her wrinkled surface, is not Daisy Perika's immediate issue. At the moment, the cantankerous old woman has all her energy focused on producing a batch of white-hot fury—which incandescent anger is directed at her amiable nephew.

Seated in an armchair beside her bed, Daisy stared straight ahead at the doorway connecting her Columbine boudoir to the darkened headquarters hallway. *If that big gourd-head so much as shows his silly face, I'll pick up where I left off last night at suppertime and tell him just what I think about a full-blooded Southern Ute man marrying a pale-as-goat-milk* matukach *woman.* A series of familiar sounds suggested that Daisy was about to have that opportunity: the sharp click-click of Charlie Moon's boot heels trodding along the upstairs hardwood hallway, followed by muffled bumps as he descended the carpeted stairway. *Good—here he comes!* Her happy anticipation was short-lived. There was a clomping stomping as the rancher made his way across the parlor, a squeaking creak as he opened the porch door, and a crisp snap as that portal to the outer world closed and latched. *He's gone outside where I can't yell at him.* And she had no doubt that . . . *He did it just to spite me.* Thus deprived of her opportunity to vent, the puffed-up old fussbudget combined a dark scowl with a sly smirk, which is no small accomplishment. *But sooner or later Charlie has to come back in again and when he does, I'll let him know how I feel about—*

This dark thought was interrupted by the ringing of the telephone on her bedside table. On the second ring, Daisy snatched up the telephone. "This is the Columbine Answering Machine Girl. I only get paid two bits a call and I don't waste breath repeating myself, so listen close: if you want to talk to my idiot nephew Charlie Moon or poor little Sarah Frank, neither one of 'em is in the house so call back tomorrow or next week or next year—I don't really give a tinker's damn—goodbye!"

A quavery voice pleaded, "Please don't hang up, Daisy—it's me."

Realizing who was on the other end of the line, the tribal elder rolled her eyes. " 'Me' could be anybody at all. A magazine salesman who wants to pick a poor old woman's pocket, some nitwit who dialed a wrong number—or a silly old French-Canadian woman who can't remember her own name." Pleased at this latter witticism, Daisy dropped the scowl and shifted to the full-smirk mode. "So which one of those are you?"

"Oh, you know who I am." A giggle. "It's me—Louise-Marie."

"I should've guessed—a wrong number if there ever was one." On a roll, Daisy was feeling better with every heartbeat. "So what'd you call me for, you want a hot tip about that big Arab camel race that's coming up in Pagosa Springs?"

"Oh my, no—I hadn't even *heard* about it." A pause. "Besides, you know that I never bet on sporting events."

"Ah, then you're hoping to trick me into telling you something I shouldn't. I know—you're gonna try to pry one of my confidential recipes outta me. No, don't tell me—let me guess. You're after my top-secret formula for green-tomato, pimento, bell-pepper, blue-corn relish that tastes so good it's sinful to take more than a teaspoonful."

"Well . . . I always did like that *delicious* relish, Daisy—it goes awfully well with scrambled eggs." A quick intake of breath. "But that's not what I called about."

Exhausted from her effort, Daisy leaned back in the armchair to rest. "Just wanted to shoot the breeze, eh?"

"Actually, I wanted to let you know that Toadie's . . . that Hester Tillman's funeral is set for day after tomorrow at two P.M."

"Don't tell me where—it'll be at a witches' church where all the mourners fly in on broomsticks."

"Oh my, no! Hester's funeral will at the Episcopal church in Durango."

Daisy snorted. "Well, you tell the priest that just to be on the safe side, he ought to drive a pine stake through Toadie's heart before he gets started." She paused to grin and "heh-heh." "That way, maybe old frog-face will stay put in her coffin."

"That's a *terrible* thing to say!"

"Not as terrible as a bunch of Episcopalians watching old Toadie turn into a big, fat bat and fly away when the priest says his 'amen.'"

"Daisy, I won't listen to another word of such nonsense." Louise-Marie sniffed, which was a sign that she was about to get her dander up. "The reason I called is that I heard about what Toad—... what Hester said to Danny Bignight just before she died. And I know you're upset about her saying she'd come back and haunt you if you don't come to her funeral." The aged woman paused to recall what her point was, and did. "But that was just Hester's way of making a joke."

Daisy shook her head and sighed. "Old Toadie couldn't make a joke if her life depended on it." *And that Pueblo Indian cop don't know how to keep his mouth shut.* The Ute elder recovered her scowl, her ire now focused on Officer Bignight's indiscretion. *If Louise-Marie knows about Toadie's threat, then so does everyone in Ignacio.*

Louise-Marie helped herself to another inhalation of crisp Ignacio air. "And I think the least you could do is show up and bring some flowers to put on her casket—or her grave." There was a slight quaver of emotion in the French-Canadian woman's voice: "Hester always liked you, and it'll hurt her feelings if you don't come to her funeral or burial." She added artfully, "You *know* that Hester was very fond of you."

THE PRIDEFUL BEHAVIOR

Say what you may of Louise-Marie LaForte's faltering mental acuity, the woman knew how to probe at Daisy Perika's several weaknesses, the chief of which was pride.

Despite the tribal elder's shortcomings, it never occurred to Daisy that anyone she had not physically attacked with a deadly weapon might actually *dislike* her. On the contrary, Charlie Moon's aunt considered herself well-nigh irresistible—a prize rose among common dandelions. "Well . . . I guess maybe the old crackpot did like me—in her peculiar way." Daisy would have enjoyed attending a gathering where she was bound to meet dozens of folks she hadn't seen in a long time and might never encounter again on this side of That River. Moreover, she knew that either Charlie Moon or Sarah would be glad to drive her to Hester Tillman's funeral and burial. But the proud old woman didn't want it to look like she was being bullied into showing up by Toadie's threat. "I've got some important things I have to do day after tomorrow." Which flimsy excuse dredged up a fragmentary memory of a half-forgotten nightmare. "Like trim my toenails."

"Oh—*shame* on you, Daisy!"

Suspecting that Louise-Marie secretly enjoyed her outrageous remarks, the old jokester cackled wickedly and cracked wise again: "And I'll be busy picking some lint out of my black stockings. But if you happen to see Toadie's homely ghost hanging around her grave, tell her I said that I never visited her when she was alive and I don't see any reason to change my habits now."

THE DETRIMENTS THEREOF?
(OF PRIDEFUL BEHAVIOR)

Quién sabe? (Who knows?)

Yes, such a response is inadequate for those adrenaline freaks who live right on the ragged edge of calamity—such edgy folk get their kicks from breaking society's rules *come what may*. And on occasion, so do we. In this instance, the temptation to answer a hypothetical question is overwhelming.

So here goes: presumably, Hester "Toadie" Tillman. (She knows.)

But aside from a ho-hum haunting (rattling chains, pitiful moaning, horrific groaning, and whatnot) that would not cause Daisy Perika to bat an eyelash, if the dearly departed has some sinister plan up her shroud sleeve for *serious* revenge, she has not yet revealed it. Which leads us to consider the dead woman's habits whilst still residing among the living: those who have crossed her and lived to tell the tale will tell you that Mrs. H. "T." Tillman is known for biding her time. For how long? Until all the cows come home—or until her intended victim is lulled into a state of dull complacency. Then (so they say)—Toadie strikes and fangs like an enraged prairie rattlesnake.

Stay tuned.

CHAPTER TWENTY-EIGHT

THE INCAUTIOUS TOURIST

The young woman behind the Bronco's steering wheel felt reasonably secure, and why not? Miss Louella Smithson had driven all the way from Kansas City without mishap. Now—with the considerable authority of Mr. Rand McNally—the map on page 20 of her new road atlas assured her that she was heading more or less northwest and would eventually end up in Granite Creek. (The town, not the chilly stream.) As she focused her intent gaze on the two-lane, "Ellie" fervently hoped so, but in her granddaddy's West Texas lingo . . . *I seem to be going every whichaway!* With the tight curves in the sinuous road, the setting sun would be directly in her eyes one moment, only to shift to the left or right, and then—presumably as some sort of celestial prank—the golden orb would pop up over her shoulder to shine blindingly in the SUV's rearview mirror. All this erratic solar bopping about made it unlikely that she would notice the vehicle that was trailing along about a quarter mile behind her. But even if she had, Miss Smithson might not have become suspicious. Unless she had taken note of something odd. Her Bronco engine badly in need of a tune-up, she was poking along at about ten miles per hour under the posted speed limit, and the vehicle behind her old SUV was matching its speed precisely—even when Louella sped up slightly when coasting downgrade . . . or puttering along on a long climb. Moreover, every other automobile that had gotten within sight had passed her old motor vehicle (and its tail) as if they were sitting still.

Pay no attention to that hopeful "old saying"—what we don't know *can* hurt us.

As the numbers on mile-marker signs regressed through the troublesome teens and eventually dwindled to single digits, her heartbeat gradually increased. At precisely nine miles from the designated center of Granite Creek and not quite seven from the city limits, Miss Smithson spotted what looked like a rest stop and slowed to ease her blue-and-white 1989 Bronco off the blacktop and into that welcoming refuge for bone-weary travelers.

As the old SUV's knobby tires crunched on white gravel that had been hauled in from a Pleistocene-era pit, Louella pulled the windshield visor down to shield her eyes from a reddening sun that (presumably for an instant's rest) was sitting atop a distant saddle-shaped butte. The fatigued tourist braked to a full stop and pushed the gearshift lever up to Park. At first glance, the cedar-dotted parking space had looked inviting. Now, her appraising gaze took in a half-moon parking lot that was bordered by the highway on the straight side and an arc of juniper, piñon, dwarf oak, and unsightly weeds on the curved bluff-side boundary. To the lady's dismay, the graveled space was lightly cluttered with longneck beer bottles, crushed soft-drink cans, and various other unseemly discards. The midwestern cynic speculated (and correctly so) that the handsome knotty-pine trash receptacle provided for the proper disposal of rubbish was virtually empty. As the worn Ford's V-8 engine chuggity-chugged along unsteadily on six or seven cylinders, Miss Smithson reflected that she had several urgent and thorny issues to consider. Though isolated, this two-acre eyesore was hardly conducive to productive contemplation. Even so, twilight was already slipping over the parking lot like a dank Mississippi Delta fog—which was all to the better. It would be easier to think once the unsightly trash was covered by the soft edge of night.

Darkness, of course, will sometimes conceal a far more unwelcome presence than cast-off beverage containers.

WHAT LOUELLA SMITHSON WAS NOT THINKING ABOUT

You already know, of course—the vehicle that had dogged her trail for almost a hundred miles.

An understandable oversight for a rank amateur, but not for a young woman who considered herself an old pro in the following game. That said, how many experienced bloodhounds expect the foxy felon at large to end up behind them?

The aforesaid felon had considered passing the rest stop and stopping a mile or so up the road to wait for Miss Smithson—then follow her into Granite Creek. But on the off chance that an opportunity might present itself to dispose of the nuisance in this lonely place, the cold-blooded soul also slowed and pulled into the graveled space behind the hopeful bounty hunter, finding partial concealment under the inky shadow of an oversize juniper.

WHAT THE SO-CALLED COWBOY ASSASSIN WAS NOT THINKING ABOUT

Jane Law, that's who—a Colorado State Trooper on routine patrol who had been gradually getting nearer to the Bronco and its tail ever since Miss Smithson and her dogged pursuer had passed through Salida. The thought of either bounty hunters or assassins never having crossed her mind, Ms. Smoky was now about a mile back and closing fast on the parked vehicles.

An understandable oversight, even for a foxy felon who knows how to turn the tables on a so-so bloodhound.

PREAMBLE TO A METAMORPHOSIS

When Louella Smithson twisted the ignition key counterclockwise a few degrees, the overheated eight-cylinder engine dieseled for a couple of cycles, coughed like a ninety-nine-year-old asthmatic drawing his final breath—and died.

This sudden absence of engine noise was jarring—sufficiently so that the Kansas City lady caught her breath. *This place is as quiet as a hundred-year-old graveyard—and about as creepy.* But, after a few deep breaths, so serenely peaceful. Which was just the prescription for her unsettled mind. *I need to rest for a few minutes so I can organize my thoughts and prepare myself.* And right at the top of the list . . . *I'll begin the process of assuming my new identity.* Which, as those extroverts who strut about upon the stage or play to the motion-picture camera well know, would involve *getting into character.*

The avocational actress smiled as she considered her upcoming role: *When I meet with those two policemen in a day or two, I'll no longer be Louella Smithson.* Which assertion raised an obvious question: who, then? Patting her unkempt hair, the imaginative thespian raised her chin in a haughty expression. *I shall be Miss . . . Miss Who?* Miss Smithson considered a half-dozen potential aliases, but not one of them seemed quite right for this career-making performance—which called for something special. (And suitable for the cover of a book.) The harder she tried, the more Louella's head ached. *I've been driving way too long without a break; I'm too tired to think straight.* But she knew just the remedy for what ailed her: *I need a hot meal, a hotter tub bath, and some peaceful downtime in a quiet room.* Problem solved. There would be ample opportunity to make the transformation after checking in to a motel. *But I don't want to waste my few minutes here.* This was (she thought) as good a time as any to review her copious files on The Case.

She thought wrong.

Having concluded that this was as good a spot as any, the assassin for hire had selected a weapon and was pulling on a pair of soft, thin-as-bat-skin leather gloves.

Oblivious to the mortal danger lurking only a few yards away, Louella Smithson fingered the lever that unlocked the driver's bucket seat from its steel track and pushed it back a few inches. For what purpose? Why, to make room in her lap for a pink laptop computer. In addition to the usual personal information one keeps on hard-disk drives, everything Miss Smithson knew—and *thought* she knew—about the so-called Cowboy Assassin and the Hooten family was stored on that useful device. Not to mention a detailed and much-edited outline of her true-crime manuscript, which was complete except for a compelling opening scene, quite a lot of exciting stuff in the middle, and the triumphant conclusion wherein she would identify the hired gun in

Granite Creek and be present for Cowboy's arrest by that pair of local lawmen whom she had come to save from certain doom—namely, Chief of Police Scott Parris and Deputy Charlie Moon.

And speaking of officers of the law . . .

State Police officer Janie Lawton slowed as she approached the rest stop, which was flagged on her mental map as a hangout for petty thieves who pilfered parked cars, small-time drug pushers, and other objectionable riffraff. Spotting two motor vehicles, she naturally ignored the shiny new one and targeted the rusty scuzzmobile—i.e., Miss Smithson's venerable Bronco. Yes, a clear case of prejudicial selection (transport profiling) but a decision that probably saved Officer Lawton's life—and most certainly preserved Miss Smithson's.

The assassin had already loaded a round into the blued-steel barrel of an automatic pistol and was about to make bad use of that lethal weapon.

Startled by the blinking lights, Louella Smithson sighed. *What now?*

As it turned out, nothing much. Merely Trooper Lawton's friendly warning not to tarry too long at the rest stop which was a known hangout for undesirables. Moreover, night was coming on and a snowstorm was rolling in from the west.

"Thank you, Officer." Louella tapped a painted fingernail on her laptop. "I have some work to do, but I promise I'll be gone before the storm shows up." And so she would.

The state trooper departed.

Louella Smithson—her mind energized by the mildly startling encounter with the police officer—turned again to the issue of a suitable persona to assume for her brief stay in Granite Creek. To that end, she opened a smallish MS Word file that listed previous aliases, each with an invented background to support the phony ID. After perusing these past deceptions, she recalled that each one had begun with the name—a suitable background story springing naturally from the ring of the moniker. And all those previous names had come to her like bolts from the blue.

This one would, too.

Using the pink-lacquered forefinger nails on each hand, Miss Smithson deftly pecked in "GRANITE CREEK ID."

That's all it took; inspiration did the rest. Creativity is a mysterious phenomenon.

Now, how the pair of dainty forefingers did fly!

Watching her potential new alias appear on the computer display, the lady smiled at one that fairly jumped out at her: Miss Whysper. *Yes—I do like the sound of that!*

Which was fortunate; her burst of inspiration had run its course.

Under "Background," and at a slower pace, she typed in: SUSAN WHYSPER WAS MY FAVORITE AUNT.

THE VILLAIN?

Long gone. Even as the trooper was offering the tourist a free weather forecast and unsolicited sage advice, the driver of the other, more-respectable vehicle had pulled away.

Was the assassin disappointed by the inconvenient arrival of the state cop? Check the box by "Yesiree!" But Cowboy endured this setback with a true professional's philosophical acceptance of a capricious Fate. *A bad break—but maybe it was for the best.* An incurable optimist, the hired gun was confident that there would be another time, a better opportunity—and quite a different outcome.

There would be. (All three.)

CHAPTER TWENTY-NINE

SUITABLE LODGING FOR A LADY

Louella Smithson eyed a helpful sign that advised the tourist that she was about to enter Granite Creek's city limits; a following sign put the limit at forty-five miles per hour. After a glance at the speedometer, she eased off the brake pedal until the aged Bronco was chugging along at a velocity just under the specified maximum. *I don't want to get off on the wrong foot with the local cops by getting a ticket.* Which concern reminded her of something else to worry about . . . *I hope Granddaddy remembered to call the local chief of police before he wandered off to his favorite fishing hole.* Old folks (bless their fuzzy minds) were prone to forget about really important business, like looking after their granddaughter's urgent interests. And not only that . . . *What does he need with a string of smelly old fish to clean when he could buy some nice fillets at the supermarket?*

The young woman's idle musings about the unfathomable eccentricities of a certain senior citizen were interrupted by the sudden appearance an iconic Holiday Inn sign. This familiar logo, combined as it was with the alluring neon glow of a VACANCY therein was irresistible. The weary traveler turned into a large parking lot that was almost filled with vehicles, the majority being pickups of various description—not a few with rifle racks mounted across the rear windows, many of which prominently displayed a Winchester carbine or a deadly serious look-alike. Capped at either end in cowboy boots and wide-brimmed felt hats, rough-looking men strolled about this way and that. A few of these tough customers had not yet seen forty winters, but most were slightly bowlegged, early models with unfiltered cigarettes hanging limply from their lips or wads of Red Man tobacco bulging in their jaws.

Miss Smithson blinked. *What's this—some kind of old-time cowboy jamboree?* A response to her query was immediately provided by the small marquee under the hotel's the main entrance (which was missing an apostrophe):

WELCOME
ROCKY MTN CATTLEMENS ASSOC
AND
WESTERN STATES BRAND INSPECTORS

She managed a wan smile. *Granddaddy would fit right in here.* And for that matter, so did the little girl inside her who'd grown up on her grandfather's small West Texas ranch. But her nostalgic thoughts were suddenly elbowed aside by an unnervingly sinister realization that the assassin who wore a cowboy hat might take this opportunity to melt into a crowd of genuine westerners. *He might even decide to check in here at the Holiday Inn.* Fear feeds upon itself. *Worse still, he might've arrived a few hours ago.* And if he had, then . . . *Cowboy could be loading his pistol in the room right across the hall from where I'll be unpacking in a few minutes.*

But how long were the odds of such a ghastly coincidence?

Of all the hotels in town, there's no reason to believe he'd pick this *one.* A sensible and reassuring conclusion. But it was impossible to dismiss the obvious fact that wherever the so-called Cowboy hung his hat in Granite Creek, it would be far more difficult to spot the hired gun among hundreds of real-McCoy convention cowboys who would be meandering around town, half of them looking like the black-hat hardcase in a grade-B Western who'd come to Dodge City to gun down clean-cut, clear-eyed U.S. Marshal Dillon. Or . . . Miss Kitty.

Since there was nothing she could do about that, the would-be bounty hunter addressed a more mundane issue. Pulling in to check-in parking at the main entrance, the edgy traveler left the Bronco engine idling unevenly and dashed inside to make sure the Vacancy sign could be relied on. She was assured that there was room at the inn; but there were only three left to chose from and these would likely be occupied within a quarter hour.

Louella Smithson promptly selected an accommodation at the rear of the hotel, where (she was advised by the helpful desk clerk), "You won't be disturbed by traffic noise, ma'am." She crossed her fingers as the dapper young man swiped her almost-maxed-out Visa card and held her breath until the plastic rectangle was accepted. The clerk gave Miss Smithson a pair of room keys, a map of the premises—and a gracious invitation to a complimentary buffet breakfast in the Gold Rush Sun Room. Capping this hospitality off with a genuinely friendly smile, he advised the famished guest that coffee, tea, and cookies were available 24/7 at that same location.

Keys and map clutched tightly in hand, Miss Smithson hurried back to her Bronco, drove around to the rear of the hostelry, and parked on the yonder side of the lot by the creek bank. As often happens when a worn-out traveler reaches her destination, she was suddenly overcome with a mind-numbing fatigue. Indeed, the longing to lean back and close her eyes was almost overpowering. *But I can't sit here in the car or I'll fall asleep.* This being so, she emerged from the Bronco with the pink laptop computer tucked under her left arm, a shabby pink suitcase firmly gripped in her right hand, and the hotel map clenched between her teeth. *Oh—where did I put those room keys?* In her jacket pocket she believed. Hoped. The groggy traveler did not actually remember putting them there, but . . . *That's where they've got to be.*

And so off she went, her face set toward the rear entrance. A playful gust of chill wind snatched her breath away. *Oh, it's so cold!* Moreover, snow was flurrying around her pale face like tiny white moths. Which reminded the tourist that her fleece-lined raincoat was in the Bronco. *Not a problem—I'll come back for it after I get the room unlocked and unpack some things.*

Not a problem. One of those phrases that we toss off so casually. On occasion, almost flippantly.

LOUELLA SMITHSON'S PROBLEM

The assassin, of course.

The vehicle that had tailed her into town was parked about fifty yards away. Lights out. Engine idling like a purring cougar.

As the intended victim entered the hotel, a pair of serenely calm eyes regarded Miss Smithson with the detached, professional interest of a cleaver-wielding butcher about to dismember a side of prime beef. Between a pair of finely tuned ears, the alert brain considered the laptop and small suitcase and made an informed conjecture: *No woman travels that light.* The head nodded knowingly. *She'll be back for something else.* Under a perfectly straight nose, the compressed, thin lips smiled without a hint of mirth. *And when she does, I'll be waiting for her.* Cowboy was confident that this day's quota of bad luck had been used up. *This time, no meddlesome cop will show up to foul things up.*

Perhaps.

But what about *two* meddlesome cops—who are already in the neighborhood?

CHAPTER THIRTY

HAVE A GOOD TIME AT THE SUNBURST PIZZA RESTAURANT!

No, this is *not* an advertisement provided in exchange for a free meal and beverage, tip included (except on Saturday evenings)—and anyone who suggests otherwise is an envious rumormonger. The headlined Granite Creek eatery happens to be the high-class feed trough where Scott Parris and Charlie Moon were dining with their lady friends when the chief of police (now officially returned to duty) grudgingly took a call from Dispatch. Possibly because he detested the interruption, Parris's share of the conversation served as an admirable model of lucid brevity: "I'm here." Six-heartbeat pause. "Got it." Disconnecting, he directed a sheepish smile at the lady sitting beside him in the booth. "Sorry, sweetie—I've got to run."

"Oh, pooh!" Tiffany effected a pretty pout. "Official police business?" (This proud holder of an earned PhD is a very discerning lady.)

Parris nodded at his knockout date, who was an assistant professor of English literature at Rocky Mountain Polytechnic. He cast a glance at Charlie Moon. "But nothing that'd interest my deputy." Grinning thinly at the lean Ute, he added, "This is strictly top-drawer stuff—way beyond Charlie's pay grade."

The intrepid poker player saw the grin and raised with a show of pearly teeth. "That's right, pardner." Parleying a hunch, Moon laid his ace of hearts on the table—faceup. "You go take care of the lady."

Well, that was a low blow! Parris stared like an about-to-be-poached buck caught in an unscrupulous hunter's pickup headlights.

Four pretty, mascaraed eyes widened.

Tiffany's pair glared at her blushing date, who was scowling at his Indian friend. She repeated Moon's provocative phrase: "The *lady*?"

"Well, she's a woman." Parris shrugged his big shoulders. "I don't know if she's necessarily a *lady.* . . ." His blush deepened. "What I mean to say is—"

"What Scott means is that she's not necessarily a *shady* lady." The merry Ute winked at Tiffany. "Let's just say she's a stranger in our fair city—someone *special,* who needs to be escorted around town and generally looked after by a big, strong, hairy-chested man."

It is not an unwarranted exaggeration to assert that Chief of Police Scott Parris was severely miffed at Moon, or that Professor Tiffany Mayfair was speechless.

Sensing an imminent explosion, Patsy Poynter hastened to defuse the tension. "My goodness, this visitor sounds very *mysterious.*"

"Oh, she is." Moon's sophomoric grin had graduated to the status of a happy, about-to-accept-a-sheepskin nine-hundred-watt smile. "You could twist Scott's arm into a pretzel and he wouldn't say a word about *who* the stranger is—*why* she's in town—or what motel she's checked in to."

This upping-the-ante provocation was sufficient to loosen Tiffany's tongue, which—when circumstances called for it—could be as sharp as a barbed obsidian arrowhead. Initially, all she could manage was one word, but she spat it out like a gourmand ejecting a distasteful morsel of overcooked seaweed. "Mo-*tel*?"

Defeated, Parris nodded glumly and repeated the information provided by his dispatcher: "Holiday Inn, room 215."

With a look at her boyfriend that curdled the undigested anchovy, green chili, and pineapple pizza and Coors Lite that had previously been so satisfyingly settled in Scott Parris's stomach, she said, "I think that I should like to meet this 'Strange Lady in Town.'" (Among her other virtues, the lettered scholar was a devoted Frankie Laine fan.)

Did the big, brawny cop stare his gorgeous date down and remind the brainy lady who was in charge and what was what?

Hah! (Enough said.)

Now beet red and knowing that he was a stone-cold-dead, shot-in-the-head six-point buck, Parris said, "All right. If you really want to meet Miss Smithson, then come along." He made the offer figuring that . . . *She won't.*

Poor, clueless cop. Of course she would.

"Thank you for the gracious invitation," saith Tiffany with cucumber coolness. Then, patting Miss Poynter's hand: "You come too, Patsy—this should be fun!"

Moon's intended was loath to involve herself in a potentially flammable dispute between Scott Parris and his high-strung girlfriend, but after a hopeful glance at her fiancé (whose wooden-Indian face showed not the slightest hint of objection), Patsy could only assent to Tiffany's invitation.

And wherever Miss Patsy Poynter goeth, Charlie Moon is obliged to follow. Which, one might suppose, might have led the humorist to conclude that his little joke had backfired. If so, one would suppose right.

As Scott Parris's blush had lightened to his facial skin's normal, healthy ruddy tint and his scowl was replaced by a "now you get yours, buddy" smirk, one might also reasonably deduce that the chief of police was not entirely displeased with this unexpected turn of events. Right again. And whatever moralists may say about the dark side of mean-spirited, petty revenge—it does create a transient sense of satisfaction. Matter of fact, Charlie Moon's presumed discomfort settled Parris's indigestion with all the soothing effect of an effervescent, fizzing Alka-Seltzer tablet.

No. Even better than that.

Make it a full pack—*two* effervescent, fizzing A-S tablets.

CHAPTER THIRTY-ONE

A RATTLED "STRANGE LADY IN TOWN"

(Not rattled just yet, but she is about to be.) We refer, of course, to the lady in room 215 at the Holiday Inn, who was deeply absorbed in a Microsoft Word file labeled ALIASES.doc on her pink laptop when someone in the hallway rapped his five-cell flashlight on the door.

Headbanger flashlight: *Bang-bang-bang!*

Rattled strange lady: "Yikes!" Quick recovery. "Who is it?"

"Wild West room service," Scott Parris bellowed. "Open up before we kick this door down and start tossin' tourists and furniture around!" (Why is he feeling so danged good? On the way over, Tiffany had given him her sizzling all-is-forgiven kiss, which is enough to make a corpse get up and dance.)

What the hell . . . The present occupant of room 215, who had no intention of being tossed around, got up from her prissy little pink computer and strode across the carpet to peer through the peephole and see a veritable *crowd* of people on the other side of the door. (If three qualifies as a crowd, so must four.) Their faces were hard to make out, but she sized the situation up right away and (as a lady is apt to do) concentrated her attention on the male contingent of the mob, one a broad-shouldered fellow wearing what appeared to be an old-fashioned fedora, the other a remarkably tall, skinny man topped off by a broad-brimmed black cowboy hat. These roughnecks were accompanied by a pair of shapely females who could've been poster girls for the Las Vegas chapter of the National Cocktail Waitress's

League. *Must be a couple of drunk cowboys and their streetwalker girlfriends who've come to pay a call on some other cowboy drunks and gotten the wrong room.* "Whom are you looking for?"

Mr. Broad-Shoulder's voice boomed through the hardwood door: "We're lookin' for *you,* ma'am." She watched a sharkish grin split his face. "I'm Scott Parris, the local Wyatt Earp, and this dangerous Indiana"—he jerked his elbow to indicate Mr. Tall-and-Skinny—"is Charlie Moon, my trusty sidekick who shoots low-down varmints first and asks questions after they're pronounced dead."

"Oh." *Of course. Chief of Police Scott Parris and Deputy Charles Moon.* She had not expected to meet them so soon or under such unnerving circumstances, but there was nothing to do but open the door just enough to eyeball the party of four. "Hello."

"Howdy, ma'am," Parris said.

The taciturn Indian merely nodded and removed his John B. Stetson lid.

At an elbowing from Tiffany, the chief of police also doffed his hat.

As the ladies smiled, the chief of police looped his muscular arm around one of the presumed cocktail waitresses and said, "This is Dr. Tiffany Mayfair, professor of something or other over at Rocky Mountain Polytechnic." He nodded to indicate Moon's date. "The other pretty lady is Granite Creek's all-American reference librarian, Miss Patsy Poynter—soon to be Mrs. Patsy Moon." Whereupon the aforesaid librarian leaned affectionately against her prospective husband. Taking note of the blank look on the stranger's face, Parris glanced at the numerals on the door again. *It's 215, but maybe I didn't hear the dispatcher right.* "I hope I didn't bang on the wrong door." He grinned like the mischievous little boy within him. "If you're not who I think you are, then I'll tell you how sorry I am and we'll be gone before you can spit in my eye twice."

"Oh, you have the correct room," she said. But there was a *but* coming up.

Scott Parris was relieved to hear this. "Well then, Miss Smith—"

"Shhh!" The lady touched a finger to her lips. Also shook her head.

"What?" Parris said.

METAMORPHOSIS INITIATED

The out-of-towner whom Parris had almost addressed as "Miss Smithson" smiled. "There was no way you could have known, but I would prefer that it was not bandied about that I'm in town. When I'm working on"—she paused to find just the right phrase, and did—"a *sensitive project,* I find it helpful to conceal my true identity."

"Oh." Parris nodded knowingly. "So you're in Granite Creek *incognito,* huh?"

"That was my intention."

Miss Smithson's smarter than her grandfather gives her credit for. "So what's your alias for this sensitive project?"

"For the duration of my business here, I shall be Susan Whysper. It was my maiden aunt's name, though our family called her 'Missy Whysper.'" Addressing the chief of police, she said, "I suggest that you address me as 'Miss Whysper.'"

"I'll do that." Scott Parris preferred the abbreviated alias to Susan Whysper and Charlie Moon did, too.

Professor Mayfair considered the whole business of using an alias unnecessarily dramatic . . . *unless she's some kind of secret agent working for the government.*

Glancing at Charlie Moon, the woman who preferred to operate incognito said (with just the hint of a sly lady-cat smile), "Or, if you prefer . . . Missy Whysper."

So she said, and so they would do, and so shall we. A strange lady in town on serious business has a right to assume any name that suits her.

CHAPTER THIRTY-TWO

THE LADY MAKES A FATEFUL DECISION

"It is very thoughtful of you to drop by," said Miss Whysper as she opened the door wide. "How did you know where I was staying?" Even as the words were slipping between her lips, she realized that . . . *I shouldn't have asked.*

Parris's face crinkled into an amused, almost supercilious smile. *What an amateur, and she writes books about crime.* "I notified every hotel, motel, and flophouse in town—and asked them to notify me when you showed up." *And every cop on the force was told to be on the lookout for an old Bronco with Missouri plates—for all the good that did.* "The bright young fella at the front desk recognized your name when you checked in—which was also on your credit card—and he called GCPD right away."

Miss Whysper sighed and rolled her eyes. "Then even the Holiday Inn is in cahoots with the local police force?"

"You betcher boots." Parris chuckled. "Anyway, the dispatcher called me, so here I am with alla my friends to say, 'Welcome to Granite Creek.'"

Moon appended an apology: "We were having supper when Scott took the call, and didn't want to break up the party—I hope you don't mind having the whole bunch of us barge in on you."

Fearing no competition from this plain-Jane sort of female, Tiffany reinforced Moon's apology: "Yes—really—if you'd like to talk to Scott alone, the rest of us won't mind waiting in the lobby."

Well—this is hardly what I had in mind, but one must take life as it comes. "No, please come in and make yourselves comfortable."

"Thank you, ma'am." Parris hated wasting even ten minutes of his treasured evening date on Ray Smithson's granddaughter. "But only for a minute or so—and only if it's no trouble."

"It is no trouble at all." Which was not entirely true, but circumstances and hospitality sometimes incline us to lean slightly to the deceitful side, and so she opened the door wide and watched the troupe march single file into room 215, which was equipped with a neatly made double bed, a pine dresser and chest of drawers trying hard to look like maple, two similarly unpretentious armchairs, a miniature couch, and a wall-mounted high-definition-television screen. Miss Whysper waved her hand to indicate the couch and chairs. "Please sit down." It had been a trying afternoon, and her tone was not especially inviting.

Parris caught the hint. "Oh, that won't be necessary." *Might as well get right to the point and get this farce over with.* "Your grandfather told me about how you write books and—"

"You're an author? What kind of books?" Wide-eyed with delight, Tiffany did not wait for a response. "I'm an English professor over at Rocky Mountain Polytechnic University, Miss Smithson—I teach a course in creative writing. Perhaps you would be interested in speaking to our students—"

"No!" Placing the finger across her lips again, the lady shook her head. "Please do *not* call me Miss Smithson."

Tiffany returned a blank look, then: "Oh, sorry—I'd already forgotten."

"It complicates my work, you see." The stern lady smiled sweetly at the completely clueless university professor. "When I am conducting research for a confidential project, I prefer to keep a low profile." She shot a glance at Tiffany's date. "Chief of Police Parris has demonstrated how easily my identity might be exposed—along with the delicate nature of my current project."

Unaccustomed to even the least reproach, Tiffany was mildly miffed. "I guess if people knew an author was in town they'd bother you with . . . with all kinds of bothersome requests . . ." *Like, "Would you talk to my creative writing class?"*

"I have never been asked to discuss my work with a university class—and frankly, the prospect is quite appealing." *Professor Barbie Doll is such an innocent.* "But at present, I prefer to remain as inconspicuous as possible."

Realizing that Miss Whysper had no intention of discussing either her true-crime book project in front of the ladies, much less the supposed killer she was presumably tracking, Parris began searching for an exit strategy. To that end, he aimed the butt end of his flashlight at the pink laptop and the pink suitcase that lay unopened on the bed. "Sorry we interrupted your unpacking."

"You didn't, actually," said Miss Whysper truthfully. "When you knocked on the door, I was about to depart." The out-of-towner sighed like the weary traveler she was. "This is a nice hotel, but rather too noisy for my tastes. I will be seeking other lodging."

"I don't think you'll find much in the way of a quiet hotel room in Granite Creek—not for the next few days." Parris glanced at Moon, who nodded his agreement. "So happens, the town's hosting the Cattlemen's Association *and* the Brand Inspectors' meetings this week, and everything's filled to the gills. You were lucky to get yourself a room here at the Holiday Inn."

"Oh, my—that is unfortunate."

"But there might be some peaceful place where we could find you a bed to sleep in." Parris shot one of those sharp looks at the Ute rancher that can only be described as *meaningful.*

Taking the hint, the hospitable westerner immediately made the offer: "You'd be more than welcome to stay at the Columbine, ma'am."

Charlie Moon's fiancée did not have a jealous bone in her body, and she trusted her man, and anyway this out-of-towner wasn't exactly magazine-cover material. Patsy Poynter smiled to signify her assent.

Nevertheless, Miss Whysper was doubtful. "The Columbine—is that a bed-and-breakfast?"

"More or less, but only for invited guests." Moon grinned. "And we serve lunch and supper too."

"The Columbine is Charlie's ranch." Parris bragged like he was top dog at the local chamber of commerce: "And you can take it from me—there's no better place to eat or get a good night's sleep in all of Granite Creek County."

Miss Whysper was charmed and amused by the offer. "That's very kind of you, Mr. Moon, but I really wouldn't want to be a bother. . . ." Her words trailed off to give him room to make the proper response.

Ever obliging, Charlie Moon assured the lady that she would not be the least bother.

Patsy Poynter provided another incentive: "You probably won't find another *decent* room in town."

Eager to get this lodging business resolved, Scott Parris commenced to describe the high points of Charlie Moon's vast cattle ranch, adding, "You'll like the Columbine—it's miles out of town and quiet as the lone prairie can get, Miss Smithson—uh, sorry, that just slipped out." The off-duty cop waved his felt fedora. "I meant to say Miss *Whisper*."

The lady arched an eyebrow. "With a *y*."

Parris returned a blank look. *What's she talking about?*

Charlie Moon leaned close to Parris's ear—and spelled it out for him.

Which the chief of police appreciated; resourceful deputies who can clarify just about any confusion that comes along are hard to come by. But there's always a *but* appended to a compliment. But . . . *I wish Charlie didn't take so much pleasure in explaining things to me.*

Mildly amused by her little tease, Miss Whysper agreed to lodge at the Columbine "for perhaps a day or two."

"Fine," the rancher said, and reached for the pink suitcase on the bed. "I'll tote this out and stash it in your Bronco."

The lady protested. "I really do appreciate your gallantry—but I prefer to carry my own luggage."

As she pulled the gaudy suitcase from his grip, Moon relinquished it gracefully and advised the do-it-herself tourist that his Expedition— with the Columbine logo on both front doors—was parked close to her car. "Soon as you're ready to leave, you can follow me to the ranch." He added as an afterthought, "On the way out of town, I'll be dropping the ladies off, and then Scott."

"That will present no difficulty," said Miss Whysper. "I am accustomed to following vehicles during the darkest nights—and this will provide me with an opportunity to inform myself about the layout of your charming little town and the rugged country surrounding it."

"Okay then." Parris glanced at his wristwatch. "Let's get going." *In a day or two, I expect she'll be ready to tell me about this alleged cop killer who's supposedly coming to town.* If not, Granite Creek's top cop would arrange an "official interview." Read: high-temperature *interrogation*—the kind that grills well-done. Having a famous ex-Texas Ranger for a granddaddy carried some weight, but there were limits to professional courtesy.

Miss Whysper was more than ready to depart, but the lady did have a request to make of the chief of police. "I'm rather embarrassed to be checking out so soon—would you mind very much informing the desk clerk that I am accepting Mr. Moon's gracious offer to stay at his ranch?"

"Not a problem." Parris donned his felt hat. "I'll see to it right away."

And he did. Within three minutes, the lodger's transfer was a done deal and under way.

CHAPTER THIRTY-THREE

SAYING ADIOS TO THE HOLIDAY INN

The lawmen and their lady friends had long since settled into the Columbine Expedition, all wondering when the Columbine's prospective houseguest would show up. When Charlie Moon noticed Miss Whysper's approach, he resisted the instinctive impulse to get out and help the lady with her luggage and laptop. He admired the woman's determined stride. *She'd just say no again—this one likes to tote her own load.* To make sure she spotted his wheels, the amiable rancher switched on the headlights and pulled his automobile halfway out of its parking place, and waited with characteristic patience for the tourist to get her car started up.

After opening the dusty old Bronco's passenger-side door, Miss Whysper placed both the pink suitcase and the color-matched laptop on the seat. Satisfied with the stability of this arrangement, the woman could not help frowning at the chaos confronting her. An automobile trip of any distance invariably results in some level of mess, but this jumble of clutter was more than an embarrassment for the Strange Lady in Town. There was no time at the moment to roll up her sleeves and attack the general disorder with gusto, but she did feel compelled to perform at least a perfunctory stab at tidying up. Toward that end, she made a slight rearrangement of the fleece-lined raincoat that was concealing some unsightly rubbish on the front floorboard—pulling one corner to cover up an old shoe. *There, that's better.* The realization that she was such a neat-freak almost made the lady blush, but with that more or less ritual task completed, Miss Whysper felt measurably better. She slammed the Bronco door shut, hurried around to the driver's side, and slipped under the wheel to crank up the old heap—which chugged unevenly, then died. *Oh, please start this time!* It seems pointless to make pleas to machines, but she did have better luck on her second try. With a sigh of relief, she proceeded to follow Charlie Moon's taillights out of the Holiday Inn parking lot.

Even relatively short car rides are often somewhat tedious, and in this instance nothing of substance would occur during the next two or three miles. Which provides an opportunity to pause, back up a few minutes—and review the recent activities of a major player whose apparel-inspired nickname and unlawful vocation have not been mentioned lately.

WHAT HAS THE COWBOY ASSASSIN BEEN UP TO?

Let it first be said that no moss grows on this seasoned pro, who has been tending to business with both eyes wide open. The earlier arrival of Charlie Moon, Scott Parris, and their good-looking lady friends at the Holiday Inn had (of course) not gone unnoticed by Cowboy. And not only that—

But wait. A matter of journalistic ethics has been brought to our attention. A number of learned essays have been written on the matter, but what it boils down to is this: one should not draw attention to the admittedly admirable skills and stratagems of those nefarious souls who earn their bread by committing capital felonies. Why? Because excessive notoriety might well drive such misguided citizens to new heights of criminality—not to mention inspiring impressionable youth into similar unhappy careers. Therefore, we shall skip over the cold-blooded killer's cunningly devious behavior whilst the happy Parris–Mayfair–Moon–Poynter foursome was exchanging pleasantries with Miss Whysper—and cut directly to the chase.

As the spunky Miss Whysper was departing from the hotel parking lot immediately behind the manly GC cops and their sweeties, the odious malefactor was also close at hand, and mulling over *what to do next*. All sorts of dreadful possibilities presented themselves, each one more appallingly appealing than the former.

Which circumstance naturally piques our curiosity.

It is folly to anticipate such an unpredictable creature, but here is an educated guess: being one of those out-of-the-box thinkers who appreciates a daunting challenge, it seems likely that the so-called Cowboy will take advantage of this unexpected twist by performing what an urbane crime-drama critic might depict as a coup de théâtre. A risky choice, but one might reasonably suppose that what the egotistical assassin has in mind is a bit of sophomoric showing off—a flaunting display of on-the-spot improvisation intended to dazzle any hard-to-please hardcases among the Granite Creek audience. This modest speculation is offered for what it is worth, but the unseemly details of the assassin's upcoming performance are necessarily opaque and will remain so until that mercurial performer has settled upon a suitably theatrical scenario—which (we suspect) is likely to bring the curtain down with a horrendous crash. This proposed finale is not so farfetched as it might seem. History is punctuated with such episodes, which have tended to end disastrously.

By way of example, d'you recall that infamous incident where Mr. John Wilkes Booth (a *sure enough* bad actor) made the grand leap from President Lincoln's balcony onto the stage of Ford's Theatre, the hammy player's closing line—and the astonished audience's reaction to this outrage?

You *do*? Extraordinary.

(You are remarkably well preserved for one of your age.)

WE RETURN TO THE TEDIOUS AUTOMOBILE TRIP

On the first leg of the journey, the ladies in Charlie Moon's Expedition spent all their time chatting excitedly about the mysterious woman who preferred to be addressed as "Miss Whysper," with no end of commentary (mostly provided by Professor Tiffany Mayfair) on such earthshaking issues as what a *smart dresser* Miss W. was (her dark blue pinstripe suit, those expensive hand-crafted black cowgirl boots, the matching black leather belt, the exquisite black-and-white cameo on the black satin strap around her neck), and observations about how her appearance might be enhanced by a few minor adjustments.

Tiffany (archly): "She really ought to discard that horrid pink suitcase and purchase a suitable set of black Moroccan leather luggage."

Patsy (sweetly): "Well, the suitcase does match her pink laptop, and perhaps Miss Whysper spends most of her income on nice clothing."

Tiffany: "She certainly doesn't spend it on a nice car—I'd be afraid to drive that old heap for a *mile*."

Patsy (hoping to put a more positive spin on their conversation): "Wasn't the way she had her hair arranged just *darling*, and so perfect for her oval face?"

Tiffany: "I still hope she will consider addressing my students." With a sniff: "Very few authors visit Granite Creek, but the ones who do are generally flattered to be invited to my creative-writing class."

And so on and so forth. Indeed, the women were so engrossed in themselves and Miss Whysper that they seemed hardly aware of their male companions. Moreover, their incessant conversation (often with both speaking at the same time) was . . . but how does one express it without being unnecessarily offensive? How about this: "Like the drone of surf in the men's ears." Not unpleasant, but neither was their stream of words particularly interesting.

Thankfully for Parris and Moon, this intense feminine exchange was abruptly terminated when the Indian pulled his vehicle to a stop at Patsy Poynter's residence, where he escorted his intended to her front door. (The couple's embrace was discreetly concealed in thickish shadows cast by branches of a bushy white mulberry tree).

Miss Whysper, who had double-parked the Bronco about a half block away, waited patiently.

From Miss Poynter's home, the small caravan motored across town to Professor Mayfair's first-floor flat in a singles' apartment building that catered to university staff, where Parris's girlfriend gave him a perfunctory kiss-off. Five minutes later, with the Bronco remaining about a hundred yards to the rear, the men arrived at Scott Parris's hilltop redbrick home, where the chief of police was dropped off with a "see you later, pardner."

With all his deliveries made, Charlie Moon rolled his big SUV out of town with the Bronco now not so far behind. A lonely male trailed by a lonelier female of the species is suggestive, but if they had been sitting side by side, their loneliness would hardly have been decreased. The pair of Ford SUVs proceeded down a long, dark highway under a cold heaven that was extravagantly sprayed with sparkling diamonds.

They finally turned into the Columbine gate and had some rough going over a few miles of bumpy ranch road.

As Moon passed the foreman's residence, he took note of the fact that the lights were turned off and that . . . *Pete Bushman's pickup isn't parked in the driveway.* The rancher concluded that . . . *Pete and Dolly must be over at the Big Hat headquarters for the night.* A reasonable guess. But after the pair of oversize motorcars crossed the creaky bridge over the Too Late Creek and were within sight of the ranch headquarters, Moon spotted Bushman's truck parked close to the front porch—like folks do when there's something to load up. Or unload.

MISS SUSAN WHYSPER OBSESSES

The lady who had assumed that name parked the Bronco under the gaunt limbs of an almost-bare cottonwood, pulled her jacket collar over her neck, and stared at the crystal-clear sky. *It will be very cold tonight.* Not that she would mind; Miss Whysper was a hardy soul and the prospect of frigid weather suited her just fine. The various and sundry cargo the SUV was carrying did not. (Suit her)

She eyed a plastic box that still contained a few of the original dozen Grandmother's Best chocolate-chip cookies. There were also several discarded Butterfinger candy-bar wrappers littering the old SUV, an open box of Ritz crackers, and a partially eaten Velveeta sandwich that had been slathered with Miracle Whip. That wasn't the worst of it, and Miss Whysper was reminded that she had some serious tidying up to do when an opportunity presented itself. *I wonder whether I ought to close the car windows tight.* She frowned. *Or should I leave them cracked a little bit?* There were pluses and minuses to be considered. To wit: *If I close them, the inside of the car might smell like road-kill in the morning.* On the other hand . . . *If I leave the windows open an inch so the old clunker can air out, the odors might attract animals.* She glanced at the Columbine headquarters building. *Like that old hound peering out from under the porch.* Which development might well prove awkward to a woman of business who needed to make a favorable impression.

Smile if you will, but this seemingly minor issue was important to the tourist, and a decision had to be made *right now* about how much frigid night air should circulate through the Bronco overnight. The time for dithering exhausted, she compromised—lowering only the driver's-side window, and by only a *half* inch.

This was one of those slice-of-life vignettes that takes longer to report than to experience, the whole episode having occupied a mere two dozen seconds of Miss Whysper's precious time. Preserving her reputation of being the sort of self-sufficient woman who has no need to lean on strong men, she did not wait for Moon to approach the Bronco and escort her to his two-story log headquarters. Indeed, a few heartbeats after the Ute had emerged from his shiny automobile and before he'd made more than a few paces toward the older SUV, Miss Whysper had grabbed the pink suitcase in her hand, jammed the matching pink laptop under her arm, and closed and locked the Bronco door—only to confront that colorful well-known local character who goes by the name of Sidewinder. Trotting amiably up to greet the stranger, the venerable hound first sniffed at her boots, then looked up with soulful, hopeful eyes that glistened in the starlight.

Miss Whysper addressed the Columbine's dignified canine with due respect: "Sorry I can't pat your head, big fellow—but as you can see, I have my hands full at the moment."

Apparently understanding her difficulty, the dog turned his attention to the rusty old horse she'd rode in on. As Sidewinder sniffed his way around the Bronco with a keen professional interest, the lady marched briskly across the yard to the spot where the rancher customarily docked his proud Columbine flagship.

As he had in the hotel room, the gallant man offered to take the lady's pink luggage—knowing that she would refuse.

Upon this occasion, however, Miss Whysper yielded the suitcase up without the least protest.

Women. Go figure.

CHAPTER THIRTY-FOUR

CHARLIE MOON'S INNER CIRCLE

Having already been introduced to Charlie Moon's stunning fiancée and (more recently) the homely Columbine hound, Miss Whysper was now about to encounter those who formed the core of the rancher's family—Aunt Daisy and Sarah Frank. And even if they were more like peripheral kin, it must be said that Mr. Moon was very fond of Columbine foreman Pete Bushman and his sweet, sugar dumpling of a wife.

Those who are acquainted with Pete might well ask, "How could Moon possibly have the slightest affection for a cranky old straw boss who delights in giving him heartburn on a regular basis?" A reasonable question. The inexplicable answer is: by the same means that enabled the amiable man to adore his irascible aunt Daisy—the ineffable *grace of God.*

Pete's better half posed no such challenge; like Sarah Frank, Mrs. Bushman was easy to love. It was typical of Dolly's selfless generosity that the hardworking old soul had spent her afternoon preparing a mouthwatering meal for other folks to enjoy. This special "going away to the Big Hat supper" was to be shared with Charlie Moon and his household. Along about dusk, when hard, stark shadows begin to get mossy-soft around the edges, Dolly had loaded the scrumptious victuals into their old pickup—which Pete cranked up for the three-hundred-yard jaunt to the Columbine headquarters.

When Daisy Perika had heard Pete's truck coming a-rumbling across the Too Late Creek bridge's loose boards, she'd muttered to no one in particular, "Well—I wonder what this is all about?" Something cooked up to vex her, no doubt.

GUESS WHO'S COME TO DINNER?

Charlie Moon opened the porch door for his guest, followed her into the parlor, and—encountering the four aforesaid members of his "Columbine family"—introduced "Miss Susan Whysper."

Which drew blank stares from those gathered there.

Charlie explained, "Miss Whysper'll be staying at the ranch for a few days while she gathers some information for a book she's writing." He expanded on this subject by stating that the book was of the true-crime genre and would have something or other to do with Granite Creek County. Moon's expression conveyed the information that he'd said about all he could about the matter; if anyone wanted to know more, they could ask the author. This presumably titillating announcement created no discernible impression upon those present. Which left the Ute's quiver empty. Never mind. A cornered Indian does not go down without a fight, be it with bare hands. In this instance, he should have run up the white flag. Desperate to break the ice, he spelled Miss W.'s unusual name out loud. Emphasizing the *y*.

The result of this inane attempt to endear his guest to the reception committee?

About what you might expect. The silence in the huge headquarters parlor was deafening. Even the wall clock's clickety ticktocks were smothered by the heaviness of the unnatural quiet. Yea, and outside on the high-prairie night, a lonely coyote had terminated her shrill yip-yippings—as if waiting for the next cowboy boot to drop. No, this was not a fortuitous coincidence; a pair of loudmouthed owls had ceased their funereal hootings, the Columbine hound was holding his doggy breath—even the crisp sigh of a chill breeze in the eaves was stilled.

Mr. Moon was both puzzled and mildly annoyed by this cool reception.

The arrival of unexpected guests was a frequent occurrence at the Columbine, but the overnighters were usually men who were Charlie's friends—and known to both Sarah and Daisy. But Miss Whysper's sudden appearance was not sufficient to account for the cool reception. The reasons were as varied and complex as the individuals.

Already crushed by Moon's engagement to Miss Poynter, Sarah stared wide-eyed at this elegantly attired female of the species. *Charlie attracts women like honey draws flies.* Moreover . . . *She's not bad-looking.*

Indeed, when not overshadowed by such eye-stunning company as Patsy Poynter and Professor Tiffany Mayfair, Miss Whysper's understated attractions became apparent: a slender but distinctively feminine figure whose supple grace suggested sly, feline instincts. Dark, semiseductive eyes set in an oval and perfectly symmetric face. And the lady had a full measure of that elusive quality that, for want of a better descriptor, shall be specified as *poise.* The sum of these attributes was sufficient to appeal both to men and to boys—and served as a warning to twenty-year-old ladies, even those whose man was already engaged to the best-looking reference librarian in twenty states. Maybe forty-eight.

Charlie Moon's aunt had no particular interest in this overdressed *matukach* woman who had invaded her private space and crashed an intimate supper with the Bushmans. Daisy Perika hoped that Miss Whysper wouldn't stay longer than it took her to catch a bad case of the flu—and didn't give two copper cents about her stupid book about lowlife crooks or whether or not she felt welcome at the Columbine. And that was only for starters; Daisy was just getting warmed up.

While Moon's glowering aunt stood with her backside to the parlor fireplace's dying embers, a heartbroken Sarah Frank avoided Charlie's eyes. But your typical Ute-Papago orphan is made of first-class material, which is also known as the *right stuff.* Gathering up all her willpower, the willowy lass murmured something that sounded like, "I'm pleased to meet you."

Pete Bushman, his speech impaired by a bulging jawful of tobacco, kept his mouth firmly shut. All things considered, this was undoubtedly the wisest course of action.

Accustomed to Pete's social shortcomings and always deferring to others before asserting herself, Dolly Bushman was nevertheless appalled at the lukewarm show of hospitality. Assuming the role of First Lady of the Columbine, the foreman's wife approached Charlie's guest with a warm smile. Dolly did her level best to make the stranger welcome with a combination of lighthearted chattering, comforting clucking, and a general fussing-about that conveyed the assurance that Moon's lady friend was as welcome as a cool drink of springwater during a seven-year drought.

Though Miss Whysper understood and appreciated Dolly's mother-hen attentions, when the traveler relieved Charlie Moon of the pink suitcase and expressed the need to "freshen up," it was apparent that she had opted for a tactical withdrawal—if not a strategic retreat.

More than a little shamed by Dolly Bushman's good example, Sarah escorted the unexpected tourist to one of the Columbine's guest bedrooms. No, not the spacious accommodations upstairs that boasted an antique cherry fourposter, an adjoining bathroom with a tiled tub big enough to float a juvenile hippo in, and a stunning view of the Buckhorn Range—which desirable quarters just happened to be directly across the hallway from the modest chamber where Charlie slept. Sarah ushered Miss Whysper to a small, shadowy *downstairs* guest bedroom with a window that overlooked an expanse of rolling prairie. This cubicle was directly across the hallway from Daisy's bedroom, and diagonal from Sarah's.

Why? Because Miss Whysper was obviously too bone-tired to climb the stairway, and this cozy guest bedroom was conveniently *only a few steps away.* It was also conveniently located near the dining room, and suppertime was only minutes away.

ENJOYING THE BUSHMANS' GOING-AWAY CELEBRATION

During the hearty evening feast that followed, and despite Daisy's continued sullen silence, the atmosphere was considerably brighter, and Miss Whysper was treated to all the heartwarming charm of genuine Columbine hospitality. The dining-table conversation centered on Pete and Dolly's move over to the Big Hat, which (Pete explained) was "just east yonder over the Buckhorn Range" and "miles closer to town than the Columbine." Dolly invited the young woman to drop by tomorrow for coffee and cookies if she got a chance. "It'll be our first day over there and we'll be all by ourselves and lonesome for some company."

Miss Whysper assured Dolly that she appreciated the gracious invitation, but declined with regrets. "I would enjoy some downtime, but I expect to be very busy tomorrow."

With the solemnity of a drunken hanging judge, Pete Bushman advised the lady that all work and no play made Jack a dull boy. Oblivious to his gender blunder and puzzled by the smiles it produced, the old man scowled under his bushy brows and helped himself to another piece of crispy fried chicken, which is a dandy remedy for acute social discomfort and any number of other perplexing anxieties.

Miss Susan Whysper was delighted to break bread with Charlie Moon's inner circle, and by the time Dolly had served up a hot-from-the-oven peach cobbler that literally made her mouth water—the lady who had been "rescued" from Granite Creek's excellent Holiday Inn was beginning to feel like a bona fide member of Mr. Moon's close-knit family. Which suited the calculating woman's purposes to a tee. In her line of work, there was nothing so beneficial as being accepted as an insider—and in this instance, without having expended the least effort. Color this self-proclaimed author of true-crime fiction self-satisfied. *I could not have insinuated myself into a more advantageous position.*

Smiling as she dipped her fork into a steaming helping of dessert, Miss Whysper summed up the personal-relationship situation thus: *There's certainly no love lost between Charlie Moon and his grumpy old aunt.* An understandable if egregious error. Glancing at Sarah, she compounded her misunderstanding: *And the sad-faced girl seems to detest the very sight of him.* The more or less clueless guest took a long, appraising look at the Bushmans. *But the foreman and his wife are close enough to be Moon's doting parents.* Something of an exaggeration, but give the lady a B+ on her third guess.

One out of three in the Correct column hardly rates a first prize for intuitive surmising, but one must allow the stranger a little slack. We all know from personal experience that first impressions are often somewhat wide of the mark. Charlie, Sarah, and the Bushmans would not have been offended by Miss Whysper's superficial evaluations. But, of course, not everyone at Charlie Moon's table would have been so charitable.

If Daisy Perika were to have her say, it would sound much like what she was thinking: *I don't like female drifters who come around looking for a free meal and someplace to flop for the night. It'd be different if Charlie had brought home a regular freeloader, like a down-on-his-luck Texas cowboy, a too-old-to-work horse thief, or even a dirty old hobo wino—but all this worthless nitwit does is write silly books.* (Imagine the tribal elder sighing and rolling her beady, ball-bearing eyes.) *But what can you expect from a full-blooded Ute Dagwood who gets himself engaged to marry a blue-eyed* matukach *Blondie?*

Not an awful lot—that's what.

CHAPTER THIRTY-FIVE

WIDE AWAKE AT THE COLUMBINE HEADQUARTERS

Fortunately, this eyes-like-poached-eggs descriptor does not apply to every soul bedded down therein. But in the interest of completeness, all four shall be considered—and in order of increasing interest.

THE MAN OF THE HOUSE

Shhh! Charlie Moon is sleeping like a little boy who has rollicked all afternoon with a frisky, fuzzy puppy. His is enjoying a deep, peaceful sleep without dreams. Which is about as fascinating as watching gray moss grow on the shady side of a boulder, so we shall leave the man to his rest and—

But hold on. What was that?

"Ooouuuueeee!" With slight variations and intonations, this blood-curdling, spine-tingling yowl was repeated several times.

On yowl number four, Charlie Moon groaned. On five, he opened his eyes and stared at the unseen beamed ceiling. *Sidewinder must be howling at the moon.* A sensible conclusion—except for one minor detail: there was no moon tonight. Except for the capitalized version, whose sleep had been so rudely disturbed.

"Ooouuuu . . . ooouueeee!"

Moon pulled the quilt over his head. *Sooner or later, he'll stop.*

Sooner. Later. The hound did not.

Having no great appreciation for this doggish serenade, the miffed rancher rolled out of bed, raised the window, and yelled at the hound, "Quiet down out there!"

Sidewinder, who had something to say and was expressing himself the only way a descendant of wolves knows how, was also miffed. And hurt. But he did cease his nighttime solo.

THE UTE-PAPAGO ORPHAN

Sarah Frank is to be counted among the insomniacs, and we know why. There is no point in belaboring the love-struck maiden's continuing melancholy about Charlie Moon's upcoming wedding to Patsy Poynter, or Sarah's indecision about when she would leave the Columbine forever, and where to go from there. Suffice it to say that the young woman has been staring at the darkened ceiling for thousands of clockish ticktocks. But nothing stays the same, and Sarah's grief will eventually be numbed by her mind's vital need for rest and the soporific effect of darkness. Her relief will, of course, necessarily be transient—at this latitude, the sun *must* come up in the morning.

THE TOURIST

The Columbine's guest was the second of the sleepless souls—and there was ample reason for her nighttime distress. Miss Whysper had a great deal on her mind, and nocturnal mental activity tends to prevent an overtired person from drifting off into blissful unconsciousness. You know how it goes: one bothersome thought leads to another of like kind, and this process repeats itself with monotonous regularity until a dreadful circle is completed, at which point the sleepless soul is obliged to tread once more along the pathway of vexing conjectures.

In this instance, the self-administered affliction proceeded as follows:

Miss Whysper's hopeful yawn was transformed into a wistful sigh. *It would be so nice to stay at the Columbine until I'm rested and up to speed.* But she knew that . . . *I really should return to Granite Creek tomorrow morning and get on with my work.* On the other hand, something useful might be accomplished right here . . . *A day or two at Mr. Moon's ranch would provide an opportunity to learn a lot about the deputy, his elderly aunt, and that young woman who seems to be so terribly unhappy.* Not so happy herself, Miss W. shivered under the genuine Daisy Perika–hand-stitched quilt. *It's awfully cold to-night . . . my toes are almost numb!* But morning was only hours away, and . . . *It's supposed to warm up tomorrow.* Which meteorological prediction called to mind the remarkably effective greenhouse effect. *Not long after sunrise, the inside of the Bronco could be toasty warm.* And already-odorous rubbish smells were noticeably worse when heated. *Maybe I should have lowered the car windows a couple of inches.* She stretched luxuriously, yawned again, and indulged in a self-confession: *I have an unhealthy tendency to worry too much.* But that went with the territory; the life of an ambitious entrepreneur was not all that it was cracked up to be. *All I do is work work work.* And no matter how carefully a lady laid her plans, complications she could not possibly have foreseen were always popping up to aggravate the situation. *Nothing in life is ever as simple as it ought to be.* But negative thinking was like walking backward, and after all . . . *I knew what I was getting into when I chose this line of work.* The bottom line was that a self-employed woman who expected to pay the rent had to put her vocation first. *So I'll leave the ranch tomorrow morning and start getting things done.* A person never knows when a golden opportunity might present itself . . . *Like Chief Parris and Mr. Moon and their lady friends dropping in on me at the hotel.* This out-of-the-blue encounter had led to the irresistible invitation to visit Mr. Moon's ranch and introductions to several other interesting people . . . *Which will make it much easier to complete my work in a satisfactory fashion.* Miss Whysper knew just what she'd do on the morrow: *I'll arrange meetings with the cops' lady friends.* Professor Mayfair and Miss Poynter both had day jobs, so tomorrow evening should be a suitable time. *And that will give me all day to take care of some other odds and ends.* Getting her work done up front was really a no-brainer. *I'll have plenty of time to kick back and relax after I return home.*

It seemed like the matter was settled.

Then, like a lady hoop snake about to swallow her tail . . . *But if I rested here for a couple of days, I'd be better prepared to do my work in Granite Creek.* Another yawn, and . . . *On the other hand . . .*

It was no wonder that the weary traveler tossed and turned for almost another hour before finally drifting off into a troubled sleep.

Having dispensed with three of the four, we may turn our attention to the last.

THE SOUTHERN UTE TRIBAL ELDER

Not unlike her nephew upstairs, Daisy Perika was, typically, unconscious only a few heartbeats after her head had made a comfortable hollow in the pillow. But hers was not to be the well-known *blessed rest of the innocent*, and anyone who dared disrupt her slumbers would be best advised to let sleeping aunties lie undisturbed—particularly when they are liable to wake up in a bad mood and put the big bite on you.

We'd like to.

But, as is so often the case with Charlie Moon's eccentric relative, Daisy's midnight experience would prove uncommonly interesting. Phase one of the disturbance began only a labored breath or two after she had switched off the table lamp by her bed and nestled her head into the feather pillow. Was she in the process of drifting off to sleep? Perhaps. But whether Daisy was wide awake or already halfway along the pathway to that eerie shadowland where *anything* can happen, the tribal elder was convinced that her rest was interrupted by something distinctly unpleasant. More to the point, something stinkingly malodorous.

Her eyes tightly closed, the old woman wrinkled her nose—her sensitive nostrils *sniffed*. She sighed. *What kind of aggravation is this?* A polecat under the floor? She did not think so. This smelled more like . . . *a mangy old coyote wearing a dead man's socks.* (Two pairs for the quadruped.)

Yes, absurdly bizarre, but we must not be overly critical of her dubious metaphor—analyzing peculiar scents can be challenging even when all our faculties are at their peak, and Daisy was weary from the day's many activities. (Creating continual trouble for others is a tiresome business.) She sniffed again and got a better whiff. *Uh-oh.* The shaman thought she recognized the characteristic odor. *It's him.*

It is so vexing when she will not be specific. Him *who*?

Daisy Perika opened her eyes. *It's the little man.*

Thank you, ma'am. (She refers to the *pitukupf,* that diminutive thousand-year-old personage who abides in an abandoned badger hole in *Cañón del Espíritu.* The very same canyon whose gargantuan mouth eternally threatens to swallow the tribal elder's reservation home whole, which cozy domicile is many miles to the south of Charlie Moon's Columbine Ranch headquarters, wherein his aunt is presently bedded down.)

As Daisy reached out to switch the lamp on, she was irked to discover a spindly little (hairy) leg dangling down on right side of her head. Upon further investigation, she discovered a like appendage on the other side. These limbs were not feetless: a pair of tiny moccasins practically brushed her wrinkled cheeks. She deduced (correctly) that the *pitukupf* was perched brazenly on the headboard of her bed. Like others of his gender, the Little Man had a tendency toward tasteless jests and unseemly appearances. But this intrusion into her boudoir was a prank too far and something had to be said.

She said it: "Your feet stink like rotten meat!"

Was her uninvited guest offended by this blunt observation? Not in the least. Evidently pining for a conversation with his old friend, the dwarf made a few introductory remarks toward that end. He began with an insightful commentary on the weather.

It shall be noted that the *pitukupf,* though fluent in several languages, prefers to converse in an archaic version of the Ute tongue that even Daisy has difficulty understanding. For that reason (and others unspecified), only the gist of their verbal exchange shall be reported.

Daisy: "What're you doing here, you sawed-off little piece of [expletive deleted]?"

Unruffled, the dwarf informed the agitated shaman that he had traveled all this distance (at no small expense) entirely for her benefit.

Daisy (rolling her eyes): "That'll be the day."

According to her night visitor, it was indeed. And after he had delivered his information and counsel, he would depart immediately for environs where his charitable intentions were appreciated.

Daisy snorted. "Have your say and *vamoose*!"

The elfin person informed his grumpy friend that she was about to be visited by the spirit of a troubled dead person.

"Hah! This sounds like that holiday ghost story—the one that European quill-pen pusher wrote down a long time ago." *What was the name of that tale?* With the benefit of a thoughtful frown, she recollected. *Oh, right.* "A Christmas Song." *Who was that* matukach *fella who wrote all those tales about ghosts and pitiful little crippled orphans and seven-year-old-pickpockets and big white whales and whatnot?* It was so vexing to disremember a famous person's name. *Ol' Herman Mole-hill?* Close (she thought), but no cigar. *David Copperfoil?* Daisy shook her head. *He was the boy that got kidnapped by those pirates.* From somewhere in the fuzzy underbrush of her memory, a raspy voice said, *You can call me Ishmael.* Maybe so, but the suspicious old soul did not much care for aliases—in her book, a character who concealed his true identity was automatically suspect. After a string of faltering heartbeats (during which interval she firmly rejected Scrooge McDuck and Ahab the Arab), her stubborn perseverance was finally rewarded. In hallowed comic-strip fashion, a yellow lightbulb popped on above the thinker's head—and the tribal elder found the eminent author's name right on the tip of her tongue. After savoring the flavor, Daisy Perika *spat it out*: "Mr. Moby Dickens—that's who he was."

Close enough. After all, nineteenth-century American and English literature was not her long suit.

Exasperated by Daisy's discourteous inattention to the urgent matter at hand, the dwarf rebuked the flippant tribal elder. She would (he suggested) be well advised to pay close attention to what the forthcoming apparition had to say—and to act upon it without delay. To do otherwise would be a great folly—and invite unmitigated disaster.

Despite her annoyance at being upbraided by this arrogant little scamp, the shaman realized that it might be unwise to ignore the *pitukupf*'s warning. "So who *is* this haunt?"

No response.

Moreover, the stink of the little man's feet was noticeably absent. As were the long-toed appendages themselves—not to mention the remainder of his miniature anatomy.

His hasty departure served to increase her suspicions. *The nasty little rascal came here just to annoy me—and to ruin my night's sleep.* Daisy Perika gritted her remaining teeth. *Well, it won't work.* The resolute old soul switched off the bedside lamp, nestled her head into the pillow again, closed her eyes, yawned enormously, and . . .

CHAPTER THIRTY-SIX

YES. PHASE TWO

As it happened (or so it seemed to the aged woman), her pleasant drifting toward sleep was interrupted by still another something or other—with a heavy emphasis on *other*. A nighttime encounter with this particular *whatever* would've made a strong man's skin crawl, his eyeballs pop halfway out of their sockets, his brave heart stop like a goose egg slamming into a brick wall at ninety miles an hour. No, please do not complicate an already ambiguous issue by asking by what means a goose egg could travel considerably faster than geese can fly. The more pertinent question is: what or whom was this jarring *other*?

We have our suspicions, but don't know for sure. Let us examine the evidence.

Exhibit one is: a low, mournful wail, not an arm's length from the pillow where Daisy's head rested so comfortably. So, did her skin crawl, her eyes pop, her heart stop? If you had such expectations, you are not acquainted with Charlie Moon's cantankerous relative. Without so much as cracking an eyelid, the aggravated sleeper groaned and said, "Oooh . . . what now?"

Do not misinterpret this query as a literal one. Right off the bat, the shaman knew *what* was in the bedroom with her. Well, more or less. Any wee-hours visitor who was so rude as to awaken a bone-tired old lady with a low, mournful wail was—without a doubt—an inconsiderate spirit who had barged in to deliberately disturb her rest. Had Mrs. Perika expressed her query more explicitly, she would have said, "Oooh . . . *who* now?"

Another pitiful, keening moan.

Recalling the *pitukupf*'s prediction, Daisy reached a reasonable conclusion: *This must be the dead person he told me about.* Which realization raised a regret: *If I'd kept my mouth shut, the haunt might've thought I was sound asleep and deaf as a brick and gone away to pester some other poor soul.* That ploy had worked before, but it was too late now. Giving up the blatant fakery, the sly tribal elder cracked one eyelid. What did she see? A filmy, amorphous haze hovering at her bedside. *I might as well get this over with.* "Okay, Casper—who're you and why're you aggravating a tired old lady who never did you any harm?"

The response was somewhat garbled, but Daisy managed to pick up the gist of what was being said. "You don't know who you are?"

The apparition popped up a knoblike head, and nodded it.

The shaman was not surprised, either by the instantly produced noggin or the spirit's identity issues As often as not, the recently dead drifted about in a state of total confusion. Poor things didn't know who they were, where they were, who they had awakened in the middle of the night—or even the fact that they were deceased. The detached souls merely wanted a warm somebody to talk to, and had probably already visited dozens of unresponsive folk until they happened upon a person who was cursed with the "gift" of seeing dead people and hearing their oftentimes-indistinct speech. Which, like it or not, did place a certain civic responsibility on those so talented. Which was one reason why Daisy pushed herself up on an elbow and launched into a explanation of the hard facts of life: "The first thing you got to get through your toadstool head is that you're *dead*!" She was about to enlarge upon this educational theme when her artful descriptor ("toadstool") reminded Daisy Perika of the threat made by one Hester "Toadie" Tillman. *I ought to have guessed right off.* "Do you remember how you died?"

The knob on the presumably muddleheaded specter nodded.

"Well don't just stand there like a big turnip, tell me!" Daisy listened to the speech that was improving with practice. *Aha! I thought so.* "So, you died inside an automobile, eh?"

The knobby protuberance nodded again, this time with noticeable fervor. The unseen mouth provided further horrid details, rounding the lurid narrative out by asserting that she was still trapped inside the vehicle, and if Daisy didn't find a way to get her out, she'd rot there like some dead animal.

"No, Toadie—you're all mixed up." Daisy shook her head. "You're *not* still inside that pickup. I know that for a fact, because Danny Bignight was there when you croaked, and he watched some people pull you out of the truck and carry you over to the ambulance." She scowled at the annoying pestilence that had invaded her bedroom. "No, don't shake your silly-looking head at me—listen to what I'm telling you! About an hour after you'd passed on, Danny Bignight showed up at my house by the mouth of *Cañón del Espíritu* and told me all about it." She paused to suck in a breath. "Danny also told me what you said you'd do if I didn't show up at your funeral and bawl my eyes out over you being dead." Daisy shook her finger at the rude intruder. "I didn't really mean what I said to Danny Bignight about spitting on your grave, but I never liked you very much when you were alive, Toadie—and I'm liking you less with every minute that passes. So you just haul your big butt out of here and—" Pause. "*What* did you say?"

The spirit repeated her querulous complaint.

"You're cold?" Daisy snorted. "Well so am I, from the neck up." Pulling the quilt to her chin, she wagged the finger again. "Now listen to me and do as I say or I'll go get a two-gallon bucket of ice-cold well water and wet you down with it." The senior citizen chuckled. "Your rotten old teeth'll chatter so hard they'll all fall out of your gums and onto the floor."

Though it seems doubtful that amorphous apparitions have decayed teeth to worry about, the cold-bath threat did seem to get the uninvited spirit's undivided attention.

Sensing that she had the Big Mo (considerable momentum), Daisy did not let up. "Now here's the deal—first of all, you go back to the Ignacio Cemetery, where your body is buried." To assist in this journey, she pointed in a southerly direction. "And when you get there, eyeball every grave marker till you spot a cheap slab of limestone that says 'Toadie Tillman Sleeps Here' on it. Then, slip back into your nice, comfy coffin and *stay* there!"

Was Daisy's helpful advice received with gratitude? No.

The dismal spirit let out an awful, high-pitched howl—which spine-jerking shriek was abruptly interrupted in midscreech by a series of gasping-choking-gurgling-gaggings—the macabre effect suggesting a hyperactive banshee being choked to death by an enraged member of the Granite Creek County Noise Abatement League.

Was Mrs. Perika startled? You bet.

The tribal elder lurched like an anteater whose yard-long tongue has just licked a tasty six-legged delicacy off a pulsating electric fence. The unnerved old soul was also vexed, provoked, and chagrined at this uncalled-for outburst from the haunt. *If you had a neck, I'd grab it and strangle you myself!* But even Daisy Perika's hard heart was touched by the specter's unfeigned display of abject misery. After a roll of her beady black eyes and a wistful sigh for bygone days when a tired woman could enjoy a good night's rest without having to wake up and counsel idiot dead people, the tribal elder added this comforting observation: "Now listen to what I say, Toadie—I know what I'm talking about because a journeyman plumber told me this years ago." When making a pitch, it often helps to quote a licensed expert.) "Colorado gets plenty cold, but it ain't Alaska." Daisy pointed at the floor. "Six feet down, our water pipes don't ever freeze. D'you know why?"

Judging from its blank expression, the specter did not have the least inkling of a clue.

About to provide one, Daisy jutted her chin. "Because even in the dead of winter, the ground is toasty *warm* down there. I guarantee it—you settle down into your pine box, you'll never shiver again."

Whether or not this confident assertion persuaded the spirit to follow Daisy's advice must—at least for the moment—remain problematic. What can be stated with certainty is this: for whatever reason, the howling-gasping-choking-gurgling-gagging apparition gave up the game—and vanished from the elderly citizen's bedroom.

Charlie Moon's exasperated auntie collapsed onto her pillow. *Oh, I'm so glad* that's *over.*

Which would be a fitting and proper conclusion to this peculiar little anecdote.

But it was not. (Over.)

CHAPTER THIRTY-SEVEN

THE HUMDRUM BEGINNING OF A
PARTICULARLY EVENTFUL DAY

And perhaps the longest day in the lives of several of the principals, though for others it would be dramatically foreshortened.

It began innocently enough in the chief of police's lonely bachelor home, with a gloomy Scott Parris dipping a tablespoon into a cold bowl of skim milk where squares of a high-fiber, factory-compacted cereal-like substance floated like debris left over after the sinking of a Lilliputian barge loaded with thumbnail-size bales of hay. Munching with a scowl, the food critic delivered his verdict on the victuals: *If this healthy crap tasted ten times better, it'd be almost as good as soggy cardboard.*

With that pithy observation, we shall leave the sour-faced gourmand to complain about his nutritious breakfast. A downer is no way to begin the day. We shall pay a morning call on a salt-of-the-earth gathering that appreciates the day's first chow-down.

But for those dyspeptics who have no appetite for rare-cooked flesh of uncertain origin, thickish spare-parts stew, and black iron pots a-bubble with overdoses of trouble—be ye forewarned that *here endeth the humdrum beginning.* (What to do? Withdraw to some sunny spot where happy little bluebirds sing, and peruse a delightful chapter or two from *The Wind in the Willows.*)

A FEW DOZEN MILES TO THE NORTHWEST

As might be expected, the day's first meal was mighty fine in the Columbine kitchen. (The formal dining room was used for lunch, supper, and high-stakes poker games.)

Charlie Moon was seated at one end of the rectangular table, with Daisy Perika and Sarah positioned at his left and right elbows (respectively). Whereabouts the lady who had arrived in the Bronco? The guest whom the hospitable rancher had rescued from the noisy Holiday Inn was seated beside the Ute-Papago orphan.

Halfway through her breakfast, the woman who preferred to be called Miss Whysper (or *Missy* Whysper when addressed by Charlie Moon) paused to touch a paper napkin to her lips. (Daintily.) "My, that is very tasty."

Moon returned a smile and a nod. "This is what we call a light cowboy breakfast. With a platter of this grub tucked under your belt, you'll be ready to rope calves, shoe horses, and bale alfalfa till lunchtime—when we turn out a serious meal."

Knowing what was expected of her, the lady laughed. "I don't know that I'll be up to any roping, shoeing, or baling—but this meal will be sufficient to last me all day."

Sarah Frank was trying awfully hard to appear cheerful, but forcing her unhappy face into a smile was an exquisitely painful process. All the poor girl could think about was Charlie Moon's upcoming wedding to pretty Patsy Poynter—and how disgustingly *happy* the pair would be together. *I hope all her blond hair falls out and she gets fat as a cow and Charlie catches a bad case of—* But, angry and vindictive as she was, Sarah was incapable of wishing any harm to the love of her young life. Not yet.

When Daisy Perika paused in the salting of her eggs to look for the pepper shaker, she happened to glance across the table at the white woman who was enjoying Columbine hospitality. The old woman frowned. *Well, what's this?* As the *matukach* woman chewed or swallowed or spoke, her pallid face (as seen through the shaman's eyes) looked like cold, dead flesh that was attempting to mimic the real McCoy. As Daisy caught a glimpse of a white skull under the taut gray skin, the tribal elder managed to stifle a shudder, but she could not suppress the macabre image that had triggered it—or the certainty that . . . *This white woman won't live to see the sun come up again.*

194

Feeling the aged Indian woman's odd stare, and spotting the salt shaker Daisy was setting aside, Miss Whysper correctly deduced what the tribal elder was looking for. She picked up the pepper shaker beside her coffee cup and passed it across the table to Charlie Moon's aunt. "Is this what you're looking for?"

Daisy Perika's right hand instinctively reached for the proffered object. As she took it, the shaman's warm fingertips touched the houseguest's cold fingers. As young, pale skin contacted its wrinkled, dark counterpart, it was as if a charge of electricity sizzled between them—and with this brief coupling Daisy *saw* someone who *wasn't there*. Eerie enough. But what made this experience *exceedingly* strange was what Daisy knew beyond a shadow of a doubt: *I'm looking at a dangerous man that this* matukach *woman has never met before—and I'm seeing him through her eyes.*

It was like watching a ninety-year-old silent movie. As the frames flickered by, Daisy saw a twilight black-and-white image of the sinister character who'd do Charlie's guest in—a dark figure in a flat-brimmed hat. The desperado in the grade-B film looked almost as skinny as her nephew, but not so tall. To blind herself to the bloody scene she knew was forthcoming, Daisy closed her eyes. This stratagem served only to make the vision crystal clear.

The heel of his hand resting on the butt of a holstered sidearm, the slender figure approached. There was an empty black holster on the gaunt man's hip—a drawn pistol in his hand.

"No—stop!" Daisy snapped.

On this curt and authoritative command, the moving-picture image froze, faded, and vaporized—the vision ending before the shooting began.

Daisy Perika opened her eyes to see Charlie Moon, Sarah Frank, and Miss Whysper all staring at her in mild surprise—the latter as through a *dead woman's eyes.*

Sarah reached across the table to put her smooth hand on Daisy's trembling paw. "Are you all right?"

The object of the girl's sympathy nodded, but Daisy could not tear her gaze from the white woman's sickly gray face. "I'm okay." *But that one ain't—she'll be cold meat before tomorrow's sun shines over the mountains.* She was tempted to warn her nephew's guest, but . . . *She wouldn't believe me.* Nor would Charlie or Sarah. *They'd all three figure me for a crazy old crank.* And even if they did believe . . . *Telling her won't change what's bound to happen.* Which led her to the conclusion that . . . *I might as well keep my mouth shut.* Even so, Daisy could not escape the nagging sense that she was shirking her responsibility. But the woman who occasionally caught glimpses of the future reminded herself that . . . *From time to time I've had a vision that turned out to be dead wrong.* This sturdy-looking white woman might live to be a hundred years old. Case closed.

Shrugging, the Ute elder spat out a lie without batting an eye. "I guess I must've slipped off into a little catnap and had a bad dream." Which reminded her of that exasperating visitation during the wee hours. *I bet this white woman would like to hear about old Toadie showing up while I was in bed asleep.* And even if she didn't . . . *Sometimes Sarah likes to hear a good, scary ghost story.*

All well and good, as far as it went—but Daisy's motives were more than a kindly intent to entertain those two ladies at the table. Her primary target was Charlie Moon.

Daisy's skeptical nephew did not (as far as she knew) believe in spirits, witches, spells, visions, or anything important that a sensible Ute ought to. *Charlie never wants to hear about the dead people who talk to me.* Which suggested a way for the mischievous old lady to spice up her otherwise bland breakfast.

CHAPTER THIRTY-EIGHT

DAISY PERIKA BAITS CHARLIE MOON

Why would an elderly woman who has benefited from so many of her nephew's kindnesses deliberately bite the hand that feeds her?

What a question—why *wouldn't* she?

But for those who demand a simple, direct answer, here it is: Daisy Perika harasses Charlie Moon because it's *fun*.

A somewhat mean-spirited form of amusement? A case could certainly be made for that point of view, and a jury of the accused's peers might well find tribal elder guilty as charged. Daisy would snort at such a decision. After all (she would ask), by what right does a dozen fussy old fuddy-duddies deprive a respectable senior citizen of a rare moment of innocent pleasure—particularly since the demise of her daily dose of Oprah? Tweaking one's uppity nephew is one of those inalienable Auntie's Privileges that is preserved in the Southern Ute Tribal Constitution.

While Charlie, Sarah, and Miss Whysper were dealing in their various ways with the stick-to-your-ribs morning meal, the tribal elder mentioned (with a calculated casualness) that in addition to their guest, the Columbine had been visited by *another* interesting person. "And only a few hours ago."

Sensing an ensuing humiliation, Sarah cringed. *Oh, I hope she doesn't embarrass me in front of our guest.* A futile hope.

Charlie Moon stirred a second helping of Tule Creek Honey into his black coffee. *Here we go again.*

Miss Whysper's ears had pricked at this report. *I didn't hear anyone come in.*

Reading the question in the tourist's eyes, Daisy added, "It was another woman." The practiced storyteller forked up a helping of scrambled eggs and gummed on it for a while. "This one showed up in my bedroom sometime after midnight."

"A rather late hour for an arrival." Miss Whysper took a ladylike sip of coffee that was mostly cream. And nibbled delicately at Daisy's delectable bait: "I suppose she's sleeping in."

"I expect so," Daisy said. *Six feet under, if Toadie did what I told her to.* She snapped off the pointy corner of a wedge of toasted Wonder bread. Masticated again. "But she's not sleeping *here.*"

Adding a quarter teaspoon of cane sugar to her cup, the guest smiled. "Oh?"

"No." Wielding a three-tine fork, Daisy speared a plump chunk of ham. "*This* woman was dead as last week's roadkill."

Her off-the-wall remark obtained a mixed result. Nothing whatever from Mr. Moon, a barely suppressed groan from Miss Sarah, and a wide-eyed stare from Miss Whysper, who was frozen with the coffee cup halfway between the table and a gaping mouth. "*Dead,* did you say?"

"You heard me right. As in *stone-cold.*" The Ute shaman waited for Charlie to offer the least hint that her report might be untrustworthy. A slightly elevated eyebrow would have been more than sufficient to provoke her counterattack. *Go ahead, you big gourd-head—make my day!* The instant he did, Daisy would strike back like an enraged viper—severely fanging her nephew.

Knowing her devious game, the poker player did not arch his eyebrow by a half millimeter, much less allow even the ghost of a smirk to find a place on his lips.

Which deliberate rebuff exasperated his expectant relative no end. So much so that Daisy lost her temper and played right into Charlie Moon's hand. "Well—what do you say to *that*, Mr. Know-It-All?"

"Please pass the biscuits," saith Mr. K-I-A, and smiled serenely at his tightly wound relative.

Daisy shoved the biscuit platter at him. *Oh—he makes me so mad!*

Miss Whysper was suspended in that state which is commonly described as speechless. But she was not without thoughts. *Three years ago, I awakened in the middle of the night to see a dead man standing by my bed. Or thought I did.*

Sarah had something to say, and said it ever so gently: "I doubt that our guest is interested in hearing a ghost story."

"Oh, you do—do you?" *Who cares what* you *think, Miss Manners!* Pointedly ignoring both Sarah and Charlie, Daisy turned her wrinkled countenance to the out-of-towner. "A lady who writes stories about cold-blooded killers ain't afraid of ghosts—is she, Miss Whisker?"

As Miss W. was about to open her mouth, Sarah nudged Charlie's aunt. "Whysper."

The snake who'd been denied the opportunity to bite her nephew shot the Ute-Papago girl a poisonous look. "I will not!" She banged her fist on the dining table. "Why should I? Nobody in this house is napping."

This small comedy provided a modicum of relief to all the diners except Daisy.

Miss Whysper's sweet smile outdid Moon's. *She is so cute.* "Please tell me about the ghostly visit."

Now that's more like it. Daisy got off to a good start, admittedly embroidering her account with a few stomach-churning bumps in the night, several spine-tingling banshee howls, and a description of the apparition that would have terrified Dracula, had the count happened by to drain a nutritious snack from some unwary contributor's vein. Having entirely captured the attention of Sarah and Miss Whysper, the storyteller launched into the raw meat of her eerie tale with the same gusto with which Charlie Moon was attacking his ham and eggs. Being of the firm opinion that a delicious meal deserves a man's entire concentration, the enthusiastic diner wasn't paying much attention to his aunt's latest ghost story.

After describing her initial conversation with the specter, Daisy was touching up and expanding upon the poor soul's belief that she was trapped in an automobile. "She said she was locked inside that truck to rot like some dead animal—and wanted me to go let her out." The storyteller was deep into the well-known groove—and about to reveal how this trapped-in-a-motor-vehicle element was the critical clue to *identifying* the ghost—when a wide-eyed Miss Whysper suffered the same sort of affliction that Sarah had experienced when Charlie Moon announced his engagement to Patsy Poynter.

That's right—Miss Whysper *choked*—as if a morsel of her hearty breakfast had made a wrong turn in her throat and ended up in that dark tunnel labeled Windpipe on the anatomist's chart. Was the lady about to experience the same sort of bronchial crisis that had humiliated Sarah? Would she require a hearty slap on the back from Charlie Moon, and if that didn't do the trick, would the distraught diner be subjected to an on-the-spot tracheotomy with the razor-sharp C101 Manix 2 Spyderco folding knife that Dr. Moon keeps in his pocket for emergency veterinary surgery? Hard to say.

But things are looking a bit dicey.

Yes! It appears that we are about to witness one of those do-or-die surgical procedures whose drama will rival the fabled appendectomies conducted on WW II diesel-powered submarines by nineteen-year-old sailors who'd never so much as lanced a painful boil.

Or perhaps not.

Things are looking up. Miss Whysper does not appear to be on the verge of projectile vomiting, nor does her pale complexion appear to be taking on that bluish tint that suggests imminent suffocation. Indeed, she seems to have washed the errant morsel down her gullet with a gulp of disgustingly pale and tepid coffee.

The medical crisis averted, our plucky storyteller was about to pick up her narrative where she had paused during the guest's distress, and regale those present with an account of how she cleverly realized that the spirit in her bedroom last night was none other than Hester "Toadie" Tillman, whose fresh corpse had—only a few days ago—been pulled from the wreckage of a pickup truck. Daisy had just opened her mouth to commence with this gripping finale when, wouldn't you know it—

The #&$@% kitchen telephone rang. (Please excuse the salty expletive; that heartfelt oath is one of Daisy's favorites.)

Charlie got up to take the call, and seated himself at the wall-mounted telephone for what promised to be an extended conversation.

After draining her coffee cup, Miss Whysper excused herself and hurried away.

Well. If Daisy's laser glare could have burned holes through expensive gabardine, human skin, flesh, et cetera, the Columbine guest would have suffered severe physical injury. Thankfully, in this instance the old woman's injurious powers were limited to the psychic kind.

Which raises the question: is there any more-hurtful insult to an enthusiastic storyteller than a sudden, cruel display of audience disinterest—and right at the critical twist of the plot? Probably not. In this instance, being deprived of delivering her masterful and self-aggrandizing finale was like a hard slap in Daisy's face. It is hard to imagine an equal calamity to the tribal elder's vanity. But the offense that Sarah Frank was about to commit was at least a close runner-up.

Aware of Aunt Daisy's anguish, the compassionate young woman reached out to pat the tribal elder's hand. "Please don't leave me hanging—I want to hear the rest of your story."

Our prior estimate of comparable distress is hereby retracted; being humored by the girl was even more mortifying than being ignored by Charlie Moon and abruptly abandoned by Miss Whysper—just as she was getting to the *good part*. Even worse, Daisy could not think of a graceful exit. The victim had no option but to continue her tale and explain how she'd deduced that the haunt was Toadie Tillman. What should have been a triumph was more like a slow, whimpering death, draining the narrator of the last grain of enthusiasm. The shaman's formerly riveting ghost story had faded to an anemic shadow of its former self—bled dry of the least essence of spine-tingling vitality.

Bad enough? Yes indeed. But the situation accelerated from worse to worser.

In an attempt to escape her embarrassment, Daisy Perika hurried to The End—when Sarah Frank patted her hand again and smiled like an indulgent mother complimenting a cute eighteen-month-old tot who has just offered Momma a hard-as-rock, dusty crust of bread in a plump, grubby hand—a nauseating morsel that the little darling had discovered under the dining table whilst foraging for a tasty beetle or moth. "My goodness—that was a *really* scary story!" Sarah effected a transparently counterfeit shudder. "Mrs. Tillman's ghost at *my* beside would've kept me awake for the rest of the night!"

Well. For a vain senior citizen, there are few humiliations more soul-piercing than being patronized by a wet-behind-the-ears do-gooder who apparently believes the pathetic elder is exhibiting symptoms of incipient senility. Daisy Perika's defeat was utterly complete. What could she do but roll her eyes at the ceiling and pose one of those pesky hypothetical questions to which there is no satisfactory reply: *Why do I even try?*

CHAPTER THIRTY-NINE

A PRELUDE TO CALAMITY

And, despite all the grim forewarnings—not one that Charlie Moon, Scott Parris, or any other lawman hereabouts could have seen coming. Only one person in Granite Creek County had a general notion of the carnage that was likely to occur before the bloody day was done, and even that murderous felon was in for a few surprises.

While he conducted a muted telephone conversation with Columbine foreman Pete Bushman (who was calling from the Big Hat Ranch), Mr. Moon was unaware of Miss Whysper's discreet departure from the dining room, Aunt Daisy's distress with her ghost story's lukewarm reception, and Sarah Frank's big-eyed gaze, which was fixed on his back. When the routine business with Mr. Bushman was completed, the rancher unfolded his long, lean frame from the straight-back oak chair by the wall-mounted telephone—and noticed the empty spot at the kitchen table. "Where'd Miss Whysper slip off to?"

"Don't ask me." Daisy barely refrained from telling her nephew where she *wished* the woman had gone. (Not heaven.)

Sarah glanced at the hallway. "To her bedroom, I think."

"Thanks." Charlie Moon headed down that twilight corridor—for once leaving Daisy and Sarah to tend to the breakfast dishes without his assistance. Tapping a calloused knuckle on the guest's bedroom door, he invited Miss Whysper to accompany him on a walk.

The lady accepted.

THE WALKAROUND
(SUBTITLE: A SHAM)

Like their breakfast, the morning stroll began innocently enough, with the proud rancher pointing his chin in various directions as he described the eighty sections of pasture over yonder, how the precipitation had been fair-to-middling lately on the eastern range, to which patch of buffalo or grama grass the Columbine cowboys would be moving a detachment of prime Herefords to graze on during the next few days—and so on and so forth. After exhausting that reservoir of conversation fodder, Charlie Moon resorted to listing the features and advantages of his "new" (three-year-old) horse barn, the comforts of the Columbine's shotgun bunkhouse, the practicality of the all-steel-machinery barn, the location of the blacksmith's shop (where quarter horses were shod and rusty old pickups repaired), and why he preferred one brand of tractor over another. Let it be noted that during this entire discourse, the lady did not yawn. Not one time. Which is evidence of either real class or incredible feminine fortitude or (more likely) a combination of both virtues. Like any deliberate man who likes to work his way gradually up to a point, Moon eventually got around to it. "Well—I suppose you'll be going into town today and start gathering material for your book."

The taciturn white woman nodded.

"So—" (No, Moon isn't quite there yet.) "I guess you'll be talking to some locals about this and that."

"Mmm-hmm." (Her first comment since coming outside.)

"When'll you get around to talking to Scott?" (He is edging up to the issue.)

"Chief Parris?" Miss Whysper paused to idly kick a pinecone with the pointy toe of her expensive western boot. With an amused smile: "Why would I want to talk to him?"

Like the legendary Clancy (ready to lower the boom), Mr. Moon stopped dead still in his boot tracks and stared at the woman. "To tell him the whole truth."

Her eyes grew large, suggesting a surprised puppy. "Truth about—"

She was about to say, "Truth about what?" when Moon stopped her with a raised palm. "Me and Scott know what you're actually up to."

An expression not unlike alarm flashed in her big eyes. "You do?"

Charlie Moon nodded. "You didn't come to Granite Creek just to gather information for your bestselling true-crime book."

"I didn't?"

He shook his head. "You're here to put the grab on a bad guy."

"Oh." She effected a nonchalant shrug. "So you know about that."

A solemn nod from Scott Parris's deputy. "We also know that this bad guy has come to town with a specific purpose in mind—and that what he intends to do here ain't likely to promote our tourist trade in Granite Creek—which is almost as important as the cattle business."

"Well . . . I suppose that's true enough." Miss Whysper nodded and sighed. "It appears that you and Chief Parris are onto me."

The gallant cowboy tipped the brim of his black John B. Stetson. "That's our business, ma'am—it's what we do." There was a wry twinkle in Moon's eye. The left one.

The lady flashed a shy, charming smile. "Please call me Missy."

"Okay, Missy." The part-time lawman cleared his throat. "Now tell me flat-out what kind of mischief this hombre has in mind." *Now I'll find out if she's a flat-out liar.*

"I don't know for sure." She met his hard gaze. "But my best guess is . . . well . . . that he intends to shoot a couple of lawmen stone-cold dead." Her smile brightened to outshine the morning sun. "Yourself and Scott Parris, of course."

Moon stared at the enigmatic female for almost a dozen heartbeats. "If and when this shooter shows up in Granite Creek, can you ID him for us?"

Another shrug. "Maybe." Another smile, neither bright nor shy. Label this one *sly*. "We'll see."

The deputy's next question ("Why does he want to take a pop at me and Scott?") was right on the tip of his tongue when their conversation was interrupted. Not by a whizzing copper-clad bullet, the sinister whisper of a flint-tipped arrow, or the maddened charge of a three-quarter-ton runaway Ford pickup with the accelerator pedal stuck, or a (three-quarter-ton) bull buffalo that'd strayed from the Columbine's herd on the far side of the river with the intent of creating horrific havoc, mindless chaos, general confusion—and having lots of good, clean fun in the process. Such terrors as those can be avoided.

CHAPTER FORTY

THE PRECISE NATURE OF THE INTERRUPTION

Which was: the usual.

Charlie Moon was sorely tempted to let the infernal instrument buzz in his pocket until the battery ran down, but his sensible right hand reached for the marvel of modern communications technology. Still, he refused to pop the clamshell cover. *Give it another few rings and whoever's calling will give up.*

Miss Whysper continued to smile at her host. "You'd better answer it—it might be something important."

With a sigh, the defeated man unfolded the device and checked the caller ID. *It's Scott.* He pressed the thing to his ear. "H'lo, pard—what's up?"

"Bad-weather signs. Are you all by yourself, Charlie?"

"No."

"Well get that way—pronto!"

"Okay." Moon smiled an apology at his guest. "Please excuse me for a minute, Miss Whysper."

"Missy." The brazen woman *winked* at him.

"Uh—right." The embarrassed fellow turned on his boot heel and ambled away a few paces. "What's the problem?"

"I don't know," Parris said. "But I just got an urgent call from the DA's office. You and me are invited to a meeting today at five P.M. sharp—and not showing up is *not an option.*"

"Pug Bullet must be awfully upset about something or other." The thought of the purse snatcher's untimely death came to mind, as did the image of a hard-eyed lawyer dispatched from the bereaved family to create serious heartburn for himself and Parris.

"Pug's outta town today, Charlie. The call was made by Miss Purvis."

Moon's brow furrowed. "We're going to have an urgent meeting with the DA's secretary?"

"Your guess is good as mine. All I can tell you is that Judy Purvis said *be* there—and the Purv was spitting out words in her you'd-better-listen-to-me-if-you-know-what's-good-for-you tone. You know what I mean, Charlie—like my third-grade teacher used when she was about to apply a dozen paddle whacks to my butt for something I did that I shouldn't've of."

Moon did know, and grinned at similar nostalgic memories. "Okay, pard." The Ute squinted to check the sun's height, then glanced at his thirty-dollar Walmart wristwatch to make sure the mechanical chronometer wasn't too far from right. "I've got some work to do here today, but I'll try to show up on time."

Parris: "Don't be late, Charlie. G'bye."

The telephone: *Click.*

Pocketing the instrument, Moon returned to his guest. There was something he'd intended to ask her, but it had slipped his mind. "I'm going to be fairly busy today, but if there's anything you need, just ask Sarah."

"Thank you. I'll be driving into Granite Creek later this morning."

He presented his poker face. "Gonna go lookin' for this cop shooter?"

"If the killer is in town, maybe I'll spot him." Miss Whysper glanced at the old Bronco, where the Columbine hound was sniffing around. "I intend to check out every hotel, restaurant, and tavern."

Moon admired the self-employed woman's positive attitude, but . . . *I doubt there'll be any bad guy to find.* "Once you've done that, you might want to drop by our fine public library—I'm sure Patsy'll be glad to show you around." Seeing her blank expression, Moon added, "Patsy Poynter—my intended. She's the research librarian."

"The library isn't on my schedule, but you've reminded me that I was hoping to arrange a visit with Miss Poynter this evening." The lady's eyes flashed. "Unless you two have a hot date."

Moon shook his head. "I'll be in town later on this afternoon, but I'll be coming back to the Columbine for supper." (He was half right.)

"Would you mind very much calling your fiancée and asking if I could drop by her home . . . say at about seven P.M.?"

"Will do." Moon immediately placed the call on his mobile phone. After Patsy had agreed to Miss Whysper's request, he turned away from the other woman and strode off three paces to exchange a few tender endearments with his sweetheart. When this happy ritual was complete, the hospitable westerner returned his entire attention to his houseguest. "It's all set."

"Thank you kindly." The lady was eyeing the Columbine canine, who appeared to be fascinated by one of the Bronco's knobby tires. "Are you sure that Miss Poynter doesn't mind my barging in?"

"She'll be glad to see you." Moon whistled at Sidewinder, but his summons was pointedly ignored by the hound, who might have still been peeved by last night's stern command to cease howling. "Patsy said she'd brew some tea and lay out a tray of ginger cookies for the occasion."

"How very sweet of her."

"If you don't get back in time for supper, I'll make sure there's something in the oven for you."

"How very sweet of *you*." Miss Whysper reached out to touch the hardworking rancher's rock-hard hand. Almost wistfully . . . as if their paths might never cross again.

Charlie Moon found this gesture uncomfortably intimate, but . . . *I guess city folks have their ways.*

"Well . . . Goodbye, then."

This parting remark also had an odd tone of finality, as if the lady had a premonition that they would not meet again. *Women sure are hard to figure.* Tipping his black hat, the Ute headed for the horse barn, where he would saddle up an old but trustworthy mount who answered to the name Paducah. The stockman's plan was to ride over to Sunrise Arroyo, where a mountain lion who was no longer sufficiently fleet of foot to run down mule deer had begun to harass Columbine calves and fat yearlings.

As the woman watched the long-legged fellow stride away to begin his day's work, she considered what a waste it would be for such a fine specimen of a man to be gunned down by an out-of-town assassin. But that need not happen. Indeed, if things in Granite Creek worked out according to her plan, such an unfortunate outcome would be avoided. Despite her jarring mood swings and a marked tendency to dither over seemingly trivial matters, when it came down to hard brass tacks like cash flow, expenses, and the proverbial *bottom line*, the resolute entrepreneur was determined to achieve her goals. In this instance, job one was to ensure that both Charlie Moon and Scott Parris would survive to awaken on additional mornings, be those dawnings chilly or warm. Her mouth curved into a smile. *For years, I hope.* A charitable thought? Given the multitude of troubles this world provides to those who reside therein for threescore years and more, perhaps one should not wish such a blessing as long life on a friend. Whatever her intent, by the time Charlie Moon was out of sight he was out of mind.

The rancher was not the only one who had work to do; it was also high time for Miss Whysper to get down to the business that had brought her all the way from southern Illinois to central Colorado. While still in bed, waiting for the sun to rise, the lady had compiled a mental to-do list, and dealing with her disreputable means of transport was the first item on her agenda. When she had the time to manage her life, this self-professed expert on crime was a well-organized woman who detested slothful behavior and could not abide a disorderly environment. Those who are apt to call a spade a spade (or a shovel) will no doubt designate Miss Whysper a cyclic neat-freak.

She unlocked the Bronco and commenced to check things out. (You know how odorous and cluttered an automobile can get on a long trip when the driver is living on candy bars, cookies, cheese sandwiches, finger-staining Cheetos, and other such nutritious stuff.) After some sniffing about (*It doesn't smell* quite *so bad as roadkill*) she spent a few minutes in a strategic tidying-up, concealing the most unsightly portion of the mess. Yes, a definite cover-up. But, like all of us who put off the bulk of today's cleanup until tomorrow, she rationalized that . . . *After I get some urgent work done, I'll deal with this crate of junk once and for all.* Perhaps. And perhaps she'd start balancing her checkbook, checking every single item on her credit-card bill, and clean out all the closets. As empty as it might have been, her resolution worked for the moment. The gratified woman slammed the SUV door, relocked it, and went marching across the yard to the headquarters. *Before I leave, I need to tend to a few things in my bedroom.*

No doubt. But *who cares?* A small dose of Miss Whysper's psyche is sufficient to give a person the fidgety jitters. We shall leave the semieccentric lady to her mundane bedroom tasks and move on to a solid-as-rock woman who has never been known to dither, display the least smidgen of self-doubt, or wonder, *Why am I here?* or *What is life all about?* She's here to take names and kick butt and have a fine time doing it. This salty old character is one of those "damn the torpedoes, full speed ahead" types with her leathery face set to the wind and her conscience stuffed into a thimble. So to speak.

As we check in, Daisy Perika is about to speak rudely to a rank stranger. And by now, you know why—just for the *fun* of it.

CHAPTER FORTY-ONE

YES, THE TELEPHONE RINGS AGAIN

No, not the one in Mr. Moon's pocket. (Recall that his instrument *buzzes*.)

The telephone that jangled was one of those embarrassingly old-fashioned ones, which was incapable of taking digital photographs, sending and receiving text messages, accessing the Internet, or playing amusing games with its owner. This plain black dial-to-call, pick-up-to-answer instrument was the same one Charlie Moon had used to chat with his foreman about twenty-six minutes ago. As we know, it is mounted on the wall in the headquarters kitchen, which is where Daisy and Sarah are putting squeaky-clean breakfast dishes into the oak cabinets over the sink.

Seeing as how Sarah had a wet platter in one hand and a soapy saucer in the other, Daisy volunteered to deal with this annoyance. Snatching the instrument off the wall, she snapped, "Columbine Ranch—eat our beef or *else*." She paused for a heartbeat to let this threat sink in, then: "If you don't, we'll hunt you down like the sissy eggplant-munching tenderfoot you are and slice you all the way from gullet to—"

"What?"

"Don't interrupt me when I'm on a roll—I was making up a brand-new motto and mission statement when you piped up and made me forget what I was going to say."

"Uh . . . all I wanted was to—"

"Who is this—some butt-head from Boise City selling life insurance or dirty magazines?"

"Oh, no, ma'am. This is Ray Smithson from down by Plainview."

Them Texans always like to tell you where they're from. "Oh, I know Plainview—that's one of the nicest towns in New Mexico." She waited. And not for long.

"Last time I checked the map," Mr. Smithson said stiffly, "Plainview was in *Texas.*"

"It don't surprise me—when you rich Texicans want yourselves a town, you go buy it and haul it home." She snickered. "I guess us poor folks in Colorado had better keep a close eye on Walsenburg and nail Trinidad to the ground with railroad spikes."

Dead silence on the other end of the line.

Which served only to encourage the animated tribal elder. "So how's the weather down there where menfolk wear ten-gallon hats and the fancy ladies eat jackrabbit hash with fried armadillo eggs?"

"It's dry." The retired lawman cleared his throat for a fresh start. "Is this Charlie Moon's ranch?"

"Last time he paid his taxes, it was. Whatta you want, Tex?"

"I'd like to speak to Mr. Moon."

"I'd like to talk to Gary Cooper if he was here, but he's not—and neither is Charlie."

"Oh. Well, then I guess I—"

"I'm Charlie's aunt Daisy, bub—you can talk to me. I know everything that goes on at the Columbine and what I don't know about my nephew ain't worth telling."

"Uh, I checked with the Granite Creek police station and the dispatcher told me my granddaughter was staying there."

Daisy's wrinkled face split in a wicked grin. *This is too easy.* "I'm sorry to hear that the girl's in the local lockup, but why d'you want to talk to Charlie about that?"

"No ma'am, you don't understand. My granddaughter's not in detention, she's—"

"So the jailbird's already got sprung, huh?"

The caller's flinty tone hinted that Ray Smithson might be getting a mite testy: "I was *told* that my granddaughter is staying out at

Charlie Moon's ranch for a few days." A belligerent pause. "Well, is she?"

"How would I know?" Daisy cackled a witchy laugh. "Does this habitual criminal write books about crooks?"

"That's her, all right." Ray Smithson was suddenly hopeful. "Is Ellie at the Columbine?"

"Sure she is." *Ellie?* Daisy frowned. *I thought she was Susan but sometimes I can't remember my own name.* "She's in her bedroom, resting, I guess."

"Does she seem okay—I mean, Ellie's not feeling poorly?"

"Poorly?" Daisy snorted. "For breakfast, that young woman ate enough eggs and ham to founder a lumberjack."

"Well—imagine that." Ray Smithson chuckled. "Last time Ellie was at my place, she'd converted from being a red-blooded American meat eater to a vegetarian."

"I'm sorry to hear it, Tex. This is a really interesting conversation—" Daisy faked a convincing yawn, "but I need to hurry off and count the flowers on my bedroom wallpaper. G'bye now."

"Please don't hang up—can I talk to my granddaughter?"

"Sure—why didn't you say so in the first place?" *This is the most fun I've had all day.* "Hold on while I go get her." Daisy left the phone hanging by its curly black cord and waddled her way down the hallway to bang her fist on Miss Whysper's bedroom door. "Hey—your grandfather's on the phone."

The door opened a crack. "What?"

"Your Texican granddaddy wants a word with you, Ellie Mae." Daisy pointed to the kitchen. "The phone's thataway."

Miss Whysper shook her head.

"You don't want to talk to the old buzzard?"

"No, I don't. Please tell him that I just left." Miss Whysper added in a whisper, "I'll call him after my business here is finished."

"Okay." Daisy waddled back the other way and picked up the telephone. "Ellie said to tell you she just hit the road, and she'll call you when she gets her business taken care of."

"Oh."

Daisy felt a pang of sympathy for the disheartened old man. "It ain't like it was when you and me was sprouts, Tex—young folk these days don't have any respect for their elders."

"When do you expect Charlie Moon?"

"Soon as I see the big gourd-head come stomping through the front door, but he's gone off somewhere or other."

"Does he have a mobile phone?"

"He does, but I can't remember the number. Anything else I can do to help you?"

"Uh—no, ma'am. I guess that's about it."

"Goodbye, then." She hung up the phone and turned to Sarah, who was scrubbing an iron skillet. "Did you already clean out the coffee-pot—or is there still some dregs in the bottom I can drink?"

Sarah hadn't and there was.

FINALLY, A BODY CAN REST

For those who prefer a degree of specificity, "finally" was five minutes later. Moreover, the atmosphere in the kitchen was serenely peaceful and, in Daisy's own words, "quiet as an abandoned badger's den under nine feet of snow." Having no intimate knowledge of shadowy subterranean domiciles, we shall yield to the tribal elder's authority.

Sarah had wandered off to her bedroom to tend to whatever a lovesick young woman occupies her lonely hours with.

Miss Whysper was (Daisy presumed) busy with whatever people do who have nothing better to occupy themselves with than such foolishness as writing dopey books about slope-browed, back-alley criminals who pack blackjacks, brass knuckles, and switchblade knives.

Not that Charlie Moon's aunt gave either Sarah or Miss Whysper much thought as she sipped contentedly at the last three ounces of coffee in the kitchen. The old woman leaned against the cushioned back of her chair. *This is the life. Just sit on my butt with a cup of Folgers brew that's strong enough to grow hair on a dead man's chest and not worry about a thing in the world.* Which pleasant reflection was sufficiently soporific to cause her eyes to close, her old head to droop, her almost-toothless mouth to gape, and the almost-empty cup to begin slipping from her fingers. . . .

You can imagine what happened next. The cup crashed to the floor to shatter into a thousand and one smithereens, waking the old woman from her doze with a spine-jerking start and an oath that doesn't bear repeating.

Daisy was saved from the cup-shattering, oath-making scenario by—still another ring of the telephone. These confounded interruptions were getting to be somewhat tedious for Charlie Moon's cantankerous auntie. She banged the cup onto the table, pushed herself up from the chair, and stalked over to a great-great-grandson of Mr. Bell's invention, jerked the handset off the cradle, and shouted, "Well, who is it *this* time?"

The caller was one of those faultlessly polite souls who feels obliged to respond to all questions. "It's me, Daisy—Patsy."

"Oh." *I guess I ought to be nice to the woman Charlie's gonna marry.* "What can I do for you, toots?"

"Well . . . I'm expecting Miss Whysper this evening, but something unexpected has come up and I have to make a quick trip over to Colorado Springs." Miss Poynter paused for a quick intake of breath and an admiring glance at her engagement ring. "I *should* get back home in time for my seven o'clock tea and cookies with Miss Whysper, but please tell Charlie's houseguest about my errand to the Springs . . . just in case I return a few minutes late."

"Okay, I'll pass it on." The tribal elder rolled her eyes. *All I am around here is a messenger.*

"Oh, thank you *so* much." Patsy made a kiss-kiss sound that nauseated the Ute elder. "Goodbye, now."

The glum Indian hung up the telephone without a word, then toddled off down the hallway to knock on Miss Whysper's bedroom door and inform the tourist of this latest fast-breaking news—only to find the guest-bedroom door open and the inner sanctum vacant. Daisy snorted. *Well, I can't tell her if she ain't here.*

True.

What the annoyed old soul *could* do was return to the kitchen and brew herself a fresh half pot of coffee. Which was her firm intention and the happy end upon which she focused her entire attention. But upon her arrival, Daisy Perika was highly chagrined to find out what was not in the red Folgers plastic canister. Ground coffee. There was nary a single, solitary grain. Nor was there a back-up supply of her favorite brand in the spacious walk-in pantry. *Well—ain't this is a helluva note!* All things considered (and from her Daisy-centered point of view), hers was an entirely justifiable complaint. After all, wasn't it Charlie Moon's legal obligation to ensure that a caffeine fix was always close at hand for his adorable auntie? (Check the box next to Yes!) And this oversight was no minor infraction. Indeed, his flagrant dereliction of nephewly duty was grounds for filing a lawsuit against her irresponsible relative. Enough said? No. As is her habit, Daisy was about to have the last word. As she slammed the pantry door: *Charlie is such a big gourd-head!*

And her day had barely gotten started.

But as troubles are measured (on the logarithmic one-to-ten Perika scale), Daisy's vexations hardly moved the needle. Or, to put it another way: for other unfortunates hereabouts, the grumpy old woman's morning would have seemed like a June picnic in Granite Creek's U.S. Grant Park. Really. With the GC Kiwanis Club providing complimentary pulled-pork BBQ with iced lemonade and Charlie Moon's Columbine Grass making music lively enough to make a ninety-year-old cowboy kick off his boots and dance in the grass like all his toes was on fire.

CHAPTER FORTY-TWO

A STRANGE GENTLEMAN IN TOWN
(AND HE'S PACKING)

The descriptor (*Strange*) is not intended to imply that the newcomer was particularly odd or even mildly eccentric. In this neck of the woods, hard-looking characters who carry deadly weapons (concealed or in plain view) are considered run-of-the-mill until they employ said weapon in a manner that is deemed either unlawful (armed robbery of the Cattleman's Bank) or unseemly (shooting up a respectable pool room just for the fun of it). Nor is the gentleman characterized as strange merely because he was a stranger—though that is getting closer to the point. Surly passersby whose faces are unknown hereabouts are as common as blackflies in July.

His appearance was strange not so much because the gent was an unknown quantity in Granite Creek—but due to the fact that he was *deliberately* concealing his identity. Yes, like that Strange Lady in Town—and for similar reasons to those that motivated m'lady to assume the moniker Miss Whysper. (Which, in neither instance, deceives those happy few of us who are *in the know*.) This particular male tourist had slipped surreptitiously into Scott Parris's jurisdiction because he was concerned about being recognized—in this instance, by a particular young woman. If Miss Louella Smithson should spot him, his sensitive and secretive mission would be foiled. Thwarted. Stymied.

Which outcome would be vexing. Annoying. Aggravating.

So what was a professional gun toter to do? This one's tactic was to melt into the crowd of rowdy cowboy tourists.

Has his ploy been successful? Thus far, it would seem so.

He is practically invisible among the dozens of big-hatted stock-men in town for meetings of the Rocky Mountain Cattlemen's Association and the Western States Brand Inspectors. Indeed, had he been of a mind to, the Strange Gentleman could have insinuated himself into the intimate company of any of those cheerful souls who were enjoying a tasty T-bone at the Sugar Bowl, a cold brew in one of eleven local bars and saloons, or a serene stroll along Copper Street to soak up the high-altitude atmosphere of a sure-enough Colorado cow town where ranchers, miners, truckers, university academics, elected public servants, and other shady characters rubbed elbows and generally got along as well as might be expected, which is to say that most recovered from wounds inflicted.

But consider this aside: aside from helping themselves to a fried chicken blue-plate special and a chilled Coors, or doing some window-shopping on the town's main business thoroughfare—every once in a while one of those conference-attendee cowboys might feel the need for a sweet, high-calorie treat. Or even a morale-raising haircut and skin-scraping straight-razor shave. This is mentioned on account of the fact that when the stranger was purchasing a double-dip chocolate ice cream cone at the corner drugstore, he inquired of the friendly counter clerk, "What's the most popular barbershop in town?"

"That'd be Fast Eddie's—hands down." The freckled youth, who had a gold-plated ring affixed to his left nostril (and spiked green hair), added a spatial dimension to his recommendation by pointing north. "Eddie's shop is about a block and a half up Copper. I get me a trim there once a month."

Despite this dubious endorsement, the out-of-towner headed in the prescribed direction, licking the ice cream as he trod along Granite Creek's bustling, boisterous, bumper-to-bumper main street.

CHAPTER FORTY-THREE

THE STRANGE GENTLEMAN IS NAMED

No, not identified. *Named.*

Yes, there is a difference.

It was the busiest hour of a hectic day when Fast Eddie and his hireling barber looked up to see the slim, elderly figure push his way through the front door of the town's top-rate clip joint. Both barbers nodded politely at the newcomer and continued with their serious work—which was not what the casual passerby might think. An astute observer would conclude that cutting hair was merely a front, that honest trade practiced only to provide a cover for their actual, less admirable vocation: exchanging gossip with locals. Beyond a glance from one of a half-dozen benchwarmers and a couple of customers waiting for their turns in the chair, the stranger was barely noticed. Which was understandable, since there was little about him to attract attention in a county where skinny old men were outfitted in OshKosh B'gosh jackets, Dickies denim shirts with pearl buttons, faded Wrangler jeans, brown leather belts with shiny brass buckles, beat-up old cowboy hats, and scuffed boots. Such characters were as common as fleas on black alley cats. Except that this stranger had iron-gray hair with prominent sideburns and was outfitted in a perfectly pressed gray suit, shiny gray cowboy boots, and a gray London Fog trench coat (which he hung on a wooden peg provided for manly outerwear). His fine gray Stetson stayed right on his head, where it belonged.

Now, to the issue of the gentleman's being *named.* The proprietor of the shop had a compulsive habit of dubbing strangers with fitting nicknames, especially those who appeared unlikely to identify themselves. This one was dead easy. *Howdy, Old Gray Wolf.* Noting that the newcomer did not doff his five-hundred-dollar cowboy hat right off the bat, Eddie marked him right off as a real-McCoy cowboy—and well heeled at that.

After sizing up the locals like the seasoned sizer-upper he was, Old Gray Wolf selected an empty chair between a pair of talkative customers and settled in for the wait without so much as a nod to the locals. In a barbershop in Denver, Colorado Springs—or even Pueblo—someone might have thought it just slightly unusual that the stern-looking elderly gentleman had hardly a word to say. But savvy out-of-towners who show up in such out-of-the way watering holes as Granite Creek generally do not speak unless spoken to. A discreet silence is particularly adhered to in old-fashioned barbershops where more than four dozen soap mugs are displayed on unpainted pine shelves, each one with a regular customer's name painted on it.

True to Fast Eddie's expectations, this steely-eyed hombre hadn't come to town to talk. The cowboy was on a drop-dead-serious mission, and fishing for information—which made it necessary to *listen.* After the old-timer had heard enough, Eddie supposed he'd know what to do next.

But, in the interests of full disclosure, it shall be noted that every once in a while the taciturn westerner did nod at an interesting remark, or grunt his agreement with a local know-it-all's assertion—and three or four times Old Gray Wolf even uttered a word or two. Carefully contrived nods, grunts, and utterings were among his crafty means of encouraging the line of talk in a specific direction. Other artful ploys included an inquisitive tilt of his head, a slightly arched brow, or, when called for—a doubtful frown.

The talkative local at his left elbow turned out to be Happy Billy Ryan, a clinically depressed real-estate agent who had not made a sale in more than fourteen months. To Ryan's keen nose for prospects, the stranger smelled like freshly minted cash money—and Ryan's hopeful eyes saw a man who ought to own a fine, Granite Creek County ranch.

The gabber on the Old Gray Wolf's right turned out to be semire-tired (formerly full-time professional loafer) "Big" Matt Bass, a 250-pound talking machine who had conversations with himself when there were no other ears around to bend. Bass figured the stranger was attending one of the two big meetings in town, and though the taciturn man might be a rancher, Bass opined that the lanky old feller was most likely a senior brand inspector. The kind that shoots a suspected cattle rustler right between the eyes and then inquires about why that Bar-Triple-X burned into the Hereford's hide looks an awful lot like it used to be a W-over-M Panhandle brand. Bass was about to open his mouth and make an astute observation on the subject of cattle thievery when. . . .

Happy Billy Ryan got in the first word. And quite a few more af-ter that. After some innocuous remarks about the weather (which could be worse), and the grass on the vast prairies west of town (not bad for this time of year), the die-hard salesman broached the sub-ject of how prices were down on rangeland now and how—if you knew whom to deal with—there were a half dozen prime spreads that could be had for a *song*.

Not at all averse to the realtor's transparent attempt to fleece him, the OGW applied his considerable talent to steering this one-sided conversation toward the biggest, finest ranch in Granite Creek County.

Happy Billy Ryan, who had no idea of Charlie Moon's recent thoughts about selling the fabled Columbine—much less that the Ute rancher had actually received an offer—opined (sagely) that Moon's big ranch was not on the market, nor ever likely to be as long as that Indian cowboy was forked-end down. On the other hand, the middle-man seller of land had a "feeling" that Charlie Moon might be willing to part with the Big Hat, and at a fair price.

While Ryan was sucking in a breath, Matt Bass used the opportu-nity to slip a word in edgewise, informing the stranger that "Ol' Charlie Moon has just moved his foreman Pete Bushman and Pete's wife Dolly over to the Big Hat."

This was news to the real estate agent, but he'd inhaled a double lungful of innervating mountain air and he expelled its good effect with: "The only reason I can think of for Charlie doin' that, Matt—is that he's fixing the place up to put on the market."

Seeing some sense in that, Matt Bass nodded his shaggy head. "Pete and Dolly Bushman are too long in the tooth to run a spread the size of the Big Hat."

Happy Billy Ryan: "And they're practically like mom and dad to Ol' Charlie. He'd trust them to spruce the place up some—maybe even show the Big Hat to potential buyers."

"Hmm," saith the Old Gray Wolf.

Ecstatic with this response, Billy Ryan touched his nose with a knowledgeable forefinger. "You can take it from me, mister—that smaller ranch will have a For Sale sign tacked on it come next month." More slyly still, and in a hoarse whisper that everyone in the barbershop could hear: "If you're interested in a buy of a lifetime, you just say the word. I'll check into it and get back to you."

The object of the pitch shrugged. Land was something the mark already had enough of, but he was interested in anything that had to do with Deputy Moon, Chief of Police Parris—and Miss Louella Smithson.

Smelling opportunity like a hound who's caught the scent of a fresh hambone, the desperate realtor kept right at it. Comfortable in his supporting role, Matt Bass piped up now and then. Within a few minutes, other locals were offering helpful and informative commentary.

By the time he'd finally eased his bony, rail-thin frame into Fast Eddie's plushy chair, the recent arrival had learned quite a lot about Mr. Moon's holdings and acquaintances, almost as much about Scott Parris, plus some spotty information about what was going on in Granite Creek—particularly during the past week. Removing his hat, the Old Gray Wolf passed it to the barber with the terse instruction: "Crown down, if you please."

"Yes sir." Eddie placed the expensive lid on a small oak table provided for those finicky customers who did not hang their hats on pegs. The Stetson was placed brim-up—so that all the old cowboy's luck wouldn't spill out. Pleased with this courtesy, the customer made his next request in a voice that was smooth as a ribbon of Japanese silk: "Would you mind turning me so I can see the street?"

"Not a problem, sir." Eddie rotated the chair ninety degrees. "How's that?"

"Fine." The senior citizen watched a pretty lass pass by, tugged along by a black toy poodle wearing a yellow collar with tiny red lights that blinked. "Just a light trim will do."

"Right. D'you want your eyebrows trimmed?"

"No, thank you." The flinty eyes under the bushy brows glinted. "You can thin my sideburns some, but don't square 'em off at the bottom—I tend to that chore myself."

"Yes sir." *And you figure I might trim one sideburn higher than the other.* Fast Eddie was a world-class talker, but a shrewd barber knows at a glance which strangers to chat up and when to hold his tongue. *This old-timer looks like a sure-enough hardcase.*

Right on, Eddie. If the aged cowboy (and he was an actual rope-twirling, bronco-busting son of a gun) had been the sort of loud-mouthed, swaggering desperado who carved notches into the grips on his .44 Colt six-shooter, the count would have exceeded a dozen—and marred the polished, hand-carved rosewood.

Considering the notable accomplishments he'd made in his chosen vocation, this particular tough customer was a modest man—and one who enjoyed life's simple pleasures. While the barber's silvery scissors snickety-clicked, the object of Eddie's tonsorial artistry entertained himself by watching parades of pedestrians and motor vehicles. But all the while, his cold gray eyes were watching for someone and something in particular. The someone was Miss Louella Smithson, the something her 1989 Ford Bronco. *She's not far away and she's getting closer.* He could feel the young woman's presence *in his bones.* But, no matter what the bones know, the old pro realized how difficult it could be to find a particular person when you didn't know what her plans were—even in a small town like Granite Creek. He didn't really expect to spot Miss Smithson cruising down the town's busy main street, but every once in a while a man who keeps his eyes wide open gets lucky. So just on the off chance, he kept a close watch on the traffic. *If she happens to spot me before I see her—there's likely to be six kinds of hell to pay.* A wry smile twisted the Old Gray Wolf's thin lips. *And I'll get the whole bill laid on my plate.*

CHAPTER FORTY-FOUR

BIG TROUBLE IS BREWING, BUT DO NOT FRET— YOUR FEDERAL GOVERNMENT HAS MATTERS WELL IN HAND

As does the local governing authority in Granite Creek County, Colorado—more specifically, the office of the district attorney, where Chief of Police Scott Parris and Deputy Charlie Moon have been summoned by a no-nonsense lady whose invitation may not be ignored.

After seating Scott and Charlie in District Attorney Pug Bullet's private conference room, the DA's capable secretary backed up two steps to put her hands on her narrow hips and cock her head (quizzically) and contemplate the result of her efforts to arrange things *just so.* The lawmen (Miss Judy Purvis thought) looked to be somewhat uncomfortable, sitting elbow-to-elbow, tiny microphones pinned to their collars, staring straight ahead at a yard-wide, high-definition, flat-screen terminal that displayed the Department of Justice logo on a serene, Mediterranean-blue background. "Okay, let's see how well you're framed." She thumbed a remote to replace the DOJ display with a live shot of the grim-faced men, staring like a pair of surly schoolboys who didn't like having their snapshots made.

"We look like a couple a two-bit criminals," Parris muttered sideways to his buddy.

Moon nodded his black Stetson. "Rustlers ready for a vigilante hanging."

Miss Purvis disapproved of such inane chitchat. "You'd fit the screen better—and look much nicer—if you removed your hats."

This time, Parris whispered to his sidekick, "Ignore the old bat, Charlie."

As he put his hat on the table, Moon whispered back, "Don't ever mess with Miss Purvis."

"Any cop who's afraid of a DA's sidekick is an egg-sucking sissy!" the chief hissed. Perhaps. But after a few heartbeats, Parris slapped his old fedora down beside the Ute's black Stetson.

The DA's secretary, who could hear a housefly larva treading on sewer slime at thirty paces (man strides, not maggot steps), shook her head. *The only difference between men and boys is that boys are cute.* Glancing at the Seth Thomas clock on the wall (whose hour, minute, and second hands specified the time of day at 4:59:07 P.M. Mountain Time), Miss Purvis switched the display back to the DOJ screen. "Okay, showtime in fifty seconds."

"The feds never start anything on time," Parris grumped. "It's their way of showing us local yokels that we don't count for pig spit." The lawman straightened the 1879 silver dollar on his bolo tie. "The three-piece suit'll be five minutes late, at the very least."

Grinning like the Man in the Moon, Moon said, "Wanna bet?"

"Two bits?"

"You're on, high roller."

As befitted the dignity of her official position, Miss Purvis disapproved of such inappropriate sport—particularly when conducted in the imposing office of the district attorney. Such behavior was uncouth. Unseemly. Very nearly indecorous. But deep inside her, a pigtailed twelve-year-old fun-loving girl hankered for a piece of the action. *Charlie Moon will win that twenty-five cents.* Miss P.'s predictions were unerringly accurate.

Sadly for the chief of police, at 5:00:00 P.M. *on the dot* the default display was replaced by a face. A female countenance, as it were. And one that was not merely pretty but heart-stoppingly gorgeous— worthy of the classic Greek sculptor's art. It smiled at the lawmen, but only one of the two experienced a skipped heartbeat.

The deputy was mildly annoyed with himself. *Why does she always have this effect on me?* (A pertinent question to pose, but one well beyond the scope of his expertise; Charlie should ask someone who knows.)

THE OLD GRAY WOLF

Even when digitized, Lila Mae McTeague's large, lustrous eyes managed to *scintillate*. "Hello, Scott . . . Charlie. Long time no see."

"Hi," Parris shot back. *I should've guessed.*

His cardiac rhythm restored, Charlie Moon managed to find his tongue. "Good evening, Special Agent McTeague." (It was evening in D.C.)

After Miss Purvis had left the meeting room to attend to other pressing duties, a few additional pleasantries were exchanged, which are neither interesting nor germane. These social niceties dispensed with, McTeague assumed her strictly business persona. "I realize that you fellows have other things to do—and so do I—so let's get on with this." She opened a glossy blue three-ring folder that was emblazoned with the FBI logo. "Bureau Intel has come up with something that may be of interest to you." After squinting, she slipped a pair of rimless spectacles over beautiful big eyes, which were a bit farsighted.

Forgetting the microphone on his collar, Parris whispered out of the corner of his mouth, "Trifocals—I betcha five cents."

"You would lose your buffalo nickel," McTeague said without looking up. "These are reading glasses that I've used for years."

Parris turned beet red. "Uh—sorry, McTeague. I was out of line."

Seeing an opportunity, Moon whispered, "She looks good in spectacles, don't you think?"

The lovely woman almost succeeded in suppressing a smile. "Thank you, Charlie—that was very gracious." She looked over her reading specs at the lawmen. "Have either of you ever heard of a Mrs. Francine Hooten?"

Parris leaned forward. "I don't think so—but the name has a familiar ring to it."

McTeague addressed the onetime boyfriend she'd dumped like a bucket of dirty dishwater: "Charlie?"

"Last week, me and Scott had a run-in with a purse snatcher by the name of LeRoy Hooten. He ended up in the morgue."

"Oh, right." Parris slapped his sunburned forehead "That's where I've heard the name." The cop wondered whether this was the preamble to some seriously bad news—such as that an assistant U.S.

attorney general was taking an interest in a suspect's allegedly wrongful death.

The same thought had crossed Charlie Moon's mind.

McTeague read the hint of alarm in Parris's blue eyes, but the Ute's face might have been carved of dark hickory. She hastened to alleviate any distress. "Francine Hooten is LeRoy Hooten's mother. The Bureau has been interested in this woman—and her notorious family—for quite a long time."

Parris exhaled a sigh of relief. "Bunch of bad apples, huh?"

"Indeed." Haunted by the recent murder of Special Agent Mary Anne Clayton and the conviction that neither Francine Hooten nor her British butler would ever be charged with this outrageous crime, McTeague presented a bitter, brittle smile. "Sufficiently so that we take a close interest in Mrs. Hooten's business affairs—and also her personal problems. What can you tell me about Mr. LeRoy Hooten's final hours in Granite Creek?"

"Well, there's not all that much to tell." *And you probably know all about it already.* Nevertheless, the chief of police did his best, and when Scott couldn't remember a detail he deferred to his Indian deputy.

Both lawmen were under the mistaken impression that all the FBI wanted was a cops-on-the-spot version of their encounter with Francine Hooten's son.

SPECIAL AGENT MCTEAGUE DROPS THE BOMB

After she'd heard all that she needed to know about how a pathetic pickpocket had met his end in Granite Creek, Colorado, the fed edged her thumb close to the detonator button. "The Bureau greatly appreciates your cooperation, gentlemen. I believe we're about finished, but before we disconnect I am authorized to read some remarks recently made by Mrs. Francine Hooten. Be advised that her comments are necessarily of a fragmentary nature—I will specify missing commentary by inserting brief pauses." Adjusting the reading glasses on the bridge of her nose, McTeague focused on a page in the notebook. "I want those two . . . suffer like I am suffering . . .

don't want . . . them killed—not until after . . . you may feel free . . . at my expense . . . arrange payment through . . . intermediary."

Both of the small-town lawmen instantly realized the connection to the so-called Cowboy Assassin, whom Miss Louella Smithson—aka Miss Susan Whysper—expected to find skulking about Granite Creek. Neither Parris nor Moon had any intention of revealing their hole card before Agent McTeague had played out her hand.

Scott Parris glared at the flat-screen display. "So what're we supposed to glean from those few words?"

"You have posed the critical question, to which a team of expert analysts has been working around the clock to provide an answer." The FBI special agent's attractive face managed to look dismal. "About three years ago, Mrs. Hooten suffered a serious fall which rendered her an invalid." McTeague removed her spectacles and laid them on the table beside the three-ring notebook. "She experiences continual severe discomfort in her lower back and legs. Medications provide moderate relief, but on a scale of one to ten, her level of pain is deemed an eight. Based upon this knowledge, Bureau Intel's assessment of Mrs. Hooten's intentions—and her express instructions to the contractor—is as follows: the two police officers whom she holds responsible for the death of her only son must be punished." She inhaled a short breath. "Punished in such a manner that they will suffer *as she suffers*." She paused to let Parris and Moon absorb this grim news.

They did.

The Ute didn't blink.

Despite a sour coldness twisting his gut, Parris affected a nonchalant shrug. "So you figure some thug with a pistol intends to *cripple* us?"

"Not I." McTeague's enigmatic face stared back. "That is Bureau Intel's majority opinion."

Noting the addition of the modifier, Charlie Moon leaned forward to peer intently at the digital image of the woman he'd once come *this* close to offering a slightly used engagement ring to—the very same ring that Patsy Poynter was now wearing. "So what's the *minority* opinion?"

Having provoked the hoped-for query from her alert ex-boyfriend, the do-it-by-the-book fed replied, "I am not authorized to reveal minority opinions." *Even when they are firmly held by forty percent of the expert analysts and myself.* She produced a Mona Lisa smile. "But you clever fellows are free to draw your own conclusions." Losing the smile, she fixed her gaze firmly on the Ute's image on the high-definition screen in the Hoover Building. *I'll call you in a few hours, Charlie, and tell you what the more likely threat is.*

Whether by ordinary lawman's intuition or some form of extra-ordinary telepathy, Moon had read the gist of the underlying message in the lady's flippant, seemingly empty remarks. Perhaps he perceived a hint from his former sweetheart's extraordinarily expressive violet eyes. By whatever means, the unspoken communication boiled down to . . . *Lila Mae knows something that she can't tell me on this secure Internet link, which is probably being recorded for Bureau records.* Would Special Agent McTeague leave him to guess what she knew? No. At least . . . *I don't think so. She wants me to call her on her mobile phone later on tonight.* Charlie Moon hoped that he could find the number he hadn't dialed in a long time. And . . . *I hope she hasn't got a new number.*

CHAPTER FORTY-FIVE

THE OLD GRAY WOLF

What was the sinister senior citizen up to during the teleconference being conducted in the Granite Creek DA's office? Nothing that would attract any unwanted attention.

About half an hour before Scott Parris and Charlie Moon were to be briefed by FBI Special Agent Lila Mae McTeague on a potential threat from some unknown gun for hire who apparently had a contract to put both of them in wheelchairs, the rangy old cowboy was whiling away his afternoon at Fast Eddie's hair-clipping shop, reclining contentedly in the barber's comfortable chair while the proprietor took his own sweet time snipping away at wiry iron-gray sideburn hairs with a pair of shiny stainless-steel scissors. Clickety-snick. Also tufts of curly ear hairs: snickety-click.

When this process was completed, the customer agreed to a shave and settled happily in while the barber added steaming-hot water to a sixty-year-old flowered soap mug and used an equally venerable brush to apply soothing, warm, sudsy foam to the lean stranger's weatherworn face. The so-called Old Gray Wolf found this nostalgic experience immensely comforting—even to the scrape of the lethal straight razor over the stubble under his chin. And except for when he was tilted back in the chair for his shave, this most singular of all the out-of-town cowboys visiting Granite Creek this week had kept his steely-eyed gaze focused on Copper Street.

As soon as his Shave-and-a-Haircut (twenty times Six Bits!) was completed and the barber duly paid and appropriately tipped, the freshly sheared tourist donned his wide-brimmed Stetson and departed—his face set toward the shiny pickup he'd rode in on. This old-timer (who couldn't have counted all the lives he'd snuffed out without pulling off his cowboy boots and over-the-calf cotton socks) was a remarkably uncomplicated man, and his plan was as straight-forward as hunting down a chicken-stealing coyote. After having given some thought to the young woman who'd hit town in the beat-up old Bronco, the OGW decided that it might be prudent to steer well clear of her. *At least until I understand more about what's going on around here.* A man in unfamiliar territory should always take some time to acquaint himself with the lay of the land. He gazed up at a graying sky. *Maybe I ought to burn some daylight outside of town.* His lips curled into a satisfied smile. *I might go take a look at some rural real estate.* Or he might not. Whatever he decided to do, there was no need to hurry; one of his favorite mottoes was "easy does it." *Tomorrow will have twenty-four hours, just like today.*

Indisputably true in the arithmetic sense intended, but one day's hours are never identical to another's. Moreover, how a fellow spends his allotted quota of minutes is a highly pertinent issue, and one that our Old Gray Wolf should have put some serious thought into. Time was slipping by like silvery minnows in a crystalline mountain stream—and well before tomorrow arrived, it was highly likely that someone's ticktocking clock would have stopped.

Correction: make that . . . *several* someones.

How many?

At the moment, the body count is problematic.

But for that final slumber—*five* is a not-so-nice, not-so-round number.

As is *three*. Which reminds us of that trio of law-enforcement officers (one in D.C., two in the Granite Creek DA's meeting room) who, as the Old Gray Wolf drove away in his pickup, were still palavering via the secure Internet link.

CHAPTER FORTY-SIX

A SMALL-TOWN LAWMAN'S NATURAL
SUSPICION OF THE FED

Scott Parris could have spent an hour and change expressing his misgivings about J. Edgar Hoover's illustrious organization, but here's what it all boiled down to: the way he sees it, every last pistol-packing employee of the FBI will withhold critical information from the local police—including two particular underpaid public servants (himself and Moon) who might be about to get their butts shot off.

Yes, that assertion does seem a bit over the top. You might well ask: for what conceivable reason would the nation's premier law-enforcement agency deny critical, buttocks-saving knowledge to a pair of their lesser colleagues? Parris will roll his eyes even as the query is posed, and yell loud enough to blow your hat off, "So the FBI can make an arrest *after* me and Charlie get popped, that's what—and then take all the credit for apprehending the perp!" A intemperate and thunderous response, but the longtime ex-Chicago lawman has a U.S. citizen's inalienable right to state his earsplitting opinion—and a pair of uncommonly powerful lungs.

In addition to his congenital distrust of Uncle Sam's finest, the Granite Creek chief of police smelled something particularly fishy about this report from Special Agent McTeague. It was not so much the gist of the thing; Francine Hooten might very well have dispatched a hired gun with instructions to seriously maim the lawmen who'd killed her son, so that they would spend the rest of their days in a wheelchair—like herself. But McTeague's elliptical remark that the crippling theory was "Bureau Intel's majority opinion" (which she'd hinted was not necessarily her own)—was galling enough to make a man want to . . . *bite the head off a rabid badger and spit it into McTeague's face!* (This was his own appalling metaphor; suffice it to say that the feat should not be attempted by amateurs. Aside from the obvious hygienic issues and the general inadvisability of spitting rabies-infected animal parts into the faces of armed-and-dangerous federal agents, one should take account of the fact that various associations dedicated to the protection of furry nonhuman creatures would be bound to make trouble for a deliberate badger decapitator.)

More to the point, Scott Parris was extremely chagrined with the fed, almost to the point of apoplexy. But not to worry; such challenges from the D.C. bureaucracy serve merely to energize our stubborn small-town cop into enthusiastic verbal combat. Charlie Moon's best buddy was primed to make a big score—by making Special Agent Know-it-all look pretty danged silly—and *for the record* on a teleconference that was undoubtedly being recorded for posterity. *I know how to pry the information out of her.* Toward that happy end, Parris produced a semisnort that served as the setup for: "I can't believe you arranged this time-consuming meeting with no more to tell us than *that.*"

A good try. Or perhaps not. But it was the cop's best shot. And as Charlie Moon had once advised his five-card-stud–playing friend, Scott Parris's best poker face was as easy to read as a Little Lulu comic book.

Not only was Parris's assertion patently false (he could believe it in a Denver minute), but the FBI agent had instantly discerned the ulterior intent behind his curt remark. She responded thus: "All I can say by way of summary is that Bureau Intel has ample reason to believe that Mrs. Hooten may have already dispatched an assassin to Granite Creek—the very same person who murdered a Chicago plainclothes detective who, several years ago and in the line of duty, shot her husband dead." McTeague thought that would take the smirk off the stocky cop's beefy face.

It did.

Scott Parris nodded, vaguely muttering to himself, "Cowboy."

Though startled, the so-cool lady did not so much as blink a perfect eyelash. But she was obliged to ask, "Where did you hear about Cowboy?

Recovering from his error, Parris returned a blank gaze. "What?"

"The Cowboy Assassin—that is a confidential Bureau designation." Her smooth-as-marble brow furrowed into a pretty frown. "What do you know about him?"

"Not a helluva lot." Parris shrugged to simulate nonchalance. "Except that me and Charlie understand he might show up in town to conduct some professional business." *Now she'll spill her guts.*

Barely managing to conceal her amusement at his transparent ploy, the FBI employee rephrased and repeated her original query: "And how did you come to understand *that*?"

"GCPD Intel." This was almost too much fun, and he could not resist tweaking the FBI agent again. "Not to mention a hot tip from an author of true-crime books who intends to work her way up to a more respectable career." *Go ahead, ask me.*

McTeague did. "And what career might that be?"

The Ute suppressed a grin. *Scott always overplays his hand.*

"Bounty hunter." Deliberate pause for effect. "Oh, I almost forgot to mention—I also have a confidential contract with a retired Texas Ranger who's been especially helpful, but keep it under your cute little FBI hat, McTeague—that info is GCPD-confidential. Your ears only."

"Of course." *He is so adorably childish.* "The next time you speak to Ray Smithson, please pass on my fond regards." With an indifference that wiped a fresh smirk off Parris's face and flushed it down the toilet, McTeague added, "And in that same vein, you may convey my compliments to his granddaughter. Please tell Miss Louella Smithson that I wish her success in both of her chosen vocations."

Staggered by this two-punch counterattack, Parris was speechless. For about one second. "That's not what she's calling herself here in Granite Creek."

McTeague feigned disinterest by glancing at the three-ring binder. "Indeed?"

"That's what I said. While Louella Smithson's here gathering material for her book, she's using the name 'Whysper.'"

The woman in D.C. arched an exquisitely plucked brow. "Whisper?"

Scott Parris shook his head. Also rolled his eyes. And sighed. Then he *spelled it out for her,* while Moon tried to swallow a grin.

"Miss *Whysper,*" McTeague murmured, and made a mental note to add that data tidbit to the Bureau's file on Louella Smithson. "Off the record, I do hope that Miss Smithson-Whysper will prove to be less of a nuisance to Granite Creek PD than she has been to the Bureau." Enjoying Parris's continuing discomfort, the fed added, "For several months, our hopeful author has been practically *stalking* Mrs. Hooten—which has created difficulties for our ongoing investigation."

Granite Creek's top cop was feeling a familiar, sinking sensation in his gut. *If McTeague's up to what I think she is, we might as well get this over with so I can go home and strangle myself to death with my bare hands.* "While Miss Whysper's in *my* town, she won't be any bother to GCPD. I'll keep a close eye on her. And if this so-called Cowboy Assassin happens to show his ugly mug in Granite Creek—me and Charlie will take care of *that* outlaw." Parris jutted his chin. *Now she'll have to put up or shut up.*

McTeague had tasted the bait and liked it. "I surely need not remind you, Chief Parris—that an assassin dispatched from Illinois to Colorado is not a matter confined to your jurisdiction." She glanced at her expensive platinum wristwatch. "Approximately forty-four minutes ago, I contacted the Denver Field Office and spoke to the special agent in charge. As a result of our brief conversation, the SAC is assuming jurisdiction of the matter in Colorado. Members of the Denver staff will be dispatched to Granite Creek tomorrow morning, which should allow plenty of time to prevent the C.A. from taking a shot at either you or Charlie. This particular hoodlum is known for taking his time in setting up a hit—Bureau Intel estimates a week to ten days."

His mouth dry as Panhandle dust during a ten-year drought, Scott Parris glared at his worthy adversary and—excluding those things a western gentleman cannot utter in the presence of a lady—could not think of a single word to say to the fed.

Sensing an opportune time to terminate the discussion, McTeague smiled at the aggravated town cop and his Southern Ute sidekick. "Unless either of you has a question or suggestion, I think that about winds it up. When the special agents arrive from Denver, the details of the role of the local police—such as they may be—will no doubt be communicated to you."

This barbed remark prompting no response from either the sullen chief of police or his taciturn deputy, Special Agent McTeague nodded at an off-screen technician—whereupon her strikingly attractive face was replaced by the DOJ logo.

Charlie Moon got up from his armchair for a satisfying stretch of sinewy arms and a wry twinkle of eye. "I'd say that went pretty well."

Still glaring at the static flat-screen display, a bearish Scott Parris barely managed a bearish growl.

How Judy Purvis was aware that the connection had been terminated shall remain a secret of her trade, but by whatever means, Miss P. knew that the conference was over. The district attorney's ever-efficient secretary arrived promptly to switch off the terminal in the meeting room and nod a curt goodbye to the pair of local cops, who got the hit-the-bricks message, donned their hats, and departed.

Within one minute flat, Chief of Police Scott Parris and Deputy Charlie Moon were striding along Copper Street in the general direction of the Sugar Bowl Restaurant, their appetites all primed and ready for some seriously tasty caloric intake such as makes the slender figure-watching set quake with horror.

WHAT IS LILA MAE MCTEAGUE UP TO?

Hard to tell—this discreet lady tends to play her cards close to the vest. And whatever clever plans she may be contriving might not matter. Regardless of all the efforts of those superalert feds who rarely miss a detail or a trick, unpredictable events have a rude habit of shouldering their way in to fluster and foil the most carefully conceived plans.

WHITHER THE OLD GRAY WOLF?

An embarrassing question. It must be admitted that for the moment, we simply *don't know*—the freshly trimmed-and-shaved tourist has given us the well-known slip. The so-called OGW has not been seen in town for some time now. He might be treating himself to a scenic tour of the more rural environs of Granite Creek County, perhaps with an eye peeled for a few hundred acres of bargain real estate. Then again, he might not.

A PLEASANT DIVERSION FROM VEXING MYSTERIES

So much, then, for the clandestine activities of FBI agents and elderly cowboys. Sooner or later, Lila Mae McTeague and the Old Gray Wolf are bound to show their hands.

In the meantime, we shall attempt to divert unwarranted attention from fuzzy peripheral issues by checking in on a couple of dependable characters whose precise location and honorable intentions are well known. Indeed, even a rank stranger in town is able to learn intimate details of their supposedly personal lives from talkative locals who have nothing better to do than while away their hours in barbershops.

CHAPTER FORTY-SEVEN

THEIR FIRST DAY AT THE BIG HAT

As he carried an overloaded box into the headquarters of the smaller of Charlie Moon's ranches, Pete Bushman was painfully aware that the dwelling was not nearly so impressive as its log counterpart over at the Columbine. Indeed, it did not even measure up to the foreman's residence that he and Dolly had occupied for decades. It was not so much that the Big Hat HQ was only a two-bedroom clapboard house with a pint-size parlor and a barely adequate kitchen; a semiretired elderly couple does not need a lot of space to rattle around in. What Pete's unease all boiled down to was that the ninety-year-old structure hadn't been lived in or kept in good repair since Harry Truman was president—and it showed. This was what those folks who advertise real estate describe (with a straight face) as a "fixer-upper" or "needing some tender loving care." Which, in this instance, meant no end of work fixing leaks in the roof, mending jury-rigged plumbing, replacing cracked windowpanes, and brushing on about forty gallons of paint—and that was just for starters. He muttered upon entering the kitchen, "It'll take a good two years' work to get this dump about one notch above Pappy Yokum's shack in Dogpatch."

Dolly looked up from her work. "What'd you say, Pete?"

"Nothin'." *There's no point in worryin' the old woman.* Despite his misgivings, Pete was determined to make the place sufficiently comfortable for himself and the missus during their declining years, which were already well under way. Burdened by the big cardboard box of brown crockery dishes and copper-bottom cookware, he grunted his way across the kitchen.

Busily scrubbing the scummy sink with a scouring pad and Ajax, Dolly stopped long enough to point her chin at an empty space on the counter under the pine cabinets. "Put it there."

The husband did as ordered, and paused to rub at the small of his back. "That was like totin' a box a rocks."

"What's that?"

"I said," he inhaled a breath, "that was like totin' a box a—"

"I heard what you said, Pete." Dolly brushed a sticky wisp of gray hair from her perspiration-soaked forehead. "What I meant was, 'What's that I *hear.*'" She cocked her good ear. "Sounds to me like a truck coming down the lane from the highway."

"I don't hear nothin'." The aching man continued to massage his sore muscles. *I wonder where she packed that little box of Bayer aspirins.* "And you only *think* you hear a pickup because you know Little Butch is supposed to haul us a load of supplies over from the Columbine sometime today." Pain tends to make a grouchy man extra-grumpy. "And if you *do* hear somethin', it might just as well be a yella Cadillac convertible."

She was about to assert that pickup trucks and big SUVs like Charlie Moon's Expedition made a different sound on the bumpy lane than regular automobiles did, but this first full day in their new home was no time to encourage an argument. Mrs. Bushman leaned to squint at a dusty windowpane, which she wiped with a wet dishrag. She pointed again with her chin. "There—take a gander at that."

Pete squinted. "Well, whatta ya know . . . there is somebody a-comin'." *Somebody's comin' and my hearin' is goin'.* Which failing was too dismal for the senior citizen to admit to. *More likely, I got too much wax in my ears.* Whatever the correct diagnosis might be, being one-upped by the old woman made the brand-new foreman of the Big Hat Ranch extra-testy. "But it's still too far away for anybody to tell whether or not it's a pickup!"

Dolly rolled her eyes. "You go help Little Butch unload his truck. I'll start up a fresh pot of coffee."

Knowing that she was likely to be right, Pete grumped his way out of the kitchen.

An inane domestic dispute? Without a doubt. But not so serious, considering that the couple tied the knot fifty-four years ago come November 26.

And in deference to the man of the house, it shall be stipulated that every once in a blue moon Dolly Bushman was wrong—at least in some particular. What was significant about the approaching vehicle—be it workaday pickup, gas-guzzling SUV, or spiffy yellow Cadillac convertible—was that the driver was *not* Little Butch Cassidy. That cheerful cowboy would show up sometime later with a bushel burlap bag of dried pinto beans, twenty pounds of cornmeal, an equal amount of flour, a half gallon of cooking oil, and a full side of prime Columbine beef from the headquarters cooler. Not to mention a nice selection of condiments, spices, jams, jellies, and other enhancements that make a home-cooked meal a couple of burps more than just lip-smackin' good.

The visitor whom Pete was going outside to meet and greet was bringing something far less palatable. Call it . . . bad news. Which is just one of the reasons why it can wait.

But not for long.

CHAPTER FORTY-EIGHT

A SUDDEN CONVERGENCE OF EVENTS

It began about an hour after the Bushmans' visitor showed up, who didn't stay long enough to enjoy a fresh cup of coffee from Dolly's kitchen. It has been observed by Mrs. Bushman, and rightly so, that "everyone these days is in such a big hurry." And so it was with the Big Hat's unexpected drop-in. But in a hurry to go where—and do what? In this instance, to Granite Creek—to conduct some pressing business. All of which raises the natural question: who was this hurried visitor who had urgent business to tend to?

AN AVID COLLECTOR, THAT'S WHO

Collector of *what*? Rest assured, neither rare postage stamps, valuable old coins, nor any manner of art—fine or otherwise. This information is deemed insufficient? Patience. All shall be revealed in the fullness of time.

CONCERNING A CREATURE OF THE ORDER *RODENTIA*, FAMILY *SCIURIDAE* (WHO PERCHES IN A CONE-SHAPED EVERGREEN OF THE GENUS *PICEA*)

But enough of this pandering to those Distinguished Professors of Zoology and Botany, who would merely sniff and make persnickety corrections to our pathetic display of pretended erudition. Having dispensed with them, here is something for the rest of us: a tufted-ear squirrel sits in a spruce.

A big ho-hum? Not sufficiently compelling?

Be forewarned, then: it is time to begin paying *very* close attention.

For one thing, this is no idle rodent. Whilst gnawing on a pungent cone whose seeds are deemed as ham and cheese on rye among her kind, she watches a two-legged creature approach the edge of a stream that was known as Granite Creek long before either the county or the incorporated township was so named.

The coated, booted, hatted bipedal creature stood stock-still for about half a minute, looking this way and that, as if to verify that no one was watching. Apparently satisfied, said biped selected two hard objects from the water's edge—one much like the other—and concealed the three-pound items stealthily in opposite coat pockets before walking away.

If bushy-tailed rodents were capable of having their say (and expressing their opinions in English), this one might have said, "Human beings are very strange creatures, indeed."

Indeed they are. We are. But more to the point, the aforementioned *fullness of time* has blossomed, and you have already guessed the revelation, which is: a collector of *rocks*.

Two of them, if you weren't counting.

Black-and-yellow-speckled granite, to be more precise—each made tolerably smooth by eleven dozen decades of slowly tumbling along in an icy-cold creek bed, all the while bumping coarse elbows with others of their durable tribe until all the rough, grainy edges rubbed off. Not a particularly interesting existence, but imagine how honored one (or two) such individuals must feel to be selected from such a multitude of her (or his) fellows for some significant purpose—which shall be revealed in a second (just-around-the-corner) fullness of time, which is to say *right away*.

SHORT AND TO THE POINT

Just minutes after the sun had set, Professor Tiffany Mayfair responded to a tentative tap-tap on her front door. As the hospitable citizen opened it with a smile, Scott Parris's lady friend was struck firmly on the forehead with a you-know-what. (Rock.) Not wishing to disturb the neighbors unduly, her courteous assailant closed Professor Mayfair's door with a barely discernible click and departed as silently as the clack-clack of hard boot heels would allow.

YE OLDE GRAY WOLF DOTH APPEAR AGAIN

It would be more colorful to assert that the out-of-towner's pickup *materialized* from the shadows of early evening—and (entirely by chance) barely thirty yards behind the 1989 Bronco piloted by that lady who prefers to call herself Missy Whysper. But such descriptors (as *materialized*) should be limited to learned articles on honest-to-goodness actual quantum mechanics, dodgy (unfalsifiable) speculations on parallel universes, and whatever category of science fantasy may suit one's taste.

As it actually happened, the driver of the pickup had made a left turn at a quiet residential intersection and immediately found himself about a quarter block behind the Bronco. The lean, elderly man behind the wheel eased the toe of his gray boot off the accelerator pedal so as not to close the distance between his vehicle and yonder SUV, which was rolling along rather slowly. "Well . . . this is a fine piece of luck."

Maybe so. But a man in his line of work had good reason to be wary of unexpected opportunities—which were liable to turn around and bite him first chance they got. *It would probably be smarter to stay as far away from her as I can, at least until I can figure out what she's up to.* On the other hand . . . *Things generally turn out fine if I just go with my instincts.*

"Fine" meant getting to tomorrow alive and spry, and his instinct at the moment was to follow Miss Louella Smithson and find out where she was going.

There was always the chance that . . . *I might see something that goes against the grain, and if I do I'll be right on the spot to sort things out.*

Most of us, be we pipe-wrench-wielding plumbers, union-card-carrying electricians, cynical law-enforcement officers—or downright bad outlaws—tend to see ourselves in a role that suits our preferred outlook on life, which is likely to be more self-serving than strictly accurate. Basically, the Old Gray Wolf saw himself as a trouble-shooter. With the emphasis on *shooter*.

In addition to this fortuitous encounter with the one woman in town who most occupied his thoughts and concerns, a couple of other surprises awaited him. The first would be Miss Whysper's destination—none other than the residence of Miss Patsy Poynter, Charlie Moon's intended. The second was—

But wait. Miss Whysper has just braked the Bronco at 250 Second Street, which is Patsy Poynter's address. She has also turned the battered SUV into the driveway—which is empty. She frowns as if saying "hmmm." The absence of a motor vehicle in the driveway might well indicate that Miss P. had not yet returned from some last-minute errand. (Or a round trip to Colorado Springs—which journey Miss Whysper was unaware of). On the other hand, it might be that Patsy's automobile was parked in the garage, where neither the so-called Miss Whysper nor the so-called Old Gray Wolf could see it.

That latter citizen cruised slowly past Miss Poynter's address and squinted as the driver emerged from the SUV. It was hard for him to see the lady with any clarity, because it was moderately dark except for starlight filtered through a swath of clouds that might rightly be described as diaphanous. (The corner streetlights were both a half block away, occupied with helpfully illuminating Stop signs.) Nevertheless, the OGW did get a good look at the woman as she mounted the front porch steps, because Patsy (whether she was inside or en route) had left the over-the-door thirty-watt yellow bulb turned on—presumably so she would be able to see—in an instance such as this—who it was that pressed the buzzer button by her front door.

Which Miss Whysper did.

Bzzz.

Turning her gaze from the buzzer button, Miss Whysper glanced at the passing pickup—and experienced an eerie sensation that the unseen driver was staring at her. Dismissing this suspicion as an amateurish case of the jitters, she pressed the button again. Longer, this time.

Bzzzzzzzzz.

She was relieved to hear the click of high heels in the darkened hallway.

The door opened.

The visitor was effectively blinded by the yellow bulb, but a familiar voice that she immediately identified as that of Charlie Moon's pretty fiancée said, "Well, hello." A silver-bell tinkle of a laugh. "Miss Whysper, I presume?"

"Yes. May I come in?"

"Sure you can, honey." Miss Poynter opened the door. "You're right on time."

CHAPTER FORTY-NINE

HE MAKES AN ON-THE-SPOT DECISION

His thin lips set tight as a steel trap, the Old Gray Wolf deliberately ran the illuminated Stop sign, made a tight (but not tight enough) U-turn in the intersection, bumped over a corner of concrete curb, uttered an oath appropriate for such a mishap—and headed back to the Poynter residence lickety-split—where he braked the pickup to a stop with a spine-jerking lurch.

Was he upset? You bet.

But a seasoned old pro does not make hasty decisions. After taking thought for about three ticktocks of his Hamilton pocket watch, the man under the cowboy hat deliberately eased the pickup forward until it *blocked the driveway exit*.

THE NEIGHBOR

An alert resident across the street had emerged onto her front porch with a small flashlight to look for the evening newspaper—and noticed the decrepit old Bronco pulling into Miss Poynter's driveway. Mrs. Buxton had also seen the shiny pickup pass by slowly, turn around at the end of the block, and return to park in front of the Poynter driveway—thus preventing the exit of the SUV.

Much like that tufted-ear squirrel gnawing on a cone in that spruce tree that abutted the small creek for which the town was named, she thought this behavior sufficiently interesting to pause and take careful note of. For a while, not much occurred that was worth gawking at—but presently her curiosity was amply rewarded.

It is accurate to assert that the ultimate event turned out to be very interesting indeed, and that Mrs. Buxton shrieked like a woman who had seated herself on a prickly pear cactus that was in full prickle. She dashed inside her cozy home, snatched up the nearest cordless phone, and dialed 911.

THE GRANITE CREEK PD DISPATCHER

"GCPD—what is the nature of your emergency?"

"This is Margery Buxton on Second Street—I want to report a fire!"

Clara Tavishuts responded in a dull monotone, "What is the location of the fire, Mrs. Buxton?"

"Oh, I don't know—I can't remember the number—but it's right across the street from my house. And I'm at . . . oh, gracious—I just can't *think.*" She closed her eyes. "I'm at 249 Second Street, so Patsy might be 248 or maybe 250—I don't know for sure."

Clara Tavishuts knew the town like the back of her hand and the names of most of the residents and their pets. "Patsy Poynter's house is on fire?"

"Yes! Well, no. Patsy's house is across the street, but it's not on fire—it's her car—well, not *her* car, but the car that parked in her driveway just a few minutes ago!"

"Please stay on the line, ma'am—I'm dispatching the fire department."

"Well, hurry!" Mrs. Buxton turned to watch the blaze flickering outside her front window. *If that car explodes and blows sky-high* (they always did on TV thrillers) *it's liable to shatter my window and the pieces of glass will slice me up like a ripe tomato!* Backing away from the window, she crouched behind the protection of an overstuffed La-Z-Boy recliner.

Within a few of the caller's racing heartbeats, Clara's voice crackled in her ear: "The firemen will be there within three minutes. Please stay inside, ma'am—a burning automobile can be extremely dangerous."

"Oh, don't you worry about *that*—I wouldn't go out there for all the tea in China!"

"Good for you." Clara's task now was to calm the distraught citizen, and the best way to do that was to keep the lady talking. "Now tell me *everything* that you know about this fire."

Mrs. Buxton did. What she actually knew was limited, but what she had *seen* proved interesting to the dispatcher. She ended her account almost breathlessly: "And after the lady came out and told the man in the pickup to move it out of her way—I didn't actually see him because it's so dark—but I'm *assuming* it was a man—nothing much happened for two or three minutes. I couldn't see the lady or the man in the pickup, but right after she walked up to the truck, I'm sure I heard a popping sound, like someone had dropped a lightbulb, and then it was quiet for a while. Finally, I heard a car door open and close—it might have been the pickup or the car parked in Patsy's driveway—I just don't know—then the pickup drove away and I thought, 'Well, *that's* over with,' and was about to come back into my house when I noticed a little fire on one side of the SUV and then *whoosh*! I mean the whole car went up in flames and I could feel the heat on my face clear across the street!" She peeked around the recliner. "I'm afraid it'll explode and blow all of my front windows out."

Clara Tavishuts had frowned at the mention of a "popping sound" and she was beginning to have an uneasy feeling about this fire report. Her intuition kicked in with: *That woman has been shot dead— and her body left to burn up in the SUV.* "Ma'am—did you recognize the lady who came out to confront the driver of the pickup?"

"Oh, no—it was too dark."

Now for the *big* question: "Could she have been Miss Poynter?"

The caller's answer was immediate: "Oh, no—this woman was about half a head taller than Patsy."

Charlie Moon's old friend closed her eyes. *Thank you, Jesus.* Thankful though she was, the dispatcher couldn't help wondering why Patsy Poynter hadn't made a 911 call to report a car on fire in her driveway. *Maybe she isn't at home.*

CHAPTER FIFTY

THE FIRST DOSE OF SERIOUSLY BAD NEWS

As Parris and Moon had just finished off a gooey, half-pound Reuben sandwich (the chief of police) and a man-size serving of the Sugar Bowl's semifamous green chili beef stew (the deputy), the stew eater's mobile phone began to buzz in his pocket.

Laying his soup spoon aside, Charlie Moon checked the caller ID. "It's Butch."

His attention focused on the dessert menu, Parris shrugged. "Wonder what that tough little cowboy wants." *I want a great big chunk of strawberry shortcake.* He glanced down at his bulging belly. *But I guess I ought to settle for a little bowl of sugar-free red Jell-O.*

"I'll ask him." Moon pressed the instrument against his right ear. "What's up, Mr. Cassidy?"

Dead silence.

"Butch—are you there?"

A long, raspy sigh rattled in Moon's ear.

Something's wrong. The owner of the Columbine Ranch frowned. "Talk to me."

"It's bad, boss." More silence, then: "*Really* bad."

The rancher felt an icy chill. Little Butch Cassidy was one of the coolest hands on the Columbine, and he *never* got drunk or exaggerated. "Has something happened to Daisy?"

"No sir."

Moon closed his eyes and prayed for another "no." "Sarah?"

"Huh-uh."

Thank you, God! He steeled himself for whatever was coming. "Spit it out, Butch."

"Okay." Quick intake of breath. "Here goes. I just showed up at the Big Hat with some provisions. It's . . ." The cowboy choked. "It's Pete . . . and Dolly."

Moon's chill dropped to forty below. "What's happened?"

"I don't rightly know." Cassidy's voice broke. "Except—except that they're both *dead.*"

"Dead?"

At Moon's mention of Daisy, Parris had laid the dessert menu aside. Now, he locked gazes with his deputy. "Who's dead?"

Moon covered the mouthpiece with his hand long enough to mutter, "Pete and Dolly."

The chief of police blanched. "How?"

Moon shrugged. The Indian's head began to spin as he considered the possibilities. *Pete could have fallen over from a heart attack or Dolly might have had a stroke.* Then the probabilities. *But not at the same time.* He addressed Butch again: "How can they *both* be dead—did they have a wreck in their pickup?"

"No sir. They're both right here in the Big Hat headquarters, sitting in the kitchen and—" Cassidy paused to swallow an unmanly cracking in his voice. "They're both dead."

Moon's numb disbelief gave way to a dark horror. *Maybe Pete shot his wife, then turned the gun on himself.* Why would his foreman do a thing like that? *Because he lost his mind.* And Charlie Moon knew who was to blame. *I should never have put Pete out to pasture—or sent them over to the Big Hat.* The rancher was unaware that he was grinding his teeth. "Dead *how*, Butch—gunshot wounds?"

"Far as I can see, there's been no shooting." Cassidy was gradually getting a grip on himself. "Some murderous bastard has knocked both of 'em in the head!" He strangled on phlegm, then coughed. "There's a bloody rolling pin on the kitchen table, boss—I'm sure it's Dolly's."

Moon tried to wrap his mind around the horrific picture Butch Cassidy was painting. *Someone shows up at the Big Hat and bludgeons a harmless old couple to death?* But why? It was too bizarre—an absurd nightmare that Moon was afraid he wasn't going to wake up from. The best friend Pete and Dolly Bushman ever had resisted the pull of the abyss by assuming his role of lawman. "You're absolutely certain that they're both dead?"

"If you could see what *I* see, you wouldn't ask me a question like that."

"Listen to me, Butch—don't touch *anything.*" Charlie Moon was getting up from the restaurant table as the chief of police did the same. "I'm at the Sugar Bowl with Scott. We'll be there inside half an hour."

"Okay, boss. Uh, just so you'll know—I already used my mobile phone to call 911. I expected to talk to Clara at GCPD, but somehow or other I got connected directly to the state police. They're sending a trooper who's already in the neighborhood." A pause while the cowboy checked his wristwatch. "He's maybe about ten minutes away. Oh—and the state cops are sending in a helicopter too, but I don't know when it'll show up."

"You did good, Butch—now just hold on for the trooper. Me'n Scott'll be on the road in thirty seconds flat."

And they would be. But not on their way to the Big Hat. For the next several hours, the state police would have to deal with that calamity.

THE SECOND DOSE

The lawmen were striding through the Sugar Bowl Restaurant's front door and about to break into a trot for Scott Parris's squad car and Charlie Moon's Expedition, when the police chief's mobile phone played a familiar tune. Not a surprise. Ever since Butch's call to Charlie Moon, Parris had been expecting a call from GCPD Dispatch. He assumed that Clara Tavishuts would advise him that the state police had reported an urgent trouble call from his deputy's smaller ranch. He answered the call with the brusque assurance that: "I'm already on top of it, Clara—me and Charlie are on our way to the Big Hat."

"Uh, I don't know anything about *that,* Chief. I'm calling because I thought you'd want to know about a reported auto fire at—"

"A car fire will have to wait," he snapped.

"Okay." The faithful dispatcher paused for a moment to display her annoyance with the boss. "But you might want to tell Charlie that the auto fire's at Patsy's home."

Parris stopped in his tracks. "Repeat that."

His dispatcher did, and added some additional details.

As Clara Tavishuts elaborated on the automobile fire, where GCPD units were already on the scene, Parris was side-mouthing bits and pieces of the urgent communication to Charlie Moon. The distressed rancher already had a dead foreman and his wife to deal with, but that double homicide was about half an hour away if they drove flat-out pedal to the floor—and the state police would have a trooper at the Big Hat in a few minutes, plus a helicopter with a detective and forensics team that would probably touch down before Moon and his best friend would show up.

Charlie Moon's decision was a no-brainer.

The Big Hat emergency was trumped by a fiancée only blocks away who might be in some kind of serious trouble.

CHAPTER FIFTY-ONE

RUSHING HEADLONG INTO PANDEMONIUM

The chief of police took the lead, clearing their way through the evening traffic. Scott Parris accomplished this task with grim determination, dual wailing sirens, a cluster of flashing red-and-blue emergency lights—and a thumb-size transponder in his hand that (at the touch of a button) greened every red light in their path. About three blocks down Copper Street, they were already moving along at a pretty good clip and "excessive acceleration" was the name of the game. It would be an exaggeration to declare that Charlie Moon was using his Columbine Expedition to literally *push* Parris's screaming black-and-white along a tad faster, but Patsy Poynter's worried sweetheart was keeping as close as he could get without nudging the squad car's rear bumper, and that sleek Chevrolet (as old-timers used to say in those bygone days of the Pony Express)—was flat-out *carrying the mail*. Only a shameless liar would assert that if they'd gone much faster, the lawmen would've shown up at their destination *before they'd left* the Sugar Bowl, but just ninety-eight seconds flat after they'd roared away from the curb, Deputy Moon and Granite Creek's top cop arrived at the outer margin of a firelight-illuminated scene of highly organized confusion.

From one end of the block to the other, the tree-lined residential street was clogged with the kind of official traffic that generally bodes ill for someone in the neighborhood. Limber up your fingers and count three fire engines, the fire chief's red Ford Explorer, a matched pair of boxy ambulances, three GCPD black-and-whites, plus two Colorado State Police cruisers. The makeshift Second Street parking lot for official vehicles was already cordoned off at both ends with yellow-and-black POLICE—DO NOT ENTER ribbons. After driving at breakneck speeds, the lawmen were obliged to park a half block from the scene of whatever calamity had occurred at Patsy Poynter's home. Moon pulled his Expedition to a jerking halt on the sidewalk, cut the ignition switch—and before the Ford V-8 engine had hit its last lick, he emerged from the Columbine flagship like a pilot ejected from a flamed-out F-15 jet-fighter aircraft. The lanky rancher hit the ground at a trot. What did he see?

About eighty yards away, a pair of EMTs were manhandling a stainless-steel gurney—whose burden was a person under a green sheet. The face was covered.

As the rancher's high-heeled cowboy boots popped on the black-top, a somber drum's voice thumped in his head, *She's dead . . . dead . . . dead . . .* The runner picked up speed as his long legs propelled him to his fiancée's address, but like a sleeper slogging through a nightmarish swamp, his feet seemed mired in muckish mud—his legs made of lead.

Mr. Moon was relieved beyond all measure and description when he saw his wife-to-be—alive and upright! Supported by the fire chief and staring like a wild creature, Patsy stumbled along. The helmeted man was shouting to be heard over the melee, "Who's the woman we found in your hallway, Miss Poynter?"

"My little sister," she wailed.

The public servant yelled again, "The EMTs will want to know her name."

"It's . . ." Suddenly angered by this noisy congregation of official-dom and their officious questions, she shouted back, "I'm so upset I'm don't even know my *own* name!" A touch of hyperbole, no doubt, but the fire chief got the message and shut his mouth.

When Patsy saw her intended approaching in long strides, she pushed the boss of the fire crew aside, took a few tentative steps to meet her sweetheart, tripped over a fire hose—and would have fallen flat on her pretty, tear-stained face had not Moon caught her in an enveloping embrace. He had the good sense not to pose a pointless, annoying question like, "What's happened here?"

But she told him straightaway: "Oh, Charlie—someone has hurt my little sister. I got a call from Daphne this morning . . . she was boarding a plane for Colorado Springs and wanted me to meet her there . . . so I hurried over there to pick her up . . . we only got back about an hour ago." She shot a wide-eyed glance at the ambulances. "I don't know whether poor Daphne's alive or dead . . ." Patsy suddenly paused like a run-down clock that had stopped—and slumped into a faint.

Moon scooped the lady up and was carrying her toward the nearest ambulance when Parris came huffing and puffing like the overweight, late-middle-aged cop he was. "My God, Charlie—this looks like a war zone. What'n hell's going on here—is Patsy injured?"

"I don't think so, but her sister's been hurt." He handed his unconscious fiancée off to a brawny emergency medical technician, who took Patsy to the ambulance, where another alert EMT was waiting with an empty gurney. Satisfied that his sweetheart was in good hands, Moon pointed his chin at the Bronco, which—despite the best efforts of enough firemen to put out a barn fire—was still sprouting a stubborn blaze near the gas tank. "And there's that."

Emergency lights persisted in their winking-blinking.

Firemen continued to shout at one another.

Petite, blond officer Alicia Martin appeared at Parris's elbow, her pale face smudged with smoke—suggesting a Tinker Bell who'd been dipped headfirst into a bucket of soot. She shouted into the boss's ear, "We've got a corpse in the SUV—charred almost beyond recognition, but the firemen believe it's a female."

His face prickling with the heat of the fire, Parris blinked at the impromptu funeral pyre and—recognizing the old Bronco—mumbled under his breath, "It'll be Miss Whysper." Realizing that there was no longer any reason to conceal the hopeful bounty hunter's true identity, he said to Martin, "It's Louella Smithson." Like his personality, the cop's logic was uncomplicated: if the corpse in Miss

Smithson's Bronco was female, the odds were a hundred to one that the victim was Ray Smithson's granddaughter. And though the situation contained an element of complexity, so it would prove to be.

Like his best friend, Charlie Moon was not what you would call a complex man—but neither was he simple. For some reason that Parris's deputy could not quite get a handle on, he felt light-headed, somewhat detached from reality—and oddly perplexed. *Something don't smell right about this.* A peculiar response; what could possibly be right about one woman burned to a crisp and another seriously— perhaps mortally—injured? But Moon must be given some slack. Even the strongest of men has his limits, and this veteran of the Second Gulf War began to experience flashbacks like those he'd endured following his ordeal in a drop zone some ninety kilometers behind Iraqi lines. Now, much like way back then, black-and-white pictures popped before his eyes like 35-mm slides projected onto a gritty silver screen— the impromptu picture show displaying no apparent chronology or logic. As if this were not sufficiently disturbing, the still shots began to couple themselves together into an erratic filmstrip that took on Technicolor tints; the various actors assuming the lively form of animated characters. Touched up by a few deft brushstrokes of fantasy and foresight, this jumbled assembly of memory vignettes began to *speak*:

Special Agent Lila Mae McTeague, her sensual lips mouthing an enigmatic murmur . . . *I am not authorized to reveal minority opinions.*

The woman in room 215 at the Holiday Inn, fashionably dressed in black pinstripe . . . *You may call me Missy Whisper.*

Patsy Poynter screaming at the fire chief . . . *I'm so upset I'm don't even know my* own *name!*

From a subliminal memory deposited in the rancher's subconscious while he had been talking to Pete Bushman on the telephone— Aunt Daisy recalling last night's nightmare: *She said she was locked inside that truck to rot like some dead animal—and wanted me to go let her out.*

Charlie Moon's solitary night-drive back to the Columbine, with the old Bronco trailing along behind in the chill starlight. (An unknown presence whispering in his ear: *We have not been properly introduced . . .*)

A faceless ex-Texas Ranger telling Scott Parris over the telephone, "I think I'll go fishing."

Sidewinder, sniffing his supersensitive hound's nose at the unshod hooves of an edgy blue-and-white bronco that was about to reward the dog with a swift kick in the head.

Miss Whysper, with black-cherry nails and lipstick, choking on her Columbine breakfast . . . *like she might strangle herself.*

The Ford Bronco, it's blue-and-white paint now blistered black . . . a cindered corpse inside—her mouth opened wide in a silent scream.

Again, Miss Whysper, determined to carry her own luggage—pulling the shabby pink suitcase from Charlie Moon's grip.

An amiable Scott Parris—checking Miss Whysper out of the Holiday Inn.

Scene-stealer Lila Mae McTeague's gorgeous face flashing onto the silver screen, her violet eyes capable of seeing him from afar . . . *Be careful, Charlie . . . sometimes things are not what they seem to be.*

This self-inflicted cinema fairly made Charlie's head spin; but, like the news-at-ten, disjointed flashbacks are not known for being either comforting or particularly informative. Deputy Moon was relieved when the unsettling experience came to an abrupt end. But, then . . .

It started up again.

Listen to Patsy and Tiffany's catty girl-chatter about Miss Whysper and her peculiar notion of color coordination.

Watch Scott Parris haul off like a star quarterback, let 'er go for the home team—and down purse snatcher LeRoy Hooten with a can of black-eyed peas.

This dubious entertainment was followed by additional (equally inane) sequences.

Capping it all off, behold Sidewinder, entering stage right—his dark muzzle lifted to the night sky, toothy mouth gaped. Is the Columbine hound performing his soul-chilling wolf imitation? Yes. More or less. But lacking the conventional lunar prop, the resourceful canine was obliged to improvise right on the spot. (There being no silvery satellite overhead, he was howling at the closest Moon at hand.)

Right—the very same Señor Luna whom Aunt Daisy (when severely vexed) referred to as *that big gourd-head.*

CHAPTER FIFTY-TWO

THE OLD PRO AND HIS ADMIRING SIDEKICKS

While Charlie Moon's mind was struggling vainly to make sense of the series of disconnected flashbacks, the medical examiner's van arrived at the opposite end of the block from where the lawmen friends had parked their vehicles.

Completely absorbed in their shared vocation, Doc Simpson and his two assistants passed by Chief of Police Parris, Deputy Moon, and Officer Martin without so much as a sideways glance. Completely immersed in their private world, the single-minded trio headed directly to the smoking SUV, where the firemen had finally doused the last flame. With no smoke to veil her gruesome countenance, the charred corpse patiently awaited the thoughtful appraisal of the skilled professional and his adoring second bananas. Arriving at the driver's door, Simpson peered into the burned-out interior and exclaimed, "My goodness—we are presented a textbook-perfect example!" (Of precisely what, the ME did not elaborate, and one hesitates to inquire for further details.) Like an old-fashioned gentleman who has just encountered an old and dear lady friend, Simpson removed his hat with due respect and smiled with genuine pleasure at the skull almost denuded of flesh.

As if she were pleased to see him, Louella Smithson's bony countenance returned a wide, garish grin.

Observing this macabre performance with a barely suppressed shudder, Scott Parris tried to recall the gist of a pithy proverb. *How does it go?* Something like . . . *Let him who enjoys his work ask for no other blessing.* Desirous of cleansing his mind of the grisly scene, the chief of police turned to his favorite GCPD uniformed cop and requested a continuation of her update.

Eager to get on with it, Officer Martin pointed her gloved hand at the boxy ambulances that were blocking the center of the street. "Patsy's going to be fine, but we don't know about her sister—Miss Daphne Poynter. The EMTs are doing their best to keep her alive."

Familiar with the drill, Parris guessed correctly that vital signs were being taken while critical information was provided via microwave link to the physician on duty at Snyder Memorial ER, who was telling the techs what to do before they started rolling to the hospital. The longtime cop imagined fluids being administered via an IV, possibly even whole blood.

Officer Alicia Martin continued to address Parris's left ear. "Patsy apparently arrived with her sister about an hour ago. The woman in the Bronco arrived much later, but only a minute or so before an incident that led to the dual assault. From what I understand, she came for a prearranged visit with Patsy."

Parris and Martin shot a questioning look at Moon, who nodded. "Patsy and Miss Whysper had a meeting set up for this evening."

Her supposition thus confirmed, Officer Martin picked up her narrative with renewed confidence. "According to a neighbor, the woman who arrived in the Bronco knocked on Patsy's door and was invited inside. Immediately after that, the porch light was turned off. It was apparently Patsy's sister who opened the door to the woman in the SUV."

"How do we know *that*?" Parris snapped.

Martin's face stiffened at this discourteous response, but she maintained her professional tone. "Because—at the time, Patsy was away on an errand to the supermarket. She returned home a couple of minutes before you and Charlie showed up."

"Uh . . . sorry, Martin." The cop with the sunburned face managed to blush. "Tell me more about the neighbor."

"According to the witness—a Mrs. Buxton, whose residence is directly across the street—" Martin pointed again "—immediately after the Bronco pulled into the Poynter driveway, another motorist showed up in a pickup. The pickup slowed, as if the driver was taking a look at the woman who'd gotten out of the Bronco."

Parris's inquiry was gentler this time. "Did the neighbor get a look at the pickup driver?"

"No sir." Officer Martin paused to gasp a breath of noxious air. "It's seems likely that the driver of the pickup had followed the Bronco here. Anyway, the pickup kept on going, but made a U-turn at the end of the block and returned to park the vehicle in front of the Poynter driveway. A woman, presumably the one who'd arrived in the SUV—it was fairly dark with the porch light out—anyway, she came out of the house and exchanged words with the pickup driver. The neighbor believes that she was requesting that he not block the Poynter driveway." Suffering somewhat from smoke inhalation, Martin paused to cough, then inhaled another breath of polluted air—and resumed her report. "The pickup stayed put and the woman walked up to the passenger side of the cab and out of sight of Mrs. Buxton—who then heard a 'popping sound' that *might* have been a gunshot, but it wasn't very loud and she couldn't see anyone. Things were quiet for a minute or so before the pickup pulled away as if nothing important had happened. But before the vehicle was out of sight, the SUV in the Poynter driveway burst into flames. The witness immediately called 911 and—" For the second time in a minute, her narrative was interrupted—but this time, not by Chief of Police Parris.

THE OLD PRO OFFERS A PROFESSIONAL OPINION

Officer Martin was upstaged by the sudden appearance of Doc Simpson, whose cherubic countenance fairly glowed with good-natured cheerfulness. After tipping his felt hat at Martin and darting a friendly glance at Moon, the medical examiner directed his remarks to the ranking police official. "Would you be interested in a preliminary finding?"

"You know I would," Scott Parris said. "So what've you got?"

"First of all, the victim in the burned-out vehicle appears to be a female." He paused, knowing that his attentive audience was waiting for the significant revelation. The medical examiner coughed, then dabbed at his pink lips with a spotless white-linen handkerchief. "I cannot be certain until I have completed a detailed examination of the remains, but I am willing to go out on a spindly limb and speculate that the cause of death was asphyxiation."

Parris was not surprised. "Smoke inhalation, eh?"

"I rather think not." The ME shook his head. "Unless I am mistaken—and I very rarely am—this is an instance of asphyxiation by strangulation."

The chief of police allowed himself a mild scowl. "How'n hell could you already know *that*?"

Gratified by this hoped-for response, Doc Simpson recited his carefully prepared and memorized oration in a deliberately annoying pedantic manner: "Unless this is the most unusual suicide that I have ever encountered, it would appear that a particularly nefarious malefactor has looped a length of wire around the victim's neck—and twisted the ends of the wire with the intent of severely interfering with pulmonary function."

"Wire?" Parris's jaw dropped. "Like for baling hay?"

Simpson shook his head at this farmhand conjecture. "The assailant used insulated wire. Solid copper, fourteen-gauge I think." The prideful performer allowed himself the merest hint of a self-satisfied smile. "Which is approximately 1.6 millimeters in diameter at a temperature of sixty-eight degrees Fahrenheit."

The old clown's really enjoying himself. "Electrical wire, huh?"

"Certainly." As if attempting to recall a significant detail, the ME paused. "I believe that fourteen-gauge is good for about fifteen amps, but I do not make a practice of staying current on electrical codes. Before replacing that outdated ceiling light fixture in your rumpus room—I refer to the one centered over your handsome pool table—you would be well advised to check the wire rating with a licensed electrician." He added, in an apologetic tone, "At this preliminary stage of my investigation, I am unable to specify either the chemical composition or original color of the heavily charred insulation on the hank of strangulation wire." With this pronouncement, the elfin man strode away to join his admiring assistants—chuckling happily as he went.

CHAPTER FIFTY-THREE

HOW DID SCOTT PARRIS REACT TO DOC SIMPSON'S PERFORMANCE?

Darkly, it would seem—like a cop who has had it *right up to here* with the irascible Dr. Wiseacre medical examiner.

Exchanging knowing glances, Charlie Moon and Officer Alicia Martin shared similar thoughts, the general gist of which was: *Scott is plenty ticked off and about to say something unseemly about Doc Simpson.*

Not so. During the ME's recitation, the chief of police had ruminated. Now, Scott Parris watched the dapper man's departure without muttering or even *thinking* an expletive. A manful effort to control his temper? No. He could not spare the brainpower required to produce a satisfactory insult. The overworked public servant was applying his entire intellect to a sober analysis of the hard facts surrounding the homicide. This process took more than a few heartbeats, but he eventually concluded that what had occurred was obvious enough. Before launching into his explanation of what'd happened in Patsy Poynter's driveway, Parris filled in Officer Martin on the highlights of recent events—starting off with the recent arrival in town of one Miss Louella Smithson, aka Miss Susan Whysper.

Chief Parris's intelligent subordinate listened intently to this revelation. Alicia Martin was particularly interested to learn that Miss Smithson/Whysper believed that she was hot on the trail of an anonymous cop killer known to the FBI as the "Cowboy Assassin," which gun for hire had presumably been dispatched to Granite Creek by purse snatcher LeRoy Hooten's mother. There was no need for Parris to mention that the obvious targets of Cowboy's get-even mission were himself and Charlie Moon.

Officer Martin, who taught Youth Sunday School at the Granite Creek First Methodist Church, offered up a heartfelt prayer: *Please, God—give me a shot at this killer before he lines up Scott or Charlie in the crosshairs!*

A laudable supplication. The answer was . . . no.

Following his introductory preamble for Martin's benefit, Scott Parris commenced to sum up his thoughts about the recent altercation at 250 Second Street: "Okay, here's how I see things playing out at Patsy's house. This so-called Cowboy Assassin hits town and one way or another, he's already found out that Miss Smithson is on his trail. While Cowboy is driving around our fair city in his pickup, he spots her old Bronco chugging along and follows the unwary lady in hopes of cornering her in some quiet spot. They end up here at Patsy's place—where the bad guy deliberately boxes her SUV in by blocking the driveway. Shortly after she's admitted to the Poynter residence by Patsy's sister, Miss Smithson notices the pickup. She comes outside and asks the guy to move it. They exchange angry words. At some point, push comes to shove and Cowboy strangles Miss Smithson with a piece of electrical wire." *Which don't explain the possible gunshot the witness says she heard, but that was probably bogus anyway.* "Patsy's sister witnesses the murder from the doorway, so Cowboy goes inside with the intention of killing her too and he might have—"

"The sister suffered a serious head injury," Officer Martin offered. "She's alive, but just barely."

Like Daisy Perika, Scott Parris hated being interrupted. *Where was I?* A frown helped him recollect. *Oh, right.* "After the perp assaults Patsy's sister, he comes back outside. Not wanting to leave a strangled corpse in the driveway, he puts Miss Smithson's remains into her Bronco. Then he pops the cap off the gas tank, stuffs something flammable into the spout—maybe a handkerchief—flicks his cigarette lighter, and touches a flame to the improvised wick. Cowboy drives away in his pickup before the Bronco goes off like a Roman candle." Parris glanced apprehensively at his deputy. *Charlie always manages to find something wrong with my notions.*

"It fits," Charlie Moon said. Sort of. *Like a pair of new boots that're a half size too small.* He fixed a hard gaze on Martin. "Did the witness across the street actually *see* the pickup driver go inside Patsy's house—or come out of it?"

"We haven't had time for a detailed interview yet, Charlie—but I don't think she did." Officer Martin shot a quick glance at her boss. "But like I said, the porch light was turned out right after Miss Smithson went inside." Martin took a moment to review Parris's grisly scenario. "After things got quiet, I doubt that Mrs. Buxton was paying much attention. A man in dark clothing could've gone into the house to assault Patsy's sister without being noticed by our eyewitness."

A grateful Scott Parris nodded his approval. *Martin is a first-rate cop.*

Moon stared at the scorched SUV. *Scott's theory must be pretty close to how it went down.* Committing two murderous assaults, concealing one of the bodies in a parked car and setting it afire—that did seem quite a lot to accomplish in a minute or so, but probably not for a seasoned professional who knew what he was doing. Even so . . . *I wonder why he'd want to burn Miss Whysper's corpse.* But the longtime lawman knew that even ordinary folks do some very strange things when stressed out. There was no telling what an edgy assassin might do in a pinch; even old pros occasionally lose their cool. *It could've gone down that way, I guess.* But Deputy Moon was not entirely convinced.

"This ain't getting us nowhere fast," Scott Parris announced obliquely. "What we need to do is find that pickup before this Cowboy strangler is a hundred miles from Granite Creek in any direction." He suddenly felt wobbly and somewhat light-headed. *Must be low blood sugar.* The long, difficult day had finally caught up with the overweight lawman, who was dithering uncertainly in that gray borderland between *middle-aged* and *over the hill.* To steady himself,

Parris leaned against Alicia Martin's GCPD black-and-white, its blue-and-red emergency lights illuminating his ruddy face with cyclic pulses alternately suggesting blood and bruises. "Officer Martin, put out a statewide alert on the pickup—"

"Already done, sir." *He looks a little shaky.* She coughed again, then inhaled a deep breath of not-so-smoky air. "Problem is, the witness didn't get a very good look at the suspect vehicle. It was too dark to see what color the truck was, and Mrs. Buxton doesn't know how big it was, much less one make of pickup from another. This Cowboy character could've been driving a pint-size Toyota or a Ford F-250. And our witness never even thought of looking at the plate."

Running out of steam, Parris managed a weak grin. "Thank you, Officer Martin—for making my day."

However diluted, a dose of comic relief was just what she needed. Alicia Martin's smoke-smudged face returned a bright, pretty smile. "Just part of the job, sir."

The moment of frivolity was short-lived.

As soon as the last word was out of her mouth, the trio of cops turned to watch the ambulances bearing the Poynter sisters pull away. Farther down the block, a fireman detached a few yards of the yellow-and-black barrier to allow the vehicles to pass without breaking the tape. Seconds later, the keening wail of their sirens pierced the chill evening air. *Like,* Officer Martin thought, *silver blades slicing ice.*

Parris turned his gaze on Moon, whose face was bereft of expression. "I'm sorry about your prospective sister-in-law, Charlie." Raising his voice, he tried to hit a hopeful note. "But we know Patsy's okay, and with a little bit of luck her sister'll pull through and be just fine." *And provide us with a good description of the bastard who bopped her on the head.*

Still gazing into the darkness where the ambulances had been swallowed up by night, Charlie Moon directed a routine query to Officer Martin: "When d'you figure the suspect pickup pulled away?"

"It must have been immediately before the neighbor called 911."

Alicia Martin checked her timepiece. "Which was about twelve minutes ago."

The deputy barely heard her response.

LOOK OUT, CHARLIE—HERE THEY COME AGAIN!

Yes, those deputy-distracting flashbacks had returned for a third run. Annoying, to say the least—especially when a man is trying hard to sort out his thoughts. But illusions have their issues, too, and sometimes it takes one a little while to get itself organized. Toward that end and during the interim, the formerly jumbled scenes had cleverly realigned themselves into chronological order along one, seamless filmstrip. Not a presentation worthy of Alfred Hitchcock; the resultant motion picture did not offer even a coherent storyline. That defect admitted, it did hint at an underlying plot. One so absurd that Moon tried to put it out of his mind. *That's way too crazy.*

Undismayed by this harsh criticism, the stubbornly sinister suggestion refused to fade to black. It looped back on itself, repeating the performance to its singular audience.

After a second viewing, Charlie Moon was compelled to admit that the notion did make a twisted kind of sense. Sufficiently so that he could not entirely dismiss the bizarre possibility. *But it sure is an awful long shot.* Which knotty conundrum resulted in one of those pesky internal conversations: *I'm probably way off base, but I ought to at least check it out.* And look like a biggest damn fool in Granite Creek County. *Which wouldn't be the first time, or the last.* But before I go off half-cocked, I should let Scott do his job. After all, I'm not the chief of police. *But I'm his deputy.* If I stick my neck out, I'm likely to get my head chopped off. *Maybe so, but that risk comes with wearing the badge and doing the job.* The outcome had never been in doubt. The man who never backed away from his responsibilities took a deep breath. *Well, here goes nothin'.* The deputy cleared his throat before addressing his best friend. "Pardner, things are happening so fast that I don't have time to explain. I'll have to ask you to trust me—and take my advice without asking any questions."

Uh-oh. "What d'you want me to do, Charlie?"

"Excepting Officer Martin, pull every GCPD uniform off this crime scene. Send every one of 'em—and every off-duty cop you can call in—over to the southeast section of town. Job one is to block off Silver Avenue from Plum Street to Fargo. Nobody gets through except law enforcement. No exceptions whatsoever."

Parris's wide eyes didn't blink. "That's it?"

"Order a silent operation. No sirens within a mile of the quarantined area." Moon added urgently, "And do it *right now*."

"You got it, buddy." Parris nodded at Alicia Martin, who promptly passed the order along.

Scott Parris watched the GCPD black-and-whites pull away, followed by one of the state-trooper cruisers. "Okay, Chuck—so what about you and me—what do we do now?"

"The hard part, pardner." The Ute stared at his best friend. "I'm not armed and you're packing that little .38 peashooter. We're liable to need some help."

Ignoring the crack about the beloved Smith & Wesson snub-nose nestled in his shoulder holster, Parris cocked his head. "Who d'you have in mind?"

Moon jerked his chin to indicate a tall, thin state policeman who deserved his reputation for getting the job done *no matter what*. And Officer Jackson was a dead shot.

Parris arched a fuzzy eyebrow. *That cop gives me the willies.* "Ice-Eyes Jackson?"

The Ute nodded.

The GCPD chief of police shrugged, but made the request to the lean trooper. Jackson immediately agreed—and without asking what was expected of him. Whatever the job was, he'd take care of business. Ice-Eyes was reputed to have shot a convenience-store robber between the eyes while mumbling, "Please drop the pistol, sir—and release the young woman." (Bang!) "Otherwise, I will be obliged to use deadly force." Probably apocryphal; neither the terrified cashier hostage nor Jackson's stand-up partner had mentioned this detail during the obligatory shooting investigation, or would confirm it later after a customer provided a fragmentary account of the trooper's alleged remarks.

Charlie Moon was pleased to have a dependable shooter to round out their team.

Scott Parris was a little uneasy as he eyed the trooper, then his best friend. "Okay, Charlie. So where do we go from here?"

His grim deputy grinned mirthlessly. *Probably to witness my all-time-greatest folly.* "You and me and Officer Jackson will pay a courtesy call on the Holiday Inn." Which hotel was located smack-dab in the center of the about-to-be cordoned-off area.

CHAPTER FIFTY-FOUR

THE CRITICAL TELEPHONE CALL

As Charlie Moon pulled his Expedition away from the Stop sign, he shot a sideways glance at the uniformed policeman in the passenger seat. In a tranquil tone that a man might use to ask a fellow diner to pass the bread, he said, "Please contact GCPD Dispatch, Officer Jackson."

Without asking why, the state trooper removed his portable radio from its belt holster, selected the proper channel, and made the connection.

As the big SUV picked up speed, Moon turned on the defroster. "Ask Clara Tavishuts to place a telephone call to Scott's lady friend—a Miss . . . no, make that *Professor* Tiffany Mayfair. Clara should advise the lady not to open her door to anyone except Scott, or me—or a uniformed police officer."

Jackson passed along Moon's polite request as a priority-one state-police directive, to be taken care of right now—any 911 calls would have to wait.

Moon enlarged upon his request: "If Professor Mayfair doesn't answer her phone, Clara should contact the condominium supervisor and ask him to check on the resident."

That instruction was also relayed to the dispatcher.

"Thank you, Officer Jackson." *I wonder what his first name is.* An unlikely but appealing possibility occurred to the whimsical Indian: *Maybe his momma took one look at her brand-new, blue-eyed baby and said to his daddy, "Let's call him Ice-Eyes."*

Jackson uttered his first words since strapping his angular frame into the Columbine SUV: "Anything else, Charlie?"

"There's a portable emergency light in the glove compartment. Use it at your discretion."

Officer Jackson found the appliance, slipped its plug into the Expedition's twelve-volt power outlet, buttoned the driver's-side window down, popped the magnetized emergency flasher onto the steel roof, and raised the window to a crack just wide enough to accommodate the electrical cable. He rested his thumb on the in-line switch.

With Scott Parris's black-and-white practically biting at his bumper, Charlie Moon alternately accelerated and slowed, watching for intersecting traffic before running several Stop signs.

As he had on the way to Patsy's home, Parris used his transponder to green the occasional red light. In between these legally allowable excesses, the deputy was exceeding the posted speed limit by as much as he could manage without significantly endangering life and limb of nearby citizens. There was not a second to lose, and the Ute's flinty face was grim, as if death was right around the next corner. *We show up a heartbeat too late, Cowboy is gone for good.* Moon realized that he might already be a thousand heartbeats tardy.

As nifty gadgets sometimes do during emergency situations, Scott Parris's traffic-light controller went on the blink. Approaching a major intersection where traffic was thick, Moon leaned on the horn as Jackson turned on the emergency flasher.

A pair of startled motorists stopped dead center in the intersection.

The situation took several agonizingly long seconds to remedy, but (despite Deputy Moon's quiet-approach stipulation) Scott Parris eventually dispersed the minor gridlock by blasting three hellish wolf wails from his siren.

The Colorado state trooper turned off the Expedition's emergency light, and on they sped toward an uncertain destiny. About a half mile from the Holiday Inn, Officer Jackson took a call from GCPD

Dispatch. Clara Tavishuts's voice on the portable transceiver was loud enough for Charlie Moon to hear about every third word.

After listening intently until the dispatcher had completed her terse report, Jackson said, "Okay—tell the supervisor to lock Miss Mayfair's door and sit tight until a uniformed police officer arrives on the scene." Softly as a lullaby murmured to an infant drifting off to sleep, he added, "But tell him it may be a little while before anyone shows up—we're all kind of busy right now with one thing and another."

Moon swerved to avoid a dressed-in-black bicyclist with neither lights nor reflectors. "I'm guessing that Parris's sweetheart didn't answer her phone." *Please tell me that when the supervisor showed up Tiffany wasn't at home.*

No such luck.

Officer Jackson made his report in a deathly flat monotone. "The condo supervisor—a retired U.S. Navy nurse—advised Clara Tavishuts that Professor Mayfair had been bludgeoned on the head, and is definitely dead. No pulse. Eyes dilated to the max. Fingers already cool to the touch." The hardened lawman allowed himself a breath of a sigh. "I guess I'd better put in a call to Scott's unit."

"No." Moon glanced in the rearview mirror, which was filled with his best friend's black-and-white. "I'll tell him."

Jackson turned his frigid gaze on the driver. "When?"

"When the time is right," Moon said. *And when I'm up to it.* "Professor Mayfair was murdered by the same person who set the Bronco on fire, and I don't want Scott to know what's happened until we've apprehended the suspect who drove away in the pickup."

"Yeah." Moon's passenger smiled thinly. "Scott'd probably freak out and shoot the bad guy dead on sight." *Which would round out the evening nicely—and serve the bastard right.*

"I expect he might." The driver peered grimly ahead. "Worse still, Scott might shoot the *wrong* citizen." It occurred to Moon that Jackson was not privy to recent events. *He deserves to know what we're going up against.* The taciturn Ute summed up the situation tersely:

"The suspect is a seriously bad character the FBI calls the 'Cowboy Assassin.' A professional shooter."

A cold-blooded pro himself, Jackson was unimpressed. "You figure this hired gun is holed up in the Holiday Inn?"

"No, I don't." *Not inside.* Moon jutted his chin. "There's Officers Knox and Slocum, setting up one of the roadblocks."

CHAPTER FIFTY-FIVE

AT THE HOLIDAY INN

As they approached the hotel's iconic roadside sign, Charlie Moon asked his passenger to please return the emergency blinker to the glove compartment.

This direction having been anticipated by Officer Jackson, the process was initiated before the words were out of the driver's mouth.

Right on Moon's tail as he slowed the Expedition, Scott Parris also eased off on the gas, allowing the elastic distance between them to stretch to two car lengths.

All three lawmen sensed some kind of showdown in the offing, and each of them reacted in his characteristic manner.

His throat seared by a sudden surge of heartburn, Chief of Police Parris gritted his teeth. *I hope I've got some Tums in my pockets.* (Not a problem; he did.)

The Ute deputy's lips whispered a four-word prayer. Charlie Moon was barely conscious of his automatic supplication. (Didn't matter. His words were heard.)

Of its own accord, Trooper Jackson's trusty right hand found his holstered sidearm and rested there with serene expectation, in eager anticipation of that moment when his brain would send a *shoot-on-sight* command. (When the time came, it would.)

Jackson: "I assume that we're looking for the suspect's vehicle."

"Mm-hm." Charlie Moon glanced left and right. "The pickup might be next door at the Quiznos—or even across the street in the strip mall." *But I don't think so.* Indeed, the Indian cowboy would have bet his fine pair of Tony Lama boots that the truck was behind the

281

Holiday Inn, where Louella Smithson had parked her old Bronco when she checked in yesterday evening. Shifting down to second gear, he eased the Columbine flagship into the hotel parking lot slowly, like a weary, bleary-eyed tourist hoping to find a convenient parking spot and then a comfortable bed.

Officer Jackson's cold blue gaze was scanning dozens of parked vehicles. *With all of these convention cowpokes in town, most of the vehicles in the Holiday Inn are pickups.* "So how'll we know when we spot the right truck?"

"It showed up just a few minutes ago, so the engine's still warm." Moon eased his pointy boot toe off the accelerator pedal and shifted to Low. "The pickup we're looking won't have any frost on the hood."

"Oh . . . right." *Thank you, Sherlock Ute.*

The latter-day consulting detective switched off the Expedition's defroster fan. "And the windshield will be clear of frost."

Thanks again. By force of habit, Jackson unholstered and checked his sidearm. As he knew it would be, the Glock's 9-mm magazine was fully loaded. With a derisive smirk, he injected a copper-jacketed round into the barrel. "So here we go, Charlie—me'n a full-blooded Ute Indian out gunning for an outlaw cowboy." *I'd sure hate to be in that unlucky hombre's boots.*

The driver nodded. *But this Cowboy ain't your average cow pie kicker.*

The state cop watched several clusters of well-booted hombres who were topped off with broad-brimmed hats, all meandering this way and that in the parking lot. A few were cold sober; but the rest had been sampling the potent liquid refreshment served up at local dispensaries. "This'll be like looking for a drunk in the Burro Alley Saloon on a Saturday night."

Ignoring the male pedestrians, the driver was looking for the suspect vehicle. "We're not likely to see the cowboy who owns the pickup strutting around with these other stockmen."

"You figure he's already holed up someplace?"

Charlie Moon switched off the noisy defroster. "I figure he'll be in his pickup."

"Doing what?" The trooper frowned. "Waiting for us to show up?"

The Ute slowed his Expedition to a crawl. "In a manner of speaking."

I sure wish Charlie would just say straight out what's on his mind. "So the shooter figures we've got him cornered—and intends to run up the white flag?"

"No. For his kind, surrender is not an option."

The state trooper's hard face split into a grin. "You believe this outlaw intends to stand and shoot it out with the police?"

Moon shook his head.

Officer Jackson was an uncomplicated man who liked things simple and straightforward. *This whole business is beginning to sound awfully squirrelly.* "Then what *do* you think?"

"I think we've found the pickup." Charlie Moon braked his SUV to a dead stop and switched off the headlights.

Close behind them, Scott Parris did the same.

There was no need for the Ute to point at what he'd spotted. Officer Jackson had also noticed the shiny new GMC pickup with *no frost on the hood*—and a freshly defrosted windshield.

Scott Parris, Charlie Moon, and Officer Jackson opened the car doors at their respective elbows almost simultaneously and slipped out like ghostly man-shadows. The trio congregated at the chief of police's black-and-white. Ready to assume charge of whatever action Charlie Moon had in mind, Parris jutted his square chin at the suspect vehicle. "Is that it?"

"I believe it is," his Indian deputy said.

Jackson was staring doubtfully at the truck. *Moon is dead wrong on at least one particular.* And he could not resist telling him so. "There's nobody in the truck, Charlie."

"Oh, he's there all right—just out of sight." Having temporarily lost interest in the pickup, Moon was now scanning the parking lot.

Parris leaned forward to squint at the GMC pickup. "Well if he's in there, I sure don't see him."

"Neither do I," the Ute said.

Figuring he'd caught on, Parris nodded knowingly. "Hunkered down, huh?"

Charlie Moon responded with a nod.

His companions drew similar conclusions:

Parris: *Ol' Charlie must've got a quick look at Cowboy right before he popped out of sight.*

Jackson: *That sharp-eyed Indian spotted the shooter before he ducked.* "He's keeping his head down and waiting for some dumb cop to peep through the window so he can blow his fool head off." Jackson's hand took a tighter grip on the butt of his holstered automatic pistol. "But we've got him cornered."

"You got that right," Parris said. "This woman-strangling, Bronco-burning yahoo ain't going *nowhere*." Despite this earnest bluster, he knew it wouldn't be a cakewalk. In a dicey situation like this, the sensible course of action was to quietly evacuate the hotel while stealthily saturating the parking lot with GCPD uniforms and state police. That process would take maybe twenty minutes, and . . . *Before we even got started we could hem that pickup in with my black-and-white and Charlie's SUV.* As soon as there was no way out, they could let the assassin know the game was up . . . *and wait him out.* For how long? Long as it takes. *Till Houston is snowed in and Tucson freezes over.*

That would be the *sensible* thing to do. But . . .

CHAPTER FIFTY-SIX

BUT WHAT?

But the edgy chief of police was not in a mood to go by the book, or to wait another minute. Why? (Granite Creek's senior police official is about to tell us.) *Once the word gets out, the FBI won't wait till morning to show up and assume jurisdiction—those feds'll be here in nothin' flat and take charge of things and make the arrest that we set up and then they'll hold a big press conference in Denver and tell the whole wide world how they nabbed a dangerous assassin in a little backwater Colorado mountain town where the local cops couldn't find their butts with both hands.* Was he going to let that happen? No way. What he had in mind was to deal with the matter *right now*.

Toward that happy goal, Scott Parris addressed the state trooper. "Here's how I see it, Jackson: the two of us circle around by the creek bank and approach the pickup from the rear. I'll slip up to the driver's-side door, you take the passenger side—but stay out of the line of fire. To get the bad guy's attention, you tap on the cab with your sidearm and yell, 'Police—open up!' When you do, I'll jerk the driver's-side door open—and shoot the outlaw five times if he so much as blinks an eye." Parris swallowed a resurgent burst of stomach acid. "But just on the off chance that I take a hit, you do whatever comes naturally."

Jackson's blue eyes sparkled. "Works for me, Chief."

Scott Parris gave his enigmatic deputy his no-nonsense, now-hear-this look. "Since you're not packing, Charlie—you stay put. Me and Jackson will take care of this badass dude in three minutes flat."

"Okay," Moon murmured. "But there'll be no need to shoot him."

The chief of police burned his best friend with a dual-laser glare. "You figure he'll fold?"

"When the chips are down, this Cowboy never bluffs or folds—but he won't pose a threat." Before stepping out on the proverbial limb, Moon inhaled deeply of the chill night air. "He's already been shot."

Recalling the popping sound the witness had reported, Parris said, "You telling me that Miss Whysper has already plugged this guy?"

"I'd be willing to bet a two-dollar bill on it," Moon said.

It would be like taking free money, but Parris was in no mood for wagering. "So you figure all the fight's gone out of him?"

"By now, he's probably dead," the deputy said.

"Let me see if I can get my mind wrapped around this." Parris refocused his gaze on the pickup. "The suspect uses his truck to block the Bronco in Patsy's driveway. Miss Whysper comes outside and tells him to park somewhere else. He stays put. Things get nasty. She pulls a pistol from her purse and shoots the guy because he wouldn't move his pickup. Is that what you're telling me?"

Moon nodded. "More or less." *Mostly less.*

"Okay. Let's say she shoots the pickup driver with the kind of small-caliber weapon a lady might carry in her purse." Parris mimicked a corny line from an old Tom Mix flick: " 'Just a flesh wound, ma'am.' "

Jackson smirked.

"This little dose of lead poisoning don't bring Cowboy down," Parris continued. "Just makes him madder'n hell. So he loops a hank of wire around his assailant's neck and strangles her to death. Noticing that Patsy's sister has witnessed this capital crime, he goes into the house to knock her on the head. Does this slow him down? Not a bit. This wounded outlaw comes back outside, dumps Miss Whysper's body into the Bronco, and sets it afire. Finally satisfied with his night's work, he drives his GMC pickup over here to the Holiday Inn," Parris pointed his chin at the vehicle, "where he's already checked in and intends to treat himself to a fine beefsteak supper and then a good night's sleep. But the wages of sin catch up with him. When the rascal parks out back of the hotel—he croaks from the minor gunshot wound. Is that what you expect me to believe?"

"Well, when you put it like that, it does sound unlikely." The deputy's attention was focused on a particular sedan in the parking lot.

Moon's flippant response annoyed his friend. "Anything you want to add to your hunch, Charlie?"

"Like what?"

"Oh, I don't know—maybe a physical description of the cowboy that Miss Whysper shot."

"There's not that much I can tell you." Six heartbeats. "Except that he'll be an elderly fellow."

"Is that all?"

"I reckon so." Another thoughtful pause. "Well . . . except for a minor detail."

"So spit it out."

"He's most likely from the Lone Star State."

"And how do you figure that?"

"Oh, just a gut feeling." Moon said. "That, and his truck has Texas plates."

Parris and Jackson squinted to make out the plate on the GMC's front bumper. Both of the lawmen envied the Indian's astonishing night-vision.

Guessing their thoughts, Moon confessed, "I spotted the out-of-state plate right before I switched off my headlights."

Parris eyed the gray GMC. "So Cowboy's from the land of the Houston Oilers and Dallas Cowboys?"

Moon nodded his black Stetson. "*This* old Cowboy is."

Officer Jackson cleared this throat.

Parris turned his glare on the state trooper. "What?"

"You two chatterboxes can talk all night if you want to." The trooper gestured dismissively with his 9-mm Glock. "But I figure it's time to go look in the horse's mouth."

"Right." The Granite Creek chief of police rummaged around in his pockets, found a package of Tums, and crunched a couple of the white disks. "But we do this according to plan. I'll jerk the driver's-side door open. If this outlaw's dead, fine and dandy. But if he puts up a fight, we settle his hash once and for all."

As they strode away into the darkness, Charlie Moon stayed firmly put. How firmly? Like century-old lichen attached to a gritty granite boulder. Ignoring the GMC pickup, Parris's stalwart deputy continued his survey of a distant spot in the parking lot. *Any minute now, all hell's gonna break loose.*

CHAPTER FIFTY-SEVEN

MEETING THE REAL MCCOY COWBOY

The reference is to that breed of boot-leather-tough hombre who works sullen longhorn cattle, rides snorty quarter horses hell-for-leather across the dusty prairie, packs a sure-enough Colt six-gun on his slender hip, and can put a .44 round dead center between a rustler's bloodshot eyes at thirty-six yards—while both shooter and shootee are in the saddle, their mounts at a dead run. (Exit wound.)

As Chief Parris and Trooper Jackson approached the GMC tailgate like the sinister shadow-men they were, a thin sliver of waxing moon provided sufficient light to illuminate their vehicular target.

Per plan, the state cop positioned himself near the passenger door.

Parris crouched uncomfortably by the driver's side, .38 snub-nose revolver in his right hand.

Despite the deputy's confident prediction of the pickup driver's harmless state, the lawmen realized that this showdown might be the *grande finale* for either or both of them. They began to harbor doubts . . . and corresponding apprehensions.

Officer Jackson: *If Charlie Moon is wrong about this outlaw being shot—he's liable to take one of us down before the other one stops his clock.* The state trooper felt ashamed for hoping that he would have the clock-stopping privilege. Even cold-blooded cops who're aptly nicknamed "Ice-Eyes" look forward to the next sunrise.

Scott Parris's concerns were somewhat more mundane: *If the pickup doors are locked, my plan ain't gonna work.* Which prospect suggested a fate worse than death by bloody bullet holes . . . *I'll look really stupid.* Untimely end or acute embarrassment, there was nothing to do now but forge ahead. *What's keeping Jackson?* Parris signaled by cocking his Smith & Wesson Police Special. The sharp click sounded like a dry stick breaking in an uninhabited forest where trees fall unheard. Parris put his left hand on the GMC door handle.

Jackson tapped the truck with his Glock, and said in a disinterested monotone, "Police—open up."

The chief of police jerked the driver's-side door open and pointed his sidearm into the cab, which was now illumined by a bright dome light. Scott Parris's intended target held no weapon in his cold, stiffening hand. "All clear, Jackson." He stuffed his revolver back into the shoulder holster.

The state trooper opened the opposite door and got a look inside.

Sitting in a puddle of sticky blood on the passenger-side floorboard, the man with a small-caliber-bullet hole in his throat looked straight ahead with a mildly puzzled expression . . . like a tuckered-out old cowpuncher who'd finally arrived at the end of his trail and didn't know what to do next.

Suitably impressed with Charlie Moon's remarkable powers of prognostication, the state cop muttered, "Well. I'll be drowned in a muddy ditch and hung out to dry."

Parris frowned at the specimen. "It's an old geezer in a cowboy hat."

Jackson: "And he sure does *look* dead."

Enough said.

No, hold on a minute. Someone else is about to express himself.

"If I'm not wrong, the corpse you're looking at is what's left of a famous ex-Texas Ranger." (It would appear that the lichen has come unstuck from the boulder.) His dark-eyed gaze still raking the far side of the parking lot, Charlie Moon had eased within three paces of the chief of police.

"Ray Smithson?" Parris shook his head. *A sure-enough Ranger always hits what he aims at—and he don't never ever tell a lie.* "It can't be, Charlie—Smithson told me he was going fishing."

"I expect he was," the deputy said. "But not in his favorite West

Texas creek." The keen-eyed Ute thought he saw a flicker of movement in the distant shadows. *Or maybe my eyes are playing tricks on me.* "Ray Smithson must've come to Granite Creek to fish around for information about a suspicious stranger who'd showed up in town—some unlikely tourist who was asking too many of the wrong kinds of questions. If Smithson got lucky, he would've set a hook into the hired gun Mrs. Hooten had sent to Granite Creek." That was, after all, the line of work the retired Texas Ranger angler knew best.

Parris could see some sense in Moon's notion. "Ol' Ranger Ray would've done whatever was necessary to protect his granddaughter."

"That's a fact," Moon said. "And the best way to do that was to keep a close eye on Louella Smithson's back. Smithson must've spotted his granddaughter's old Bronco this evening and followed it to Patsy's house."

This assertion by Moon raised a pertinent question. Though he hated to nitpick, Parris asked it: "But why would Smithson's own granddaughter shoot him, Charlie—and over a parking spot?"

"It don't seem very likely, does it?" Charlie Moon saw it again. Movement in the semidarkness. *That could be the Cowboy I'm looking for.*

Scott Parris was not born yesterday, and the Ute's theory about the dead man's being the famous ex-Texas ranger from Plainview, Texas, seemed like an awfully far reach. *Charlie Moon could sell ice cubes to an Eskimo.* After a doubtful glance at his enigmatic deputy, Parris went to check out a piece of allegedly supporting evidence. Squatting by the GMC pickup's front bumper, he narrowed his blue eyes. No surprise. *That's a Texas plate all right.* But that didn't prove that the driver was Ray Smithson. *What with these two conventions, I bet there are a dozen Texas pickups in the parking lot.* Which raised another pertinent question: *So how could Charlie be so danged sure that—*

Why did Scott Parris not complete this thought? Because the solution to the conundrum was about ten inches from his nose. His gaze had been drawn to the license plate's mounting frame, which advertised the name of a GMC–Chevrolet dealer in *Plainview.* The chief of police shook his head and grinned. *Ol' Charlie don't miss a trick, and he's gone and done it again.* As he grunted himself up from the painful squat, Granite Creek's heavyweight top cop opened his mouth to congratulate his clever deputy—when Charlie Moon uttered two electrifying words.

CHAPTER FIFTY-EIGHT

A BRIEF BUT MEMORABLE ENCOUNTER

So what were the deputy's two electrifying words? "Over there."

Not much as phrases go, but the effect was no less than . . . *kilovoltic.*

Charlie Moon aimed his forefinger at the far end of the Holiday Inn parking lot. A dome light had just flashed on, suggesting that someone had opened a car door. As the door was closed with a barely audible click, the light went out. An ordinary enough event in a parked automobile, but the longtime Ute lawman's *that's it* instinct had kicked in. The Indian uttered two more words that sparked his companions into instant action: "Let's go."

About sixty paces away, they observed one of those despicable mixed metaphors that set the teeth on edge: a sleek sedan beetling along, lights out—at a snail's pace.

As the formidable trio of lawmen strode along shoulder-to-shoulder, Moon addressed the big, brawny town cop on his left: "Please leave that little .38 in your shoulder holster, Scott—don't use it unless you absolutely have to."

That don't make any sense. "Why should I—"

"Because we need to take this suspect alive." That was not quite a half-truth, and Moon added another fraction that still didn't quite bring the sum up to a whole *one*: "It's important that you don't fire a shot." Moon knew that the Granite Creek mayor was just itching to rid himself of Scott Parris and any old excuse would do. *If you kill somebody that's suspected of murdering your sweetheart, your days as chief of police will be numbered.* Ignoring his friend's grumbling protest,

Moon turned his head to mumble to Officer Jackson, "If the driver so much as lays a finger on a firearm, you know what to do."

Ice-Eyes did and could and would—and he could hardly *wait*. His expression was that of a little boy about to open a gift on Christmas morning. *This is turning out better than I'd hoped.*

Indeed, things might have turned out just fine, but at precisely the worst possible moment, a GCPD black-and-white pulled into the parking lot behind the hotel—emergency lights flashing.

At this jarring development, the suspect sedan stopped dead still. As they might've said back in olden times when five cents was serious money, "on a half dime."

How a human being under pressure can just *know* things remains one of those murky mysteries well beyond our ken, but Charlie Moon *knew* that the driver was trying to decide whether to hide in the shadows or make a mad dash for it. The gambling man hoped for a compromise choice, and suggested it to the suspect . . . *Ease away real slow—like you had nowhere in particular to go and all night to get there.* Which would give the Indian time to come up with a plan. He picked up his pace. *But if you're not inclined to hang around—don't drive away like some little old lady on her way to church—make a run for it and don't stop for hell or high water!* That way, the perp would run right into one of the roadblocks.

Even before Moon offered this telepathic advice to the driver in the immobile automobile, Parris and Jackson had turned to wave the errant cop car to a stop.

As they did, the suspect sedan began to ease away at a doodlebug crawl.

Moon grinned. *That's it . . . don't go breaking any speed limits just yet—not till I get close enough to—*To do what? The unarmed deputy did not have the least germ of an idea.

But his right hand and his lean legs did.

Without looking back or giving the least thought to the possible consequences of his reckless actions, the keyed-up Ute picked up a big chunk of loose asphalt and broke into a hard run—directly at the sedan that was pulling away toward the far side of the hotel. This less-than-subtle approach did not go unnoticed by the other party.

When the driver saw the long-legged man running like he was about to break a record for the hundred-yard dash, a reaction occurred that the sprinter had not expected. The automobile turned abruptly and headed directly *at* Charlie Moon—picking up speed as the distance between them closed.

Having no desire to play moth with the automobile's gleaming grille, the hopeful athlete stopped in his tracks and did what any red-blooded American sports fan would do: he assumed the classic pitcher's stance, wound up like a seasoned pro, whispered a three-word prayer, unleashed his best knuckleball at the vehicle with all his strength, and slipped—no, not to fall down like Scott Parris had in the icy supermarket parking lot; Moon slipped between two parked cars. And just as the asphalt missile connected with the oncoming sedan's windshield—which shattered white with a jumbo-size spider crack.

Understandably startled by this unforeseen development, the driver lost control of the sleek motor vehicle, which promptly careened into a sturdy-as-the-Rock-of-Gibraltar concrete base of a twenty-four-foot-tall light pole, which steel reed began to swing back and forth like a coconut palm in a tropical storm.

Moon gritted his teeth at the sound of the collision. The poker player figured the odds at ninety-nine to one that he knew who was behind the wheel of the totaled product of a Detroit assembly line. But . . . *With my luck, Cowboy drove away ten minutes ago and this'll turn out to be a hotshot Philadelphia trial lawyer on vacation who hates Colorado cops and his great-great-granddaddy was scalped by a Ute Indian.* Moreover (Moon imagined), the attorney would have . . . *a perfect record of suing halfwit deputies for every dime they've got socked away and all the real estate they own and then some.*

Which extravagant image, as one might expect, did not accurately depict the driver of the wrecked sedan.

Nevertheless, things were about to get more than moderately

interesting for Mr. Moon and his two lawman comrades, who had lost interest in the GCPD black-and-white with the still-flashing lights. The state trooper and the chief of police were rapidly closing in on the scene of the serious motor-vehicle accident—for which Scott Parris's unpredictable deputy was entirely responsible.

CHAPTER FIFTY-NINE

IT AIN'T OVER TILL—

The point is, the assassin for hire in the wrecked rental car was neither dead nor seriously injured. One might rightly assign credit (or blame?) for this outcome to the well-designed air bag that had exploded from the steering wheel at the instant of impact, thereby protecting the driver from the full force of the tooth-jarring, eyeball-popping collision. This unhappy outcome will be no great surprise to those erudites among us who are informed by numerous "thrillers"; such literary scholars know all too well that extremely dangerous villains are never dead when by all rights they should be. Those bloodthirsty brutes are not only *very much alive*—they are ready, willing, and able to create serious mischief before their eventual demise at the hand of the good guy.

Lacking this expert knowledge that can be gained only by intensive study of carefully contrived fiction, neither Charlie Moon nor Scott Parris nor Officer Jackson, was concerned about a sudden and deadly attack from the passenger in the totaled vehicle. But do not look askance at these public servants; their misplaced confidence was hardly surprising. Counting the pair of befuddled GCPD officers in the unwelcome squad car, there were five determined cops pitted against one cold-blooded felon who wasn't likely to have any fight left. The lawmen's bias was that in real-life situations, those who experience head-on encounters with concrete bases of lampposts are normally dazed and discombobulated for at least a few minutes, and cannot correctly answer such questions as "What year is it?"; "Who is the current president of the United States?"; or "Where do you want your body sent, hairball?" And even if this particular accident victim's brain was functioning like a fine Swiss clockwork, the odds against a comeback were daunting.

In all fairness to the constables, it shall be stated for the record that the driver *was* somewhat addled by the collision. Which fact obliges us—despite the assassin's admitted moral shortcomings—to give credit where credit is due. As soon as the driver's bruised and swollen eyes opened and her vision began to clear, she saw the fuzzy images of three large men approaching her wrecked rental car—and understood the utter hopelessness of the situation. Did she wilt like a picked-last-week black-eyed Susan in a vase of tepid tap water, and wait to be cuffed and led away like a common criminal?

You know that she did not.

Acting more on stubbornness than instinct, the plucky lady produced a .32-caliber silenced Browning automatic pistol—the same weapon with which she had shot the troublesome pickup driver—when Ray Smithson inquired, "What'n hell are *you* doing driving my granddaughter's Bronco?" Thus armed, she managed to push the car door open with her left elbow, get both feet firmly onto the asphalt, and aim her sidearm at the widest of the oncoming male targets—which was Scott Parris, who was fumbling for the .38 nestled in his shoulder holster.

As it happened, Daisy Perika was not present to witness this verifying climax of her breakfast-vision, and shout, "No—stop!" And even if she had been, the tribal elder would not have uttered a word to prevent a shooting that was bound to happen. And even if she had protested, the slender, single-minded state trooper under the flat-brimmed Smoky hat would not have paid Daisy's plea for the woman's life the slightest heed.

—IT'S OVER . . . ALMOST
(EXCEPT FOR THE HARD PART)

Approximately a quarter second before Miss Whysper could pull the trigger on Scott Parris, a 9-mm round erupted from the barrel of Officer "Ice-Eyes" Jackson's sidearm. The spinning projectile passed through the delicate bridge of her nose and drilled through that marvelously complex tissue behind the nasal sinuses where sweet dreams and horrific nightmares alike are produced. The requisite damage done, the half-spent lump of lead popped out of the posterior side of her head to ricochet off the roof of the severely dented rental sedan—to sail off to who knows or cares where. (For those who do, into the resinous trunk of that stunted, twisted cedar over there—the one beside the stumpy red fireplug.)

Her lights thus snuffed out, her earthly sojourn finished, the assassin dropped like a bag of rocks. A fitting end? It would seem so.

All three lawmen had good reason to be satisfied with the outcome, but it would be premature to celebrate Miss Whysper's going away. This day's night was about to get darker still for some. You know who, and can count them on one finger—and a thumb.

CHAPTER SIXTY

THE HARD PART?

Not just yet. Charlie Moon is working his way up to that dismal duty ever so slowly . . . imagine the rancher pouring old, cold sorghum molasses from a crockery jug onto a winter's morning stack of piping-hot flapjacks.

Before our deliberate deputy gets around to that sticky business, Scott Parris has a reasonable request to make of his best friend. But not before expressing his heartfelt appreciation to the Colorado state policeman whose pistol still smoked in his rock-steady hand. "Thank you, Officer Jackson."

"You are welcome, Chief Parris." As Ice-Eyes holstered his weapon, he realized that this day's work was about done, and the man's thoughts naturally turned to personal matters. Such as what he might enjoy for supper. *A medium-rare T-bone at the Sugar Bowl?* That'd sure hit the well-known spot. *And a baked spud with sour cream and chives.* Plus a couple of hot sourdough rolls soaked with real butter. *I'll wash it all down with big mug of black coffee.*

THE CHIEF OF POLICE EXPRESSES A DESIRE FOR CLARIFICATION

Having expressed his gratitude to Jackson, Scott Parris turned his attention to the deputy who'd insisted that he refrain from shooting the suspect. True, none of them suspected that the driver in the wrecked car might pose a deadly threat, but . . . *Charlie Moon's advice almost got me killed.* And the Ute was not known for putting a brother lawman's life in jeopardy. Which curious circumstance raised that universal question so often posed by betrayed lovers, four-year-olds who delight in vexing their long-suffering mothers— and old friends who are simply puzzled.

Reading the *why* in his friend's blue eyes, Parris's deputy cast a meaningful glance at the state-police officer.

Recognizing the make-yourself-scarce signal and realizing why Charlie Moon needed some time alone with his friend, Jackson mumbled something about the necessity of reporting his shooting of an armed suspect at the Holiday Inn. After casting a sorrowful glance at the GCPD chief of police, the state trooper strode away to put in the call.

Barely aware of Jackson's departure, Scott Parris also ignored the commotion the car wreck and shooting had created among various police and civilian spectators. Having filtered out all this superfluous background noise, he put the question directly to Charlie Moon: "Why didn't you want me to shoot her?"

"My mistake, pardner—a bad call, I guess." The most forthright man the ex-Chicago cop had ever encountered was avoiding his gaze. "But all things considered, I figured it was best if someone else did it." *And I'd left my pistol at home.*

Knowing half an answer when he heard one, Parris snorted. "It's high time for some straight talk, Charlie."

"Okay, pard." Moon looked him right in the eyes. "But you're not going to like what I've got to say." An understatement that Parris would remember until the day he drew his final breath.

WHAT CHARLIE MOON HAD TO SAY

He commenced with a question: "D'you recall what Special Agent McTeague told us about Mrs. Hooten wanting you and me to suffer like she had?"

Their afternoon teleconference with the fed seemed ages away—a previous lifetime. "Lemme think." Parris closed his eyes in an effort to recollect, and did. "Oh, right—the old crank's confined to a wheelchair. She wants you and me to end up the same way, so she sends a shooter to cripple both of us." The thought of getting kneecapped with a .32-caliber chunk of red-hot lead, or his spine shattered with a bigger number than that, was more scary than getting shot stone-cold dead. The macho cop shrugged off the threat. "So what—she's a nutty old woman who doted on her lowlife, purse-snatching, son-of-a-bitch son, who'd be alive today if the jackass hadn't plied his trade here in Granite Creek. What do we care *what* she said?" *Now that the shooter's dead.*

Ignoring his friend's more or less hypothetical query, Moon continued. "When Mrs. Hooten said we ought to suffer *like she had,* I figure she meant it literally—but in a different sense."

"Don't make this too hard for me, Charlie." The spent cop leaned against the assassin's wrecked automobile. "It's been a kind of busy afternoon, and my thinker is running on fumes." His gaze locked with Miss Whysper's blank stare. *I wonder what goes wrong, for a smart young woman like that to take up killing folks to make a living.*

Ignoring the warm corpse at their feet, Moon continued. "The notion that Mrs. Hooten wanted us crippled was Bureau Intelligence's majority opinion." Taking professional note of the 9-mm hole between Missy Whysper's eyes, he could not help admiring Jackson's marksmanship. "McTeague wasn't authorized to pass on the *minority* view, but I'd lay ten-to-one odds that she leaned toward that one—and wanted us to figure it out for ourselves."

"I'm so tired I couldn't add two to three and get four. I mean *five.*" Parris tried to rub imaginary sand from his eyes. "Tell me straight-out what's on your mind."

"It's just a best guess, but here's how it looks to me. The way Mrs. Hooten sees it, we're a couple of brutal cops who deliberately killed her son." The Indian turned a dark gaze on his friend. "That score has to be settled, and she's an old-fashioned mother who prefers the 'eye for eye, tooth for tooth' kind of justice." The Ute felt a frigid breeze caress the back of his neck. "The best way to make us suffer the way *she's* suffering would be to send a hired gun to kill *our* sons."

"Well, maybe so." Numb as his brain was, a salient factoid occurred to Scott Parris. The lonely bachelor felt obliged to share it. "I don't have a son." He managed an anemic smile. "And unless you've been keeping a deep secret from your best buddy for all these years—neither do you."

"I don't have a son, pard—and neither one of us has a daughter." The deputy helped himself to a breath of chill night air. "Or any close family left."

Parris was beginning to get a glimmer of what was brewing in the Indian's brain. "But you practically have yourself a wife."

"That's a fact." Loath to continue along this dreary pathway, Moon refreshed himself with a happy thought: *And next month, I will have one.* He cleared his throat. "I also have—or *used* to have a foreman. And Pete had himself a fine wife."

Parris stared at the dead assassin, blinking twice. "You figure it was Miss Whysper that murdered the Bushmans?"

Moon nodded. "Last night at supper, Dolly invited our Columbine houseguest over to the Big Hat today for coffee. The invitation was declined." The rancher lifted his chin to gaze at a sooty-dark sky. *Somewhere up yonder, maybe a billion light-years away, stars are twinkling.* "But sometime this afternoon, the Bushmans both died from a blow on the head—just like LeRoy Hooten."

"Okay. Let's say Miss Whysper offed the Bushmans." Heaving a great sigh, the town cop posed another question: "But why didn't she raise a hand against either Daisy or Sarah?"

"Professional killers aren't generally suicidal," Moon murmured. "A double murder at the Columbine was too risky. But if Sarah or Daisy had been away from the ranch today . . ."

"Okay." Parris glared at the corpse. "But it still don't add up, Charlie. Just last evening, we found this woman in Miss Smithson's hotel room. And when I went downstairs to check her out, the name on the register was Louella Smithson."

"And like you said a few minutes ago, Miss Smithson wouldn't be likely to shoot her granddaddy dead." The rancher eyed the assassin's corpse with detached professional interest, as if examining a coyote he'd killed for raiding the chicken pen. "Which raises a couple of pertinent questions. What was Miss Whysper doing in Miss Smithson's hotel room—and where is the real Louella Smithson?"

Parris shrugged. "Beats me."

The Indian turned his face toward the direction from which they'd come. "Miss Smithson's body is back at Patsy's house—in that burned-out Bronco."

"Oh, right." Having temporarily forgotten about that particular corpse, the Caucasian lawman felt a surge of nausea. *I'd have to get better to die.* "So how'd the corpse get there?"

"That's where Miss Whysper left it last evening."

"You figure she followed Ray Smithson's granddaughter to the Holiday Inn?"

"Sure. And then into the lobby, and to her room." Count three Charlie Moon heartbeats. "Maybe the assassin intended to do the job there, but for one reason or another she didn't have the opportunity." Two more heartbeats. "But Miss Smithson must've gone back outside to get something out of her car. That has to be where it happened."

"Okay." Parris closed his eyes long enough to view the hideous picture. "Whysper follows Smithson back out to the parking lot, and probably loops the wire around her neck just as she opens the Bronco door." Imagining the horror of being strangled to death, the lawman tried to swallow past a constriction in his throat. He could not quite manage it.

Moon picked up on the story. "Miss Whysper took the keys to the Bronco and the hotel room off her victim, and left Miss Smithson in the Bronco. Then—cool as you please—she went back inside to see what she could find in room 215. She probably wanted to find out how much Miss Smithson knew about her, and who she might've shared her knowledge with." Charlie Moon glanced at the Hertz sticker on the wrecked sedan. "If the four of us hadn't shown up while she was still in Miss Smithson's hotel room—reading whatever interesting stuff she could find on her victim's pink laptop computer—I expect she'd have driven off in her rental car a few minutes later." Parris's deputy took a brief look at the Holiday Inn's rear windows, where dozens of curious cattlemen tourists were gazing into the parking lot and wondering *what in tarnation* was going on out there. "Miss Whysper would've hightailed it in her own wheels right after we left, but I invited her to stay the night at the Columbine while she *researched her book.*"

"Well," Parris admitted, "her staying at your ranch was my idea." *But this is getting crazier and crazier.* "Being cool is one thing, Charlie. But it's hard to believe that Miss Whysper drove that old Bronco all the way to your ranch last evening—with Louella Smithson's corpse *still inside.*"

"She didn't have much choice, pardner—if she'd left the old heap here in the parking lot, someone might've spotted the dead body after the sun come up." *And soon as she parked it at the Columbine, Sidewinder picked up a scent of human remains—and all that howling late that night was his way of telling me about it.* The Ute made a promise to himself: *From now on, I'll pay more attention to what dogs have to say.*

Scott Parris was still trying to wrap his head around Charlie Moon's grisly scenario. "And today, the assassin hauls Miss Smithson's cold cadaver *back* to town?"

The deputy nodded. "With a short stopover at the Big Hat, where she took care of some business."

"That is *really* cold-blooded." The hard-bitten lawman, who thought he'd seen and heard just about everything a man could encounter in his line of work, could not suppress a shudder. "She must've taken us for a couple of idiots." An additional embarrassing detail occurred to Parris. "Miss Whysper couldn't very well check out of the Holiday Inn—because she'd never checked in. So she finagled the local chief of police into checking Louella Smithson out."

"Last night, she was on her toes all right." *But something upset Miss Whysper this morning at breakfast.* The Ute paused as he recalled the ghost story his aunt had recounted during that meal. Something about a dead woman who'd come to Daisy's bedside last night, and claimed she was locked inside a truck somewhere. Like other rugged SUVs, the stolen Bronco that Miss Whysper had driven to the Columbine was classified as a *truck.* Was it a mere coincidence that the murderer had gotten choked on something from her plate—or had his guest been startled by the suggestion that Louella Smithson's disembodied presence had drifted into the Columbine headquarters last night—to tell Daisy that her corpse was outside in the Bronco? Perhaps Miss Whysper had shared Aunt Daisy's belief in haunts who make their appearance during those dark hours when their dim light might be seen. And then, lurking in that darkest closet of his mind, was the unthinkable possibility.

It whispered to him from behind a securely locked door: *Maybe Louella Smithson's spirit really* did *visit Daisy.*

This suggestion was summarily dismissed.

Charlie Moon did not care to go there. If a man doesn't want to slip off the deep end and never come up again, he has to draw the line somewhere.

CHAPTER SIXTY-ONE

ALMOST THERE

While Charlie Moon mused about his aunt Daisy's ghostly experiences and other imponderables, Scott Parris hardly had a thought in his head; the lawman stared blankly at nothing whatever. *I could lay down right here in the parking lot and go to sleep.* To slumber dreamlessly forever . . . to awaken never. "I'm sorry, Charlie." He lowered his head and groaned. "But I'm worn out. All this is just too much to deal with."

It ain't over yet, pardner. "Take a break Scott; rest your bones and brain."

Parris seated himself on a section of front bumper that projected from the wreckage.

To Charlie Moon's practiced eye, his best friend resembled an over-the-hill, weak-in-the knees heavyweight contender who'd taken too many hard punches. A light tap on the chin and Parris might go down for the full count. But there was no way out—somebody was bound to land the knockout blow. Moon assumed (and rightly so) that the officers who'd arrived in the GCPD black-and-white had been sent to break the horrific news about Tiffany Mayfair's murder to the chief of police. The reason for the deputy's dark suspicion? Just this: the uniformed cops, understandably loath to perform their thankless duty, had remained securely in their unit—putting off the unhappy encounter with the boss for as long as possible. But delaying a dose of unpleasant medicine only makes the eventual remedy that much harder to spoon out . . . and to swallow. So Charlie Moon was elected, and the man in the black hat knew that . . . *One way or another, I've got to get this business over and done with.* But not until Scott at least had a chance to catch his breath.

Somewhere off in the darkness, a lonesome, home-alone, back-yard beagle barked twice and then whined.

Nearer by, a pickup's radio suddenly boomed full-blast with a sad 1950s Hank Williams ballad. (Old Hank was so lonely he could *cry.*)

The hound let out a prolonged, mournful howl—as if crooning a melancholy duet with his forlorn soul mate. As oftentimes happens after nightfall, the heartfelt canine yodel seemed uncannily appropriate.

Behind an open hotel window, a drunken woman's shrill laugh cut through the night like a steak knife slicing off a raw slice of blackest despair.

The Ute waited with characteristic patience. Stolid as a knotty-pine Indian stationed in front of a cigar store, Charlie Moon counted his heavy heartbeats.

On ventricular contraction number forty-two, the stone mask slipped off Parris's face. He rubbed at his eyes.

Moon: "You feeling some better, pardner?"

"Almost as good as death warmed over." As he got to his feet, Scott Parris returned Moon's gaze and was startled to see the bleak expression there. *Charlie has something else that needs telling.* The lawman who didn't want to hear any more bad news today could not help asking, "So what's gnawing at you?"

Presented with the invitation he'd been waiting for—and dreading—the deputy held his tongue. Say what you will of tired old maxims and tedious clichés, there are occasions when silence does speak louder than words. The Ute's tight lips fairly screamed.

The chief of police was aware of a slight buzz in his ears, a dreadful tingling in his fingertips. "There's something about Whysper you haven't told me."

The time had come. Moon pointed his boot toe at the silenced .32-caliber automatic just inches from the assassin's hand. "When you banged on that hotel-room door last night, we're lucky that Cowboy didn't think we'd showed up to make an arrest—and shoot us dead."

"Yeah." The white cop stared dumbly at the lethal weapon.

The Ute angler dangled the terrible bait: "If it'd been *just you and me* at the door, we probably wouldn't be here anymore."

"Yeah." Scott Parris didn't bite. "Good thing Whysper realized that we took her for Louella Smithson." *That was a sure-enough close call.*

He sure ain't making this easy. Like a blind man stepping into quicksand, Charlie Moon pressed on. "Once she realized our mistake, Miss Whysper must've figured she'd hit the jackpot. She's in Miss Smithson's hotel room for a few minutes, checking out her victim's personal effects—and you and me show up like a couple of clowns . . . *with our lady friends.*" The deputy held his breath. *Please. Take the hint.*

"Right." Parris helped himself to a half portion of the suggestion. "And when she learns that you're engaged to Patsy, the hired gun knows right away who one of her intended victims is. But tonight, she mistook Patsy's sister for—" This thought was interrupted by a wrenching coldness that twisted his gut. *It's unlikely, but just to be on the safe side . . .* "I'd better call Tiffany and make sure she's all right."

Moon heard his mouth say, "That call has already been made, pardner."

"Thanks, Charlie—you think of everything." The exhausted cop closed his eyes. "I'm glad that this is all over and done with."

Charlie Moon averted his gaze from his friend's haggard face. "I wish it was." And, *I wish I was someplace ten thousand miles from here so somebody else would have to tell you.*

NOW FOR THE HARD PART

Scott Parris's bull neck was sore from shaking his head, but he did it again. "The murderer's laying here stone-cold dead at our feet—Patsy and Tiffany are okay—and as far as we know, Patsy's sister will survive." *And we already know the Bushmans are dead.* "So what's the big problem I *don't* know about?"

As he tried to find his voice, Charlie Moon was fearful that he wouldn't be able to pull this off.

Parris was also afraid; his fear increased when he saw the Indian's deathly grim expression.

"I'm sorry, pard. Clara Tavishuts made the call to check on Professor Mayfair, but . . ." That was all Moon could get past his lips.

It was sufficient.

"Oh, God . . . *no.*" Having taken the hit square on the chin, Tiffany Mayfair's sweetheart reeled and grabbed at the wrecked sedan's open door.

Charlie Moon reached out to steady his friend.

The stricken man blinked at the darkness, and his voice was hoarse with dread. "Tiffany . . . you're telling me she's actually *dead*?" Such a horror did not seem possible.

Moon nodded.

Light-years beyond a rage that he could not express without slipping into madness, Scott Parris was rescued by his brain—which shifted into mind-survival mode.

The deputy was chilled to see his old friend revert to his former Chicago PD persona—a gruff, big-city cop inquiring about a run-of-the-mill homicide.

"So how'd Whysper do it, Charlie—gunshot?"

"No. Same as with Pete, Dolly—and Patsy's sister. A blow to the head."

"Like the purse snatcher got his." Eye for eye. Tooth for tooth. *All this because I tossed a damn can of black-eyed peas at a petty criminal who wasn't worth lizard spit!* Ever so gradually, Parris returned to himself. One salty bead at a time, the tough guy's eyes filled with bitter tears, and his husky voice made a plea: "Tiffany must've died . . . passed quickly." *Please tell me she did.*

"Of course she did, pard. It was all over before the lady knew what'd happened." *But she must've seen it coming.* The deputy recalled an incident a long time ago in Ignacio when a delivery van running a Stop sign had hit his bicycle. Time had slowed in the instant of impact; a fractional second stretched into a minute—and then the lights went out. But that was way back when and this was right now.

"One dead assassin." As Parris toed the pistol away from Miss Whysper's stiffening fingers, he counted the others. Louella Smithson, whom he'd never met. Her fine old Texas Ranger granddaddy.

Pete and Dolly Bushman. And of course . . . Tiffany. "Five upstanding citizens to one lowlife—that ain't a very good score for the home team, Charlie."

"That it's not, pard."

Yes, Parris's count was short, but neither he nor his deputy was aware of the brutal murder of upstanding citizen number six. The cold, gray corpse of Special Agent Mary Anne Clayton, aka Marcella Clay, lay on a stainless-steel tray in an unspecified federal morgue in Prince George County. Was this outstanding public servant to be forgotten by her government? Perish the very thought. And neither would the woman who had dispatched the assassin to Granite Creek County. The Agent Clayton case would not be closed until the remains of Francine Hooten were six feet under the sod, and an anonymous—

But should such an unseemly, unofficial ritual be revealed?

You bet.

The Agent Clayton case would not be closed until the remains of Francine Hooten were six feet under the sod and an anonymous special agent (who'd selected the cherished short straw) had *urinated on Mrs. Hooten's grave.*

But that victory celebration was somewhere far over the yonder horizon. In the meantime, what about the Colorado lawmen? They had suffered through a month-long day; there was nothing more to say. Not with words.

During the ensuing silence, Scott Parris wept openly, his heavy shoulders heaving with every sob.

No less wounded than his best friend, Charlie Moon didn't taste the salty blood he'd bitten from his lip.

CHAPTER SIXTY-TWO

SAYING GOODBYE
(VARIATIONS ON A THEME)

We are assured (by those *in the know*) that funerals in whatever form serve the worthy function of comforting the bereaved, and in many instances this is no doubt so. But what about those silent players who occupy center stage at these solemn rituals? More to the point—do the spirits of the dearly departed linger long enough to witness the final ceremonies performed in their honor?

For some of us, the question of ghosts remains one of those open issues—perhaps to be resolved when we are eventually privileged (or not) to view the subject from a distinctly different perspective.

Those who are convinced that matter "is all that is or ever was or ever will be" will smile (or even sneer) at such a naïve question. But note that by actual count, some 82 percent of these no-nonsense folk talk to dogs, cats—and grave markers.

There are, of course, firmly opposing views that are based upon sacred tradition, impressive anecdotal evidence, and compelling personal experience.

Fascinating as it might be to examine these conflicting opinions in great depth and with considerable sensitivity, we prefer to proceed as all moderns do when it is necessary to settle a knotty issue. We shall take a poll. No, do not anticipate an extremely annoying robocall at 10:00 P.M. This is strictly a shoestring operation, so in the interest of economy this survey of the population will not be strictly scientific—our sample size is *one*. (PhD statisticians will please resist the compelling urge to offer helpful advice.)

Who is this randomly selected, perfectly average citizen who will have the awesome responsibility of accurately representing hundreds of millions? A hint: her initials are D.P.

THE RESULTS ARE IN

Here they are:

It would never occur to Daisy Perika to question the existence of disembodied spirits; as we already know, she is intimately acquainted with dozens of them. And as to the question of whether these wispy wraiths habitually linger in the vicinity of their funerals, the tribal elder knows for a *fact* that they do. According to the old woman who can see dead people (so she ought to know), the ghostly presence usually remains near the corpse for several days after death has undone the tie that binds mortal flesh to that essence of personality which *cannot die.* And why shouldn't they enjoy their big send-off? The Southern Ute tribal elder will look you right in the eye and tell you that any ghost who was born in the good old U.S. of A. has a constitutional right to attend her (or his) own going-away celebration if she (or he) is of a mind to—and then hover around until the burial is a done deal. Do not waste time arguing the point with Charlie Moon's irascible auntie, who will advise you as follows: "Anybody who don't understand that is a big gourd-head!" So Daisy has asserted on several occasions to Charlie Moon or any other well-intentioned ignoramus who happened to aggravate her by raising vexing questions about "what anybody with half a brain knows."

But the truth of a matter of honest doubt is not determined by who shouts the loudest. Until the matter is finally settled, we may consider apparently conflicting testimony from presumably reliable witnesses. (Daisy insists on being heard again on this subject, and firstly.)

FOND FAREWELLS TO THE CANTANKEROUS COLUMBINE FOREMAN AND HIS SWEET WIFE

In addition to a crowd of local citizens from all walks of life, practically every ranching family in GC County turned out for Pete and Dolly Bushman's graveside service. The solemnities were performed at the Columbine's small cemetery, which is located atop Pine Knob. Even the eldest of the old-timers managed to ride a horse through the cold, rolling, waist-deep river that waters Charlie Moon's Herefords and alfalfa crop, and not a few of those hardy souls will have crossed over that final River before another winter passes.

How many spirits did Daisy Perika see lurking around the fresh grave site? Dolly and Pete were present (so she says), and the tribal elder reports the visible presence of a half-dozen others. Four of these told the old woman that they'd been buried on the barren hilltop by her nephew. (Such claims cannot be verified; only one of the graves the Ute had filled was provided with a marker—and for good reason.) The shaman also sensed a gathering of *unseen* specters, and these outnumbered the visible spirits. It was Daisy's professional opinion that this latter congregation had been haunting the lonely old graveyard for a long time before the Columbine Ranch was established.

SAYING ADIOS TO THE EX-TEXAS RANGER
AND HIS FAVORITE GRANDDAUGHTER

About a week after Pete and Dolly were laid to rest on the Knob, Charlie Moon and Scott Parris were among dozens of lawmen—mostly Texas Rangers, middle-aged and retired—who attended the burial service for Ray and Louella Smithson on Ray's little ranch out west of Plainview. Neither Charlie nor Scott had anything uncanny to report, and if anyone among the local mourners saw a ghost, that taciturn Texan kept it to himself.

But something did happen that may be worth mentioning. We'll let an old gent by the name of "Turkey" Bob Wilson tell it: "Just as six strong men was a-lowerin' Ray's pine box into that sandy slot in the ground, why here come this rip-roarin' dust devil—and I tell you, it like to blew the short whiskers right offa my chin!" When asked what he made of this curious event, Mr. Wilson replied, "Oh, there's no figurin' these West Texas whirlwinds—I s'pose it dropped by just to make ol' Ray's send-off interestin'."

Perhaps so.

But more than one old lawman held on to his Stetson and thought as he grinned, *It's Ray Smithson's way of sayin', "See you later, ol' friends—somewhere down yonder where the trail ends."*

THE PROFESSOR'S MEMORIAL SERVICE

We refer to the solemn send-off for Ms. Tiffany Mayfair, which staid farewell was conducted in a New England township that shall remain unnamed. Picture-postcard-perfect village though it was, Scott Parris *did not want to go there*. That's what the recently bereaved boyfriend assured himself after he was not invited to attend the affair—which privilege was limited to immediate family members and a few select friends. This latter group pointedly did *not* include an uncouth ex-Chicago cop boyfriend who was four years older than Tiffany's daddy. Scott is getting somewhat long in the tooth to be romancing a fluffy-headed youth, but any honest rowdy in Granite Creek will tell you that Chief Parris is *every bit* as couth as any other big-fisted, hard-hitting hombre you're likely to meet on Copper Street. (And this hardcase is liable to deck you for looking at him crosswise.)

But enough about Scott Parris. The scholarly issue being addressed herein is whether (or not) anyone present at the going-away sensed something that suggested the presence of Tiffany's spiritual essence. (Such as a whiff of her favorite perfume.)

The answer is: we flat *don't know*. Within such hermetically sealed inner circles as that of the Mayfair clan, it is virtually impossible to find a reliable informant.

EXIT ONE LEROY HOOTEN

As her son's earthly remains were deposited in the weedy rose garden behind the crumbling family mansion, Francine Hooten was the only person present to witness the interment. Unless you count Cushing, the butler (who remained a respectful distance away), and the hired man with the rented backhoe, who Francine did not (count him). She did pay the latter citizen the agreed five-hundred-dollar (cash money) fee for digging the eight-by-three-by-six-foot (deep) hole, lowering the bronze casket, and filling it. (The hole, not the casket.) Francine also tipped the hireling a crisp new twenty-dollar bill for tamping the mound of dirt down neatly before chugging away in the sturdy Bobcat.

Though Mrs. Hooten had risked a great deal to avenge her son's death, during the burial she did not shed a single salty tear. Cold-hearted? Perhaps. But do not dismiss the wheelchair-bound woman as a lonely widow who has been bested and beaten. Francine's defeat is real and hard to bear—but temporary. Before she goes away, the lady is determined to have her final say.

Did the mother see her son's ghost? No.

But we shall take note of the fact that the gravedigger was happy to depart from the desolate burial spot. Whether or not he'd spotted something a man would rather not see cannot be determined with certainty. But as soon as he'd returned the backhoe to Polk's Heavy Equipment Rentals & Floral Gifts (a nifty pop-and-mom shop), he dropped in at his favorite tavern. Nothing unusual about that. Except that the sober citizen who chugged down maybe a half-dozen beers in an entire year treated himself to a couple of shots of straight Jack Daniel's. Then a couple more. Before long, the hardworking man had squandered a significant portion of the day's profits at Duncan's Bar & Grill. Before much longer, he fell off the stool, sprawling unconscious on the filthy barroom floor. The higher-class drunks laughed at the unfortunate soul and made unseemly remarks.

Which doesn't prove that Mr. Gravedigger saw anything scary when he put Mr. LeRoy Hooten under the sod.

MISSY WHYSPER, AKA THE COWBOY ASSASSIN

During the next several months, the Federal Bureau of Investigation would apply every means available to modern forensic science in an effort to identify her body. Yes, without success.

Evidently, neither the woman's fingerprints, toe prints, nor DNA profile had been recorded in any database available to the Bureau. There had been some minor dental work done on three molars and a cracked bicuspid, but all attempts to locate the skilled dentist would come to naught. The shady lady had nine known aliases, almost as many Social Security numbers, and motor vehicle driver's licenses from seven states—plus Alberta.

Aside from a three-minute ecumenical service provided by a semi-retired Anglican FBI chaplain, Miss Whysper would have no formal send-off to the Eternal Mystery. Her unclaimed corpse will reside in the Bureau's facility in Chicago until it is identified. Or (and this is more likely) forgotten.

As far as we know, no one at the FBI has reported seeing a spirit hovering above her earthly remains. But those feds who tote sidearms and eat bank robbers for breakfast and kidnappers for lunch are a tight-lipped bunch.

CHAPTER SIXTY-THREE

THE GAME-CHANGING DELIVERY

No, not a red-hot fastball sizzlin' over home plate, the introduction of a lovable infant to the light of day, or any kind of murky metaphor you can call to mind. This was one of those *literal* deliveries—and by FedEx. Here comes the truck right this minute—roaring down the Columbine lane, kicking up brown gravel and gritty dust like a wild-eyed bull buffalo on a dead run toward anyplace under the sun but where he's acomin' from.

A marginal note: those high-octane parcel-delivery drivers are endowed with loads of get-up-and-go. They also have tight schedules to meet and not two ticktocks of the clock to waste. Not a few of 'em (and this was one) enjoy making the dramatic high-velocity entrance and do not mind scattering flocks of nervous turkeys, honking geese, or chickens of any description.

Sad to say, Charlie Moon does not keep any feathered livestock.

The sturdy van rolled into the Columbine headquarters yard at high noon *on the dot*. The hyper driver was out of her seat about one heartbeat after the vehicle braked to a stop under a gaunt, lonesome lady cottonwood who's been standing right on the spot for ninety-two years without ever receiving a single string-tied parcel, scented love letter—or as much as a penny postcard from someone who wished she were here. Or there. Whichever.

Such visits were not unusual. An operation the size of the Columbine Land and Cattle Company received at least a dozen parcels weekly from UPS and their major competitor. Charlie Moon knew all the drivers by name and temperament. The AAA member also knew that by the sweat of her brow, this particular FedEx employee was supporting an alcoholic husband, a doped-up, dropped-out daughter, and (on the plus side) two darling grandchildren.

Moon stepped outside the west door of the headquarters to meet this lean, hard-muscled, late-middle-aged woman. He waved as she approached with an armload of cardboard boxes and inquired as she deposited her burden on the redwood-planked porch, "How's the family, Paula?"

The hardworking lady paused long enough to roll her eyes heavenward and say, "As well as can be expected—you got any outgoing today?"

"No, but I'll have a couple of boxes on Friday."

"Works for me." She was already marching away to the idling van. "See you then, Charlie."

THE EAVESDROPPER

Why was Daisy Perika at a parlor window, peering out between slightly parted curtains? Possibly because the arrival of a delivery truck was generally the high point of the tribal elder's day. That, and the fact that the old woman took an almost childish delight in spying on her nephew—or anyone else who might have private business to conduct. As it turns out, Charlie did. Even though he didn't know it.

WHAT HE HAD DREADED

As Charlie Moon knelt to gather up the parcels, he spotted the return address on a smallish item and his heart almost stopped. But *almost* is a long way from cardiac arrest, and this development was not entirely unexpected. *She hardly ever answers the phone when I call and never returns my messages.* Leaving the other deliveries untouched, he took the deadly thing to the porch swing and seated himself— the rusty suspension chains creaking under his weight. He had no desire to open this parcel that would destroy his last hopes, but his nimble fingers were busy doing just that. And before the prospective jilt-ee could blink, there it was—nestled inside in a comfy bed of Bubble Wrap. The familiar hinged, velvet-covered, satin-lined box.

There was also a small, pink envelope—factory-scented to enhance the wild-rose pattern printed on it. To the grim-faced recipient's nostrils, the fragrance was *funereal*.

THE RECRUIT

Astonished at her good fortune, Daisy turned to jerk her head at Sarah Frank—a gesture whose unmistakable meaning was, "Come over here *right now!*"

THE KISS-OFF

Setting the jewelry box aside on the swing, Charlie Moon opened the envelope with all the enthusiasm of an about-to-be-lynched rustler who was obliged to dig his own grave. The tear-stained note inside—it was too brief to be considered a letter—would contain no surprises. The doomed groom already knew more or less what his erstwhile fiancée would have penned. And so he made no attempt to read it carefully, as would a man who had some hope left. As he scanned the brief epistle, the disconnected phrases impressed the gist of the message upon his numb consciousness.

> *Dear Charlie . . . Daphne is improving slowly . . . long period of convalescence . . . I'm really needed here . . . rented my Granite Creek home to a sweet couple . . . with an option to buy . . . given the circumstances . . . doesn't seem fair to keep your ring . . . so I'm returning it . . . maybe someday we'll . . . so sorry, Charlie . . . Love and Kisses . . . Patsy*

Both in explanations and kindness, this rejection was superior to the previous two—and more hurtful than both combined. But the fair-minded man realized that Patsy was not to blame: she'd come very close to losing her sister in Granite Creek. *She might not ever set foot in town again.*

It was Miss Whysper who'd brought all these troubles with her, and the assassin whom Francine Hooten had sent to Granite Creek County had already paid with her life. But what really got the bad business started was the arrival of her thieving son, who just happened to snatch a purse in the supermarket parking lot *at the very moment* when Scott Parris was close at hand. And the chief of police had made a one-in-a-thousand toss of a can of peas that connected with LeRoy Hooten's skull.

Anywhere along the way, the merest intervention of fate might have altered this dismal future. A kind word from a Granite Creek passerby to LeRoy Hooten. Scott's aim being not quite perfect. The mere fluttering of the proverbial butterfly's wings. But nothing of the sort had occurred, and Moon reminded himself that this note from Patsy was not the worst of the bad outcomes. The names of those who were dead in the wake of Miss Whysper's cruel rampage passed by his dark eyes. Pete and Dolly Bushman. Tiffany Mayfair. Miss Louella Smithson. Ex-Texas Ranger Ray Smithson. Not only had Moon provided the murderer with Columbine hospitality . . . *I didn't have a clue about what was going on until she'd already murdered five people.* He shook his head. *Some deputy I am.*

The injured man wanted to fight back—to punch some loudmouth bully in the face and knock his rotten yellow teeth all over the barroom floor—but this was a defeat without a punchable adversary. Searching for someone or some*thing* to strike back at, Moon's gaze was inevitably drawn to the velvet box.

The discarded lover thumbed the lid open to glare at an ill-starred circle of gold that sparkled with a single small diamond, that icy eye glittering at him with cold insolence. The noble metal was as corroded brass, the precious setting a faceted fragment of glass. There was a tiny residue of superstition buried deeply in the rational man's mind. It bubbled up from the black muck to suggest that this circular symbol of eternal love was a phony—a talisman of misfortune whose sinister function was to lure him into romantic alliances that were predestined to fail. Offer this cursed thing to an intelligent, honey-sweet, attractive woman, and the lady would walk away and leave him lonelier than ever.

Being the sort of fellow who preferred immediate action to tedious cerebration or unmanly self-pity, he snapped the damn box shut, stuffed the hated thing into his jacket pocket, lurched up from the swing, leaped off the porch rather than use the steps—and strode away like a resolute man on a deadly serious mission. Which he was.

CHAPTER SIXTY-FOUR

CHARLIE MOON'S NEW BEGINNING

Like all genuine transformations, this one could not be had without a kind of death—one that would sever the silver strand that connected Mr. Moon's tomorrows to all his yesterdays. The determined man stopped at the riverbank, removed the boxed engagement ring from his pocket, and opened the lid for a final look and a heartfelt promise, which he uttered aloud: "I'll never make *that* mistake again."

You know what he's going to do.

But for those who don't, imagine Chief of Police Parris about to fling his purloined can of peas—or Deputy Moon chucking a chunk of asphalt at an oncoming automobile. The plan was much the same in this instance, except that Charlie Moon's easy target was a fifty-foot-wide river rather than a purse snatcher's coconut-size head or a Chevrolet sedan's windshield. Watch the long, lean man grip the ring box in his right hand, wind up like a Colorado Rockies pitcher atop the mound in Coors Field, stretch his sinewy arm back a yard behind his head like ol' Jason Hammel about to lay a smokin' sizzler knee-high and dead center across home plate, and—

"No!"

(Who has dared interrupt this heart-stopping drama?)

Charlie Moon would also like to know. Frozen in midpitch, the promising rookie from Granite Creek County took a look over his shoulder—in the general direction of second base.

"Shame on you!" Sarah Frank snatched the box from his hand.

He blinked at the angry lass whose dark eyes flashed with white-hot fire. "What'd I do?"

Silly question. "You were going to throw it away."

Charlie Moon did not need to be informed of that fact, and he was up to here with various women who had nothing better to do than aggravate him. "So what?" With uncharacteristic sternness, he explained, "The dang thing's mine and I can do whatever I want to with it."

Sarah stamped her foot. "No you *can't*!"

Such an assertion as this stumps a red-blooded male American who firmly believes in the sanctity of private property, not to mention all the cherished rights pertaining thereto. So the best Moon could come up with was, "Why not?" This was a sincere question, and one that instantly discombobulated the tightly wound young lady into a speechless state.

But only for a heartbeat. "Well . . ." Add two more heartbeats. "Because."

Which snappy comeback called for a witty riposte: "Because *why*?" *Gotcha now.*

No he didn't. "Because . . . it's a *sin!*"

Well. Despite his admitted deficiencies, Mr. Moon was a practicing Christian who took his religion seriously. He had never stolen anything since he was delivered from alcoholism by the Grace of God, and he had never killed a man except in defense of himself or another citizen. Moreover, the Catholic confessed all his sins regularly and repented with utmost sincerity. All this being so, he was puzzled by the girl's charge. "Why?"

"Why what?" Sarah's state of discombobulation had not entirely abated.

Having regained a measure of his characteristic serenity, the Ute lived up to his reputation for being an uncommonly patient man. "Why is it a sin for me to pitch something that's mine into the river?"

Sarah looked to heaven for an answer, which was immediately forthcoming (from the opposing realm), and instantly relayed it to the alleged sinner: "Because it could be sold and the money given to the poor." *There.*

Charlie Moon smiled upon his sweet-as-honey persecutor, who

had just quoted Judas Iscariot. But the boxed engagement ring was not pure nard in an alabaster flask that *she who had been forgiven much* would use to anoint the feet of God's Messiah. Nevertheless, Sarah did have a point, and Moon had cooled off some and was able to see the foolishness in the rash act she had interrupted. Sort of. "Okay." He pointed at the box clasped tightly in her hands. "*You* sell the ring and put the money in the poor box at church." But even as he proposed a solution that seemed worthy of a latter-day Solomon, the kind man saw a shadow pass over the girl's face. Moon realized that he'd hurt her feelings. *Poor kid, she wants to put it in her jewelry box with all those other trinkets.* Sufficient injury had been suffered for the day, so he added, "But don't sell it right away."

Confused by these seemingly wishy-washy instructions, the youth waited for clarification.

Which was immediately forthcoming.

"From what I hear on the street, consumer demand for used jewelry is close to rock-bottom right now." Charlie Moon cocked his head sideways, as if in deep thought. "But sooner or later, the market is bound to get bullish."

Sarah nodded.

"So I'd advise you to hold on to it until the price of engagement rings peaks."

"Whatever you say." But Sarah posed a sensible question: "How'll I know when that happens? I mean . . . the ring might be worth a thousand dollars one day and double that in another week."

"Don't worry about that." The rancher assumed an expression of manly confidence. "I know something about the cattle market and how it fluctuates—and beef on the hoof is not all that much different from pork bellies, wheat, gold, or diamonds." He gave the girl a light, one-armed hug. "*I'll* tell you when to sell it."

"Okay." But there was that *one more thing* and Sarah's eyes were full of hope, her girlish innocence now transformed into sly, feminine guile: "Should we keep it in the attic safe till then?"

"Nah." Charlie Moon shrugged. "That trinket has spent way too much time in the dark already. You pick a good place for it."

That was the right answer, and she knew just where. *But I wouldn't dare.* "Really?"

"Sure." Poor, clueless fellow.

Sarah Frank opened the box, removed the engagement ring, and slipped it onto her supple brown finger, where the diamond shone like a miniature supernova and the gold glistened like King Midas had just put the Big Touch on it—and it was a perfect fit. *Oh, I could just die!*

Thankfully, she did not.

The ecstatic young woman grabbed the tall, lean man in a hug around the neck, pulled herself up to kiss her astonished benefactor *right on the mouth,* released him into a dumb numbness that paralyzed Charlie Moon from head to toe—and ran away toward the big log house, almost bowling Daisy Perika aside.

The tribal elder, who had crept close enough to overhear the conversation, was shaking her head. *There ain't a man alive that can outsmart the silliest girl you ever saw.*

CHAPTER SIXTY-FIVE

WEEKS LATER AT THE COLUMBINE
APPROXIMATELY 10:02 A.M. PLUS 16 SECONDS

But who cares a nickel or a dime about precise time? Not Charlie Moon, who was in the headquarters parlor, reclining in his favorite rocking chair. And speaking of specie, the Indian did not give one penny's worth of attention to the ticktocking clock on the mantelpiece.

All things considered, this was a restful interlude for a hardworking man who needed a few hours alone. There had not been a knock-down, drag-out brawl in the bunkhouse for almost four days, no reports of busted windmills, sick cattle falling like flies from some mysterious malady, or cougars on the prowl for prime beef. Moreover, Mr. Moon was all alone. Sarah Frank was away, attending some class or other at Rocky Mountain Polytechnic University, and best of all—Aunt Daisy was spending an entire week in her reservation home.

As he took advantage of this uncommon respite from life's various and sundry vexations, Moon's eyes were closed, his long legs stretched out, his bare feet propped on the hearth and warmed by a famished blaze that was licking at tasty chunks of resinous pine. Mighty fine? You bet. But do not jump to the conclusion that the rancher was malingering. This one was not even dozing. So what was he doing? The man in the rocker was waiting for the telephone to ring.

By and by, it did. Seven times.

No, the peaceful soul did not get up from his comfortable chair and stroll over there to where the communications instrument jangled. And why should he? Charlie Moon figured he knew who was calling, the reason why, and more or less what Scott Parris had to say.

Before ring number eight could sound, the answering machine kicked in. After Parris listened impatiently to the standard Columbine greeting, he barked at the man in the chair, "Charlie, I know you're there. Now here's the deal—what I need to tell you about is *confidential police business*, so I can't leave it on your machine. Now pick up the phone, dammit—so I won't have to drive all the way out to the ranch!" The chief of police continued to fume, fret, and fuss until his minute was up.

As Señor Luna yawned, his eyes remained closed. Behind the lids, he was looking forward to the forthcoming visit from his best friend, but now he would complete his restful midmorning siesta. Imagine sixteen solid minutes of deep, dreamless sleep.

TIME HAS PASSED

A wide-awake Charlie Moon was in the headquarters kitchen, getting the six-burner propane range primed and ready for action. In a little while, there would be pig meat sizzling deliciously in a black iron skillet, seasoned legumes bubbling contentedly in a stainless-steel sauce pan, and black, brackish brew blurpity-blurping rhythmically in a blue-enameled percolator. Accompanying these satisfying sounds would be a breathtaking aroma wafting up from the oven vent. But that would be then, and this was right now. At present, an eighth inch of olive oil simmered in the skillet, the sauce pan was empty as a dead man's fixed stare, and not a flicker of a blue flame blazed underneath the coffeepot. But the oven was already hot and a bowl of sticky biscuit mix was ready to spoon onto a sooty cookie sheet.

Being alone in the house and in no particular hurry to commence with the feast, the Ute occupied himself by setting the table with two brown-as-Big-Muddy-Creek stoneware crockery platters, a pair of matching mugs, silver forks and spoons that had belonged to his mother, and a couple of bone-handled hunting knives such as suspicious housewives sharpen when their tomcat men are still out at 2:00 A.M. As he occupied himself with these tasks, the man of the house was expecting another call—this one on his cellular telephone. Which was why Mr. Moon was not the least bit surprised when the instrument in his shirt pocket buzzed like a spinning lead slug does when it drones past your ear; a sound you're happy you can hear because when you don't, you are no longer here.

Figuring the odds at about twenty to one, the poker player connected without checking the caller ID. Scott Parris's keen-eared deputy knew he was right when he heard the high-rpm roar of the GCPD black-and-white's supercharged V-8 engine. *He's mad as a hornet and on his way here.* "Howdy, pardner."

"Howdy yourself! Why didn't you answer the phone when I called almost an hour ago?"

"I was indisposed." Moon's free hand laid a can opener on the table. "I'm guessing you got yours too."

"I sure did," Parris growled. "When Mr. UPS showed up with a parcel from that purse-snatching son of a bitch's murderous momma, my first thought was that she'd sent me an improvised explosive device that'd blow my fat head all the way to Kingdom Come if I so much as cracked the lid." The cop snorted. "But after taking thought, I realized that a lady who mails a gentleman a homemade bomb does not generally put her right name and return address onto the box."

"Not unless she wants the gentleman to know *which* lady bought his ticket before he takes that last train to Glory." The deputy allowed himself a crooked smile. "I thought her note was a nice touch."

Despite his annoyance, Parris snickered. "Yeah—'It is difficult to shop for a public servant whose tastes and preferences are unknown to me. Nevertheless, I hope that this small gift will suffice until I forward something more appropriate.'"

"Despite some minor character flaws, Mrs. Hooten has a sense of humor."

"And she intends to have the last laugh, Charlie. Sooner or later, she'll send another assassin to shoot us fulla holes."

The same thought had crossed Moon's mind. "Sooner or later, we'll both end up dead from old age."

"So what d'you intend to do with your gift, Charlie—put it on the parlor mantelpiece with your other trophies, souvenirs, and mementos?"

"Nope." The rancher removed a butcher-paper-wrapped package from the refrigerator. "I intend to forget all about dead felons and their vengeful mothers, and just do what comes naturally."

"Hah—you're goin' to feed your face!"

"I wouldn't put it that crudely, but I am about to whip me up a light midday meal." He paused to give his friend time to think about that.

Parris did, and licked his lips. *Lunch sure sounds good.*

"After some grub, maybe I'll mosey over to Lake Jessie and wet a line."

Fishing sounds good, too. But even for Moon's ardent-angler buddy, there were more-immediate priorities than hooking finned creatures: Parris's mouth had begun to water. "So what's for lunch, Chucky?"

"Nothing special, pard. Just some thick-cut pork chops, as many buttered biscuits as I can choke down, a big bowl of ice cream—and fresh coffee. Oh, I almost forgot to mention the best dish of all—" Moon grinned at his distant friend. "But I wouldn't want to spoil the surprise."

It had already been a trying day, what with a shouting meeting with the halfwit mayor whose meddling wife was determined that all GCPD officers should start wearing big white cowboy hats ("It will help the tourist trade"), Officer Knox punching out a mouthy tourist who called him a gun-toting fascist Nazi swine (an insult to decent pigs everywhere), and a sweet little old bespectacled lady who drove her shiny new Chevrolet Volt over a nun's parked bicycle. Not to mention the parcel received from the purse snatcher's brazen momma. With all these unsavory events on his mind, the edgy chief of police's hundred-watt brain was overloaded and running in its dim-bulb mode. But when Parris caught on to what the Ute was alluding to, he laughed like a braying mule. "You are *kidding* me!"

"I'm serious as a twenty-year drought, pard—and hungry as a grizzly who's just woke up to smell the spring flowers. I'm ready to take a bite out of anything that looks like food and can't outrun me."

"Don't you dare start without me." The chief of police pressed the accelerator pedal to the floorboard. "When'll lunch be ready?"

"How long'll it take you to get here?"

"Lemme see." Parris caught a glimpse of a thirty-mile-marker sign with a .44-caliber bullet hole dead center through the zero. "I'm about nine miles from the Columbine gate." *And then there's that long, bumpy gravel road to the headquarters.* "Maybe half an hour."

"Lunch'll be ready by the time you belly up to the table."

"How many pork chops have you got?"

"Two for me, two more for you. There'll be a big pot of cowboy coffee, enough sourdough biscuits to sink a small canoe, a half gallon of store-bought peach ice cream, and of course we'll have us a fine mess of—" Moon adjusted the propane flame under the skillet. "Did you bring your gift from the purse snatcher's momma?"

"No, dang it." Parris grimaced as a plump moth splattered on his windshield. "Mine's back at the house."

"Not a problem, pard. With all the other grub, I expect we can make do with one can of black-eyed peas."

CHAPTER SIXTY-SIX

THE SHAMAN WALKS IN *CAÑÓN DEL ESPÍRITU*

We're not talking about a Sunday-afternoon stroll in the park; Daisy Perika's spindly legs ached and her shortened breaths came in painful gasps. Was our determined hiker discouraged? Certainly not. The tribal elder (with tongue firmly in cheek) assured herself that . . . "If I'm all tuckered out, it's *not* because I'm getting feeble." Why did she waste a precious breath by speaking aloud what she could have *thought* at no incremental cost? The answer is: the aged recluse was feeling lonely, and her offhand remark was offered in hopes of striking up a neighborly conversation with one of the canyon's longtime inhabitants.

If one of the more gullible local haunts had taken the bait and asked the Ute elder what the problem was—if not the natural infirmity of having lasted too many winters—the senior citizen would have asserted that with every year that passed, this tiresome expedition into the shadowy canyon was getting longer. Literally—by about two dozen paces. Moreover, the grade of the climb was increasing about a degree per annum. It was (Daisy would insist) as if the unseen hand of some sadistic prankster was gradually stretching the sinuous deer path—and elevating the rocky canyon floor that lay before her. (That same perverse trickster who shrinks newspaper print so that aging folk are obliged to squint.)

Sad to say, none of the resident spirits offered such an accommodating inquiry—which omission served only to increase her exhaustion.

For the eighteenth time in as many minutes, Daisy paused to lean on her oak walking staff. While inhaling a refreshing tonic of the crisp autumn air, she mused about how easily this mortal life can slip away. *I could have a heart attack and fall down flat on my face and die and nobody would even know I was missing for weeks.* She scowled at the injustice of it. *Maybe months.* By and by, Charlie Moon might wonder, "Why haven't I heard a word from ol' Aunt What's-her-name since sometime last year?" After taking care of important matters (like making sure his already-fattened cows were well fed) her nephew (the big gourd-head!) would eventually get around to driving down to her remote reservation home, and finding her hideous corpse. *By then, them damned old coyotes would've had their fill and left the rest to the buzzards and magpies, who'd pick my eyeballs out of their sockets.* The morbid old soul could visualize the grisly scene with crystal clarity. *All that'd be left would be some cracked bones with all the marrow sucked out, a half-dozen nubby little teeth, and a hank of gray hair.*

As her taciturn grandfather used to say about a century ago— "Maybe so."

But, as it had for many decades, her old heart kept right on apumping. When she had breath enough, the old woman resumed her slow ascent.

Daisy Perika's intended destination?

The tribal elder was going to visit an old friend. No, not the sort of friend she'd want to be snowed in with during a midwinter blizzard. Put the emphasis on *old.* Think a thousand years or so. That's right: the shaman was paying a call on the *pitukupf.* For what purpose? It was a journey of conscience. Yes, Daisy does have one, though that indispensable faculty wasted away due to insufficient exercise. Every once in a while—probably just to make its presence known—that minuscule residue of her happy childhood would raise its small voice and whisper some folderol to the crotchety old soul about duty, kindness, and patience—even *humility,* for goodness' sake! Charlie Moon's irascible aunt mockingly called her better self "Daisy Do-right," her virtuous invisible sister's unsolicited advice "pesky naggings." Daisy D-r's hopeful exhortations would generally go in one ear and right out the other and be forgotten in a heartbeat, but upon occasion (such as during the past twenty hours) the small voice would persist.

If the elderly woman wanted to get a wink of restful sleep, there was nothing to do then but obey. Which, in this instance, required a long, tiresome walk into *Cañón del Espíritu*.

What did Daisy Do-right require of her? That shall become clear soon enough.

The abandoned badger hole that had been homesteaded by the dwarf is yonder in the smallish clearing, just beyond that cluster of bushy junipers. Reclining beside the entrance is a recently fallen ponderosa. (Within the seemingly ageless walls of *Cañón del Espíritu*, "recently" means "within the past few decades.") When she arrives, Daisy will seat herself on that rotting, fungus-encrusted log and wait for the *pitukupf's* appearance. While she does . . .

TIME WILL PASS

While it did, the old woman leaned her head against the sturdy walking stick and dozed. She also snored intermittently, and dreamed fitfully about her mother—who was telling an oft-heard tale about how Coyote stole a string of catfish from a Navajo child. Thankfully, the dozer did not fall off the log. Thankfully for the dwarf, that is. For if Daisy had taken a comical topple, the Little Man would almost certainly have laughed. And if he had uttered the least chuckle, chortle, or snigger—the old woman would have gotten a firm grip on her big stick and *knocked his fool head clean off.*

Which would necessarily have been the end of the story, their forthcoming conversation being forever lost to posterity. As it happened, the dwarf awakened the tribal elder by tickling her nose with a fuzzy Apache-plume blossom that he had plucked specifically for that whimsical purpose. Subsequently, the preamble to the one-act play went something like this:

Daisy Perika (rubbing her eyes sleepily): "Ahhhh!—why'd you do that?"

The *pitukupf* stated his reason (succinctly).

Mrs. P.: "Well I didn't need you to wake me up." She yawns. "I open my eyes when I'm done sleeping."

The Little Man inquired as to the purpose of her visit.

(Good for him; now we are getting to the meat of the matter.)

Settling herself more comfortably on the pine-log bench, the old woman opened her mouth . . . and hesitated. *This ain't going to be easy.* In a pathetic ploy to delay the painful ordeal, she cast a furtive gaze this way and that. Swatted at an annoying gnat. Daisy also dithered, shilly-shallied, and vacillated—and in alphabetical order. Which vain subterfuges rapidly got tedious. *I might as well get this silly business over and done with.* "Thing is . . ." After a final wavering, she spat the distasteful mouthful out: "I thought I ought to come over here and apologize to you."

Well.

Was the elfin personage stunned? Yes. Like a poetical soul who pauses in a flower-strewn meadow, bends to gaze at a dainty little daisy, and is greeted (rearward) by the lowered head and horns of a playful one-ton longhorn bull trotting along at about twelve miles per.

Perhaps the elderly neighbor was forgetful, but in all his long association with the Ute woman (which had begun when Daisy was a bright-eyed child), the *pitukupf* could not recall hearing the least word of apology, regret, or any other expression of contrition slip between her lips. So it was not surprising that, after reaming excess wax out of his left ear with the long nail of a gnarly forefinger, he asked his guest to repeat what she had allegedly said.

She did. And, urged on by her conscience, Daisy enlarged upon her confession: "When you came to my Columbine bedroom a few weeks ago and warned me to be on the lookout for a haunt, well . . . I guess I should've paid more attention." Having made her basic apology, she felt entitled to an excuse: "I was awfully tired and sleepy—it was hard to think straight."

Equally surprised and gratified by this unprecedented admission of human frailty, the *pitukupf* said that he hoped his information had proven helpful.

"It should've." Daisy allowed herself a sigh. "But when that ghost showed up, she looked more like a bloated toadstool than a young woman. That's why I took Miss Smithson for Hester 'Toadie' Tillman. You know who I mean—ol' Toadie died in that pickup truck accident over by Ignacio."

Nodding to signify that he was aware of Mrs. Tillman's fatal accident, the dwarf admitted (with uncharacteristic generosity) that the error on Daisy's part was understandable.

The tribal elder should have appreciated this small kindness, but it irked her to be patronized by a sawed-off know-it-all who (after all) did bear a measure of responsibility for this case of mistaken identity. The cranky woman knew that she should let the matter lie; even a helpful suggestion might be taken amiss by the volatile dwarf. But nasty old habits die hard. Despite urgent exhortations from Daisy Doright, she simply *could not resist* the temptation to offer some constructive advice to this conceited little pipsqueak. "From time to time, when you have something important to tell me—it'd be nice if you'd add a helpful detail." She glared at the *pitukupf*. "Like what a person's *name* was."

The dwarf appeared to be genuinely puzzled.

Daisy elaborated: "If you'd told me to expect Miss Smithson's ghost, that would've helped some."

The Little Man hastened to demur. As it happened, the dead woman was from out of state. That being the case, he did not (so he claimed) know the spirit's name.

Certain that he was lying between his pointy little yellow possum teeth, Daisy snapped back, "Well, you must've known she was a dead woman whose body was in that rusty old Bronco parked in Charlie's yard—it wouldn't have made your forked tongue fall out to tell me *that*!"

It never helps to lose one's temper.

From this point, their conversation deteriorated into a lively exchange of charges, countercharges, finger waggings, pointed reminders of previous offenses (some going back to the early 1930s), and finally—unseemly allusions to the other party's venerable ancestors, comparing the dearly departed to various diseased quadrupeds, sharp-toothed serpents—even the loathsome larvae of pestilent insects. It would be indelicate to provide a detailed description. (But for those few who hanker for one: mangy coyotes, treacherous rattlesnakes, and ugly maggots.)

It is hard to find anything positive to report about this unfortunate exchange, but in the interest of promoting the illusion of an upbeat conclusion, some attempt must be made. Try this woolly euphemism on for size:

Like all unpleasant events in our transitory existence, this one finally came to an end.

Still somewhat of a downer?

Point taken. What we need here is an upbeat adverb. One pops immediately to mind.

Happily, the two old-timers finally ran out of steam. Thus exhausted, they were in the mood to mend fences. No, they did not embrace. Neither was there an exchange of comradely handshakes. But as she withdrew from the field of conflict, Daisy did offer a genuinely friendly smile with her fond farewell: "See you later, little neighbor." *When I ain't got nothing better to do—like grow a big, hairy wart on the tip of my nose.*

How did the *pitukupf* respond? In that faultless, archaic-Ute dialect with which he customarily communicated, the diminutive gentleman expressed his heartfelt wish that the Ute elder would arrive home safe and sound. *To find her fine house burned to the ground.*

EPILOGUE
CLOSURE

The conclusion to Charlie Moon's romance with the reference librarian occurred on a fine September afternoon, when the mobile phone buzzed inside his jacket pocket. He frowned at the caller ID, and was about to return the communications instrument to his pocket when he realized that . . . *This is as good a time as any for a final goodbye.* "Hello, Patsy—how's your sister getting along?"

"Why *hello,* Charlie—Daphne's doing fine." The lady's bright voice did not conceal her inner tension. "Aren't you going to ask how I am?"

"So how are you?"

"Oh, okay I guess." After waiting vainly for a response, she added, "I'm in Granite Creek for a few hours to pick up some belongings I'd left at my house . . . and . . . well . . . to tie up some loose ends."

The loose end nodded. "That can take some doing."

Pretty Patsy Poynter sighed like a warm southern breeze. "You know how it is—moving away can be *such* a pain."

"Mmm-hmm. I know how it is." *But tell me all about it.*

What she had to say for the following minute or so is of no more interest to us than it was to Mr. Moon. Pretty Patsy chatted about this and that and whatnot before getting around to the issue that had prompted her call. "Oh, by the way—when I was coming out of the public library today, *who* do you think I almost bumped into on Copper Street?"

The gentleman admitted his ignorance, but concealed the fact that he did not really give a damn.

"Well, it was Sarah Frank—she is such a *sweet* little child."

Uh-oh. Moon waited for the other dainty high-heeled shoe to drop. It did. "And Sarah was wearing an *engagement ring*."

He arched an eyebrow. *So that's what this is all about.*

"And the thing that struck me as such a strange coincidence was that it looked very much like mine—" She cleared her throat. "Well, I mean like the ring that you gave me."

Moon nodded at his mental image of the gorgeous woman. "The one you returned by FedEx."

"Well . . . yes. But let's not get into all that sad business right now." Patsy inhaled a deep breath and homed back in on the burning subject like a heat-seeking Miss Missile. "Anyway, when I asked the adorable girl who the lucky man was—she wouldn't tell me."

The unlucky man grinned. *Maybe Sarah figured it was none of your business.*

Patsy Poynter affected a conspiratorial tone, as if two sensible adults were discussing a silly juvenile. "Well, not *right off* she wouldn't. But when I pressed, Sarah looked me right in the eye and said, 'Charlie gave it to me.' Moon's ex produced a brittle little laugh. "Well, what do you think about *that?*"

The designated fiancé sighed. *I think this is gonna be a long, interesting engagement.*

"Charlie—are you there?"

"Sure." *A man has to be somewhere.*

"Well . . . about that ring you *supposedly* gave Sarah . . . are you going to tell me what that's all about—or just leave me to guess?"

"Yes."

. . . .

. . . .

Click.

. . . .

Click.